BR... ...S

...DING

EMERGENCY DOCTOR AND CINDERELLA

BY
MELANIE MILBURNE

MILLS & BOON

A Proposal in A&E!

Drama, Desirable Doctors and Diamond Rings!

In the high-octane world of the Emergency Room, these commanding doctors are locked in a daily battle to save the lives of their patients.

Focused, intense and assertive, they must keep their emotions on rigid lockdown. Until two irresistible women unexpectedly blow them away…
and suddenly electricity in the A&E rockets sky-high!

But as the sizzling tension threatens to boil over, these doctors will need something special—and sparkly!— to convince these women they're seriously in love!

THE NURSE'S BROODING BOSS
by Laura Iding

and

EMERGENCY DOCTOR AND CINDERELLA
by Melanie Milburne

THE NURSE'S
BROODING BOSS

BY
LAURA IDING

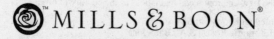

MILLS & BOON

To the wonderful, wild, wacky women of CAFA.
I look forward to seeing you every year.

First published in Great Britain 2010
Harlequin Mills & Boon Limited,
Eton House, 18-24 Paradise Road, Richmond, Surrey TW9 1SR

© Laura Iding 2010

ISBN: 978 0 263 87877 6

Printed and bound in Spain
by Litografia Rosés, S.A., Barcelona

Dear Reader

Many of us have done things in our past that we regret. Unfortunately there is no way to go back and fix the mistakes we've made, so somehow we end up finding a way to live with them.

But what if the mistake is something that has far-reaching consequences? Life and death consequences? This is the main dilemma facing Elana and Brock in their touching story of love and forgiveness.

Brock Madison was driving his car when Elana's sister pulled out in front of him. The crash wasn't his fault, but Elana's sister died at the scene despite his efforts to save her. Nine years later, Elana finds herself working for Brock at Trinity Medical Center's Emergency Department. They are both dedicated to their careers, but will they let go of the pain from the past in order to find love and happiness?

I hope you enjoy THE NURSE'S BROODING BOSS. I love to hear from my readers, so please stop by and visit me at www.lauraiding.com

Happy Reading!

Laura

Laura Iding loved reading as a child, and when she ran out of books she readily made up her own, completing a little detective mini-series when she was twelve. But, despite her aspirations for being an author, her parents insisted she look into a 'real' career. So the summer after she turned thirteen she volunteered as a Candy Striper, and fell in love with nursing. Now, after twenty years of experience in trauma/critical care, she's thrilled to combine her career and her hobby into one—writing Medical™ Romances for Mills & Boon®. Laura lives in the northern part of the United States, and spends all her spare time with her two teenage kids (help!)—a daughter and a son—and her husband. Enjoy!

Recent titles by the same author:

CHAPTER ONE

ELANA SCHULTZ dashed into the emergency department of Trinity Medical Center, heading straight for the time clock, swiping her badge at exactly three o'clock in the afternoon.

On time. Barely. Breathing a sigh of relief that she'd made it, she quickly stuffed her purse into her staff locker and crossed over to the arena where the charge nurse was going through the shift assignments.

"Elana, you and Raine will take the trauma bay," Stacey informed them. "Suzette, you're taking the urgent care area. Emma, you're arena team one. Liz, you're arena team two…"

"How was your long weekend?" Raine asked in a hushed whisper so as not to interrupt Stacey's monologue.

"Good. Everything went well. I'll fill you in later," Elana whispered back.

"Any questions about the assignments?" Stacey asked, looking up from her clipboard. After a moment of silence she nodded. "All right, there are twenty-seven patients on the board, with eleven still waiting to be seen. The trauma bay is currently empty; the last patient has been dispatched to the medical ICU. It's been a busy day, but not too crazy. Let's hope it stays that way for our shift." Stacey set her clipboard aside. "Call me if you need help."

That was their cue to leave. The group of nurses broke up, scattering to their various assignments.

"How's your aunt Chloe?" Raine asked as she fell into step beside Elana on their way to the trauma bay.

"She's much better. Her cardiac stent procedure went off without a hitch." Technically, Chloe Jenkins wasn't Elana's blood relative, she was Elana's foster mother, the last and by far the best in a string of horrible experiences. If not for Chloe, Elana knew there was a very good chance she would have ended up on the streets.

She owed Chloe her life.

"I'm so glad she's doing all right," Raine said softly.

Elana smiled. "Me too. You know how close I am to Chloe." Her mother, Louisa Schultz, had been in a nursing home since Elana was fifteen after suffering a complete relapse of her nervous breakdown. Her mother's emotional state had collapsed after Elana's father had walked out on them. She'd gotten better slowly over time until Felicity's death had sent her into a deep emotional breakdown. Elana still loved her mother and faithfully visited every weekend, but it had been nine years, and her mother still hadn't spoken a single word.

"You missed the big announcement while you were gone," Raine said.

Elana raised a brow and took the trauma pager from the first shift trauma nurse, who looked all too eager to give it up. "What? We're all getting pay raises?"

"Yeah, right." Raine let out a snort of laughter. "No.

There's a new doctor on staff. He started the day after you left, as a matter of fact."

Elana shrugged, sweeping a gaze over the trauma bay. She got along fine with the doctors she worked with, but she didn't go ga-ga over them like some of the other nurses did. Most of the doctors were married anyway, and the ones who weren't were—in her opinion—single for a reason.

"I'm telling you, Elana, he's hot. And he's single. At least, I'm pretty sure he is—Suzette was pumping him for personal information."

Their trauma pagers went off simultaneously, interrupting Raine's story. Elana read the text message.

Motor vehicle crash, 23 y/o female trauma victim ejected from the car, intubated on the scene. ETA two minutes.

Motor vehicle crash. Female trauma victim ejected from the car. Just like Felicity had been.

Elana swallowed hard and clipped her pager back onto the waistband of her scrub pants. Even after nine years, any reminder about her sister's tragic death made her feel sad. With her mother's emotional collapse and her absent father, Elana's life had spiraled downhill. Thank heavens for Chloe, who'd rescued her before she was too far gone.

"I wonder if he's working today?" Raine asked.

It took her a minute to figure out Raine was still talking about the new doctor.

"How do you know he's single?" Elana asked.

"Because Suzette talked to him. Weren't you listening? He's young, just turned thirty, and he's hot. Like, steamy hot."

No, she hadn't been listening. Elana shrugged again and crossed over to the supply cabinet, opening drawers and ensuring the day shift staff had restocked everything after the last trauma patient had been transferred up to the medical ICU.

"There he is," Raine hissed.

Before she could turn to look, the double doors of the ambulance bay burst open. Two paramedics wheeled in the young female trauma patient. Elana took her place at the right side of the patient, while Raine took the left. Trauma resuscitations were not as chaotic as they were made to look on television. Every person had their role to play, and predesignated responsibilities, depending on where they stood. Elana tended to take the right side because she liked doing the vital signs and initial assessment.

"Two liters of Ringer's lactate are going into respective antecubital eighteen-gauge IVs. Suspected cervical fracture, limbs flaccid at the scene, C-collar in place. Intubated in the field with a seven-point-five endotracheal tube."

Elana connected the patient to the heart monitor, listening as the paramedics rattled off the pertinent information. The new doctor stood at the foot of the bed, but Elana's attention was riveted on the patient. This young woman was older than Felicity had been, but only by a couple of years.

A suspected cervical fracture. Possibly paralyzed for life. How awful. Felicity had died at the scene of her accident, but, really, which fate was worse? Staring down at the young woman's blood-streaked face, Elana wasn't sure.

She did a quick assessment, getting the first set of vital signs and doing a quick listen to the patient's heart and lungs. When she finished, she flipped her stethoscope around her neck. "Vitals are low, BP 76/40, pulse tachy at 122, pupils sluggish but reactive and equal in size. Lungs coarse but bilateral breath sounds noted." She glanced up at the new physician and froze.

Brock Madison.

Her chest tightened, and she had to remind herself to breathe. No, it couldn't be. She had to be mistaken. She hadn't seen him in years. Maybe this guy just looked like an older version of the Brock Madison she remembered.

"Do you want to continue the Ringer's lactate solution, Dr Madison?" Raine asked.

"Yes, although we may need to transfuse a unit of blood too."

The room spun, and Elana had to grab onto the side rail to keep herself upright. Dr Madison. Brock Madison was the new doctor on staff.

And he was also the driver of the car that had hit her sister's vehicle nine years ago. The man who'd caused Felicity's death.

Brock hid his surprise at seeing Elana Schultz again, although the shocked expression on her face mirrored the turmoil in his gut. With an effort, he forced himself to ignore his personal problems and concentrate on the young trauma victim before him.

"Start with two units of O-negative blood," Brock ordered. "We need to get her stabilized before we send her to the CT scanner to evaluate the extent of her injuries."

Raine did as he asked, but Elana simply stood there, hanging onto the side rail and staring down at the patient, clearly in shock. As much as he appreciated what she must be going through, at this critical juncture he needed the entire trauma team to be working together. He moved closer, keeping his voice low so it wouldn't carry. "Elana, if you can't do this, please find someone to take your place."

She snapped her head around to look at him. The fierce expression flaring in her eyes nearly made him take a step backward. After a moment's hesitation, she glanced away, took a deep breath and let it out slowly, unclasping her tense fingers from the side rail. "I'm fine. Do you want a full set of labs?"

"Yes. We need to know if she's bleeding internally." Brock couldn't help admiring the way Elana jumped back into the trauma resuscitation. He'd known she'd graduated from college with a nursing degree because he'd kept tabs on Felicity's younger sister over the years. But he hadn't realized Elana had taken a position here at Trinity. Ironic that she'd chosen to work in the emergency department, providing care to trauma patients. Like her sister.

And yet hadn't he gone into emergency medicine for the same reasons?

He watched as she drew a set of blood gases and then filled another four lab tubes with blood. Reassured that Elana was doing all right, he turned his attention back to the patient. He was somewhat worried about the young woman's lung function, but, even more, he needed to know what her hematocrit and hemoglobin levels were.

"Get me those H & H results stat. In the meantime, let's make sure there are no other obvious sites of bleeding."

Elana and Raine worked well together, he noted. Since arriving at Trinity Medical Center, he'd been impressed with how well the emergency and trauma center staff gelled, from the techs to the nurses up to and including the physicians. A true team approach. Things hadn't been quite this cohesive in his former position.

Within a few minutes, Elana reported new vitals. "BP up to 84/42, pulse a little less tachy at 117. We're making some headway."

He nodded, agreeing with her assessment. If they could get this patient's blood pressure up to the nineties, he'd be satisfied enough to send her to the CT scanner. If she needed emergency surgery on her spine, he didn't want to delay care. On the other hand, he didn't want her to crash in the CT scanner, either.

"We have the H & H results," Elana announced. "Hemoglobin is 7.8 and hematocrit is 29."

"Give another two units of O-negative blood, Raine," he ordered. "Keep running the fluids too; I'd like to see her systolic blood pressure over ninety. I'm going to call Radiology to make sure they're ready for her. One of you is going to need to go with her to the CT scanner."

"I'll go," Elana volunteered.

He gave a brief nod, turned on his heel and walked to the nearest phone. Within moments he had everything arranged with the radiologist on call.

His gaze settled back on Elana, watching her as she worked. With her jet-black hair pulled into a long ponytail, her high cheekbones and olive-toned skin, a gift from her Hispanic mother, she was stunningly beautiful. She'd grown up from the gangly teenager she'd been nine years ago.

And she had every reason to hate him.

The familiar guilt surged like bile in the back of his throat. He tore his gaze away and swallowed hard, trying to focus on the monitor above the female trauma patient's head. This wasn't the time or the place to wallow in the mistakes of the past.

"Blood pressure is up to 95 systolic after the first unit of blood. We still have one more unit to give, but she seems to have stabilized for now. Do you want me to take her for a CT scan?" Elana asked.

He nodded, the lump lodged in the back of his throat making it impossible to speak.

She didn't need to be asked twice. Within moments, she and Raine had the patient disconnected from the main monitor and reconnected to the portable one they used for transporting patients. As Elana whisked the patient away, he found himself wondering if she'd volunteered to go to the CT scan for the sole purpose of getting away from him.

Possibly. No, probably. Damn. The last thing he wanted to do was to cause Elana any more grief. He certainly didn't want her to quit her job because of him. She must love trauma nursing to have chosen to work here, and Trinity Medical Center was the only level-one trauma center in Southeastern Wisconsin.

He sighed and scrubbed his hand over his face. Talk

about his rotten timing. If he'd known Elana was working here, he could have handled their first meeting a little differently.

No, who was he trying to kid? There was nothing he could have done to make this meeting easier for her. The scalding look she'd sent him had stabbed deep. He'd leave himself if not for the fact that his brother needed him. And the fact that he'd signed a twelve-month contract.

"So, Dr Madison, how do you like it here at Trinity so far?" Raine asked, cleaning up the area around the trauma bay.

He cleared his throat. "It's great. I'm glad I made the move from Minneapolis."

"Minneapolis's loss is our gain," Raine said with a smile.

Raine was pretty enough with her dark red hair and her bright green eyes, but he wasn't interested in the signals she was sending out. He didn't date, especially anyone who might be interested in a future. He couldn't help glancing at his watch, wondering where Elana was.

He wished they could talk. There had to be some way to ease the tension that shimmered between them.

For years he'd longed for a chance to explain. To redeem himself in her eyes if at all possible.

So much for seeking forgiveness. Remembering the banked fury in her dark eyes, he knew there was no chance in hell Elana would give him that option.

He didn't deserve her forgiveness.

"How much longer?" Elana asked, casting a worried glance at her patient. The young patient's name was

Jamie Edgar, and her blood pressure was starting to slip downward.

"Ten minutes," the tech assured her.

She increased the flow of the fluids to help maintain Jamie's blood pressure. Keeping busy was helping her to forget about Brock Madison, who happened to be waiting for them in the trauma bay.

What on earth had she done to deserve this? Why after all these years was it her misfortune to have to work with the man she despised?

She rubbed her aching temple, hearing Chloe admonishing her in her mind. *Don't talk like that, young lady. Brock Madison wasn't the person at fault in the accident, your sister was. She pulled out right in front of him! It's certainly not his fault Felicity died.*

In some tiny corner of her mind Elana knew Chloe was right. Her sister had pulled out onto the busy highway in front of Brock without warning. But he'd also been speeding, at least according to one of the witnesses on the scene. Brock's father had been a cop at the time, and everyone thought his dad had pulled strings to cover up the truth.

Including Elana.

Besides, did it matter? The irrevocable fact remained that Brock stole Felicity's life.

Nothing on earth could change that.

And now she'd be forced to work with the man she detested.

"There, we're all finished." The radiology tech broke into her troubled thoughts. "Do you want me to call the ED to let them know you're on your way back?"

She forced a smile. "Sure, that would be great."

Jamie's blood pressure slipped a little further, and Elana quickened her pace, pushing the gurney as fast as she dared, keeping one eye on the monitor and the other on the hallway. Luckily, the radiology department was not far from the emergency department.

"I'm losing her blood pressure," Elana announced as she entered the trauma bay.

"Hang another unit of O-neg blood. The spine surgeons are on their way down. The radiologist already called me with the CT results. She has a severe compression fracture in her cervical spine. If they can operate quickly, they might be able to minimize the damage to the spinal cord."

Elana nodded, indicating she'd heard him. Relieved that the spine damage may not be permanent, she made sure Jamie was ready for the OR, taking off her rings and her necklace and putting them into a valuables envelope to be stored in the hospital safe.

The OR team showed up and took over the case, taking Jamie straight up to surgery. Once her patient was gone, Elana felt the all too familiar letdown. She enjoyed trauma nursing, but there was a part of her that had considered moving to the critical care area so that she could follow the trauma cases more closely. She'd miss the thrill of caring for patients coming in right from the scene, but it would also be great to see some of these patients actually recover.

"Elana? Are you all right?"

She glanced at Brock, her stomach knotting with apprehension. How could she be all right with him around? She needed to get away from him. Far, far away. "Of course. Excuse me while I restock the supplies before the next trauma call comes in."

"I'll do it," Raine offered, glancing between Elana and Brock with frank curiosity.

She ground her teeth together, wishing Raine wouldn't try to be quite so helpful. Since Raine hurried to do the stocking, and Brock simply stood there, watching her with concern, she turned and headed towards the staff lounge. Unfortunately she wasn't going to get the privacy she needed since Brock was right behind her.

"What do you want?" she asked, spinning around to face him and crossing her arms over her chest defensively.

"First of all, I wanted to say I'm sorry. I had absolutely no idea you worked here." Brock's sincere expression didn't succeed in soothing her annoyance. Maybe she had noticed the shock in his eyes when he'd recognized her, but she was the one who'd lost a sister. "I moved home for family reasons, not to torment you."

"Doesn't matter to me where you work," she said in a stiff, formal tone. "You stay out of my way, and I'll stay out of yours."

He stared at her for a long moment, and she struggled not to squirm beneath his intense scrutiny. She could see why Raine had called him steamy hot. He wore his chocolate-brown hair a little longer than was fashionable, but with his chiseled jaw and strong chin he was ruggedly attractive. To everyone else, maybe. Not to her. "If that's what you want. But it might help if we could spend some time talking things through."

Talk things through? She blinked. Was he serious? The nerve of him acting as though talking things out would somehow bring Felicity back. She curled her fingers into fists, her nails digging into the palm of her hand, and for a moment she relished the tiny flash of pain.

Maybe they had to work together, but, as far as she was concerned, there would never be anything remotely personal between them.

"No. I don't think so."

He frowned. "Why not?"

"Because there is absolutely nothing you have to say that I want to hear." With that, she turned, leaving a gaping Brock standing behind her as she walked away.

CHAPTER TWO

FINISHING her shift, while being stuck in the trauma bay with Brock Madison, was the hardest thing Elana had had to do since moving into her first foster home at the tender age of fifteen.

He'd wanted to talk things through.

Yeah. Right. To make himself feel better, no doubt.

Elana swallowed hard, trying without success to keep from ruminating over Brock Madison. Even when he wasn't in the immediate area, she'd found herself searching for him. If only so she could find a way to stay as far away from him as possible.

Raine was right: Brock was devastatingly attractive. Too much so. In those brief moments when he'd pinned her with his sizzling blue gaze, she'd nearly forgotten how much she hated him.

Brock had matured over the years. She shouldn't have been surprised; it wasn't as if she was the same angry and confused fifteen-year-old, either. But for some reason, her brain had always pictured him as the young, reckless college student who'd been speeding down the highway when Felicity pulled out in front of him.

For years she'd railed against the unfairness of it all. Brock had essentially walked away from the crash with only a couple of minor injuries—a broken collarbone and a few cracked ribs—while Felicity had died at the scene.

Enough. She needed to stop wallowing in the past. She threw herself into her work with a vengeance. Elana thought she'd successfully hidden her feelings towards Brock, but at the end of their shift, Raine cornered her in the staff lounge.

"All right, give. What is up with you and Dr Madison?"

Elana raised a brow, trying to keep her expression impassive. "Nothing."

Raine rolled her eyes. "Yeah, sure, and I'm Princess Stephanie. Come on, Elana. It's obvious you two know each other. For one thing, he called you by name before anyone had introduced you. And then he followed you to the staff lounge to talk to you in private. Did the two of you have a relationship in the past or what?"

Relationship? Good Lord, nothing could be further from the truth. "No. I barely know the guy."

"I don't believe you." Raine swiped her badge through the time clock, and Elana followed suit. "I'm not blind. There's a definite tension between you."

Elana suppressed a sigh, knowing Raine would continue to badger her endlessly unless she explained. "Remember when I told you my sister died in a car crash nine years ago?"

Raine frowned. "Yes." Then her eyes rounded. "Was your sister dating Brock at the time?"

"No. Worse." Elana walked into the staff locker room to retrieve her purse. She slammed the locker door shut with more force than was necessary. "Brock was the driver of the car that hit her."

"No! Really?" Raine's mouth dropped open in disbelief. "You have got to be kidding me."

"I wish I was." Elana's expression was grim, and she dropped onto the bench, her shoulders slumping with sudden fatigue. Keeping up the pretense that everything was okay when it really wasn't had been exhausting. "I don't know if I can do this, Raine," she whispered. "I don't think I can work with him."

Raine sat down beside her, putting a comforting arm around her shoulders. "Don't make any rash decisions, Elana. I'm sure this has been a shock, but Brock Madison seems to be a really good doctor. Maybe you need to give him a chance."

Give him a chance? Why? What about Felicity's chance? Her sister's life had ended far too young, and it was all Brock's fault.

She didn't want to give him a chance. Logically, Elana knew Raine might be right, since Chloe would have told her the same thing. But letting go of the past wasn't easy. Those dark years after her sister's death had been so awful. She winced and rubbed her pounding temple. "I can't," she murmured.

"Elana, you can. You're an adult now, and you're strong. Remember I'm always here for you if you need to talk." Raine gave her a quick hug. "Call me anytime."

Elana flashed a weak smile. "Thanks."

They gathered their things and headed outside to the staff parking lot. The night air was chilly for April, and she hunched her shoulders against the breeze, having left her coat in the car in her rush to get to work on time.

That night Elana couldn't sleep. Because there was no way she was going to be able to work with Brock. And she mourned the fact that her career as a trauma nurse was likely over.

"Brock? Do you have a minute?"

Elana's voice made him stop and turn in amazement. She'd called out to him. Voluntarily. Her dark eyes were warm and welcoming, making her even more beautiful than the first time he'd seen her at work. "Elana. It's great to see you."

Her tremulous smile made his chest tighten with anticipation. "I've been looking all over for you, Brock. I wanted to say I'm sorry. I'm so sorry for the way I treated you the other day. I had no right to be angry with you."

"I—don't know what to say. Does this mean you've forgiven me?" He could barely allow himself to hope.

She smiled. "Yes, Brock. I forgive you."

The incessant ringing of his phone pulled him from the dream. With a low groan of regret, Brock pried his eyes open, searching for his cell phone. Whoever was calling him this early in the morning had better have a good reason.

He'd wanted to stay asleep. To spend more time with the Elana in his dreams. The beautiful, smiling Elana who didn't blame him for her sister's death.

"Yeah?" He opened his phone without looking at the screen to see who was calling.

"Brock? You gotta help me, man." He could barely

hear his younger brother Joel's voice over the shrill wailing of a baby in the background. "I can't take it any more. Tucker's crying non-stop. There has to be something wrong with him. Something bad. He cries all the time!"

Wincing at the desperation in his brother's tone, he swung out of bed. Joel had got his girlfriend, Lacey, pregnant, and while Brock admired his brother's efforts, Joel was obviously struggling in his attempt to do the right thing. "Try to relax. Babies can sense when something is wrong. Tucker is only seven weeks old; maybe he's a little colicky. Does he seem better riding in the car? Or in the baby swing?"

"No. Nothing works." Joel's tone rose in agitation. "He just cries and cries. I'm telling you, there's something seriously wrong!"

Brock scrubbed a hand over his chin. Joel was only twenty-two, but his girlfriend, Lacey, was even younger, just six months past nineteen. They were young and finding it difficult to handle the responsibility of a brand-new family. Hence Brock's decision to move back to Milwaukee. Especially after hearing their father had refused to offer Joel any financial help. He felt bad for Joel. The screaming baby in the background was already getting on his nerves, and he wasn't there with them. "All right, maybe there is something going on with the baby other than just colic. You and Lacey need to take Tucker to the doctor for a check-up."

"We thought you could look at him," Joel said. "Since neither of us has health insurance."

"There's a low-income family clinic that caters for mothers and babies in Lacey's position," Brock explained patiently. "I don't mind taking a look at Tucker, but I'm not a peds expert. And I can't run lab tests on him to see if he has some sort of infection. Or do a chest X-ray of his lungs if he needs one. You could bring him to the ED while I'm working, but that will end up costing you more than simply going to the clinic. I really think you should go where they can offer the most help."

"All right. Where is this so-called clinic?" Joel asked in defeat.

Brock gave him the directions, wondering if the hospital had failed to give Lacey this information after she'd given birth. They certainly should have done more to help these two young kids, especially knowing Lacey's financial situation. They'd qualify for food support as well as basic health-care needs.

"You're going to be fine, Joel," he tried to reassure his brother.

"I don't know," Joel protested. "I'm not as strong as you, Brock."

"Yes, you are." He wished he could give his brother the self-confidence he needed. "You're stronger than you know."

"I'll talk to you later," Joel said evasively.

He didn't push, knowing Joel was under a huge amount of stress. Their father had basically tossed Joel onto the street. Brock had helped them move into a small duplex apartment and paid the security deposit along with the first three months of rent. Joel was only working part-time at a gas station, so Brock had also been trying to help his brother find a full-time job, one that would ideally provide decent benefits. Raising a child in this day and age without health insurance was not easy.

He stared at his phone. Should he have offered to take Tucker to the clinic? No, as much as he wanted to help his brother, he couldn't do everything for Joel. His brother would become more self-confident if he grew up a bit and took some responsibility.

After tossing his cell phone back down on his discarded clothes, Brock flopped back down on his bed, throwing his arm up over his eyes. He wished he could fall back asleep, picking up the dream with Elana where he'd left off. For a few brief moments, her forgiveness had swept away the dark cloud of guilt, making him feel light-hearted and happy.

But it was only a dream. In reality, Elana hadn't forgiven him for the accident that had stolen her sister's life. And, considering the way their conversation had ended so abruptly yesterday, he had to acknowledge she never would.

He knew he needed to let it go, but the sting of her rejection continued to gnaw at him. Why he was letting it bother him, he had no idea. He'd carried the guilt of that night for a long time. Had changed his major to medicine the semester after the accident, vowing to make a difference in other people's lives.

He'd also done what he could for Elana. More than she realized. Yet nothing he could do would bring Felicity back.

Her sister's death had haunted him for years. No reason for that to change now.

The best thing he could do for Elana was to stay far

away from her. He'd caused her enough pain. He refused to cause any more.

Elana hadn't slept well, but her fatigue didn't keep her in bed for long. Today was Wednesday, the day she was scheduled to work a four-hour stint volunteering at the low-income family clinic providing care to people who didn't have access to better health care.

Normally she enjoyed her hours at the clinic, as there was something immensely satisfying about helping people in need. Some of the cases were heart-wrenching, the pregnant mothers trying to overcome their addictions, or the young people who'd contracted HIV, but there were also a lot of people who just needed a helping hand.

Today her head pounded with a dull ache she'd had ever since she'd woken up that morning. No doubt a result of a restless night, which was all Brock Madison's fault.

But she wasn't going to think about him. Brock was just another ED doctor she'd have to work with. And if he liked trauma, then maybe she'd ask Stacey to assign her to one of the arena teams for a while. At least until she figured out what her options were.

Staying in the ED long-term was clearly not going to work. She needed to find a new career and fast.

Shaking off her depressing thoughts, Elana drove her tiny compact car down to the clinic. The clinic was in the middle of the low-income district, several miles from her tiny apartment. The clinic had to be close to where people in need lived because many of these clients didn't have cars or other means of reliable transportation.

Finding a parking space was always a challenge. As

she walked inside the clinic, she discovered Tina Kaplan was the receptionist on duty.

"Hi, Tina. How are you today?"

"Great, Elana. How is your aunt Chloe doing?"

All of the staff at the New Beginnings Clinic knew Chloe, her foster mother, had volunteered her time here as a receptionist while Elana was growing up. Elana was glad that she could now return the favor, carrying on her foster mother's tradition. "She's wonderful. The cardiac stent went very well."

"I'm so glad." Tina handed over the list of patients who were already waiting to be seen. Their clients often began lining up at the door a half hour before the clinic officially opened.

"Me too." Elana took the list and scanned it, as always checking to see which of her previous clients might be making a return visit. "Thanks, Tina. Who's the doctor coming in today?"

"Hmm." Tina glanced up at the handwritten schedule. "Looks like Liz Jacoby is the MD on the schedule today."

Liz was an exceptionally talented African-American woman who donated a lot of her time to the New Beginnings Clinic. Most of their clients didn't know that Liz Jacoby was also a nationally renowned breast cancer physician. Elana loved working with her. Her dull headache began to fade. "Excellent. We should have a good day, then."

"When do you want me to start sending patients back?" Tina asked.

"Give me five minutes to make sure everything is well stocked, and then you can let 'em rip."

Tina laughed, and Elana smiled as she headed back to the exam room. She routinely saw the patients first and then got the physician involved in their care as needed. Their system would have worked better with more volunteers, but so far, other than Raine, she hadn't convinced any of her other co-workers to help by donating their time.

The first few patients came through with simple enough concerns. One woman had a bad cough with a fever that Elana suspected was a case of bronchitis turning into pneumonia. The next two patients were severely dehydrated from the stomach flu that was making its way through the city. Another young man came in with a serious burn on his forearm, with a story she absolutely did not believe.

"Jackson, there is no way you got this burn from a lighter falling on your arm," she told him sternly. "Do you really think I'm that stupid? I can tell this is a gasoline burn. So why don't you tell me what really happened?"

The young man refused to talk. Elana sighed and applied a generous amount of ointment to the burn, wrapping it with gauze to keep it clean and dry. Maybe Liz would be able to pry more information out of the taciturn young man.

"Elana?" Tina called from the other side of the door.

"Yes?"

"How much longer? There's a young woman and a crying baby that need to get in to see you right away."

That didn't sound too good. She reached over and opened the door. "I'm nearly finished. Jackson just needs to see Dr Jacoby while I get his wound supplies together."

"I'll do it. Tell me what he needs."

Elana raised a brow. "What's going on? Is the baby that sick?"

"I don't know, but the mother is crying almost as hard as the baby." Tina's eyes were full of compassionate concern. "I can't stand it."

"All right, get him ten rolls of gauze and a jar of burns cream. Jackson, you need to change this dressing twice a day and return here to the clinic in five days, do you understand? We need to make sure that burn doesn't get infected."

"Yes, ma'am."

Tina hustled the young man out of the exam room, taking him over to see the doctor. Elana quickly threw out the paper strip from the exam table and wiped down the surface with a disposable bleach cloth. Within two minutes, a young waif-thin girl lugging a crying baby on her shoulder came into the room.

"Good morning, I'm the nurse here, my name is Elana. What's going on today?"

The young woman's eyes were swollen and red from her weeping. "He just keeps crying and crying. I don't know what I'm doing wrong," she murmured.

"There now, I'm sure it's nothing you're doing wrong," Elana said firmly. "What's your name? Do you mind if I hold him for a minute?"

Letting out a loud sniffle, the young woman handed the baby over. "I'm Lacey, and his name is Tucker. He's seven weeks old."

"Hi, Tucker," Elana crooned, gently nuzzling the baby, testing the temperature of his skin. He did feel warm, but that could just as easily be because of the crying. She loved babies, another reason she volunteered her time here. Giving him one last nuzzle, she laid him on the exam table and undid his diaper, looking for obvious signs of irritation, like diaper rash, before using her stethoscope to listen to his heart and lungs.

Not an easy task while he was crying.

"Are you breast-feeding?" Elana asked, her heart going out to the waif-thin girl. The baby sounded a bit congested, but it could be merely the result of his non-stop crying. His ears didn't look red, ruling out an ear infection.

"No. We give him whatever formula is on sale at the store," Lacey admitted.

"That might be your problem," Elana said gently. "Colicky babies don't tolerate dairy-based formula, and you should really stick to one brand. I want you to try the soy-based formula, and nothing else. I'll give you some free samples here."

"Are you sure it's nothing more serious?" Lacey asked, swiping her nose on her sleeve. The motion pushed up the sleeve of her shirt, revealing a few bloody cuts on her forearm. As if she sensed Elana's gaze, she quickly covered the area back up again. "I can't believe Tucker is crying this much just because of colic."

Elana wanted to ask about the suspicious marks she saw on Lacey's arm, but at the moment little Tucker was her primary concern. "Don't underestimate colic, Lacey. I've seen many mothers reduced to tears over inconsolably crying babies. There are many ways to treat colic. First let me get a soy-based formula sample for you to try, okay?"

Lacey sniffled again and nodded.

"I'll be right back." Elana handed her the baby and hurried over to their jam-packed supply cabinet and found a six-pack of soy-based cans of formula and a disposable bottle. After quickly preparing the bottle, she brought it back to the exam room.

"Here, see if he'll take this," she instructed.

Lacey held the baby in the crook of her arm and tried the bottle. At first Tucker sucked greedily, then, after a few minutes, he turned his head away and began crying again.

"See how he's hungry but then turns away? That's another classic sign of colic, too much gas. We can give him some anti-gas medicine in an eyedropper that should work. And I will get Dr Jacoby to take a listen to him just to be sure there's nothing else going on." Elana hesitated and then carefully asked, "Do you have anyone to help you, Lacey? Or are you raising Tucker all alone?"

Lacey shrugged, trying to get Tucker to take the bottle again. "Joel, the baby's father, is trying to help me, but he can't stand it when Tucker cries."

Oh, boy. Sounded like Joel and Lacey needed a lot of help. And she couldn't dismiss those cuts on Lacey's arms. She understood how hopelessness could suffocate your soul.

"Lacey, I'm here for you. I'd like you to come back in two days and bring Joel with you. You both need to learn how to deal with a colicky baby. I've heard using a baby swing alongside a noisy vacuum cleaner works, and car rides. Once Tucker gets the dairy products out of his system and starts on the anti-gas medication, he should be better."

"Joel's brother is a doctor, and even he thought there might be something more wrong with the baby," Lacey said defensively.

She frowned at Lacey's tone. Did the poor girl feel as if she wasn't a good mother because she couldn't handle the baby's crying? "Really? Is his brother a pediatric specialist?"

"No, but Brock works in the emergency department at Trinity Medical Center."

Brock? Had she heard correctly? Her stomach clenched, and she forced herself to ask, "What's Joel's last name?"

"Madison. Joel Madison."

CHAPTER THREE

Later that day, Elana couldn't stop thinking about Lacey's plight. The cuts on that poor girl's forearm haunted her. Lacey needed help. For herself and for her baby. More than just a quick clinic visit.

No matter how much she wanted to stay far away from Brock, she simply couldn't ignore her conscience. Lacey was obviously in serious trouble; the telltale cuts on her forearm were not to be taken lightly. And Tucker was Brock's nephew. Hadn't Brock mentioned that he'd moved home to deal with some family issues?

There was no way around it. She needed to talk to Brock. To let him know her concerns about Lacey, Joel and their baby.

When she arrived at work, she walked into the arena and was surprised to discover they were busier than usual for a Wednesday evening. Patients streamed in seemingly from nowhere.

She couldn't deny a hint of relief at the reprieve. There was no time to talk to anyone, not when so many patients were in need of assistance. She jumped into the fray, helping to move patients through the system. But just when they'd started to catch up, a local discount store reported a serious gas leak. Dozens of people flooded the ED to be ruled out for potential carbon monoxide poisoning.

Luckily, most of the discount store patrons weren't too sick, but each patient had to be registered, screened, treated and released, taking up a significant amount of time and energy. Elana had been pulled from the trauma bay to help, giving her what should have been a welcome break from working with Brock Madison.

Except she still really needed to talk to him about Lacey. At least, that was what she told herself when she found she was constantly looking for him.

"Do we have any more carbon monoxide poisoning cases left?" Raine asked, coming over to stand beside Elana, who was finishing up the charting on her soon-to-be-discharged patient. "Because if I don't get a chance to eat something soon, I'm going to pass out myself."

"I don't think so," Elana said, glancing up at the central board listing the status of all their patients. "According to Stacey, we were expecting to see twenty-three patients, and I'm sure we've moved at least that many through already."

"I hope so," Raine muttered with a low groan. "At least this influx of patients has made the shift go by fast."

"No kidding. Why don't you take a break? I'll cover for you," Elana offered. "Then, when you're finished, I'll go."

"Thanks. Give me at least fifteen minutes."

"Take twenty," Elana said generously. "We deserve it."

Even though the immediate urgency of the discount store gas leak had passed, there were still quite a few patients to see. Since the trauma bay was quiet, Elana continued to help out in the arena.

When she nearly tripped over Brock, she realized Stacey had reassigned Brock to the arena too. Probably to help with the influx of patients.

"Elana? Can you send a pregnancy test on the female patient in room two?" he asked.

"Sure. Is she one of the carbon monoxide exposure patients?"

He nodded. "She's a bit worried she might be pregnant."

Understandable. She hurried over to do what he'd asked. Unfortunately there wasn't time to ask him about Lacey because her second patient began complaining of tight chest pain.

"I think you'd better take a look at this guy, Mr Reeves, in room eighteen," she told Brock. "He has new-onset chest pain; we just did an ECG and sent labs. I think he needs to be moved into the trauma bay."

Brock didn't hesitate. "Let's take a look."

The elderly gentleman had come in originally because of a fall, but now, with this new onset of chest pain, Elana guessed it was more likely his fall had been caused by his heart problems in the first place.

"Definitely signs of ST depression, according to his twelve-lead ECG," Brock murmured. "Let's get him into the trauma bay so we have more access to equipment. I'll call Cardiology so we can get this guy into the cath lab asap."

Elana nodded, quickly explaining to Mr Reeves their plan. When she asked about his support systems, she learned his wife had passed away a year ago from colon cancer and he had two kids, a son and a daughter. He didn't want to bother his kids, though, claiming they had their own families to worry about.

"I really think we need to call them," she urged. "You may be having a small heart attack. I'm sure your son and daughter would want to know." And hopefully they were decent kids who would come in to support their father.

Mr Reeves grudgingly agreed, and Elana quickly called the son, Kirk, who willingly took responsibility for getting in touch with his sister, Lisa. Satisfied her elderly patient wouldn't be alone for long, she hurried back to his side.

"Your son, Kirk, is on his way," she told him. "And he's going to call Lisa too."

"Thanks," he whispered. His face had gone pale, and there was a fine sheen of sweat on his brow.

"Are you having more pain?" she asked in concern.

"Maybe a little," he grudgingly admitted.

Catching Brock's eye, she waved him over. "Mr Reeves is having pain; can I give him more morphine?"

"Absolutely. Give him five milligrams and move up to ten as needed. Draw a troponin level if you haven't already. The cardiologist is on his way down."

"I already drew the troponin with the rest of the labs; we should have the results any minute." She hurried over to the medication machine to withdraw the narcotics for her patient.

Mr Reeves visibly relaxed after he received the additional pain medication. His troponin level was elevated, so the cardiologist wasted no time in arranging for transport to the cardiac cath lab.

"Wait," Mr Reeves protested. "I need to wait for my son."

"You can't wait, Mr Reeves," Elana said gently. "There isn't time; the quicker they can get your heart fixed, the less damage you'll have. I promise I'll talk to Kirk when he gets here. Your son will be in the waiting room when you're all finished, okay?"

"Okay," he reluctantly agreed.

"Nice job," Brock murmured as the cardiology team wheeled Mr Reeves away. "You handled that very well."

His offhand praise made her blush. "Er, thanks." They'd been so busy since the start of their shift, the stilted awkwardness between them from the day before had vanished. She wasn't sure it was a good thing. Could she really just pretend Felicity's death meant nothing?

No. But at the same time, there were other, more important things to worry about. Like the situation with Lacey, Tucker and Brock's brother.

Gathering her courage, she looked him in the eye. "Brock, do you have a few minutes after our shift to talk?"

He looked surprised, but readily agreed. "Of course. I can be available at any time you need."

His eagerness made her feel guilty. Did he think they were going to rehash the past? Not likely. She hesitated, wondering if maybe she should give him a hint as to what she wanted to discuss.

"Elana, I'm glad you're willing to talk to me," Brock said in a low voice before she could think of a way to ease into the topic of his brother. "I haven't been able to get you out of my mind."

Really? Her cheeks felt hot all over again, and she cursed herself for succumbing to his charm. She wasn't the least bit attracted to Brock Madison, and she didn't need his approval to feel confident in her nursing skills.

"Elana? I'm back," Raine said, walking up to them. "It's your turn to take a break."

She took the chance to escape gratefully. "Thanks, I'm starved. See you later," she said to Brock before hurrying away.

Good grief, she needed to pull herself together, and quick. The purpose of her chat with Brock was solely to explain her concerns about Lacey and Tucker.

Once she'd let Brock know what was going on with Lacey and Tucker, she'd have no reason to speak to him on a personal level again.

Brock couldn't control the wide grin on his face as he either helped dispatch patients home or admitted them to the hospital, depending on the extent of their illness.

Even though he doubted that Elana was totally going to let him off the hook the way she had in his dreams, he was thrilled she was finally going to give him a chance to explain.

Nine years ago he'd gone to Felicity's funeral, but that attempt to talk to Elana and her mother had ended in disaster. Her mother had all but tossed him out of the church, creating such a scene that he'd escaped before the police were called.

Good thing, since his policeman father had nearly boxed his ears after the accident as it was.

Months later, he'd tried to talk to them again, only

to find Elana's mother's house was for sale. He'd soon discovered Louisa had suffered a complete nervous breakdown and Elana had been placed in foster care.

Shaken by the events that seemed to keep getting worse instead of better, he'd made it his business from that point forward to keep tabs on Elana from afar. Guilt had been his constant companion during those months following the accident, despite the results of Felicity's autopsy. Those seconds before she'd pulled out in front of him had replayed over and over in his mind.

When he'd entered medical school, he'd buried his guilt and poured his energies into his studies. He'd graduated top of his class, but he couldn't have cared less.

He'd been determined to save lives. It was the only way he could live with himself.

Brock took a ten-minute break, checking his phone for voice mail messages, surprised to find a message from Lacey. She'd sounded upset, crying again, as she'd begged him to call her back.

Glancing at his watch, he realized she'd called almost thirty minutes ago. Wincing at the delay, he quickly dialed her number, hoping she hadn't gotten bad news regarding Tucker's health.

"Lacey? It's Brock. What's wrong?"

"Oh, Brock, I don't know what to do. Joel's gone," Lacey said between hiccupping sobs.

Brock frowned. "What do you mean, he's gone? Gone to work? Is there something wrong with Tucker?"

"I took Tucker to the clinic, like you said. They did some tests, gave me medicine for him and told me to use different formula because he probably has colic.

When I came home, I thought Joel was at work, but a couple of hours ago, they called here looking for him."

A warning chill snaked down his back. Joel couldn't have taken off, could he? Surely he wouldn't risk losing his job, not when he had a baby to support. "Okay, don't panic," he said soothingly, hiding the depth of his concern. "I know Joel has been having a tough time lately. He probably just needed a little break. He's likely having a drink or two with a couple of his buddies."

"That's what I thought too, at first," Lacey said. "But I've called all his friends—no one has seen him all day. I even went to the bowling alley, his favorite hangout, but he hasn't been there either. I'm scared, Brock. What am I going to do if he's gone for good?"

Elana swiped out at the end of her shift and then glanced around, searching for Brock. He'd promised to meet her in the staff lounge after work, but it was possible he was still finishing up. The physicians couldn't leave until they were assured all the patients were safe. The hand-over of care was easier for the nurses, though, since there were more nurses assigned per shift than doctors.

Nervous, she swiped her damp palms on the sides of her scrubs. A brief conversation with Brock shouldn't cause an anxiety attack. Especially since this talk wasn't remotely personal. This was about Lacey. The young mother and her son hadn't been far from her thoughts all evening.

"Do you want to walk out to the parking lot to-gether?" Raine asked.

"Nah, go ahead without me. I have a few things I

have to do yet," Elana hedged, avoiding direct eye contact with her closest friend.

"Like what?" Raine demanded, oblivious to Elana's subtle hint. "You've swiped out, haven't you? What else is there to do? It's not like you can make phone calls or run errands at eleven-thirty at night."

Elana suppressed a sigh. "There was a patient at the clinic today that has me worried. I need a few minutes to run the issue past Brock, that's all."

"Oh. I see." Elana didn't appreciate the knowing glint in Raine's eye. "I'm sure *Brock* will be more than happy to help you out."

"It's not like that, Raine," she snapped. "This isn't a personal issue. I barely know the man."

Raine arched one brow in disbelief. "Sure, Elana. Whatever you say. Heck, I think it's great you're talking to him. That means you're giving him a chance. Hey, maybe you can get him to volunteer a few shifts a month at the clinic too."

Oh, no. Absolutely not. No way was she asking Brock to volunteer at the clinic. Working with him in the emergency department was bad enough. The clinic was her refuge. She didn't want him anywhere near the place.

After Raine had finally left, she let out a sigh of relief and plopped into a chair to wait for Brock. She'd give him another five minutes before she went searching for him. She was tired and didn't have all night.

Yet she refused to leave without telling him her concerns about Lacey.

When he finally came in, he looked terrible. He

wasn't smiling, his face drawn into harsh lines. He looked about as exhausted as she felt.

For a minute she wavered. Maybe this wasn't exactly the time to dump her concerns on him.

But just as quickly she stiffened her resolve. This wasn't about Brock; he could take care of himself. Tucker was the vulnerable one. Not that Lacey was an awful mother, but she was definitely struggling.

"Hi, Elana. Sorry I'm late," Brock said with a forced smile.

"No problem. It was a rough night for everyone, I think." Making small talk with Brock felt weird. Truthfully, until the day they'd worked together in the trauma room, they hadn't exchanged more than half a dozen words to each other, and none of them pleasant or friendly. At least on her part.

A hint of embarrassment crept under her skin when she remembered how she'd lashed out at him all those years ago at Felicity's funeral. She pushed the memories of the past aside.

She cleared her throat, swiping her hands on her scrubs again. "I'm sorry to bother you, but there's a problem I think you need to know about."

His dark brows pulled together in a frown. "A problem?"

"Yes. I volunteer at the New Beginnings Clinic down in the low-income district. Earlier today, a very distraught young woman brought in her colicky baby to be evaluated by the doctor."

Brock's spine straightened, and the expression on his face became noncommittal. "Lacey and Tucker."

She was surprised he'd guessed, but that only made it easier to speak her mind. "Yes. You need to know I'm really concerned about them. Especially Lacey."

"Why? Because there was something wrong with Tucker? She's not hurting him or anything is she?" Brock asked in a rush.

"No! No, it's not that." Although she could understand why he might jump to that conclusion. Working in the ED, they sometimes saw cases of child abuse. "Tucker has a bad case of colic, but she was making it worse by giving him different kinds of formula. I helped her switch him over to a soy-based product and gave her some anti-gas medication for him. But your brother, the baby's father, didn't come to the appointment with her."

Brock's shoulders slumped with apparent relief that abuse wasn't the issue. "Yeah, I'm not surprised," he muttered.

He was being far to blasé about the entire situation. She leaned forward, willing him to understand. "Listen to me. I noticed several small cuts on Lacey's arm. She covered them up right away, but I didn't imagine them. She's not coping very well with motherhood. I think she might be cutting herself, purposefully inflicting pain."

"What?" Brock stared at her in disbelief. "Are you telling me she's suicidal?"

Elana didn't want to have this conversation, she really didn't. But hadn't she learned the hard way how ignoring a problem only made it worse? "Young adults who are known to be cutters aren't suicidal per se, but it is a sign of being unable to cope. They cut themselves because it's one area of their life they can actually control. And cutting themselves seems to help relieve guilt, in a bizarre way."

"You sound like you're familiar with this affliction," Brock said, his gaze intense.

She swallowed hard. She knew far more than she wanted to about kids who used harmful ways to cope. Been there and done that.

And it was all Brock's fault.

For a moment darkness threatened. She pushed the sensation away. "I know a little about it."

"I see." He stared at her, a flash of real regret intermixed with guilt shadowing his eyes. Could it be that the accident had affected him more than she realized?

Disturbed by the possibility, she stared down at her hands. Had Brock really suffered too? Maybe, but so what? He'd been able to walk away. She hadn't. Besides, she needed to focus on the issue at hand.

Lacey and Tucker.

"Brock, you need to make your brother understand how his son needs him. Joel and Lacey should take a parenting class; there are resources to help them." She silently pleaded with him to take her advice seriously. "I honestly don't think Lacey is stable enough, or capable enough to raise Tucker alone."

"Yeah, well, unfortunately, that's going to be a problem," Brock admitted, his expression grim. "Lacey just called me less than an hour ago. She's freaking out because apparently my brother, Joel, went AWOL. She hasn't seen him all day, and no one seems to know where he is."

CHAPTER FOUR

"LACEY has been home alone with Tucker all day?" Elana couldn't control the surge of panic as she stared at Brock in horror. "We have to get over there right away."

"Maybe you're right." He glanced at her, his gaze serious. "I know it's a lot to ask, but since you've established a bond with Lacey, she might feel better if you came along."

She hesitated and then steeled her resolve. Lacey needed her. "Of course I'll come with you."

"Thanks."

Ten minutes later she found herself seated in the passenger seat of Brock's SUV as he drove to Lacey's small duplex. She twisted her hands in her lap and stole a glimpse at him. His gaze was glued to the road, his face drawn into a deep frown. She found it difficult to breathe; his presence was large and overpowering in the tight confines of the car.

There was no way to know what was going through his mind. She told herself she didn't care, but couldn't quite make herself believe it. He'd immediately jumped to help Lacey, and she was reluctantly impressed with his willingness to do whatever was necessary.

The silence was deafening. For the life of her, she couldn't think of anything to say. She barely knew him. Brock the emergency medicine physician was a complete enigma to her.

Not that she'd known Brock the reckless college student either.

Her aunt Chloe had discouraged her from blindly believing the rumors about Brock's speeding. The normal speed limit on that stretch of highway where the accident had occurred was forty-five miles per hour. More than fast enough to have caused a fatal accident without speeding.

Elana had refused to listen. It was easier to hate Brock for her messed-up life than to hate her disabled mother. Or her dead sister.

She glanced at the dashboard, noticing he drove well within the speed limit. Of course, she would too if she'd caused a young girl to die.

Her chest tightened with a spurt of empathy. How awful to know you'd taken a life. She couldn't imagine how difficult that must have been.

Wait a minute. Why was she feeling sorry for Brock? His guilt, one way or the other, wasn't her concern.

Turning her attention to Lacey and Tucker, she glanced at the clock. Almost midnight. Did Brock know where to find his brother, Joel? She hoped so. She wouldn't mind staying with Lacey while he went searching for him.

Brock pulled into the driveway of a rather dilapidated building a few minutes later. The lights were on in the upper-level apartment, and Brock softly rapped on the door, as if trying not to wake the occupants of the lower apartment.

Lacey answered the door a few minutes later. There was no sign of Tucker, which caused a tingle of alarm to skate down Elana's back.

For Brock too, apparently, because the first thing he said was, "Where's the baby?"

"Sleeping." Lacey seemed surprised yet happy to see Elana. "Come in."

They trooped up the stairs to the apartment. The interior was a bit of a mess, clothes scattered around and dirty dishes piled on top of the scarred coffee table. Elana's fingers itched to clean up. Instead she turned her back on the mess, facing Tucker's young mother.

"Hi, Lacey. Do you remember me from the clinic? My name is Elana, and I work with Brock in the emergency department."

Lacey slowly nodded. "I remember. The gas medicine seems to be helping. Tucker napped for a full two hours this afternoon."

Elana smiled. "I'm so glad. I'm sure the new formula will help too."

"Do you mind if we look in on the baby?" Brock asked, still wearing his scowling frown. "We promise not to wake him."

Lacey lifted a thin shoulder in a half shrug. "I guess. He's probably going to wake up in another hour or so anyway to eat. He's been getting up to eat every four hours."

The resigned expression on the young woman's face bothered Elana. Was Lacey already imaging what it was going to be like to raise Tucker all by herself? She was glad the woman didn't seem too desperate, yet she also knew how easy it was to hide your true feelings.

She darted a glance at Brock, and he nodded at her unspoken question, gesturing towards the bedroom door that Lacey had left partially open. She tiptoed into Tucker's room, gazing down at the sleeping baby nestled in the crib, lying on his back, with a rolled-up blanket tucked behind him.

Brock and Lacey spoke in low tones, no doubt discussing where Joel might be. She longed to pick up the baby, but knew better than to disturb the sleeping infant. If Lacey was right, he'd be awake soon enough anyway.

She left the room quietly, closing the door soundlessly behind her. "He seems to be sleeping pretty well," she announced, coming back into the living room.

Brock was on his cell phone, calling one of Joel's friends. After several fruitless calls, he snapped his phone shut in defeat.

"I'm sorry, Lacey. There's nothing more I can do to find him tonight," he said in a resigned tone.

Lacey looked as if she wanted to cry. "I know."

Brock let out a heavy sigh. "Go and pack a bag full of whatever you and the baby will need for a few days," he said. "You and Tucker will be better off staying at my place until we find my brother."

Brock sat on Lacey's sofa, broodingly watching as Lacey began packing their things together. He didn't mind helping out, but he couldn't quell a sense of panic. Moving Lacey and Tucker to his place was a drastic step. What if they didn't find Joel right away? How long would this arrangement have to last? He didn't have any idea, but he also didn't have any other options. He couldn't leave Lacey to cope on her own.

Dammit, where in the hell was Joel?

Brock had to swallow his seething frustration. He couldn't help being annoyed with his brother. He'd come home to give Joel a helping hand, but Joel needed to do his part too. Disappearing was not holding up his end of the deal.

He scrubbed a hand over his jaw. Had their dad been right to deny Joel any financial help after the baby was born? Maybe Brock's offer to help was only enabling Joel to shirk his responsibilities.

No. Joel needed support. And Elana's concerns were well founded. It was no secret to him that Lacey was having trouble coping, but he hadn't realized the full extent of her problems. Deliberately cutting herself in some twisted need to be in control was scary.

And how had Elana known those sorts of details? Just from working as a nurse in the emergency department or because of her own troubled teenage years?

It was difficult to think about how Elana had struggled back then, losing her sister and then her mother. She'd certainly been a casualty in the entire mess. He'd hoped that Elana was ready to talk, had foolishly looked forward to their meeting after work, only to be taken aback by her concerns regarding Lacey and Tucker.

How long had she been working at the New Beginnings Clinic? He couldn't help admiring her willingness to help those in need. Patients like Lacey would certainly flourish under her care. Elana was a beautiful woman, inside and out. He was amazed at how accomplished she was. Selfishly, he wished he could get to know Elana better.

But that wasn't likely.

Tucker woke up, crying softly at first but then swinging into a full-blown wail. Lacey became flustered, dropping her bag and rushing over to him as if something awful would happen if the baby cried too long.

"Here, why don't you let me take care of him for you," Elana said, following Lacey into the bedroom. "That way you can keep gathering all your stuff together."

Brock wondered if he should offer to help too, but when Elana changed the baby's diapers and competently whisked him off to the kitchen to make a bottle, he decided she had things under control.

The way Elana cooed at his nephew, pressing kisses to the top of his head even as he cried, captured his gaze. When she finally settled down in the rocking chair, quieting the baby with the bottle, a bolt of desire shot straight to his groin.

What in the world was wrong with him? He'd no business thinking of Elana in a personal way, as a woman he might be interested in. Yet, suddenly, he couldn't tear his eyes from the picture she made gazing serenely at Tucker. Since when did he get aroused watching a beautiful woman rock a baby?

Since never. He must be overly tired. Talk about being self-destructive. Elana hated him. Being attracted to her was crazy. She deserved a family of her own.

But he didn't. There was no way he'd ever consider having children. Ever.

He tore his gaze away and jumped to his feet. He needed to do something. Anything. When he saw Lacey lugging the swing towards the door, he bit back a protest and crossed over to take it from her.

"I'll carry that down to the car for you," he said quickly. "Does it fold up somehow?"

"I think so. Joel put it together for me," Lacey said.

Wrestling with the baby swing gave him something to do. But, even so, he found his gaze resting on Elana and Tucker more than once.

When he saw the amount of stuff Lacey was packing, including the swing, a portable cradle, the infant car seat, the box of diapers and their suitcases full of clothes, a surge of panic grabbed him by the throat. He'd only asked her to come for a few days, not to move in permanently.

He was going to kill Joel when he found him. No, scratch that plan; he couldn't kill his brother because then Lacey and Tucker would really be his responsibility. But, dammit, Joel needed to stop running away from his mistakes.

He finally figured out how to get the baby swing folded up to a point it would fit in the trunk of his car. He hauled it downstairs and then returned for the portable crib. After making several more trips down to the car, he had most of the stuff packed up.

"Is there anything else?" he asked Lacey, watching from the corner of his eye as Elana finished feeding Tucker, holding him on her shoulder and rubbing his back, urging him to burp. Did babies burp on command?

He didn't think so. But when Tucker let out a loud belch, he couldn't help but grin.

"I think so," Lacey said hesitantly, wringing her hands together nervously. "Babies sure need a lot of stuff, don't they?"

"You're not kidding," Brock muttered. He forced himself to sound positive. "It's probably good enough for now. We can always come back if you did forget something. And I'm sure Joel will be back soon."

"Yeah. You're probably right," Lacey said in a voice that lacked conviction.

"Do you have the anti-gas medicine?" Elana asked, crossing over to them, still holding the baby.

Lacey's face crumpled. "No. I forgot. And I don't think I packed the formula either."

"Here, Brock." She thrust the baby at him. "Come on, Lacey, let's make one last sweep of the house."

He wanted to protest, but the women disappeared into the kitchen faster than he could blink. Holding his breath, he stared down at his nephew. It wasn't as if he'd never held a baby; infants occasionally ended up in the ED, although not for long since they didn't waste any time transferring them over to Children's Memorial Hospital, located right across the street.

After the accident, he'd refused to contemplate having a family of his own. Children. After stealing Felicity's life, he knew he didn't deserve a family.

Yet he couldn't ignore his nephew. Tucker looked up at him with a solemn, steady gaze. Brock smiled nervously. "Hey, there. You're being a good baby, aren't you? No crying now, and let's try to keep it that way, hmm?"

Tucker blinked and then waved his hands, as if he wanted to say something but obviously couldn't. When Brock put his hand out, the baby grabbed his finger with a surprisingly tight grip.

And when Tucker smiled, the icy reserve around Brock's heart melted into a gooey pile of slush. For the first time, he realized how much he'd given up that day he'd crashed into Felicity's car.

Elana's breath hitched in her chest when she came out of the kitchen and caught sight of the enthralled expression on Brock's face as he gazed down at his nephew.

She tightened her grip on the cans of formula she carried so they didn't slip and crash to the floor.

What was she thinking to react like this? Maybe she could respect Brock's talent as a physician, but she couldn't be attracted to him. Obviously being with him like this outside the hospital was dangerous. It was almost too easy to forget how he'd recklessly killed her sister.

Felicity. She'd idolized her older sister, especially since Felicity had often looked out for Elana when their mother wasn't quite capable. Felicity had been so vibrant, so full of life. Everyone had loved her, Elana most of all.

She drew a ragged breath. *Don't go back. You're a different person now.*

Distance. She needed distance. She needed to get as far away from Brock as possible.

"Do you and Lacey have everything now?" Brock asked.

She put down the cans of formula and curled her

fingers into tight fists, the prick of her fingernails help-ing to sharpen her focus.

"Elana?" he asked again.

"Yes," she croaked. Lacey crossed over to put Tucker into his car seat, giving him his medicine once he was settled in.

"Let's go, then." Brock reached down to pick up the car seat by the handle, holding the door for them so they could head out to the car.

"Put your seat belt on," he said to Lacey after she'd gotten Tucker's car seat fastened.

Elana caught Lacey rolling her eyes, but the young woman didn't protest as she complied with his wishes. Elana had already buckled herself in.

So Brock was fanatical about seat belts. That made sense; working in trauma, you learned the patients who weren't secured in their seat belts, nine times out of ten, suffered more severe injuries than those who complied with the law.

Like Felicity. Chloe had pointed out several times that her sister might have survived the crash if she had been wearing her seat belt. Her neck had been broken when she'd been ejected from the car.

Brock's fault. It was all Brock's fault.

Wasn't it?

Elana huddled in her seat, her head spinning. She wanted to tell Brock to drop her off first, so she could get away from him, but she should really go to make sure Lacey was settled in before leaving.

She would take a taxi home. Anything to get away from him.

Brock seemed grateful for her help as they proceeded to unpack all the items they'd just stored in the back of his SUV. By the time they had everything set up, it was two o'clock in the morning.

The good news was that Tucker had fallen asleep on the short drive over to Brock's. Brock had carefully carried the sleeping baby inside and set him in the corner of the spare bedroom, where Lacey would also have to sleep.

"That anti-gas medicine really works," Lacey whispered, her gaze full of relief. "If only Joel could see Tucker now, he'd know things weren't so bad."

"Do you think that's why he left?" Elana quietly asked. Brock was still hauling stuff inside while they unpacked.

Lacey nodded. "It was so awful with Tucker crying all the time. Nothing helped. Feeding him, changing his diaper, rocking him, nothing. Joel couldn't take it any more."

Elana tightened her lips, wanting to point out that Lacey had struggled too but hadn't taken the easy way out by walking away. "Brock will find him, you'll see," she said instead.

"I hope so. I've always been a little afraid of Brock, but he's been nice so far tonight."

Afraid? Elana almost choked out a laugh. She was afraid of Brock too. Of getting close to him. Of not hating him as much as she should. "There's no reason to be afraid," Elana assured her. "I think he's irritated with Joel's disappearing act, but he would never hurt you or Tucker."

"I know. But I still don't think he likes me much,"

Lacey said, yawning widely, her eyes drooping with exhaustion.

"Get some sleep while Tucker's down," Elana advised. "You'll cope better if you get some rest too. I'll finish putting this stuff away. You can take care of the rest in the morning."

"All right." Lacey offered a shy smile. "Good night, Elana. Thanks for all your help. I don't think I could have done it without you."

Touched, Elana reached over to give Lacey a quick hug. "You're very welcome, Lacey. I'm always available if you need me. Call me any time."

Elana finished setting up the formula, bottles and the medicine along the kitchen counter so that Lacey could easily find them when Tucker woke up hungry in the morning. Brock was still putting the baby swing back together, looking up in surprise when she headed for the door.

"Wait, I'll drive you home," he said, abandoning his project and jumping to his feet.

"No, don't bother. I called a taxi."

He frowned, and she could tell he wasn't happy with her decision. "There's no need to waste your hard-earned money on a taxi," he said testily.

Her sanity was well worth the expense. She edged closer to the door. "It's better for Lacey if you stay here."

He stared at her. "Better for Lacey? Or for you?"

She stopped and squared her shoulders defiantly. "Does it matter?"

"Yes, it does." His voice was soft and compelling. "I never wanted to hurt you, Elana."

"Too late," she whispered. "Good night, Brock." She turned and slipped out the door, overwhelmingly relieved when he didn't follow.

But in the taxi she looked down in surprise at the crimson stains on her fingers. She opened her palms, realizing with a shock that she was bleeding from several spots in her hands where she'd broken the skin with her nails.

Her stomach churned, and for a moment black spots danced before her eyes. She struggled to take a deep breath.

Brock's return was pushing her to the edge of her fragile self-control.

CHAPTER FIVE

BROCK bowed his head, fighting every instinct in his body screaming at him to follow Elana. *Too late*. Her whispered words were seared into his memory. He knew they were true. He was too late. He'd already hurt her.

He stayed where he was, picking up a piece of the swing and continuing to put the various parts back together.

What did his needs matter?

He didn't sleep well; Elana's tortured expression followed him into his dreams. Nightmares. Over the next couple of nights, he lay awake, not falling asleep until the wee hours of the morning, only to be woken up by Tucker's crying.

By the second day, he groaned and shoved his head under the pillow, but it was no use. Logically he knew the little guy was just hungry, and crying was the only way Tucker had to make his needs known. But that shrill tone sent an immediate shock to his system, yanking him out of a deep sleep quicker than any alarm clock.

And then there was Lacey, who tiptoed around him, jumping like a scared rabbit every time he walked into a room. Tucker still had his colicky crying jags, which only made things worse, as Lacey literally went nuts trying to get him to quiet down. He finally told her to let him cry, which made her break down sobbing herself.

Yeah, Lacey's coping strategies were pretty much non-existent. He kept trying to reassure her that everything would be fine, but after he'd spent his entire day off searching for Joel, without any luck, he found that line hard to believe himself.

When he'd exhausted every contact he had for his brother, Brock was forced to admit Joel had taken off on purpose. This wasn't just a case of his brother needing a break from his seemingly overwhelming responsibilities, getting drunk, overdoing it, and passing out with one of his buddies.

His brother was really gone. As in leaving his girlfriend and infant son to fend for themselves gone.

Or, more likely, leaving without a backward glance because Joel knew Brock would pick up the pieces of his mess and make things right.

To make matters worse, Brock was worried about leaving Lacey home alone with the baby while he went to work Friday night.

He wished he could call Elana; it was obvious to him the two women had bonded the night he'd moved Lacey and Tucker into his house. But Elana didn't want to see him. Or talk to him. Or be anywhere near him.

Clearly, she'd taken a taxi home rather than allowing him to drive her.

So he pulled out the phone book and sat at his kitchen table and made two phone calls. One to a private investigator, hiring a guy named Rufus Kingsley to search for Joel. And the other to a nanny service, hiring a woman to come over to the house while he was gone to help Lacey care for Tucker.

Maybe hiring a nanny was going a bit overboard; Lacey might actually do fine once she stopped freaking out about Tucker's crying disturbing him. But he couldn't help noticing she'd spent a lot of time in the bathroom earlier that morning, and he kept imagining the cuts Elana had seen on Lacey's arm.

He hadn't gotten so much as a glimpse of them himself because Lacey wore those long-sleeved T-shirts that hung all the way down to her bony wrists.

Before he went to work, he went back into the bathroom and stared at the razor over the sink, wondering if it was in the same position where he'd left it or if Lacey had moved it. Muttering under his breath, he took the razor and the blades, hiding them both in his room.

"You hired a nanny?" Lacey asked, staring defiantly at him for the first time since he'd moved her to his house. The nanny in question was standing in the living room, watching them curiously.

Warily he nodded. "Yeah. I thought maybe you could use some time for yourself. To—I don't know—take a bubble bath or go shopping or something."

Lacey stared at him as if he'd told her to strip naked and dance for a room full of old men. "I can take care of Tucker myself."

He suppressed a sigh, glancing at the nanny, a motherly-looking woman whose expression held a note of faint disdain. It had never occurred to him that Lacey would rebel against the idea. "I know you can take care of Tucker yourself. But I'm going to be gone for a long time, and I thought you'd like a little help." And maybe wouldn't feel the need to cut yourself, he silently added.

"Thanks, but I don't need any help." Lacey stoutly crossed her arms over her chest.

Brock wavered, inwardly debating. He didn't have time for an argument. If he didn't leave soon, he'd be late for work. The stubborn expression on Lacey's face forced him to cave in to her wishes, against his better judgment.

"All right," he said, hoping he wasn't making a mistake in trusting her. "If you're sure."

"I'm sure."

He turned to the nanny and pulled out his wallet. "I'll pay for the day, but you're not needed here after all. Thanks anyway."

"Hrumph," she said, clear disproval etched on her features as she hitched her purse on her shoulder and took the cash he offered. "I guess you can call me again if the situation changes."

Lacey glowered at the woman, her gaze clearly saying the situation would not change in her lifetime, leaving Brock to escort the woman out of the house. He glanced back at Lacey. "I'll be at work if you need me."

She nodded. "We'll be fine."

He hoped so. He carried enough guilt; he didn't need something bad happening to Lacey on top of everything else. Closing the door behind him, he hurried to his car, ducking his head against the April showers pouring from the sky and pounding the pavement.

The gloomy weather matched his mood. Lacey was

likely relieved to have him out of the way, and Elana was no doubt dreading working with him. There wasn't much he could do about the latter, other than try to stay out of Elana's way.

And hope that it was enough.

Elana cursed her luck when she discovered she'd been assigned to work in the trauma bay with Brock. She'd asked for her assignment to be changed, but there were no other trauma-trained nurses working in the arena for her to switch with. Nurses had to work in the arena for at least a year before they could be trained in trauma.

In the past few days, she'd been happy with the reprieve of seeing Brock. She'd vowed not to let him drag her back down into the depths of despair. That night in the taxi, when she'd noticed her blood-stained fingers, she'd realized how close she'd been to losing it.

The very next morning, she'd stopped in at the human resources department to formally request a transfer to the critical care unit. She'd been hoping that they'd take her right away, but she was told she needed to wait for the manager to call.

That was some days ago, and still she hadn't gotten a call. Now she had to work with Brock again. At least it was Friday night, one of the busiest nights of the week, so there wouldn't be a lot of down time.

Brock walked into the trauma bay, deep grooves of exhaustion lining his face, and immediately her thoughts went to Lacey and Tucker. Where they doing all right? Or had something happened?

Surely he'd come and tell her if something was wrong with Lacey or Tucker. Wouldn't he?

Working with Brock wasn't nearly as bad as she'd feared. His leadership style was more collegial than not. If she didn't think about it too much, she could forget her animosity towards him and fall into a synchronized rhythm. And when two patients arrived, sporting identical gunshot wounds, it was a good thing she could anticipate exactly what he needed.

"Give me the latest set of vitals, Elana," he said when she'd completed her assessment.

"BP 88/42, pulse tachy at 118. Respirations up a bit at 30, but not labored." She glanced up at the IVs, not having the luxury of Raine's help as she was busy in the other trauma bay with her own patient, and Brock was going back and forth, leading both resuscitations at the same time. "Do you want more fluids? Or blood products?"

"Blood products," Brock announced. "Keep the left PIV running with normal saline, but start with one unit of O-negative packed cells on the right until we get the lab results back. The bullet is still lodged somewhere in his belly; the trauma surgeon on call should be here soon."

"Got it," Elana said, having already reached for the unit of packed red blood cells. She automatically drew a full set of labs once she'd hung the blood, keeping an eye on the patient's bedside monitor as she handed the tubes of blood to the ED tech.

Their side-by-side gunshot victims were soon dispatched upstairs, one to the OR for surgery, the other to the ICU to wait for his turn in the OR, since both penetrating wounds were serious but not immediately life-threatening. The worst part came when the respective family members of the victims began arguing loudly, escalating into a full-blown physical altercation in the waiting room.

Once the cops had hauled the offenders away, each side blaming the other for starting the fight, things quickly settled back to normal.

"Takes all kinds," Brock muttered under his breath.

"You're not kidding," Elana couldn't help but agree.

His sizzling blue gaze clung to hers, making her breath catch in her throat. For a moment it felt as if they were the only two people alone in the entire department. She took a hasty step back. Professionalism was one thing, but allowing Brock to get too close was something completely different.

The light in Brock's eyes dimmed when she turned away, and she was hit by an unexpected pang of regret. If things had been different, maybe…

No. Don't go there.

Thankfully the trauma pager went off, announcing another arrival. Soon afterwards, they received another one. The trauma bay was hopping, but they were able to move patients through the system pretty well.

Towards the end of their shift, they got a call about a young eighteen-year-old patient who'd overdosed on wine and pain pills found in her mother's medicine cabinet.

"Didn't her mother listen to those commercials warning parents to lock up their prescription meds?" Raine plaintively asked in a low tone to Elana.

"I guess not." Elana took her place on the right side

of the patient, gasping when she saw the young woman carried a slight resemblance to Lacey.

"Get a nasogastric tube down her, stat," Brock ordered. "Get the activated charcoal ready to go."

Elana did her assessment while Raine prepared to place the tube. "Her pupils are dilated and very sluggish. She's not responsive to verbal stimuli or pain. BP low at 78/40."

"We need a full toxicology screen, Elana. We don't know if she took more than the empty bottle of painkillers that her mother found on the floor next to her."

Brock's terse tone convinced her that he'd noticed the slight resemblance to Lacey too. Elana could only imagine how depressed this young woman must have been to take such drastic steps. Or maybe it was simply a cry for help.

A silent plea that could end in disaster.

Raine passed the nasogastric tube down into the girl's stomach, pumping the first diluted bottle of activated charcoal through the tube as quickly as possible.

Once she'd sent the tox screen, Elana helped Raine with the mess. Because shortly after the first contents hit their patient's stomach, the girl began retching violently.

"It's okay, Ariel. We're going to get that poison out of your system," Elana said, smoothing the girl's limp blonde hair away from her face. "You're going to be okay."

Ariel Peterson cried between bouts of retching. Elana didn't mind the mess so much; having Ariel crying and throwing up was better than having her comatose from the drugs.

"Here's the results of the tox screen," the tech said, handing her the slip of paper from the lab.

"Nothing more than the narcotic and the alcohol,

and those levels aren't as bad as they could be," Elana announced, catching Brock's gaze. "Her mother found her early enough."

"Thank God," he muttered. "I'm going to arrange an ICU bed for her. We can hold off with the next dose of charcoal as long as she stays responsive."

Elana nodded, relieved to know Ariel would survive after all.

She and Raine transferred Ariel to the ICU. Miraculously, Elana had come out of the resuscitation without a single charcoal stain. Raine hadn't been quite so lucky.

"Next time, I'm taking the right side of an overdose patient," Raine muttered darkly, grimacing at the black streaks running down the side of her leg.

"Hey, at least it's the end of our shift," Elana pointed out. "Could be worse. Give me your trauma pager, and then you can grab a new pair of scrubs before you head home."

"Don't worry, I will." Raine handed off her pager and veered off towards the OR locker rooms. "See you later."

Elana lifted a hand and hurried back downstairs. She gave a brief report and handed off the two trauma pagers to the on-coming night-shift nurses. When she walked into the staff lounge, she saw Brock was on his cell phone.

"I'm glad the baby is doing better, Lacey. Get some sleep. I'll see you in the morning."

Lacey? She'd been about to leave, but concern over Lacey and Tucker had her walking further into the room. "Is everything all right with Lacey?" she asked once he'd hung up his phone.

"Yeah. I guess." He let out a heavy sigh. "Seeing

Ariel gave me a sick feeling about Lacey, but she swears she's fine."

"I know, I have to admit I worried about the same thing," Elana admitted. "I'm glad to hear things are going better."

"I tried to hire a nanny to stay with her while I'm at work, but Lacey freaked."

A nanny? He really didn't understand women at all. She raised a brow. "Generous of you, but I'm not surprised. I'm sure she took that move as proof you don't trust her to be alone with the baby."

"What am I supposed to do?" Brock asked in a vexed tone. "I had to hide my razors, for God's sake."

"But Lacey wouldn't hurt Tucker," she reminded him gently. "She's only been hurting herself."

"Maybe. But I didn't want to take any chances."

She couldn't blame him for being worried. Self-mutilation could easily escalate into something more. She veered away from those dark thoughts. "I take it you haven't found Joel yet?"

"No." Brock sank into a chair, his shoulders slumping in defeat. "I spent my entire day off yesterday looking for him, but no luck. I ended up hiring a private investigator to find him."

Wow. It seemed he'd been busy. And concerned. No wonder he'd looked so exhausted earlier. As much as she wanted to avoid him, she realized she couldn't walk away. Hesitantly she took a seat across from him. "You can't force him to be a father."

"I know. But it's not fair for Lacey and Tucker to suffer either."

He was right. She couldn't argue that one.

"Lacey keeps telling me that Tucker is better, that he's not crying as much, but I think she's fooling herself," Brock continued. "He really is colicky; the poor kid cried for nearly an hour straight before he finally fell asleep in his swing." He raised his resigned gaze to hers. "I'm worried about her."

"Lacey isn't going to end up like Ariel," she said softly. "We won't let her."

"We?" Brock arched a brow. "You've done more than enough, Elana. Lacey and Tucker are not your problem, they're mine."

"She was my patient in the clinic," she reminded him. She didn't add how much Lacey reminded Elana of herself at that age. Chloe had saved her, but who was going to save Lacey? Elana wasn't sure Brock even understood what the poor girl needed. His trying to hire a nanny was proof of that.

No, she refused to abandon Lacey.

"Lacey trusts me. I'd like to help."

"You already have been a huge help to her," Brock agreed. "I owe you for that. I guess I can understand why Lacey finds it easier to talk to you than to me."

"I don't mind."

There was a moment of companionable silence. The animosity she normally felt toward Brock seemed to have vanished. She was amazed at how easy it was to discuss Lacey's issues.

Much easier than discussing her own thoughts and feelings, that was for sure.

"I guess I should get going," she murmured, feeling

a little like the traitor who'd consorted with the enemy. She rose to her feet and headed for the door.

"Elana?" Brock's voice stopped her.

"Yes?" She turned back towards him.

"Thank you. I know I don't deserve your kindness, but I want you to know how much I appreciate your help."

She shrugged, shaken by his sincere gratitude. He seemed so different from the man she'd hated for all those years after Felicity's death.

"If I ask you a question, will you tell me the truth?" she asked.

His eyes widened in surprise. "Of course," he said gruffly.

She gathered her courage. "There were rumors about you speeding that night," she said in a rush before she could change her mind. "That your father, the cop, covered for you so you wouldn't go to jail."

She didn't have to explain what night she was talking about: he knew. "I wasn't. I swear to you, Elana, I wasn't speeding. If you knew my father, you'd understand the last thing he'd ever do is cover up for me."

She hesitated, wishing she could believe him. "No matter how difficult your relationship with your father, I'm sure he wouldn't be so cold as to put you in jail."

He let out a harsh laugh. "Don't bet on it. Elana, do you know why I had to move back home to Milwaukee?" When she shook her head, he continued. "Because my father lashed out at Joel after he got Lacey pregnant. Our old man basically threw him out onto the street with nothing but the clothes on his back. Joel called me in a panic because the cheapest apartment he could afford didn't allow kids. I came home because my father refused to give him a dime."

Elana didn't know what to say. The stark statement rang true.

"I wasn't speeding, Elana. But I also know that there's nothing I can say to make up for what happened. You have no idea how much that night has haunted me."

Yes, she did. Because that night haunted her too.

"I tried to save her. I had a broken clavicle—the bone was poking right out of the skin—but I still did CPR at the scene until help arrived. The image of your sister's face will be ingrained in my mind for the rest of my life."

Tears burned in her eyes, her throat clogged with regret. She'd loved her sister. Yet it was just as clear that Brock hadn't escaped unscathed. He looked at her expectantly, but she couldn't say the words he wanted to hear.

I forgive you.

Blindly she turned away, but Brock was there, grasping her hand to stop her.

"Don't cry, Elana," he said in a low, husky voice. "Please don't cry."

When he reached up to wipe her tears away, her breath caught in her throat. The brush of his fingers against her skin was like an electrical shock, sending a tingling wave of awareness dancing down her spine.

He was close. Too close. The male scent of him, a hint of aftershave mixed with honest sweat, enveloped her. For long moments they stared deeply into each other's eyes, as if held by an invisible string that was slowly tightening, drawing them together.

She was shocked by the abrupt desire to throw herself into his arms, seeking comfort.

"I have to go," she said in a strangled whisper, breaking out of his grasp. As she hurried away, she could feel his intense gaze boring into her back.

And it took every ounce of willpower to keep on walking.

CHAPTER SIX

BROCK took several deep breaths, realizing he'd nearly crossed the line with Elana, big-time. He'd wanted nothing more than to pull her into his arms. Would have offered her comfort and anything else she'd needed.

Shaky, as if he'd shot-gunned a six-pack of the highest octane energy drink, he scrubbed his hands over his face. The enticing vanilla scent of her lingered in the air, messing with his head.

It was crazy. Completely insane. But there was no point in lying to himself.

He wanted more than her forgiveness.

He wanted her.

Even knowing how much she hated him, would do anything to avoid being with him, he still wanted her.

Pathetic. Self-destructive. Hopeless. He shook his head at his own foolishness.

All this time she'd thought he was speeding the night her sister had pulled out in front of him. No wonder she'd been so upset. He clearly remembered the insults she'd screamed at him when he'd shown up at Felicity's funeral. Now he understood a little better why she'd been so angry.

He'd told Elana the truth. He hadn't been speeding. But he had no way of knowing if she believed him or not.

And even if she did, what did it matter? The end result was the same. She wouldn't forgive him. Hell, he didn't forgive himself.

He'd thrown himself into his work, sacrificing his personal life to save others. Trying to make up for losing Felicity.

So why was he longing for a relationship now? With the one woman he could never have? He needed to stay away from Elana, now more than ever. For one thing, he wasn't sure he could trust himself around her: his body didn't listen to logic. And there was always the extremely remote possibility that if she ever did want more from him, he'd succumb. He'd never deny her.

Which would be bad since his track record with women sucked. He'd indulged in the occasional one-night stand, hating himself afterwards. Elana deserved someone better. Someone who could offer her a life. A future. He needed to get the turmoil of wanting Elana out of his head, and fast.

Before he managed to hurt her all over again.

The next morning, Brock dragged himself out of bed early because Tucker was crying louder and longer than usual.

Yeah, the kid had colic, but even after a few days with his nephew, Brock could tell the difference between his colicky cry and this sharper, desperate one.

Bleary-eyed, he shuffled into the kitchen, searching

for coffee. Lacey jumped when he walked in, spilling her cup of tea. As she hurried to wipe up the mess, he squelched the urge to apologize for walking through his own house, trying to smile at her reassuringly. "Hey, Lacey. Seems like Tucker's having a rough morning."

The baby was propped in his infant seat on top of the kitchen table. Her face immediately crumpled. "I don't know what's wrong with him," she wailed brokenly. "I carried him around for an hour, tried feeding him and changing him. I just don't know what's wrong."

"Hey, it's okay. You're a great mom, honest. This isn't your fault. Here, I'll take a look at him, okay?" He made a rash promise, forgoing the need for coffee as he unhooked Tucker from his seat and lifted him in his arms. "We can always take him back to the clinic too if needed."

"Okay." Her puffy, reddened eyes filled with hope. Not good, since he was hardly a miracle worker: there was no magic touch to make the baby stop crying.

Tucker didn't quiet down for him either, the wailing much louder with the baby on his shoulder, close to his ear. Tucker felt warm, his nose and throat far more congested than they'd been a few days ago. Carrying Tucker into his bedroom, Brock fished out his stethoscope, wishing he owned a pediatric ophthalmoscope.

Setting Tucker on his bed, he did his best to examine him with the limited equipment he had. He'd bet Tucker's ears were red and inflamed, but he couldn't prove it since he didn't have a pediatric scope. The baby's lungs definitely sounded a bit congested too.

He doubted Lacey had given Tucker any over-the-counter medication but Brock thought the baby could benefit from getting a decongestant into his system. Tucker also seemed to be a bit dehydrated.

"We need to take him back to the clinic," he told Lacey, bringing Tucker back into the kitchen. "He might have an ear infection, and, if so, he'll need a course of antibiotics."

"All right." She reached up for the baby, the sleeve of her right arm sliding up a bit to reveal two thin cuts on her forearm, somewhat scabbed over but still looking fairly recent.

He froze.

Should he call Elana? He wanted to. He felt out of his depth with Lacey's cutting behavior. Yet was this bad enough to bother Elana with on a Saturday? After all, Lacey's cuts weren't bleeding or anything. At least not the ones he'd caught a glimpse of. He'd almost pulled out his phone before he realized he didn't have Elana's number. He'd have to call the ED to get it.

Tempted, he hesitated. He forced himself to think rationally. Did he want to call Elana for Lacey's sake? Or for his own?

To make himself feel better. Disturbed, he stuck the phone back in his pocket and handed Lacey the baby. He fetched his wallet and car keys as Lacey put Tucker into his infant carrier.

He could handle this crisis without Elana's help. He drove to the New Beginnings Clinic, telling himself that leaving Elana out of his problems was the right thing to do. He could always mention the cuts on Lacey's arm the next time he saw her at work.

The clinic was packed, and he did his best to wait patiently in line until it was their turn, even though he wanted to march in there, demanding Tucker be seen next.

"Lacey and Tucker?" the petite receptionist called out. "You're next. Follow me."

Surprised that they were taken so quickly, although it was possible the receptionist behind the desk couldn't take Tucker's crying any more than he could, he gratefully followed Lacey and the baby into the tiny exam room.

A nurse turned to face them when they came in.

His jaw dropped to his chest in surprise when he saw Elana.

"Lacey!" Elana looked just as surprised to see them. Her gaze skittered over him and landed on Lacey and Tucker. She frowned. "What's wrong?"

"Tucker's crying again, but it's different this time, Elana." Lacey shocked him by speaking up for herself. "Honest, it's not the same colicky cry as before."

Brock felt the need to stick up for Lacey. "She's right, you can definitely tell the difference."

"I believe you, Lacey," Elana assured her, barely glancing at him.

"I examined him at home, but I didn't have a pediatric ophthalmoscope," Brock explained. "So I couldn't look at his ears. The way he's acting, though, I'm betting he has bilateral ear infections."

This time, she didn't ignore him. "Thanks, Brock. I'll take a quick look, and then I'll get Dr Liz in here right away."

Feeling unusually useless—normally he was the one in charge within a medical situation—he stepped back and tucked his hands into the pockets of his jeans. Elana was focused on Tucker, using the pediatric ophthalmoscope to peer into his ears. With her silky dark hair pulled back into a ponytail, he found it difficult to tear his gaze away from the graceful curve of her neck.

"Brock's right," Elana murmured a few minutes later. "Hold on to Tucker, Lacey, while I get Dr Liz."

Dr Liz Jacoby was a statuesque woman who took charge the minute she entered the room. Impressed with her gentle, yet no-nonsense manner, he was pleased when she quickly concurred with his diagnosis.

"This little guy needs a full course of antibiotics," she announced. "Good thing you brought him in when you did."

"Maybe I should have taken him straight to Trinity Medical Center's ED, where I work. I'm Dr Brock Madison," he introduced himself belatedly.

"Personally, I'm glad you came here." Liz's wide gaze sharpened on him. "You're the new guy, aren't you? Recruited from Minneapolis? I've heard you're a good addition to the emergency department team." Liz Jacoby flashed a brilliantly white smile. "So what do you think of my little clinic, hmm? If you're interested, we're always looking for new doctors to volunteer their time."

There was a loud crash as Elana dropped a tray of instruments she'd been carrying to the sink. He couldn't help but notice the flash of horror on her face. Obviously, Elana didn't want him anywhere near the clinic.

"I'll think about it," he hedged, unwilling to flat-out refuse when he knew that clinics like this depended on volunteers to stay afloat. "At the moment, I'm pretty busy helping Lacey and Tucker."

Liz frowned, casting a quick glance at Elana, who had knelt to pick up the instruments from the floor. "I understand, but it's an open invitation if anything changes. Even one or two shifts a month would help."

"Sure thing," he said, unable to refuse.

Elana took the tray to the sink, her back stiff, radiating disapproval.

Liz handed him the prescription for Tucker's antibiotics.

"Thanks," he murmured.

They were making their way out of the exam room when Raine rushed in.

"Thanks for covering for me, Elana. See, I told you I'd be here in plenty of time for you to go visit your mom at the nursing home."

Visit her mother? Brock ushered Lacey and Tucker toward the lobby, stealing a quick glance back at Elana. He wished he had the time to reassure her he wouldn't volunteer at the New Beginnings Clinic if she didn't want him to. But she was busy talking to Raine, and Tucker needed his medicine sooner rather than later, so he left.

He wondered if Elana's mother was still in the same nursing home as she had been eight and a half years ago. Chances were good she was.

When Lacey mentioned she needed more soy-based formula, Brock headed to the nearest pharmacy instead of going to the hospital for cheaper antibiotics. As they waited for the script to be filled, he decided it would be best to stock up on some needed supplies. Rehydration solutions to help keep Tucker hydrated, lung decongestant medicine, a case of soy-based formula, a pack of diapers and, last but not least, the antibiotics.

Eighty-three dollars and ninety-six cents later, he grimly acknowledged that caring for an infant was far more expensive than he'd ever realized, and the antibiotics were the cheapest item in the cart.

No wonder Joel had felt overwhelmed.

The New Beginnings Clinic offering free medical care was only a drop in the bucket of what a new mother needed to provide for a baby.

He wished he could help at the clinic. But he wouldn't risk causing Elana any more distress. Surely there was some other way he could donate his time. Some cause that would still benefit people like Lacey and Tucker.

Brock dropped Lacey and Tucker off at home, making sure they had everything they needed. He reinforced with Lacey that the liquid antibiotic needed to be kept in the refrigerator between doses.

Glancing at his watch, he decided he had a couple of hours before he needed to get to the hospital for his shift. Before he fully realized his intent, he found himself heading for the Cottage Grove Nursing Home.

He'd hang around outside until Elana finished visiting with her mother. Surely she'd feel better once he'd convinced her he had no intention of encroaching on her work at the clinic.

No matter how much it pained him, he'd promise to stay out of her way from this point forward.

* * *

Elana bypassed her usual stop at the nurses' station for an update though her mother's condition rarely changed. Outside her mother's room, she took a deep breath and pasted a cheery smile on her face to buoy her spirits before walking in.

The aides had gotten her mother up out of bed and seated in her rocking chair by the window. They'd also taken pains to dress her up in her favorite bright pink housecoat in honor of Elana's visit.

"Hi, Mom, it's so good to see you." Elana crossed over to give her mother a hug and kiss before taking a seat beside her. She took her mother's hand in hers and captured her mother's gaze. "How have you been? Are they still taking good care of you here?"

Her mother held her gaze and tightened her grip twice in their communication code. One squeeze meant no but two squeezes meant yes. Her mother's emotional status had been extremely fragile: her first nervous breakdown had occurred right after their father had taken off. After Felicity's death, her mother had retreated further, hiding from everything painful in a world of silence.

The doctors had been wonderful; they'd made a little progress over the years, getting her mother to make eye contact and respond to verbal commands, but the process seemed to go so slowly.

She longed to hear her mother's voice.

"I'm glad things are going good, Mom." She forced herself to sound cheerful. "You know, I think it's time to get you some new pictures. These prints have been up for almost three months now. Well past time for a change in scenery."

Her mother glanced at the splashy, colorful prints Elana had put up on the wall, but then turned away. Her mother's fingers tightened around hers once. No.

"Come on, Mom. You love art, remember?" Elana imagined her mother was feeling as if she shouldn't bother, but, in reality, buying new pictures for her mother made Elana feel as if she were doing something, even if it was something as simple as buying new prints. The medical staff had used art therapy to encourage her mother to stay connected to the world. So far, her mother had made several watercolor paintings, so she liked to think the new therapy was working.

Her mother looked away, and Elana wished she knew what was going on in her mother's mind. Carrying on yes-and-no conversations were heart-wrenchingly difficult.

"Don't you think new pictures would be a nice change?"

After what seemed like forever, her mother squeezed her hand twice. Yes. Elana relaxed, hoping this was a sign of more progress.

She went through her usual conversation tidbits, telling her mother about her work at the clinic and some of her patients, keeping the stories as upbeat as possible. Her mother answered the occasional question with yes or no hand squeezes.

When she ran out of chatty things to say, she stared at her mother's hand in hers. It was at times like this she missed her mother the most. When she needed a confidant.

She winced at her selfish thought. Her mother's emotional health had been fragile for years; it wasn't her mother's fault she had difficulty coping with the added stress of her sister's death.

"I met Brock Madison," she finally said in a low voice, hoping and praying her mother wouldn't react negatively to Brock's name. "Do you remember him?"

She risked a glance at her mother's face. Her mother's gaze was clear, alert. She squeezed her fingers twice. Yes.

Elana was surprised her mother didn't appear to be upset. Was this a good sign? Maybe that art therapy was working better than she'd imagined.

"He claims he wasn't speeding that night," Elana continued, needing to get some of this inner turmoil out of her system. "He said the last thing his dad would do is to cover up for him, and I think I'm starting to believe him. Did you know he's a doctor now?"

One squeeze. No, her mother hadn't known Brock was a doctor. Encouraged by the intensity of her mother's gaze, and feeling as if they were actually having a meaningful conversation, she continued.

"We work together in the emergency department. He's a really good doctor. He gives everything he has to save his patients."

Her mother's gaze clung to hers, and Elana had the sense her mother wanted to say something. She waited a few minutes, but the words remained locked deep inside.

Nervously she licked her lips. "I don't know what to think, Mom. I know everything is his fault, yet I can't seem to hate him as much as I used to."

"Life's short," her mother suddenly rasped. "Hate isn't worth it."

Elana sucked in a shocked breath, her eyes stinging

with tears. She'd spoken! Her mother had actually spoken! She struggled not to make too much of a big deal of the event, even though she wanted to dance around the room, screaming with joy.

"I know life is too short, Mom. You're right—wasting time on negative energy doesn't help anyone." She reached over to engulf her mother in a tight hug. "I love you, Mom. I love you so much."

"Love you, Elana," her mother whispered.

Elana's eyes welled with tears again. Things were going to be fine. She just knew it.

And she couldn't help wondering if her mother's breakthrough had something to do with her confessions about Brock. This was the first time she'd ever really opened up about her thoughts and fears.

Maybe she should have confided in her mother sooner.

"I have to go to work, Mom," she said regretfully when she'd stayed as long as she dared. "But I'll be back soon, I promise."

Her mother squeezed her hand twice, and Elana hoped and prayed that now that her mother had spoken, she'd only continue to improve.

She held her emotions in check long enough to update the nurses, who promised to let the doctor know. Yet she couldn't help feeling guilty, as if she could have impacted her mother's health sooner if she'd only opened up to her.

Her throat swelled with tears, and suddenly she couldn't stay in the nursing home for another second. She flew towards the door, throwing it wide open in her haste to get outside.

And barreled straight into Brock's arms.

"Elana?" Brock caught her close, preventing her from taking a header into the concrete sidewalk, his expression full of alarm. "What is it? What's wrong?"

"Nothing! Leave me alone. I'm fine!" She twisted, trying to break away, but he was much stronger and only tightened his grip.

"You're not fine. You're crying. Tell me what's wrong."

"Good tears," she whispered, trying to swipe them away in an attempt to get a hold of herself, but the sobs in her chest struggled to break loose. "She spoke! After all these years, my mother finally spoke!"

Despite the fact that she considered Brock the enemy, she collapsed against him, burying her face against his chest and letting go, crying as if she might never stop.

CHAPTER SEVEN

BROCK held Elana close, inwardly reeling at the news. Her mother had spoken? It sounded like good news, but the way she continued to cry worried him. He could feel dampness on his shirt from the force of her tears. He closed his eyes, the familiar snake of guilt uncoiling in his gut, twisting and turning.

Her mother might be improving, but he couldn't ignore the fact that his actions had caused her mother to withdraw from the world in the first place.

Yet another reason for Elana to hate him.

He didn't for one minute believe Elana had forgiven him just because she'd broken down crying in his arms. Especially when, all too soon, the maelstrom of her tears subsided, and she broke away, furiously swiping at her face.

"Sorry about the waterworks," she muttered, sniffling loudly and digging in her purse for a tissue. "I don't know what's wrong with me."

"Don't." He realised his tone must have been sharper than he'd intended when her shocked gaze snapped up to his. "You have nothing to apologize for," he said, trying to soften the edge of his tone. "Nothing."

She stared at him for a long minute, then pulled out a tissue and blew her nose. Hard.

Hating the feeling of helplessness, he glanced back toward the Cottage Grove Nursing Home. "She's really talking?"

Elana's tremulous smile broke his heart. "Well, she said a few words. But I think it's a sign she's finally healing."

He hoped so too, more than Elana could ever know. He was afraid to hope, but tried to remain positive. Elana was happy, which was all that mattered.

"What are you doing here?" she asked, glancing around as if surprised to realize they were still standing on the sidewalk outside the nursing home.

"I came to see you."

"Me? Why?" Now her gaze was full of narrow suspicion. Their moment of brief closeness faded. "Can't you just leave me alone?"

Her frank annoyance bothered him. "Yes. That's exactly why I came to find you. I wanted to ease your mind about Dr Liz's offer. I have no intention of volunteering my time at the New Beginnings Clinic."

"Sure, make me be the bad guy with Dr Liz." Elana's gaze filled with disgust. "She needs doctors like you more than nurses like me."

He let out a frustrated breath. "So what are you saying? You want me to take her up on the offer?"

"Doesn't matter to me." She gave an unconvincing careless shrug. "We won't be working together much longer. I'm transferring to a position in the ICU as soon as it's available."

"No!" The vehement protest slipped out before he could stop it. "Don't leave trauma nursing." *Not because of me.*

She glanced away as if she could barely stand the idea of leaving the ED herself. "I have to go. I'm working second shift tonight, and I'm already running late."

So was he. Knowing he'd see her in less than an hour gave him the strength to step back. Hadn't he promised to stay away? "Are you sure you're okay? Maybe I should drive you home."

"I'm fine. My mother is on the road to recovery, so I'm happy." She did look better; there was a rosy flush to her cheeks that had been missing earlier. "Goodbye, Brock."

"Take care of yourself, Elana."

He watched her as she walked away, heading back across the street and into the parking lot where she'd left her car. He knew giving Elana the distance she craved was the right thing to do. She seemed thrilled about her mother's progress, yet she was still angry with him.

He was beginning to realize Elana would never heal from her emotional scars. Not until she put the past behind her once and for all.

Elana worked very hard, without much success, to shake off the rippling effect of that momentary madness in Brock's arms.

What was wrong with her? Why did she seem to be unequivocally drawn to the one man who was absolutely wrong for her? Why couldn't she figure out a way to pry him out of her life once and for all?

Despite her shower, the unique scent of him, musky male intermixed with soap, clouded her senses. When he'd cradled her in his arms, it had been all too easy to forget who he really was.

She didn't want to admit she was hopelessly infatuated with the enemy.

When she walked into the arena, he was standing in front of the census board, talking to a nurse named Eric. He didn't glance at her as she went past.

Assuming Brock was assigned to the arena, she was relieved to learn she'd been assigned to the trauma bay again. Telling Brock her plans of moving to the ICU had backfired. His plea for her not to go still echoed in her mind. He was right: she did love trauma nursing. Yet she was just as certain she'd learn to love critical care too.

Raine had the day off, leaving Eric Towne as her partner in trauma for the shift.

There was still a patient in the trauma bay waiting to be transferred to the ICU. An elderly woman, who was intubated and on a ventilator as a result of contracting tetanus.

"I don't understand," her husband said, obviously stressed out over the seriousness of his wife's illness. "I thought tetanus wasn't a problem any more. That people didn't get lockjaw like they used to."

"They don't if you continue to get your tetanus booster shots every ten years," Dr Laurel Carmen said gently. "Your wife loves to garden, but you said yourself she sustained a severe cut on her finger a few weeks ago.

She didn't come in for a tetanus shot and hasn't had one in almost twenty years."

The elderly man's shoulders slumped. "I should have made her come in," he murmured. "But it was just a small cut."

Elana approached Dani, the day shift nurse who was caring for Mrs James, their tetanus patient. "Is there something I can do to help you get her transferred upstairs?" she asked.

"I have everything caught up; we're just waiting for a bed."

"I'll see what I can do." Elana went to the nearest phone, calling up to the medical ICU to find out how much longer before they'd get a bed.

"Housekeeping is in there right now cleaning it," the ICU nurse informed her. "Why don't you give me report? By the time we're done, she should be finished with the room."

"Okay, hang on a minute." Elana called Dani over and handed her the phone. "They're asking for report. You can leave when you're finished; I'll get Mrs James packed up and transported upstairs."

"Thanks," Dani said gratefully.

The trauma bay remained busy with a steady stream of patients, not too surprising for a Saturday night. She was upset to discover Brock was moved into the trauma bay to help with the strong influx of patients. Being so close to him in the confined space was difficult. If she didn't know better, she'd think he was following her on purpose.

Yet she couldn't deny he'd come out to her mother's nursing home just to let her know he wouldn't volunteer at the New Beginnings Clinic. Because she'd betrayed her true feelings by dropping that tray of instruments on the floor when Dr Liz had tried recruiting him.

He was tormenting her with his kindness and under-standing. She wasn't sure how much more she could take.

The awkwardness between her and Brock grew more noticeable the harder they tried to stay out of each other's way.

She reached for the patient's clipboard at the same time he did. A tingly awareness shot up her arm as their fingers touched.

She snatched hers back quickly, avoiding his gaze.

"Get me a chest X-ray stat," Brock said tersely. "I have a bad feeling about this guy's abdominal pain."

Elana hurried to carry out his orders, wondering what diagnosis he was considering but not brave enough to ask.

"What are you thinking?" Eric asked, as if reading her mind. "Hot gall bladder? Or appendicitis?"

"Neither. Possible abdominal aortic aneurysm. We need to get him to surgery asap before it dissects."

Why he couldn't have told them that from the begin-ning, she wasn't sure, but Elana wasted no time in getting the requested X-rays. And after the films were done, and the diagnosis confirmed, Brock continued to give orders.

"Keep his blood pressure under control with the labetalol. I don't want to see anything higher than 120 systolic, understand?"

She nodded, noticing how he avoided speaking her name. She missed the camaraderie they had the other day.

Before she'd collapsed like a weeping willow in his arms.

The surgeons came down to evaluate Roger Ames, their abdominal aortic aneurysm patient, and soon they were getting him ready for the operating room. His aneurysm hadn't dissected yet, but time was of the essence. Ruptured aneurysms had a very poor survival rate.

When their patient was safely in the OR, she helped Eric clean up the mess, putting things away and restocking the supplies. Brock left to briefly talk to Roger's family, letting the wife know her husband was heading to surgery.

"Eric, how are your twin boys doing?" she asked, hoping to use her colleague to break the stilted silence that hovered when Brock returned to the trauma bay.

"The terrors of Towne?" he joked. "They're great. Although Mandy is ready to pull her hair out now that they're three and have discovered the word NO. It's their favorite word, by the way. Between the two of them I bet they say no a hundred times a day."

She had to laugh. She noticed that Brock was listening to their light conversation, a slight grin on his face, although he remained silent, not joining in. "The terrible threes are something, aren't they?"

"You're not kidding. Mandy's been threatening to go back to work, leaving me to stay home with them until they're in school." Eric's wife was a respiratory therapist, but she'd only worked one day a week since the twins were born.

She was about to say something about Tucker, to bring Brock into the conversation, but he interrupted before she could say a word.

"I'm going to the arena. Call if you need me." Brock headed towards the door.

She watched him, telling herself this was what she'd wanted, to be left alone. So why did she want very badly to follow him? Because she was a glutton for punishment?

"What is up with you and Doc Madison?" Eric asked.

She scowled, swinging around to face him. "Have you been talking to Raine?"

"No!" Eric raised his hands up in surrender. "But seriously, Elana, the tension radiates between you guys like we're standing in the middle of a nuclear power plant. So what gives?"

"Nothing." Okay, so maybe that was a lie, but she wasn't about to blab about her personal life to her colleague.

"Fine." Eric seemed annoyed. "If you want to pretend nothing is wrong then, hey, go ahead. Don't let me be the one to burst your bubble."

With a sigh, she lifted a hand to massage the tight muscles in the back of her neck, knowing Eric was right. Things had been tense with Brock, and pretending everything was fine wasn't helping.

She needed to get away. She needed that transfer to the ICU. Maybe she could ask her boss to help get the wheels moving on that paperwork so the process would go a little faster. Surely it would be easier to forget about Brock when she wasn't seeing him every day.

At that moment their pagers went off, announcing

a new arrival, effectively bringing their personal conversation to an end.

The message on their pagers read:

Twenty-two-year-old male pedestrian struck by a car, BP 62/30, pulse 144 and irregular, coded once and intubated in the field.

Didn't sound promising. Brock must have gotten the page too, since he joined them in the trauma bay a few minutes later, his expression grim.

When the ambulance doors burst open, she noticed their patient was covered in blood from head to toe, bleeding from various sites. In the battle between pedestrians and vehicles, the pedestrians were often the losers. From the very beginning, Elana knew this patient's outcome wasn't going to be much different.

But Brock was just as determined to do everything possible to prolong the inevitable outcome.

"Eric, get more plasma and blood running now," he snapped. "Elana, I need a chest tube tray: he's bleeding into his lungs."

She nodded, setting the chest tube tray on the overbed table, opening the tray while keeping the contents inside sterile. Brock expertly inserted the chest tube, and almost instantly blood poured through the clear tubing, filling the plastic receptacle at an alarming pace.

"His pressure is dropping, only fifty-four systolic," Elana said.

"Get more blood. I want four units on the rapid infuser at all times," Brock ordered. "Get me the thoracic surgery team stat. This kid needs the OR."

She briefly met Eric's gaze, both silently acknowledging there was no way this kid was going to make it to the OR. But pushing her instinctive beliefs aside, she made the phone call and then hurried over to help Eric hang more blood, working in tandem on the rapid infuser.

Their patient's blood pressure continued to fall. And then, when the thoracic surgeon walked in, the young man lost his heart rhythm altogether.

"Start CPR," Brock demanded.

Elana jumped up on a stool so she could reach the patient and began doing chest compressions. The image of Brock doing this for Felicity, with a broken collarbone sticking out of his chest, flashed in her mind. Eric took over with the breathing, using the ambu bag to provide deep breaths. She kept up a steady stream of compressions, checking the heart monitor overhead to make sure she was getting good circulation from her efforts.

"He's gone, Brock," the thoracic surgeon said. "I wouldn't take him to surgery in this condition anyway. He's bleeding from everywhere, likely into his head and his abdomen as well as into his chest. There's nothing we can do."

Elana continued to do CPR, after Eric gave epinephrine through the IV, until Brock said, "All right, stop CPR."

She paused, glancing up at the monitor. Flat-line pulse. Completely absent blood pressure. She let out a heavy sigh.

"Time of death, ten forty-five p.m." Brock's voice was hard, tense, as he stripped off his bloody gloves and grabbed the death notice out of the chart. He scribbled his name on the bottom and then stalked away.

Elana helped Eric clean up the patient, whose family had yet to be notified, but she kept looking for Brock, wondering where he was. She tried to tell herself Brock's issues were none of her business, but she couldn't seem to shut off her concern. When they'd finished cleaning up the patient, waiting for transportation to the morgue, she slipped out of the trauma bay. Following her instincts, she headed towards the staff lounge, catching sight of Brock sitting on the small sofa, his head cradled in his hands.

She felt sick to her stomach, seeing him so miserable. Once she'd wanted him to hurt as much as she did. Now she knew that wasn't true.

Seeing Brock suffer didn't make her feel one bit better.

He was taking the young man's death very hard. Did he always react like this when he lost a patient? She watched him for a minute, realizing he'd probably rather be alone, but, as before, unable to simply walk away.

Had it been just a few short hours since he'd held her when she'd cried outside her mother's nursing home?

"Brock? Are you okay?" she asked, cautiously venturing into the room.

He lifted his head, his expression haggard. "Yeah."

She didn't believe him. He looked awful, and suddenly she understood. He lived for his work, pouring every bit of himself into his patients' lives, taking every death as a personal failure. "Don't do this," she pleaded in a low tone. "It's not your fault. He was gone before he got here."

A flash of anguish flitted across his face before he glanced away. "I know that. I'm not blaming myself."

Yes, he was. The stark desolation on his face proved it. He hated losing even one patient, although every doctor knew that it was impossible to save everyone.

Why did he let it affect him so much? Because of the past? Because of her sister?

She remembered how she'd been at the beginning of her career when she'd lost a patient. "During my first six months in the ED, I lost my first patient. She was in her mid-thirties, but I kept seeing Felicity's face instead of hers."

For a moment his stunned gaze collided with hers. And she realized he was doing the same thing.

She and Brock had more in common than she'd ever imagined.

Chloe had tried to tell her that he'd suffered too, but she'd refused to believe. Hadn't understood how much she'd needed to blame Brock.

Because the only other option was to blame Felicity. For being reckless in pulling out in front of Brock. For being careless in not wearing her seat belt.

For leaving Elana when she'd needed her older sister the most.

The realization shook her to the core. She didn't want to think about how lost she'd been. At the moment, Brock was more important.

"This isn't the first patient I've lost," he murmured, rubbing a hand over his jaw. "And I'm sure it won't be the last."

Didn't he ever remember the patients he'd saved?

"Jamie Edgar, the spinal fracture patient, is doing fine; she still has some limited mobility, but the spine surgeons have complete confidence she'll regain most of her limb function. Mr Reeves, our heart attack patient, is scheduled to go home tomorrow; he's doing great. Our twin gun-shot victims are also fine, although hospital administration has kept them on opposite ends of the hospital to keep their families from running into each other and causing more fights." She paused, knowing she was forgetting one. "Oh, yes, and Ariel Peterson is doing better too after her drug overdose; her parents have agreed to take her in for therapy."

"So?" Brock had frowned as she'd rattled off just a few of the patients they'd cared for over the past few days. "Saving lives is what we do. What's your point?"

"Focusing on the few losses among so many successes is counterproductive. Stop punishing yourself for losing a patient. Especially one that had so many strikes against him."

He stared at her for a moment, his guilt clearly reflected in his eyes.

"And maybe it's time to stop punishing yourself for Felicity's death."

He glanced away, letting out a harsh laugh. "Strange advice coming from the woman who hasn't been able to forgive me."

Feeling sucker-punched, she drew in a sharp breath. "Maybe you're right."

He winced and shook his head. "No, don't listen to me. It's been a rough night. I don't know what I'm talking about."

"Yes, you do. Because you're right." She remembered what Eric had said to her less than an hour ago. Pretending everything was fine was hardly healthy. She thought about the hours of pain she'd suffered, the relentless anger as she'd entered the foster-home system. Until Chloe.

Her foster mother had been right all along. She'd thought she'd put the past behind her, but in reality she'd only been pretending. On the surface. Not accepting the truth deep inside where it counted.

Brock Madison wasn't the awful person she'd depicted all these years. Even her mother didn't blame him! Why was she holding back?

"I forgive you."

CHAPTER EIGHT

HE COULDN'T believe what he was hearing. Had she really meant what she'd just said? "It's okay, Elana. You don't have to say things you don't mean to make me feel better. I know I don't deserve your forgiveness."

She let out a heavy sigh. "I'm not putting the past behind me for your sake, Brock. I'm doing it for mine. I think it's time I move forward with my life, don't you?"

"Yes." He was happy for her and seriously hoped she could really follow through. "I'm glad. You deserve to be happy."

Tilting her head to the side, she sent him a puzzled glance. "And you don't?"

He hesitated, unsure how to respond. "Sure, I guess."

He must not have sounded convincing because she gave him a skeptical look. "Have you ever been in a serious relationship?"

"No." He didn't want to have this conversation. He'd rather bask in the knowledge that Elana had forgiven him, even if only for her own sake.

"I see." Her expression was troubled, and he didn't like to think she could read his guilt-ridden mind.

"There hasn't been time," he protested, even though he knew it wasn't really true. "Besides, saving lives is far more important."

"More important than living your own life?" she asked.

Yes. But he didn't say it out loud.

"One isn't mutually exclusive of the other," she said softly.

"I know." Logically he did know, but deep down he couldn't quite accept it. Especially when he thought about those breathtaking moments when their fingers had tangled on the clipboard. Maybe he was thinking about having a personal life for the first time in years, but Elana was off-limits.

Just because she'd forgiven him, didn't mean she wanted to be friends with him. Or more.

Definitely not more.

"I'll see you at work, Brock." She stood and headed towards the door.

He wanted to call her back but forced himself to let her go. He needed to get over his fascination with Elana once and for all. She was a beautiful, successful woman. One he could admire from afar.

He'd find consolation in knowing that now that she'd forgiven him, she wouldn't have to leave the ED and trauma nursing.

His house was dark when he pulled into the driveway, indicating Lacey and Tucker were sleeping.

A flash of guilt plagued him as he walked inside. He should have called Lacey to find out how Tucker was doing. He was sure the baby would be fine once he had a couple of doses of antibiotics on board, and it wasn't as if he'd had a lot of spare time, since the trauma bay had been jumping, but, still, he should have called.

His brother should be here too, dammit. He'd have to call Rufus Kingsley, the private investigator he'd hired, to see if the guy had made any progress on finding Joel.

Exhausted, he didn't stop by Lacey's room to look in on them. The house was blissfully silent. Carefully, so as not to wake them, he tiptoed past their room, heading for his.

He closed his eyes, hoping the turmoil in his brain would ease with some badly needed sleep.

But, instead, he dreamed about Elana. Only, this time, his subconscious hadn't been satisfied with her gift of forgiveness. He'd wanted more. And when she melted into his arms, she wasn't crying. She was gazing up at him in wonder, wrapping her arms around his neck and kissing him.

He was sweating when Tucker's crying woke him up the next morning at six sharp. Groaning, he turned over and pulled his pillow over his head to drown out the sound. More than anything he wanted to go back to the steamy, erotic Elana of his dreams. Even if she was just a figment of his imagination.

But what if Lacey needed help? What if the baby really wasn't doing any better?

The image of a ready and willing Elana evaporated, and he dragged himself upright and yanked on a pair of sweats.

Blinking the remains of sleep from his eyes, he made his way into the kitchen. Lacey glanced up when he walked in, and he considered it progress when she didn't jump like a scared squirrel.

"Are the antibiotics staying down?" he asked, eyeing the crying baby propped on the table.

"Yesterday the medicine stayed down, but this morning he threw them up," Lacey said, her eyes mirroring his exhaustion. Immediately he felt guilty about wanting to sleep in. Obviously rest and relaxation wasn't an option for Lacey. "I wasn't sure if I should try to get him to take another dose or not."

"I wouldn't," he said, scrubbing a hand over his face. "Did he get up during the night?"

Lacey nodded, her expression still troubled. "I fed him right away so he wouldn't wake you up."

Considerate. Lacey must still feel as if she was imposing. She didn't ask about Joel, though. He wondered if she feared his brother was gone for good.

"Give him some of the rehydration solution," he suggested. "If he's throwing up, he might be a bit dehydrated."

"All right." Lacey pulled herself up from the table to get a bottle of the sugar water. Brock had to admit, if Tucker didn't start feeling better soon, they'd have to take him to the hospital for IV antibiotics.

He needed to get Elana out of his mind. She didn't need him, but Lacey and Tucker did.

And Tucker's health took priority over his useless dreams.

Brock called Rufus Kingsley, leaving a message for the PI to call him back. Rufus called back within the hour.

"I think I might know where your boy has gone," he said in lieu of a greeting. "Does your uncle have a cabin in the middle of the woods in Marshfield, Wisconsin?"

"Yeah." Why hadn't he considered the possibility of the cabin? His uncle and his father used it for deer hunting, a sport Brock couldn't get into, but Joel used to go up with them every year. "Do you think that's where he is?"

"Possibility, although from what I hear, it's not exactly a nice place to live year-round. April is still pretty cold at night; if he's there, I'm sure he's freezing his butt off. I'm heading there now and will let you know."

Finally, progress on finding his brother. Elana's words came back to him. *You can't force him to be a father.* Muffling the voice in his head, he agreed, "Sounds good. I don't know exactly where it is, but my uncle Joe will probably tell you. His number is in the book."

"Already on it," Rufus said. "I'll keep you posted."

"Thanks." When Brock hung up, he saw Lacey had been listening in. "We might know where Joel is."

"I heard." The expression in her eyes didn't change. Maybe she already knew that finding Joel didn't mean the end to her problems. There was no guarantee he'd be back to help her with Tucker.

Brock turned his attention to Tucker. The baby wasn't eating very well and had stopped taking the sugar water.

After trying without success to get the baby to take any form of nourishment, he gave up. Three hours had passed, and Tucker had only gotten worse instead of better.

"Lacey, we need to take Tucker to the hospital," he said, trying to hide the extent of his concern. "I think he needs IV fluids and IV antibiotics."

"Okay." Her listless response wasn't encouraging. But she rose to her feet and began dressing the baby in his quilted jacket before securing him safely in his infant car seat.

He drove Lacey and Tucker to Children's Memorial Hospital, located opposite the Trinity Medical Center. Because of Tucker's young age, the triage nurse didn't make them wait but hustled them straight back to one of the empty ED rooms. Since Lacey was still looking frazzled, he took the baby into his arms, unzipping his outfit so he wouldn't get too warm.

"What's going on with this little guy?" Dr Barb Wynn asked as she came into the room.

He recognized the doctor from an emergency medicine conference in Las Vegas last year, even though he didn't really know the woman personally. He was happy to see a familiar face. "He has bilateral ear infections but isn't keeping the antibiotics down. I think he's dehydrated and may need IV fluids."

"So why did you come to see me if you have everything all figured out?" Barb teased, taking the baby so she could set him on the edge of the crib to examine him.

"Because you're the pediatric expert, and I'm not," Brock said dryly. "And as long as you're looking at him, his lungs have sounded a bit congested as well; it's possible there's more going on than just a bilateral ear infection."

"Hmm." Barb Wynn listened to Tucker's heart and lungs. "I agree; I don't like the way he sounds," she admitted. "His ear infections may have already progressed to something more serious, like bronchitis or pneumonia. We'll get a chest X-ray and some blood cultures. I'll have one of the nurses come in to start an IV."

Lacey made a small sound of protest but didn't voice

her concern. Brock belatedly introduced them. "Lacey is Tucker's mom; my brother, Joel, is the father. Joel's not available at the moment."

"Nice to meet you, Lacey. Don't worry, we'll take good care of Tucker, I promise."

Lacey's attempt at a smile was truly pathetic. As Barb Wynn left to get her orders written, he tried to put her at ease, suspecting she was blaming herself for not being a good mother.

"This isn't your fault, Lacey. Kids get sick all the time. Once Tucker gets a few doses of IV antibiotics, he'll be much better, you'll see."

"I'm sure you're right," Lacey said in a quiet voice.

"Of course I'm right." Brock glanced at his vibrating phone. "I'll be right back, all right?"

Without waiting for her to respond, he opened his phone and walked out towards the waiting room so his cell phone wouldn't interfere with any of the monitoring equipment.

"Hello?"

"Brock? Rufus here. I'm at your uncle's cabin. The good news is that Joel has been here: the fire in the fireplace is fresh, and there are muddy footprints outside. The bad news is that he's gone."

Gone? How was that possible? He glanced back through the doorway leading into the emergency department and the small room where he'd left Tucker and Lacey. Even now, he could hear the baby crying, no doubt as he was getting poked with the IV.

Joel should be here, supporting Lacey. And Tucker.

Where on earth could his brother be?

* * *

Elana went into work early on Monday, a few hours before the start of her shift. She'd decided to come in early to complete some education modules that she hadn't quite finished, since sitting around at home and thinking about Brock was driving her crazy.

She'd meant what she'd said about forgiving him for her own sake rather than his. But saying the words, and believing them deep down where it counted, was much more difficult. She'd wanted to find Chloe, since talking to her foster mother had always helped in the past, but Chloe, well on the road to recovery from her operation, was helping to set up a charity function at the local church. And Elana was scheduled to work.

Raine was in the arena, her eyes widening in surprise when she saw Elana. "What are you doing here? Did you get called in early too?"

"No, just thought I'd finish that disaster planning module that's due the end of the quarter," Elana said. She glanced around, hoping she wasn't being too obvious. "Have you seen Brock?"

"Ah, yeah, in fact I have." Raine's expression was pained, and she grabbed Elana's arm, tugging her into the break room. "Look, Elana, I don't know how to tell you this."

Perplexed, she arched a brow. "Tell me what?"

"Brock's here. In the cafeteria." Raine's eyes were grim. "I just saw him down there while I was getting lunch, and you need to know, he's not alone. He's sitting with—a woman."

Elana's heart stumbled in her chest. Brock was with another woman? She swallowed hard, feeling sick.

She'd gotten the impression he wasn't seeing anyone. That he'd given up on having a personal life at all. The stab of jealousy struck deep.

"She's not at all the sort of woman I'd expect him to be with," Raine continued. "She's too young, rail thin, with stringy blonde hair. Pretty enough, I guess, if a guy is into the lost-waif type."

Lacey. Irrational relief flooded her. Raine's description fit Lacey to a T. "Was there a baby with them?"

Raine's eyes rounded comically. "Oh, my God, you mean to tell me Dr Madison has a kid?" she squeaked.

"No, the baby is his brother's child," Elana explained quickly. "And I think the woman he's with is Lacey, his brother's girlfriend. Don't you remember? They were at the clinic this past Saturday."

Raine didn't look entirely convinced. "No, I don't remember. For your sake I hope you're right."

"Brock's personal life isn't any of my business," she said, even though she knew she wasn't being truthful. Because she did care if there was a special woman in Brock's life. More than she should.

"Yeah, right." Raine rolled her eyes.

Elana ignored her. "I think I'll run down to check on them. It's odd they're here in the cafeteria." She tried to sound nonchalant so Raine wouldn't guess at how invested she was in Lacey's situation. The poor girl had already been through so much.

A horrible thought hit hard. What if they'd found Joel? And he was right now a patient up in the ICU?

"Don't say I didn't warn you," Raine said.

Elana gave a distracted nod, turned and left. Thankfully she hadn't swiped in yet to officially start work.

Bypassing the pokey elevator in favor of the stairs, she ran down to the cafeteria, not even realizing she was holding her breath as she scanned the crowd, looking for Brock. When she saw him sitting in a booth along the back wall, facing Lacey, she let out her pent-up breath in a rush.

She'd been right. He wasn't with another woman. She frowned when she realized Tucker's infant seat wasn't anywhere in sight.

They were arguing, or, to be technically correct, Brock was arguing while Lacey just sat with her thin shoulders hunched defensively.

"Why are you being so stubborn?" he asked, clearly annoyed as he pushed a set of car keys across the table towards Lacey. "This is your chance to take a break, to do something for yourself. You know Tucker's in good hands."

Lacey's eyes were downcast, as if she could barely hold Brock's gaze. "I don't need a break. I told you, I'm fine."

"You're fine." Brock let out a rough laugh. In an abrupt move, he reached across the table and grabbed her arm, roughly pushing up her sleeve to expose the cut oozing on her forearm. "Sure, you're fine. If you're so fine, why are you cutting yourself, huh?"

Lacey twisted her arm from his grip, shrinking further back against the seat. Elana sucked in a harsh breath at the flash of pure panic in Lacey's eyes. She hurried forward.

"Hi, Lacey, Brock. What are you guys doing here?" She smiled brightly, ignoring the tension as she glanced around. "Where's Tucker?"

There was a long moment of silence before Brock turned to her. "Tucker has pneumonia; he's been admitted to Children's Memorial."

"Oh, no, I'm sorry. I didn't know." Truly distressed by the news, she glanced at Lacey, who looked much worse than Raine had described her. The poor thing looked as if she hadn't gotten any sleep in days. "Is he doing all right?"

Brock nodded, again answering for Lacey. "He was admitted yesterday and he's on IV antibiotics. They're pleased with his progress so far."

Lacey's hand shot out, her fingers curling around the keys Brock had shoved in her direction. "I think I will borrow your car; I do have a few errands to run."

Brock looked surprised at Lacey's change of heart. "Good. I'm glad."

"Excuse me," Lacey whispered, easing out of the booth. She clutched her ragged purse beneath her arm and left.

Elana watched her for a moment before turning to Brock. "You scared her to death," she accused as she slid into Lacey's vacated spot.

"I didn't mean to." Brock looked truly bewildered.

"It's your anger that scares her," Elana explained. "She thinks you don't like her."

Brock scrubbed his face with his hands. He didn't look as if he'd gotten much sleep, either. "Of course I like her. She's the mother of my nephew. I'm trying to support her as best I can."

"Lacey needs to know you don't resent her. And that you'll be there for the long haul."

Brock grimaced. "You're probably right. The private investigator I hired found where Joel had been staying at a remote cabin in the north woods that my uncle owns, but Joel's not there now. I'm sure that information isn't making Lacey feel any better."

"You're right, and yet you chose this moment to confront her about the cuts on her arm."

"Am I supposed to ignore what she's doing to herself?" he asked. "Why do you think I was so insistent that she take the keys?"

She let out a heavy sigh. Brock's intentions had been good, but his technique needed work. "I don't know what to tell you. Lacey needs help. Maybe there are some counseling services for low-income families. I'll ask around, see what's available."

"Thank you," Brock said quietly. "I appreciate your help."

There was an awkward moment of silence. She knew she should go back up to the ED to work on her modules, but she didn't move. She hadn't seen Brock alone since the night they'd worked together and he'd lost his young patient.

Since she'd told him she'd forgiven him.

Since she'd realized he'd planned to sacrifice his own life in order to save others.

"Elana, did you mean what you said?" Brock's intense gaze bored into hers. The noisy, crowded cafeteria faded away, making her feel as if they were the only two people in the room. "About trying to find a way to forgive me?"

"Yes." She flashed a crooked smile. "Sometimes it's easy to forget when we're sitting here like this, talking about Lacey and Tucker. But other times—" she gave a helpless shrug "—it's not as easy to forget. And then I find myself thinking the worst."

Brock nodded, his expression serious. "I understand. And I want you to know how much it means to me that you're willing to try. You were right, though, to do it for you, not for me."

She almost shook her head because he was wrong. Brock needed her forgiveness as much as she needed to give it. What a messed-up pair they were.

She bit back a protest when he stood. "I have to get back to Tucker," he said in a low voice.

Stifling her regret, Elana stood too. "Are you working tonight?"

"Yeah, although you'll probably be glad to hear I'm working a shorter shift; I'm splitting the time with Nathan Forrester." His lopsided smile did funny things to her stomach.

When he turned to walk away, Elana realized, with a start, that he was wrong. Again.

She wasn't glad to hear he was working a short shift. As irrational as it was, she looked forward to working with Brock.

She missed him when he wasn't there.

CHAPTER NINE

ELANA was assigned to the trauma room with Brock. From the beginning of their shift, it was busy. Their first two patients were elderly women with severe flu symptoms.

It took a while to get the patients admitted to the ICU, where they belonged, because every critical care bed was full. Finally, after almost two hours, Elana was able to transfer both patients upstairs.

By the time she'd returned, the trauma pager was going off again. Brock met her in the trauma bay, a slight frown marring his forehead.

"Motor vehicle crash," he said in a low tone.

She nodded, having read the text message herself.

Female driver, Janey Thompson, in critical condition after long extrication.

"Get ready," Brock murmured.

She took a deep breath just as the doors of the trauma bay burst open. Two paramedics wheeled their patient in, and, as Janey Thompson drew closer, Elana looked down, and her heart lodged in her throat.

Janey Thompson was young. Far younger than she'd expected. Beneath the blood stains and open gash on her forehead, Janey couldn't have been much more than sixteen.

"Dear God," Brock said in a low, shocked tone. She knew he was remembering her sister, Felicity. "Give me the latest set of vitals."

The paramedics rattled them off. "BP low at 66/32. Heart rate extremely tachy at 155 beats per minute. She was intubated in the field, and we've had fluids wide open during the ride over here."

Elana swallowed hard. This young girl already had so many strikes against her. She feared their efforts would be in vain.

"Get two units of O-negative blood in her stat, Elana," Brock ordered, his expression grim. "We are not going to lose her."

She believed him. With renewed energy, she reached for the two units of packed red blood cells and hung them on the rapid infuser. Since Eric Towne was preoccupied with another patient from the same crash, she and Brock worked over young Janey together.

As the blood was flowing in, she performed a quick assessment. "Brock, take a look. The right side of her chest is tense and hard; I think she has a tension pneumothorax."

At that moment, the monitor overhead began alarming. They'd lost her blood pressure!

"Get me an eighteen gauge needle," he ordered, ripping off the girl's blouse to expose her ribs.

Elana whipped open the top drawer of the supply

cabinet and grabbed the needle. Without taking the time to prep the skin, Brock yanked on gloves and stabbed the needle between the patient's fourth and fifth ribs.

"It's working," Elana said urgently, her eyes glued to the monitor. "Her blood pressure is coming back up."

"We need a chest tube set up." Brock's expression was still tense. "I think she's bleeding into her chest. And I want a CT surgery consult."

She was already pulling out the chest tube insertion tray. Brock had taken care of the immediate crisis with the tension pneumothorax, but Janey wasn't out of the woods yet.

Brock inserted the chest tube, and immediately the tubing filled with blood. Elana called the operator to order a stat surgery consult.

Between them, they worked in tandem over Janey Thompson, giving fluids and blood, for well over an hour. Sweat was dripping down her spine when they finally had Janey stabilized enough for surgery.

"Let's get her up to the OR," Brock said.

With a nod, she disconnected the young girl from the monitor above the bed and connected her to the portable device they used for transports. She wasn't at all surprised when Brock helped her to wheel Janey upstairs.

The surgical team met them right outside the OR doors. With one last look at Janey's pale face, Elana stepped back and let the OR team take over.

For a long moment, Brock didn't move.

"You did it," Elana whispered, touching his hand lightly. "You saved her."

Brock slowly shook his head, a relieved half smile

curving his mouth. "Not just me. You too. We saved her, Elana. Together."

"Together," she echoed. Janey had a fighting chance to make it, thanks to her and Brock's teamwork. Maybe it could always be this way between them? Maybe this was meant to be?

In companionable silence, they headed back down to the trauma room.

Dr Nathan Forrester was already there, waiting for them. "Hey, Brock, I was able to get here a little early, so you're free to get out of here."

She struggled to hide her dismay. She'd forgotten about Brock's plans to work a short shift.

"I appreciate it, Nate." Brock glanced at Elana, his blue gaze intense, and for a brief moment, he made her feel as if they were all alone in the room. "Thanks again for all your help, Elana."

"You're welcome." She licked suddenly dry lips, wishing he didn't have to go. She tried to remember they were both simply doing their jobs, but it seemed like so much more.

Because together they'd made an awesome team.

The rest of Elana's shift dragged by. Not that Dr Forrester wasn't a good doctor, because he was. But, somehow, working the trauma bay with him wasn't nearly as exciting as working with Brock. His intensity drew out the best in the rest of them.

"Elana?" The unit clerk called out to her as she was about to head to the locker room. "You have a call on line two."

She frowned, wondering who would call her this late. Chloe? She quickened her step and picked up the closest phone. "Hello?"

"Elana? It's Brock. I need your help."

Her fingers tightened on the phone. "Tucker? Is he okay?"

"Tucker's fine, but Lacey's gone. She's not answering her phone, and I haven't seen her since I gave her my car keys at lunchtime."

"Gone?" Elana frowned. Surely Brock was exaggerating. "Are you sure?"

"I need a ride," Brock said bluntly. "I'm still at Children's. Are you able to drive me home when you're finished with work?"

"Of course. I'm finished now. Give me five minutes, and I'll pick you up outside."

Elana hung up the phone, her mind whirling. There had to be some sort of explanation. Lacey wouldn't just take off, leaving Tucker behind, especially in Brock's car. Lacey was intimidated by Brock.

There must be some mistake. More likely, Lacey had gone back to Brock's house and had fallen sound asleep. The poor thing probably hadn't had a decent night's sleep since before Tucker was born.

She hurried to the parking garage. Minutes later, she pulled up at the front door of Children's Memorial Hospital. Brock strode out, and he would have been devastatingly handsome in his worn blue jeans and navy-blue shirt if not for the dark frown etched on his features.

"I appreciate the lift," he said brusquely.

"No problem." His broad shoulders bumped into hers as he leaned back and over to put his seat belt on. She grabbed the steering wheel tightly, hyperaware of his overwhelming presence in her small car. Everything felt different now that she'd forgiven him. Especially after the closeness they'd shared working over Janey. "How long do you think they're going to keep Tucker in the hospital?"

"The plan at this point is to keep him for three days on IV antibiotics before switching him to oral medication. If he does well, he could potentially come home as early as Wednesday."

"That's good to know." Elana glanced at him. "You tried calling Lacey at home?"

"At least a dozen times." His expression turned even darker, and Elana knew he was thinking the worst.

She didn't argue because nothing she could say would make him feel any better. Ten minutes later, when she pulled into his driveway, she saw the garage door was closed and there were no lights on anywhere inside the house.

It certainly looked as if no one was home.

Brock jumped out of the car before she'd even put it in park, using his key to access the house. She quickly followed him inside, suddenly feeling extremely apprehensive. Their young patient, Ariel Peterson, had taken an overdose of drugs. What if Lacey had done something similar?

"Lacey? Are you here?" Brock shouted as he strode through the house, flipping on light switches wherever he went. He headed straight into Lacey's room but came back out so fast Elana knew he hadn't found her.

Brock headed through the living room into the kitchen and through to the garage, probably checking the garage for his car. With her pulse pounding, Elana forced herself to check the bathroom, pushing back the shower curtain to look inside the bathtub, making sure Lacey wasn't lying there. Then she even went so far as to check Brock's room but didn't find any evidence that Lacey had been there, either.

"She took off and left her son," Brock said grimly when they met back in the living room. "I just checked her bedroom again. Some of her stuff is gone, along with the small suitcase she had, but Tucker's things are all here."

"I can't believe it," she murmured. This truly didn't look good, and she would have easily bet money that Lacey would never willingly abandon her child. "Maybe she just lost track of time. I'm sure she'll be back."

His bark of laughter held no humor. "Yeah, that's what I told her when Joel took off, and you can see how well that worked out for me. At least Joel didn't steal my car."

"You gave her the keys," Elana pointed out. "That's not stealing. Besides, even the police wouldn't do anything anyway, not until she's been gone twenty-four hours. We haven't seen her since noon, and it's close to midnight now. I'm sure she'll show up sometime tomorrow." At least, she hoped so.

Brock rubbed a hand along the back of his neck. "I really screwed everything up, didn't I?"

"No." When he grimaced, obviously not believing

her, she shrugged. "Maybe. But Lacey is tougher than you think."

His shoulders slumped, and he sank down on the sofa, looking like a man defeated. "You were right, earlier. I shouldn't have confronted her about the cuts on her arm. I don't know what I was thinking."

Hearing the self-recrimination in his tone, she sat down beside him. "Hey, don't be too hard on yourself. You moved here just to support your brother and Lacey. That counts for something."

He slowly shook his head. "I lost my temper and snapped at her. No wonder she took off."

"Do you know anything about her background?" she asked, changing the subject. "Does Lacey have family in the area?"

"I have no idea. She's been pretty quiet about her past. But I do care about her," he said, lifting his head to meet her gaze. "I care about Lacey and Tucker. And I care about Joel too, even though I've been irritated with him since he left."

"Understandable, don't you think?" she asked softly, taking his hand in hers and giving it a reassuring squeeze.

He lifted their clasped hands and brushed a kiss across her knuckles, the soft caress sending tingles down her spine. She couldn't have moved away from him now if her life depended on it.

"The minute I realized Lacey was gone, I wanted to call you. This is the second time you've come to my rescue, Elana."

Her mouth went dry, but she tried to smile. "Like I said before, I don't mind."

Brock closed his eyes and sat back against the sofa. She sat back too, intending to stay only for a few more minutes. He put his arm around her shoulders and hugged her close. The gesture was nice. Comforting. She should leave to go home, but she didn't want to. She liked being here with Brock.

Secretly savoring the embrace, her eyes drifted closed, and she wished for the impossible.

When Brock opened his eyes several hours later to see the bright sunlight streaming in through the windows, he realized they'd fallen asleep on his sofa. Elana's soft body was pressed against him, the curves of her body achingly noticeable through her thin scrubs. Somehow, during the night, they must have stretched out on the sofa, instinctively seeking a more comfortable position.

Her warm vanilla scent teased his senses. Brock knew he should move, especially now that every nerve in his body had zinged to awareness, his groin tightening with primitive need, making his jeans uncomfortably snug. Holding Elana in his arms felt good. Better than good. Fantastic.

He wanted her. More than he'd ever wanted any other woman in a really long time. He'd been determined to stay away from her, but he was fighting a losing battle. Because he didn't want to stay away. He liked working with her. The way they'd saved Janey had given him hope. Had made him realize how great it was working with Elana.

Or maybe it was enough to simply be with Elana.

Breathing in her scent, he didn't move, unwilling to do anything that might bring this slice of heaven to an end. When Elana shifted, pressing her body against his, he held his breath. Her hand splayed in the center of his chest, the heat of her palm burning through the thin fabric of his shirt. He froze, hoping and praying she wouldn't wake up.

Not yet.

Her hand lightly caressed him, her fingertips making lazy circles that sent a shaft of desire straight to his groin. Holding her like this was pure, agonizing torture.

But he didn't want to be anywhere else.

Elana shifted again, her lips skimming the line of his jaw, and in that moment, it occurred to him that she might be awake.

Was it possible?

After everything that had happened in the past twenty-four hours, was it possible she was really awake? Wanting him as much as he wanted her?

Afraid to breathe, he trailed his hand up along her arm, wishing the thin, long-sleeved T-shirt she wore beneath her scrubs would vanish, so he could relish the silky softness of her skin. His fingers brushed along the side of her breast, and she reflexively arched against him, as if seeking more.

He lifted his head to glance down at her, to make sure she wasn't still asleep and unaware of what was happening. When she gazed up at him, he knew she was silently encouraging him to continue. He lowered his head and captured her mouth in a dizzying kiss.

Her fingers curled in the fabric of his shirt, not to push him away, but to hold on to him, as she, hesitantly at first, and then with more boldness, kissed him back.

CHAPTER TEN

BROCK'S heart soared. Drowning in the taste of her, he slanted his mouth over hers, deepening the kiss. He wanted Elana more than he wanted to breathe.

He could have stayed like this forever. But the heat of her skin beckoned.

Slowly, he slid a hand beneath her scrubs, seeking the softness beneath. She stiffened and drew back, gasping for breath. "Wait."

Wait? He forced himself to stop, to pull back, even though every nerve in his body wanted more. He lifted his head and gulped desperately needed oxygen into his lungs. "What's wrong?"

"Nothing. Everything." Elana pushed against his chest again, and this time he reluctantly released her. She smoothed a hand through her hair. "I—we can't do this."

He tried to gather his scattered thoughts. Had he imagined her response? He didn't think so.

"I can't believe I fell asleep," she continued. "Gosh, it's later than I thought. I really need to get home."

He didn't know what he'd done to cause her to back

away, but there was no denying that, despite her sweet response, she now regretted their kiss.

The way she avoided his gaze bothered him. He put a hand on her arm to keep her from bolting for the door. "Do I need to apologize, Elana? If so, I'm sorry. I never meant to make you feel uncomfortable."

She tugged from his grasp and leaped to her feet, straightening her clothes. "You didn't make me uncomfortable," she said, although the rush of color in her cheeks belied her words. "I just don't want you to think I stayed—for this."

"We fell asleep. It's not a crime." He stared at her for a moment, quickly figuring out that she hadn't been awake as long as he'd thought. She'd enjoyed their kiss, but he'd let things get a little too far out of control.

His fault, not hers. But after that kiss, he didn't want her to leave. "I'm sorry," he said again. "Would you please stay for breakfast?" Brock slowly rose to his feet. "You'd actually be doing me a favor since I'm going to need a ride back to Children's Memorial anyway."

"Oh." She hesitated, looking like a scared fawn ready to bolt. "I—uh, sure. I guess I can take you back to the hospital; it's on my way."

"So you'll let me make you breakfast?" he asked hopefully, wishing he could do something to help her relax. No matter what she said, he had obviously made her uncomfortable, and for that he was sorry. "The bathroom is right down the hall, and you can help yourself to whatever you need; there's a new toothbrush in the cabinet."

"All right, you can make me breakfast," she acquiesced. "And I will borrow your bathroom if you don't mind."

"Take all the time you need." When she disappeared into the bathroom, he scrubbed his hands over his face, grateful for the time to pull himself together.

That kiss had shaken him. Had tied his stomach into knots and left him wanting more.

But Elana wasn't at ease with him, and, really, could he blame her? She'd barely had time to come to grips with forgiving him, much less understand why he'd kissed her senseless.

He needed to take things slowly. To give her time to get used to him. As a friend and, maybe in time, as something more.

He didn't feel the same sense of panic he usually did when faced with an attractive woman he'd wanted to get to know better. He usually avoided relationships. But for the first time in his life, he couldn't make himself back away, even though he knew he didn't deserve her.

Keeping busy in the kitchen, making omelets for breakfast, helped him stay focused, but when Elana returned, with her face scrubbed free of makeup and her hair brushed, gently framing her face, darned if he didn't feel another shaft of desire.

She was so beautiful, his gut ached.

"Coffee?" he asked in a low, husky tone.

"Yes, please."

He pulled another mug out of the cupboard, taking several deep breaths to steady his hands as he poured her a cup. He knew she preferred flavored creamer, but he didn't have any. "I'm sorry, but I only have milk," he said, pushing the container towards her.

"That's fine." Again, she avoided his direct gaze, and he wondered what she was thinking. Did she regret the heated kiss they'd shared?

"Are you planning to call the police about Lacey taking your car?" she asked as he slid twin ham-and-cheese omelets on two plates, one for each of them, and set them on the table.

"No. But I might call Rufus, the private investigator," he said. "I do need to get my car back eventually. But I'd rather give Lacey a chance to return the vehicle on her own. And I'm truly more worried about what might happen to Tucker than about the stupid car."

"I'm glad," Elana murmured. She stared at him for a long moment before she turned her attention to her food. Softly she added, "You're a nice man, Brock."

The bite of omelet lodged in the back of his throat.

No, he wasn't a nice man. Because if she knew what erotic thoughts had been going through his mind all morning, Elana would surely turn and run as fast as she could in the opposite direction.

And he wouldn't blame her one bit.

Elana tried to eat her omelet, anxious to act as if everything was normal, but, in reality, the effects of Brock's kiss had left her badly shaken.

Brock may have started the kiss, but she'd been more than a willing participant. Until the moment he'd slid his hand beneath her scrubs, reminding her how long it had been since she'd been naked and vulnerable with a man.

Too long.

Forever.

She shied away from that thought.

"This is great," she said, forcing enthusiasm into her tone, even though for all she could tell, she might be eating sawdust. She swallowed hard, anxious to finish so she could get out of Brock's house. Away from the sofa that mocked her.

Her cell phone rang, drawing her gaze back to her purse that was still on the sofa. Odd, she wasn't expecting a call. "Excuse me," she murmured.

She went into the living room and fished her phone out from the depths of her purse. The number on the screen indicated the call was from the hospital. Her boss asking her to come in early? She hesitated, tempted to let it go to voice mail.

"Hello?"

"Elana? This is Claire, the manager of the ICU. I received your transfer request from Human Resources. Would you have time this afternoon to stop in for an interview?"

She flashed a guilty glance at Brock, who was watching her. This was the call she'd been waiting for, only now she wasn't sure she still was interested in transferring out of the ED. Away from Brock. Working with Brock as they'd taken care of Janey had been extremely rewarding.

She didn't want to leave him.

But she wasn't going to make a hasty decision. It certainly wouldn't hurt to find out more about the position before making a final decision. "Ah, sure. I can do that."

"How about two o'clock?" Claire asked.

"That will be fine." She turned to reach for a pen and paper from her purse.

"Great. My office is on the fourth floor, right across from the ICU. You can't miss it."

She hastily scribbled two o'clock and fourth floor on a scrap piece of paper. "Thanks, I'll see you then." She flipped her phone shut and tossed it back in her purse.

"Problems?" Brock asked when she came back to the kitchen table.

"No, just work." She swallowed her cold omelet, feeling guilty for not telling Brock the truth. But it seemed foolish to bring up the possibility of her transfer when she wasn't even sure she was going to take it. "I have to go in for a meeting."

"I see." She was grateful he let the subject drop.

She finished her food and pushed away her empty plate. "Thanks for breakfast, Brock. You're a great cook."

"You're welcome." As if sensing how desperately she wanted to leave, he stood and carried their empty dishes to the sink. "Would you give me a few minutes to shower and change before we leave?"

"Of course." She smiled weakly, thankful when he'd finally left her alone. For a moment she buried her face in her hands, stifling a low groan.

What had she been thinking, kissing Brock like that? She'd wantonly pressed against him. Had very nearly thrown caution to the wind and begged for more.

Maybe she should consider that transfer. Because now that she'd kissed Brock, she was acutely aware of him. As a man she was attracted to.

She'd opened herself up to a personal relationship during her college years, but that leap of faith had blown up in her face. She'd never trusted anyone like that again.

Yet here she was, considering placing her trust in Brock. The one man who had the power to hurt her worse than she'd ever been hurt before.

Because she cared about him. Too much for her own good.

Elana drove Brock to Children's Memorial, struggling to maintain the light friendly tone.

"Do you want to come up with me to see Tucker?" Brock asked as she pulled up in front of the hospital.

"Not right now, maybe later," she hedged.

"If you have time, come over after your meeting," he suggested. "I'll be hanging out here for most of the day; I want to talk to the pediatrician when he makes rounds."

"You're not working tonight?" Elana asked.

He shook his head. "Are you?"

"No, I'm off too." Amazing how their schedules seemed to match perfectly. She flashed him a smile. "Take care, Brock. I'll probably see you later."

"Thanks for the ride." He took her hand, gave it a squeeze, and then reluctantly let go and climbed from the car.

"Goodbye." She waved as she pulled away.

Elana headed home, her thoughts in turmoil as she stepped into the shower. The hot spray didn't wash away her sudden doubts.

Was she crazy to even think about staying in the emergency department with Brock?

Maybe. She needed to talk to Raine. Or Chloe. Her foster mother had always been there for Elana when she needed someone to talk to. If anyone could make sense of the confused madness that defined her feelings for Brock, Chloe could.

She threw on a sweater and jeans, allowing her hair to air-dry as she hurried back outside.

"Elana! How nice of you to stop by." Chloe greeted her warmly.

"Oh, Chloe." Elana closed her eyes and savored her foster mother's exuberant embrace, returning the tight hug, inhaling the familiar, comforting scent of roses. Over these past few years, Chloe had become synonymous with home. Elana loved and cared about her mother, but it was Chloe's gentle, no-nonsense attitude that had kept her grounded when times were tough.

Feeling better already, Elana grinned and stepped back from the hug. "How are you feeling?"

"I'm fine." Chloe waved off Elana's concern and gestured for her to come into the living room. They sat down on the sofa, which was soft and threadbare from years of use. Elana turned to face her foster mother, seeking any hint of fatigue or lingering pain. "Completely back to normal."

Reassured that Chloe at least looked well rested, she raised a skeptical brow. "I hope you're following that low-fat diet Dr Ames recommended."

"Of course." Chloe answered so quickly, Elana suspected she was fudging the truth. Chloe loved fried foods and had agreed to try to cut back after her cardiac stent placement. "But enough about my medical issues; I'd rather talk about you. How are you doing? What's new at work?"

She didn't bother sidestepping the issue. "Chloe, you're not going to believe this, but I have two big things to tell you. First of all, my mom started to speak. And secondly, Brock Madison is the new emergency medicine doctor on staff."

Chloe's eyes grew wide. "Oh, my. How wonderful for you about your mother. But Brock Madison? Heavens, how are you holding up?"

"It's been difficult." Elana lifted a shoulder in a slight shrug. "At first, it was impossible. I put in for a transfer to critical care. But the more I work with him, the more I realize he's changed. I don't hate him, Chloe," she said in a rush. "I've wasted so many years, hating him. Even my mother told me not to hate him."

"There, now." Chloe took her hand and squeezed it tight. "You were young. And so full of pain."

Tears pricked her eyelids, and she blinked them back. "I needed someone to blame, and Brock was the perfect target."

"And now?" Chloe asked softly.

"I don't blame him." She drew a deep breath, anxious to tell Chloe everything. "I can't blame him because I've seen firsthand how he's suffered too. He doesn't deal well with losing patients. And he treats every new patient like a challenge he's not going to lose."

"So he's a good doctor."

"Yes. He's a good doctor. And a good man. He's dedicated his entire life to saving others." She swallowed hard, determined to tell Chloe everything. "I like him. Too much."

Chloe's eyes widened at the implication. "You're attracted to him." It wasn't a question.

"Yes." She couldn't deny it. "I kissed him. But I have an interview this afternoon with the manager of the ICU." Elana jammed her fingers through her damp hair. "Chloe, help me. What should I do?"

"I can't answer that, Elana. Only you can."

Typical—even when she was young, Chloe had made her face her feelings. "I don't know," she whispered helplessly. "I like working with Brock. I think we make a good team."

"So what's stopping you?"

"Fear." Saying it out loud didn't sound as ridiculous as she'd thought. "I'm afraid. Of caring too much. I kissed him, Chloe. And that kiss could have led to something more. Maybe I should transfer to critical care."

"So you're starting this relationship already believing Brock will hurt you?"

"Yes. No." She shook her head. "I don't know."

"There are no guarantees in any relationship, Elana. I don't think you should leave because you're thinking the worst."

Chloe was right: she was already planning for a contingency in case things didn't work out. "Maybe you're right," she agreed.

"Of course I'm right."

Chloe's certainty made her chuckle. "I guess it's just not easy for me to trust him."

"It could be that he feels the same way. Aren't you afraid you'll be the one to hurt him?" Chloe asked.

"No." The idea had never entered her mind. "He has nurses tripping over themselves to get his attention. He could have anyone he wanted." And she couldn't imagine he really wanted her. Especially since he didn't know the truth about her past.

"Then why did he kiss you?" Chloe asked reasonably. "Don't sell yourself short, Elana. Maybe Brock Madison has kept an eye on you throughout the years."

"No. He was just as surprised to see me working in the ED as I was to see him." The expression on his face when he'd recognized her had been priceless. If she'd been in the right frame of mind to appreciate it. "I'm sure he moved away in the first place because it would be easier to forget."

Chloe pursed her lips for a moment. "Do you really think so?"

She shrugged, remembering how he'd looked when they'd lost the young pedestrian hit by the car. "Maybe not. He's intense. I doubt he ever forgot."

"Elana, I think it's time you knew the truth."

"About what?"

"Your college scholarship." Chloe grimaced. "Brock Madison didn't want you to know, but he sponsored your scholarship."

"What?" She couldn't wrap her mind around the news. "How?"

"He supplied the money," Chloe said simply. "I'm not sure how he did it, although I suspect he doubled the amount of his own student loans to come up with the necessary amount. But, in the end, he went through the university to ensure his scholarship was awarded to you."

"But that's impossible." Dumbfounded, Elana stared at her foster mother.

"He didn't want you to know. And I've honored his request, until now."

"I don't know what to say," Elana murmured, still in shock. Brock had sponsored her scholarship. Likely out of guilt. For years she'd hated him, had blamed him for everything that had gone wrong in her life. Ironic to realize that, without his help, she wouldn't be where she was today. "I never suspected."

"I tried telling you he wasn't a bad person," Chloe reminded her. "But I'm glad you've found a way to forgive him on your own."

She nodded. She had forgiven him, and suddenly that was the easy part. How was she supposed to handle talking to him now that she knew the truth? Humbled, she looked up at Chloe. "I feel like I should pay him back."

Chloe quizzically tilted her head to the side. "Why don't you try trusting him instead?"

Trusting him. With her body and maybe with her heart. She thought about their heated kiss. Maybe Brock could heal her once and for all. "Okay, I'll trust him."

"Follow your heart, Elana." Chloe smiled at her with approval. "Always follow your heart."

"I will, Chloe." She gave her foster mother a warm hug.

Elana dressed in a navy-blue suit, one of the few outfits she owned that was appropriate for a job interview.

She'd talk to Claire, but, in reality, she'd already made her decision.

She was going to stay in the ED with Brock.

Claire was nice enough, and when the only position she had was the graveyard shift, it was even easier to decline. As Claire walked her down to the lobby, she asked Elana to keep in touch if anything changed.

"I will. Thanks, Claire."

Brock walked into the lobby, looking surprised to see her standing there with Claire. He narrowed his gaze when he took in her formal attire, immediately realizing she hadn't been truthful about her meeting. She winced, unable to hide the flash of guilt.

"Elana?" He immediately strode towards her. "Wait. Don't make any rash decisions. Let's talk about this first, okay?"

"Brock, this isn't what you think…" she tried to reassure him.

"You're making a mistake," he interrupted, not letting her finish. "Have dinner with me, please? Things have been intense since Lacey vanished, and I could use a break. I borrowed a friend's car. I can pick you up at six. Please, give me a chance."

How could she not? And he was right: things had been intense with Lacey gone. Remembering her promise to Chloe and to her own mother, Elana nodded. "All right, Brock. I'll have dinner with you tonight."

CHAPTER ELEVEN

BROCK finished up with Tucker and then drove Nathan's car home, clenching the steering wheel tightly. He couldn't believe Elana had gone to a job interview. Despite her claims that she'd forgiven him, she was still planning to leave trauma nursing.

Ha. Not if he had anything to say about it.

When he arrived at home, he wasn't too surprised to find that Lacey still hadn't returned.

Maybe he ought to call the police after all. Something could have happened to Lacey. She could be a patient in a hospital somewhere…or worse.

Pushing his troubled thoughts aside, Brock showered again and shaved before changing into slacks and a dress shirt. Elana deserved to go someplace special.

Fancy, yet intimate.

Feeling uncharacteristically nervous, he drove to her house. She met him at her apartment door, wearing a long-sleeved siren-red dress that clung to her generous curves and flared at the knee. He stared at her, his mouth martini dry as he struggled to keep a rein on his desire.

This was his chance to convince her to change her mind, not give her another reason to leave.

"You look stunning," he murmured.

She flashed a shy smile. "Thank you. It was fun dressing up for a change."

She hovered in the doorway, as if afraid to ask him in, so he escorted her back out to the car, wishing there was some way to put her at ease.

"You know, you didn't have to do this," Elana said as he headed toward the restaurant. "I didn't accept the transfer."

"You didn't?" He threw her a startled glance. "Really?"

"Really. I thought about it but decided that I'd rather stay right where I am. For now."

He took a deep breath, relaxing a bit at the news. "I'm glad, Elana. You had me worried for a minute."

"I know. I should have told you the truth about the job interview."

"What made you change your mind?" he asked, curious.

There was a moment of silence before she turned towards him. "You."

Him? His breath lodged in his throat. "I'm glad. This morning I was worried that I'd scared you off."

"Maybe a little at first." She surprised him by acknowledging the truth. "I don't have a lot of experience with relationships."

He almost wanted to laugh, since his experience with relationships was nonexistent too. For years he'd carried so much guilt; he hadn't believed he deserved happiness. A future. But somehow those old arguments didn't seem to matter at the moment. He reached over and took her hand. "Me either. So I guess we'll learn, together."

Her smile was tremulous. "Sounds good."

Her trust humbled him. He didn't want her to ever be afraid, which meant he needed to go slow. Very slow.

"Excellent. So let's enjoy dinner, then." Feeling more confident, he handed over the keys to the valet-parking attendant and escorted Elana upstairs to the plush restaurant overlooking the shores of Lake Michigan.

Elana captured more than one man's gaze as she walked past, but she seemed oblivious to the attention. Their table was small and cozy, with an awesome view of the sunset over the water.

"It's spectacular," Elana murmured, gazing at the rippling waves on the great lake.

"Not nearly as spectacular as you," he said, barely giving the breathtaking view a glance.

She blushed, and he reminded himself to take things slow and easy. There was no rush. He requested a bottle of red wine and was pleased when Elana seemed to enjoy it.

"What made you move to Minneapolis?" she asked, sipping her wine.

"That's where I was matched." She inclined her head, indicating she knew about the match process where every medical student from all the graduating classes went through a complicated system of requesting their first, second and third choices for residency programs across the country. It was involved, yet seemed to work.

"Because you wanted to do trauma?" she asked.

"Yes, because I wanted to do emergency medicine and trauma. Once I finished my residency in the Twin Cities, I decided to stay on as an attending physician."

She stared at her wine. "So it wasn't a conscious decision on your part to avoid staying here after the accident?"

"I went to medical school here," he reminded her. "No, of course I wasn't avoiding Milwaukee. My family lived here. Joel and I were pretty close despite the age gap. Chicago, Milwaukee and Minneapolis were my top three choices, although not necessarily in that order."

The waiter brought their salads, adding fresh ground pepper with a flourish. They ate in silence for a few minutes.

"I went to college here in Milwaukee too," Elana murmured. "But you probably already knew that."

Warily he nodded. "Yeah, I guessed as much," he said evasively.

She gave him an exasperated look. "Brock, Chloe told me about the scholarship you provided."

He gulped, swallowing a whole cherry tomato and nearly choking in the process. "She did?"

"Yes." Elana paused and then leaned forward. "I don't know what to say. A mere thank-you doesn't seem to be enough."

Her gratitude made him mad. Chloe Jenkins shouldn't have opened her big mouth. "Don't. I never wanted you to know where the money came from. For God's sake, Elana, don't you think it was the least I could do? After everything you went through?"

"No, I think you went above and beyond the call of duty." Elana pushed her empty salad plate away. "Chloe was a lifesaver, but now I owe you a debt of gratitude as well."

"No, you don't." This was exactly why he hadn't wanted her to know. "Gratitude isn't what I want from you, Elana."

She nodded slowly. "I know. But you already have my forgiveness."

His heart stumbled in his chest. He should be grateful, but he wanted more than just her forgiveness. He wanted everything she was willing to give. And more. Yet he needed to step warily.

Elana tilted her head to the side. "Did you see the movie *Pay It Forward*?"

"Yes." He dragged his mind to the present.

"Well, that's what I've decided to do. I have some money saved up, and I've decided to use it to offer a scholarship to someone else. I'd like to give another underprivileged child the chance I had to go to college." Her wistful smile broke his heart. "I'd like to call it the Felicity Schultz Memorial Scholarship."

Stunned, he stared at her. Surely she could use the money for a down payment on a house or towards a new car? But the fact that she wanted to honor her sister, the way he'd tried to do, humbled him. "You're incredible. I think that's a great idea," he managed.

Her smile lit up her face, hitting him with the force of a tsunami. "Thank you. I think so too."

He wanted her. Wanted her so badly, he ached with need. The waiter served the rest of their meal, but Brock couldn't have told anyone what they ate, even though when the waiter took his plate away, it was empty. Every nerve in his body shimmered with amplified desire.

Elana declined dessert, so they left the restaurant shortly thereafter. He'd promised her they'd go slow, but he didn't want to take her home. Not yet.

"I have some wine at home if you'd be willing to come over for a bit. Or I can take you home if you'd rather. It's up to you, Elana."

She bit her lip and hesitated. "I'd like to come over for a bit."

He was startled, fully expecting the opposite. "Are you sure?"

A small smile played along her lips. "I'm sure."

Nearly dizzy with relief, he headed to his place. He pulled into the driveway and then went around to help her from the car. Slow. He was going to take this slow.

Slow would kill him, but better that than scaring her.

Inside, he flicked on a light and gestured to the sofa. "Have a seat. Can I get you something to drink? Wine? Or a soft drink?"

"No, I don't think so." She caught his hand, preventing him from going into the kitchen. "What I'd really like is for you to kiss me again."

Heaven help him, he'd promised to go slow. Yet how could he keep himself under control when she looked at him like that? Her moist lips were parted softly, inviting him to take her up on the offer.

As if he could do anything else?

"Elana," he whispered, pulling her into his arms and holding her close as if she were the rarest, most fragile vase on earth. He dipped his head, his mouth hovering over hers. "Please be sure."

"I'm sure." She rose up on her tiptoes, closing the space between them to press her mouth to his.

A kaleidoscope of color burst behind his eyelids as her mouth teased his, the tip of her tongue outlining his lips seductively. He kept chanting inwardly, *go slow, go slow*, but the razor edge of desire soon overwhelmed rational thought.

He pulled her against him, deepening the kiss, drowning in the honeyed depths of her mouth. His blood pounded in his chest, but he didn't stop. He'd waited forever for this, and now that he had her in his arms, he didn't want to let go.

She wrapped her arms around his neck, returning his kiss with fervor. Trying not to scare her, yet unable to hold back, he slid his hands beneath her bottom and lifted her higher, so she fit snugly against him.

She let out a moan when he released her mouth and trailed a line of kisses down the side of her neck. As thin as her sexy little red dress was, he was annoyed by the barrier, wanting nothing but her silky soft skin between them.

"Here?" she whispered, and it was then he realized he'd pressed her up against the living room wall.

He realized what he was doing and froze. What was wrong with him? His first time with Elana shouldn't be like this. She deserved better. Far better. Gasping for breath, he desperately tried to control his raging need.

"Hold on," he said gruffly, lifting her higher in his arms and carrying her down the hall to his bedroom.

"I could have walked," she murmured, her breath near his ear causing shivers of awareness.

"Maybe, but this way I don't have to let you go." He tried to smile but failed. He was more serious than he let on. Letting her go wasn't an option. The very idea brought a rush of panic.

One step at a time, he reminded himself. When he reached the edge of his king-sized bed, he let her go so she could stand on her own two feet. He kissed her again, gently this time, enjoying the softness of her mouth.

"Are you sure about this?" he asked, determined to give her one last chance to change her mind.

"Yes."

"And you'll tell me if I do something you don't like?" He couldn't bear the thought of hurting her.

"You won't." She sounded confident.

He wished he felt as much. With the moonlight streaming through his window, he could see a small smile tugging at the corner of her mouth. She lifted her hands and began opening the buttons on his dress shirt, one by one. Her fingers lightly brushed against his skin, making him crazy imagining the possibility of those hands touching him all over.

Going slow was no longer an option. He yanked off his shirt, without giving her time to finish with the buttons. Shucking off his pants, he stood there in a pair of navy boxers, his need evident. When he reached for her dress, she stepped back out of reach and slowly, oh, so slowly, drew the garment off, revealing her silky olive skin and a skimpy red bra and matching thong.

"Elana." He wished he'd turned on a light, so he could see every precious inch of her. He could barely tear his gaze away, frustrated with the inadequacy of mere words. Beautiful. Stunning. Sexy. None of the adjectives he could name came even close to describing her.

"Brock," she echoed, although her teasing smile reassured him. "Come to bed."

Lord knew he wasn't going to make her ask twice.

When Brock carried her into the bedroom, Elana was grateful he'd left the lights off. The room wasn't completely dark, but dark enough that she didn't need to worry about him seeing too much.

Deep down, she could admit she'd chosen the sexy red dress just for this reason. Brock had only seen her wearing scrubs or jeans. She'd wanted to look nice for him. Attractive. Sexy.

Considering her lack of experience, she was hoping the dress would give her the courage to seduce him.

The shadowy moonlight gave her the boldness to strip down to her underwear, and she reveled in his stark, hungry gaze. Seconds later they were naked.

She pushed aside the brief flash of vulnerability. She hadn't been with a man for a long time, but she wasn't nervous with Brock. Not any more. This was exactly where she wanted to be. The bed was soft beneath her, and the sheets smelled like him, musky and male.

He lavished kisses along her breasts, and she thought she was going to lose her mind. Her nipples peaked, begging for more. He lightly stroked them with his tongue, but then he trailed kisses down her abdomen to the inside of her thighs, and she knew she wasn't going to survive.

She whimpered when he parted her thighs and pressed his mouth there, where no man had ever kissed her before. She cried out, her hips bucking off the bed as her orgasm hit hard. Brock didn't stop, though he took his time, loving her, kissing her and rekindling her desire.

"Brock, please," she begged as she wrapped her legs around his waist.

"Shh, we have all night," he promised. But he did grab a condom, and after sheathing himself, he settled between her legs and probed her opening.

She was ready. More than ready. It seemed she'd waited her entire life for him.

"Now. Please." Her impatience made him chuckle, but when he finally granted her wish and slid deep, neither one of them was laughing.

Intense, sensational pleasure filled her body, her nerve endings tingling even as she strained against him, seeking more. And this time, when her orgasm took her sailing over the edge, Brock was right there with her.

She held his head to her breast when he collapsed against her, his harsh breathing audible over the roaring of her pulse. Shaken, she stared at the ceiling.

No man had ever loved her the way Brock just had. And she was very much afraid she'd never be satisfied with anything less than the intense closeness they'd just shared.

CHAPTER TWELVE

ELANA lost track of how many times Brock made love to her throughout the rest of the night. Each time surprisingly better, tender and yet more intense than the last.

He held her close, even while they were asleep. She'd always preferred to keep her own personal space around her, but, somehow, with Brock, she didn't mind so much. Even more amazing, she found she was able to fall asleep despite his heavy weight pressing against her.

When the morning light streamed in through Brock's bedroom window, she swallowed a groan and stretched her aching muscles. The bright light of day brought her old insecurities to the surface, so she quietly slid from his bed, trying not to disturb him.

Feeling acutely self-conscious, she picked up his shirt, thankful it covered her down to her knees. She made her way quietly to his bathroom.

Emerging a few minutes later, she searched for her dress, wishing she'd brought along some comfy, casual clothes to wear. Brock's cell phone rang loudly, startling her so badly she let out a high-pitched squeak.

"What are you doing?" Brock asked sleepily, ignoring his cell phone as he stared at her. "Sneaking out on me?"

"No, I was going to cook something for breakfast." She felt a little guilty because she had, for a split second, considered sneaking out on him. His cell phone continued to ring. "You'd better answer that," she said, gesturing to the phone while still holding the wrinkled red dress in front of her. "What if it's Lacey or, what's his name, Rufus?"

Brock muttered a curse under his breath and dug in his discarded pants for his phone. It had stopped ringing by the time he grabbed it. He stared at the screen. "I can't believe it. I missed Joel's call."

The sheet pooled at his waist as he punched Redial. She had trouble keeping her gaze off his chest as he waited for Joel to answer. "Joel? I'm so glad you called. I've been looking all over for you. Are you all right? Where are you?"

Elana held her breath, blatantly listening to Brock's side of the conversation with his missing brother.

"Yeah, I know things have been rough," Brock said, scrubbing a hand over his jaw as he talked. "Tucker needs you, Joel. You were right: his crying was an indication of something more. He's in the hospital, being treated for pneumonia." There was another pause as Joel said something.

"Yeah, don't worry. He's doing better, I swear. I wouldn't lie to you, Joel."

Elana edged closer, wishing she could hear what Joel was saying. "Is Lacey with him?" she whispered.

"Joel, listen, Tucker needs you. Hurry home, okay?

No, don't hang up! Dammit!" Brock stared at his phone in dismay. "I can't believe he just did that."

"What? Where is he? Is Lacey with him?"

"No, Lacey isn't with him. He told me he's tried to call her, but she didn't answer her phone. He said to tell her he loves her and that he'll be back soon." Brock's tone was laced with helplessness. "I didn't get a chance to tell him Lacey disappeared too."

"You could try calling him back."

"No. He's in Pelican Point. One of his buddies got him an interview with a home remodeling company that pays better than what he used to make at the gas station."

"Well, that's progress." Elana sank down onto the bed beside Brock.

"Yeah. Progress." He let out a heavy sigh. "I only wish he would have told me his plans before he took off. At the very least, he should have told Lacey."

"He wasn't thinking clearly, I'm sure. He was probably feeling trapped," Elana said, relieved that they'd at least heard from Joel. Now if only they knew where Lacey was, things would be back to normal.

"No kidding." Brock's tone was dry.

"He needed a break, and then when he realized he couldn't simply run away from his problems, decided to look for a better paying job," Elana rationalized.

"You're right." Brock grinned, obviously in a better mood now that he'd heard from his brother. "He promised to call me back in a few days once he finds out for sure about this home remodeling job. Says the owner is willing to make him some sort of apprentice."

An apprentice sounded promising.

"Do you think he and Lacey will move to Pelican Point?" She knew Brock would miss Tucker if that happened.

"I don't know. Maybe. I could help them find a place, get them settled so they're not starting out too financially in debt. Or they could commute for a while, until they save up for a house."

Brock to the rescue. Again. First her scholarship, then getting himself through medical school, and now supporting his brother and his nephew. She leaned forward and gave him a quick kiss. "I'm glad Joel called. See? You didn't need that private investigator after all. And I bet Lacey will be back soon too."

He pulled her close, returning her kiss with passion. "Now I remember where we were before my brother rudely interrupted us," he murmured between kisses.

She was tempted to give in and crawl back into bed with him. Yet she was worried about her scars. And she hadn't been lying earlier. She was really hungry. Must be all the calories they'd burned throughout the night.

"Where are you going?" he complained when she pulled away. He held on to her hand, refusing to let go.

She grinned. "I promised to make you breakfast, didn't I? I always keep my promises."

"Wearing only my shirt?" he asked with a frankly hopeful gaze.

She let out a wry chuckle. "Well, it's either your shirt or my dress, since that's all I have." Elana stood and turned away, draping her dress over the bottom of the bed. She'd wait to change until after she'd had a chance to eat. Maybe then she'd borrow Brock's shower.

"Hurry up," she added as she walked away, buttoning up his shirt. "Because I'm hungry enough to eat your portion too."

"You wouldn't be that cruel," he protested. After a few minutes, she heard the water running in the bathroom.

No, she wouldn't be that cruel. She smiled and hummed to herself as she gathered the ingredients to make French toast.

So this was how it felt to be happy.

Brock used the bathroom and then hurried out to share breakfast with Elana.

"Smells wonderful," he said, pleased that she'd made the effort to cook for him. Not that he thought it was a woman's job. Far from it. He'd taught himself to cook years ago. "Thanks, Elana."

"You're welcome," she said in a muffled voice. There was only half a piece of French toast left on her plate, and a surplus of syrup indicated she'd already eaten her share.

"You're amazing. I like a woman with a hearty appetite." He helped himself to several slices of French toast and took the seat across from her. The way she looked, wearing nothing but his white dress shirt, the dusky tips of her breasts visible through the cotton fabric, made him hungry for something other than food.

The night they'd shared had been amazing. He wanted nothing more than to spend the rest of the day with her.

"How many more would you like?" Elana asked, getting up from the table and going over to the electric frying pan.

"This is enough for me, thanks."

She frowned at him over her shoulder. "Something wrong with my cooking?"

"Of course not, you went above and beyond making breakfast." How could he explain he was too keyed up about having her in his home to eat? "I should have cooked for you."

"Next time," Elana murmured.

"Absolutely," he agreed, thrilled at the thought of there being a next time. He couldn't deny he was feeling very possessive where she was concerned.

"You've mentioned your dad a few times," Elana said as she returned to her seat across from him at the table. "But you haven't mentioned your mother."

His family. Of course Elana wanted to talk about his family. A chunk of French toast lodged in his throat, and he swallowed with an effort. "That's because she passed away my first year of medical school."

"I'm sorry, Brock." Elana's empathetic expression made him feel ashamed. After everything she'd been through, his family issues were nothing. "I'm guessing your father didn't handle it very well."

He lifted a shoulder in a careless shrug. "Dad was always the disciplinarian of the house. Believe it or not, I was the one who tended to follow the rules. Joel, on the other hand, rebelled."

"You were close," she guessed.

He nodded. "After Mom died, I think things between my dad and my brother got even worse. I felt bad I couldn't be there for Joel when he needed me."

"I can imagine." Elana stared down at her plate for a minute. "Give him a chance, Brock. He'll come around."

"I know." His brother had more of a chance of coming around than his father did. "Tucker's crying really bothered Joel. I'm sure he took off because he was afraid of turning out like our father."

Elana sucked in a harsh breath. "Are you saying—your father hit you?"

"Not really," he answered honestly. "But he did use his tongue as a weapon, saying hurtful things." He didn't go into detail, trying to shelter her as best he could. "I often wondered why my mother stayed and put up with him."

"Maybe she loved him," Elana said, her troubled gaze meeting his. "Maybe she loved you and your brother too much to leave."

His gut clenched, and he automatically shook his head. "I don't understand that kind of love."

"I do."

He snapped his head up to look at her in surprise.

Elana continued in a low voice. "I was a sullen, angry teenager, but Chloe still loved me. And I thank God every day for bringing her into my life."

He winced, realizing the extent of his blunder. "I'm sorry, Elana. You're right—"

"I'm going to take a shower," she interrupted. "Excuse me."

She stood and practically ran from the room, taking the mangled mess of his heart with her. For a moment all he could do was to curse at himself under his breath.

What was wrong with him? Why didn't he learn to think before he spoke?

Elana would surely leave now that he'd insulted her.

Suddenly, he couldn't bear the idea. He wasn't going to let her go. Not without a fight. Maybe he was an idiot, opening his mouth and blabbing about things he didn't know anything about, but he could learn.

He loved her. The realization hit him, hard.

He loved her!

Shaky, he splayed his hands on the table. Okay, he loved. That didn't mean Elana was ready to hear the truth about his feelings. They'd only just made love.

But he could show her, with actions rather than words.

He wolfed down the rest of his breakfast and then hovered for a moment outside the bathroom door. Images of a naked Elana in the shower tortured him, but, somehow, he knew this wasn't the time or the place to encroach on her personal space.

He told himself to leave her alone. To wait until she was finished, but then the shower turned off, and a few seconds later he heard a yelp and a loud thud.

"Elana?" He opened the door a crack. When he saw her lying on the floor, her face drawn in pain as she clutched her knee, he didn't hesitate but barged the rest of the way in. "What happened?"

"I was stupid. I reached for the towel, slipped on a wet spot in the floor, and jammed my knee." She leaned against the sink, clutching a towel to her chest. He didn't have the heart to tell her the small cloth didn't provide much cover.

"Let me see," he said, dropping to his knees to examine her. Her skin was silky soft, and he found it difficult to concentrate. He focused on the swollen spot on her knee. "We need some ice. This is going to bruise."

"I hope it doesn't get to the point I can't work."

He traced the swollen area carefully. "It feels super-ficial." This close to the front of her thighs, he noticed the scars. Numerous thin white lines, about an inch long, running in parallel lines up the surface of both legs.

Puzzled, he ran his finger up the length of her leg. Glancing up, he saw similar scars on her arms. Had she been in an accident too? "My God, Elana. What on earth happened to you?"

She froze, her muscles going stiff. At first he didn't understand the significance, but then she jerked away from him, nearly giving herself another vicious bruise as she leaped over him in her haste to reach the door.

"Elana?" The cold air was nothing like the icy fist of sheer panic that squeezed his heart. "What is it? What's wrong?"

Seeing the tortured expression in her eyes moments before she bolted from the bathroom, he suddenly under-stood. Mentally, he smacked himself for being so stupid.

She'd known about Lacey's cutting herself, in a des-perate need for control, because Elana had done the same thing.

Those thin, faint scars on her skin were evidence of her self-inflicted cuts.

How could she have forgotten her scars?

Limping, she ran into Brock's bedroom and swiped the towel over her body before tossing it aside. She grabbed her dress, her fingers shaking so bad she nearly dropped it.

With a determined yank, she pulled the wrinkled

fabric over her head, without bothering to track down her undergarments.

She had to get out of here. Now.

Where were her shoes?

Her stomach lurched, and she had to swallow hard to keep from throwing up the French toast she'd eaten. Her shoes were on opposite sides of the room, and after she found them both, she jammed her feet into the ridiculously high-heeled pumps, wincing as the stupid shoes made her knee hurt worse, and headed for the door.

Only to stop abruptly, completely horrified to see Brock standing there, blocking her means of escape.

"Elana, please wait." He stood there, his expression anguished. "Don't go."

She momentarily closed her eyes, wishing she could just disappear, that this nightmare would be over. But she knew clicking her ruby heels together wasn't going to work to get her home. Gathering every ounce of self-control, she opened her eyes and struggled to find her voice. "Move out of my way."

He didn't budge. "I caused this to happen to you?" he asked hoarsely, his gaze full of self-recrimination. His fingers were clenched into white-knuckled fists. "I did this?"

No matter how mortified she was that he'd discovered the truth, she couldn't let him take the blame. He hadn't shied away from her scars in horror.

He was taking responsibility for them.

But they weren't his fault. Not really. Chloe had made sure she'd known she wasn't the only kid in the world to be dealt a lousy hand. What a person did with the cards they'd been given was no one's fault but their own.

She knew that now.

She forced herself to meet his gaze. "No. I did this to myself."

CHAPTER THIRTEEN

"I'M SORRY," Brock murmured, venturing closer, his expression still tortured. "I'm so sorry."

If he kept apologizing like this, she was going to lose it. She angled her chin, desperately trying to hang on to her anger, to remain strong. "I already told you it's not your fault. Please, just let me go."

"I can't." Brock remained exactly where he stood, still blocking the doorway leading out of his bedroom. "Not like this."

What did he want from her? Blood? A touch of hysteria bubbled in her chest. "Why not? My ugly scars have nothing to do with you."

"They're not ugly, Elana. I hate knowing you suffered, but those scars are not ugly." His gaze narrowed in anger. "Who told you they were? Some idiot past lover?"

She resented how he seemed to read her so easily, and she lifted a shoulder in a careless shrug. "Doesn't matter. I know they're ugly. I see the evidence every day."

"Yet you hide them from the rest of the world," he said in a low voice. "Wearing long sleeves beneath your scrubs. Why didn't you say anything to me about them?" Brock took another step into the room, his imploring gaze eroding the edges of her resistance. "After expressing your concerns about Lacey, why didn't you tell me what happened to you?"

What happened to her? As if her scars were some sort of bizarre accident, rather than the intentional self-mutilation she knew them to be? "I'm not proud of what I did to myself, Brock. Do you have any idea how difficult it's been for me to pull my life back together?"

"I can only imagine, and knowing what you've accomplished only makes me respect you more." His tone was firm, and a tiny part of her longed to believe.

But respect? Hardly. He had no idea.

"I know you're a strong woman, Elana," he continued. "You've shown me your strength in a variety of ways, not least of which the way you volunteer your time to take care of others." His brows pulled together in a puzzled frown. "You're the strongest woman I've ever known, which is why I don't understand why you believe those scars are something to be ashamed of."

Obviously, he didn't get it. Didn't understand the burden she carried. And she was finished talking about this. "I'm going home, Brock. Move out of my way."

"Elana, please, don't do this. Don't throw away what we shared last night."

"We had sex last night," she said bluntly. Wonderful, glorious sex—at least that's how she thought of it until he'd noticed her scars and all her old insecurities had rushed back. "Because I wanted to."

A flicker of uncertainty flashed in his eyes, and she squashed a niggle of self-doubt for downplaying the closeness they'd shared. "It was more than sex for me," he said slowly. "We made love. All night long."

Her mouth went dry. He didn't mean that. Not really.

Brock's gaze grew fierce. "Did you hear what I said, Elana? What we shared was making love. I love you. Scars and all, I love you."

He loved her? No, she didn't believe it. He couldn't be serious. "You don't know what you're saying."

"Yes, I do. I love you." He took another step forward, and she immediately backed away. "Please don't leave. Stay. Talk to me."

How could he love her? He was only saying that because he didn't really understand. Didn't know the darkness that had haunted her for so long.

"We've been talking," she protested, suddenly weary. "Talking isn't going to change anything. You're only saying all this because you feel bad. Because you think you're somehow responsible for these scars. But you're not. What can I say to convince you?"

"You could stay. You could let me hold you." He reached out towards her.

Flinching from his touch, she shook her head. If he touched her, held her, she'd lose what little control she had left. "Look, this isn't personal. I just need a little time, some space."

"It's not personal? I tell you I love you, and you think this isn't personal?" For the first time, a note of anger tinted his tone. "Hell, I hate to tell you, but having you walk away from me feels pretty damn personal, Elana."

She'd hurt him, even though she hadn't meant to. She remembered what Chloe had asked: if she was worried she might be the one to hurt him. Yet she was the one with the scars. With the horrible past. None of this was making any sense.

She just wanted some time alone. To think. To try to figure things out.

His phone rang again, and she glanced at the device clipped to the waistband of his jeans. "Aren't you going to get that?"

Stubbornly he shook his head. "They'll call back, I'm sure."

"What if it's Lacey this time?"

He glanced down, uncertainty shadowing his gaze.

"She'll think you're mad at her if you ignore her."

He muttered a curse under his breath. "I'll talk to her later. Right now, I think it's best if I do take you home."

She'd almost forgotten she didn't have her car. She almost insisted on taking a taxi but didn't want to hurt Brock any more than she already had by refusing something as simple as a ride. She gave a jerky nod. "Fine."

When he disappeared into the living room, she quickly searched for her undergarments. Changing fast, she took off the dress, put on her bra and underwear, and then pulled her dress back on.

Being properly dressed made her feel better. She headed out to the living room, forcing herself to sit on the edge of the sofa to wait.

Brock emerged from the kitchen, his phone in his hand, his expression wary.

"What's wrong?" she asked, suddenly worried. She jumped to her feet. "Lacey? Has something happened to Lacey?"

"No, this was the pediatrician from Children's Memorial. Tucker is ready to be discharged."

"Oh." She relaxed a bit. "That's good news."

He grimaced. "It's good for Tucker, but I'm going to need help, Elana. How am I going to care for a baby on my own without Lacey? I've always avoided kids. I know it's a lot to ask, but will you help me?" Deep down, he knew he could have just hired a nanny, but what he really wanted was Elana.

Help him? She couldn't. He was asking too much of her.

So then why hadn't she told him no?

Elana rode with Brock to the hospital to pick up Tucker, telling herself that she'd help him get things settled with the baby at home before she left.

While he was driving, he tossed his phone at her. "Try Lacey again, would you?"

She opened his phone and found Lacey's number. Lacey's cell phone went straight to voice mail.

"No answer," she said, snapping his phone shut.

His mouth tightened, but he didn't say anything.

She wanted to reassure him that Lacey would be back, that she'd return his car and step up to take care of her son, but, at this point, words were useless. The longer Lacey stayed away, the worse things looked. She knew only too well how the inevitable darkness could warp a person's perceptions.

She hoped and prayed Lacey was okay.

Wordlessly, they took the elevators up to the sixth floor. Entering Tucker's room, they found the nurse in with him.

"I'm glad you're here," she said in relief, thrusting

the baby at Brock. "I wanted to get this little guy discharged before my next patient came in."

Brock held Tucker in his arms, only the tiniest hint of panic in his gaze. "He's finished with his IV antibiotics?" he asked, noting the absence of an IV.

"Yes, we switched him to oral meds this morning, and he seems to be doing fine. The doctor said you should continue the oral antibiotics for another week. Really, he shouldn't have any other problems; he's been an angel."

"Well, he doesn't seem to be crying much," Brock murmured.

Elana crossed over to pick up the diaper bag Lacey must have left and slung the strap over her shoulder.

Brock held Tucker as the nurse rattled on about the last time he'd eaten. She couldn't tear her gaze from Brock. The enthralled expression on his face, as he gently stroked a finger down Tucker's cheek, hit her low in the stomach, stealing her breath.

Brock couldn't have looked any more natural if Tucker were his own son. And in that moment, she caught a glimpse of the future. A tiny shred of hope.

The family she'd always dreamed about.

Gently, so as not to wake him, Brock lifted Tucker and set him in his infant car seat, bypassing his quilted jacket, since the day was warm and sunny. After buckling Tucker into the seat, he covered the car seat with a blanket, the way he'd watched Lacey do.

He cast a glance at Elana, knowing he'd pushed his luck by asking her to stay and help him.

It was the only thing he could think of that might

convince her to stay. She would stay for Lacey's sake. And maybe for Tucker's.

But not his. And certainly not for herself.

"Here's the prescription," the nurse said, shoving a slip of paper at him. "You can get this filled at any pharmacy. And all the rest of Tucker's discharge instructions are on this sheet here."

Clearly, the nurse was eager to be on her way. He couldn't totally blame her, since she did mention having a new admission.

"Thanks. I'm sure we'll be fine."

Elana shot a surprised glance at him but didn't say anything.

He lifted the infant carrier and gestured to the door. "Ready?" he asked. "We can stop at a drugstore on the way home."

He imagined she flinched when he said the word *home*. He had to swallow hard to stop himself from making a bigger fool of himself than he already had. He'd told Elana that he loved her.

Clearly she didn't believe him.

And he had no way of knowing what to say to convince her.

Elana didn't say much, other than offering to stay in the car with the baby while he ran into the local pharmacy to pick up Tucker's liquid antibiotics.

The minute he carried Tucker inside the house, though, the baby woke up and began to cry.

"Hey, what's wrong?" he said in alarm as he unbuckled the baby from his car seat. "You were doing so much better."

Elana watched from the doorway, as if she were just waiting for the right moment to leave. And suddenly he realized he shouldn't try to make her stay. Taking advantage of her innate kindness.

He'd only wanted another chance to talk to her. To make her understand what he was barely able to comprehend himself.

How much he loved her. And how together they really had a chance of making things work.

But if Tucker was going to keep crying, they weren't going to have any time alone. And his tiny nephew was his problem, not hers.

"Elana, you don't have to stay; we'll be fine."

"Are you sure?" The deep furrows in her brow indicated she wasn't convinced. When Tucker continued to wail, she pushed away from the door. "I'll make a bottle of formula for you to try. Maybe he's hungry."

She disappeared into the kitchen before he could protest. He walked around the living room in a feeble attempt to get Tucker to calm down. When she came back, she handed him a warmed bottle, so he awkwardly sat on the end of the sofa and tried to get Tucker to eat.

He wasn't interested. In seconds he was crying again.

"Here, let me try."

He handed over the baby, and Elana must have had some sort of magic touch, because Tucker settled down to suck on his bottle.

"How did you do that?" he muttered.

"I don't know. Maybe he could tell you weren't comfortable with him." She smiled down at Tucker, bending to gently kiss his head.

Lucky Tucker to be in Elana's arms. He wished more than anything he'd handled things differently that morning. But he hadn't. God help him, he'd never once thought she'd inflicted those cuts herself.

He took a deep breath and tried to concentrate on the matter at hand. Tucker. Soon he'd be alone with Tucker.

"He'd better get used to me," he said with a frown. "Because right now, I'm all he's got."

Elana glanced up at him, her expression troubled. "What if Lacey doesn't come back? Do you think Joel will still come back to take over?"

He couldn't hide the flash of panic in his eyes. "I don't know. Maybe."

Her gaze clouded with doubt. He couldn't blame her. The way Joel had taken off in the first place made him doubt his brother too.

"Maybe I was wrong, Brock," Elana said, smoothing a hand over Tucker's head. "I've been thinking we should call the police. What if something happened to Lacey, like a car accident or something worse?"

He stared at her for a minute. "Don't you think we would hear about it if she was in a car crash?"

"Not if no one's found her and she's too sick to make a phone call." Elana's brow puckered in a frown. "Call the police. Tell them how Lacey took off. Report your car stolen."

He was shocked at her sudden turn of heart. "Elana, don't you think that will make things worse for Lacey?"

Elana turned away, burying her face against Tucker. "I don't know," she said in a muffled yet agonized voice.

He understood what she was really afraid of. Elana

carried scars just like Lacey's. She knew better than anyone what was going on in Lacey's troubled mind. "You don't think she's coming back."

She lifted her head to look at him, her gaze full of desperate fear. "I'm not sure. And I'm afraid that if your brother knows she's gone, then he might not come back either. And then what will happen?"

Taking the bottle from Tucker's mouth, she sat him in her lap and rubbed his back until he burped. He looked away from his nephew's sweet, innocent face, his chest tightening.

"They'll be back." He wished he sounded more convincing.

"What if they don't come back?" she persisted. "What would happen to Tucker? Would you adopt him? Give him the loving home and family he needs?"

Brock swallowed hard, unable to respond. He knew he should tell her what she wanted to hear, but he couldn't. Just the thought of raising a child made him feel sick to his stomach.

He'd already stolen one young woman's life. And look what had happened to Elana. The scars weren't the worst of it, he knew. They were only a reminder of how she'd been through hell and back.

No, he couldn't do it.

And suddenly he realized that loving Elana wasn't enough. He didn't have anything to offer. Not if she had her heart and soul set on having a family.

Elana felt her heart squeeze painfully in her chest when she saw the stricken look in Brock's eyes. Not wanting children was one thing, but to give up Tucker? No, she couldn't believe it. "You'd give him up to strangers?" she asked in a hoarse whisper.

"It won't come to that," he said finally, sidestepping her question. He looked away, avoiding her gaze as he gestured to Lacey's room. "The portable crib is still set up in there if you'd like to put him down."

"Sure." Regretfully, she carried the baby to Lacey's room, leaving the light off and only using the illumination from the hallway to find the crib.

She carefully set him down on his back, covering his body with a blanket. He stirred a bit but didn't wake up. She stared at him for a long minute, thinking he was the most beautiful baby she'd ever seen.

How could Brock even think of giving him up? Inwardly reeling, she tried to comprehend what was going through his mind. What had he said earlier? He'd always avoided kids? Did he seriously plan to live the rest of his life without children?

Sure he did. Because all this time he had lived his life only for his patients. He'd never planned on having a future of his own.

He couldn't love her. He couldn't possibly love her if he thought she wouldn't one day want to have babies of her own.

She heard the muffled thud of a car door slamming shut.

Visitors? With a curious frown, she walked back out to the living room to find Brock opening up the front door.

"Lacey!" Brock exclaimed in relief. "I'm so glad you're back."

"Where is he?" Lacey barely spared Brock a

glance, searching the room frantically for her son. "Where's Tucker?"

"I just put him down in the crib," Elana said, trying to reassure Lacey. "He's fine, doing great, in fact. We just picked him up from the hospital today."

"I need to see him," Lacey said, quickly heading for the bedroom.

Elana glanced at Brock.

The relief in his eyes was starkly overwhelming.

Lacey was back and obviously planned to take over Tucker's care.

There was no reason for her to stay.

CHAPTER FOURTEEN

"TUCKER is really doing better?" Lacey asked, coming back into the room.

Elana forced a smile. "Actually, he is a lot better. Has hardly cried at all since the antibiotics have started working on curing the pneumonia."

"I'm glad." Lacey looked relieved.

"Where in the heck have you been?" Brock demanded.

"I went home to see my mother," Lacey admitted. "Obviously, you probably guessed I haven't been home in a long time. In almost two years, to be exact. I don't much care for my stepfather, but my mom seemed glad to see me."

"I'm proud of you for going, Lacey." Elana reached out to gently touch her arm. "I'm sure that must have been difficult."

Lacey shrugged, but Elana could tell the visit home hadn't been casual or easy. "She wants to meet Tucker and Joel sometime, and maybe I'll arrange for her to come visit without my stepfather." She glanced glumly around Brock's house. "I guess Joel hasn't been back yet, huh?"

"He called this morning, actually," Brock said with

a reassuring smile. "Wanted me to tell you he loves you and that he's hoping to land a new job as an apprentice for a home remodeling company."

"Really?" Lacey's eyes brightened. "He said he loved me?"

"I swear." He crossed his heart and cocked an eyebrow. "Maybe if you'd turned on your cell phone, he would have called you directly."

Lacey flushed. "I know. I'm sorry. I forgot my cell phone battery charger here. I guess I was just so desperate to get away." She looked uncomfortable, as if remembering their argument in the cafeteria.

"You're here now, Lacey, and that's all that matters," Elana pointed out.

"I missed Tucker so much," Lacey admitted, her eyes glimmering with a hint of tears. "More than I thought I would. When I went to the hospital and saw some strange baby in Tucker's room, I freaked out. It took a while for the nurse to calm me down enough to let me know you guys had brought him home."

As much as Elana wanted to leave, had in fact edged closer to the doorway, she couldn't just abandon Lacey. She put a comforting arm around the young mother's slim shoulders. "It's okay. Everything is going to be just fine."

Lacey hugged Elana back, but her gaze was still centered on Brock. "My mom gave me some money; it's not a lot but enough to hold me over until Joel comes home."

"Lacey, don't worry about the money. That's not what's important." Brock's gaze momentarily dropped to her forearms. "You are what matters. I'm willing to help in any way I can."

Lacey must have noticed his gaze because her chin came up a notch. "You were right; I have been cutting myself. It started a long time ago, for reasons that don't matter any more. But I'm getting better. I haven't cut myself in over a week. I'm trying to be a good mother to Tucker."

Elana was amazed Lacey blurted out the truth like that. "No one ever said you weren't a good mother, Lacey," Elana hastened to point out.

"Of course not. I was just worried about you," Brock added lamely. His alarmed gaze collided with Elana's, practically begging her for help and guidance in handling Lacey's revelation.

She swallowed hard, wondering what she was supposed to say. She was hardly an expert.

Yet suddenly she understood exactly what she needed to do.

"Lacey, I want to show you something." Elana stepped away, slowly pulling up the long sleeves of her dress, exposing her arms. "I know exactly what you're going through. Because I used to cut myself too."

"You did?" Lacey's eyes widened with undisguised amazement. She reached out to tentatively stroke the telltale raised ridges of Elana's scars. "Just like me?"

She nodded. The scars weren't exactly badges of honor, but in a way they were a sign of hope. Of healing. "Just like you. For reasons that don't matter any more to me, either. But you can beat it, Lacey. I learned to stop, and I have all the confidence in the world you can too."

"I hope so," Lacey said in an awed and somewhat hesitant tone. "I really hope so."

"I'll help you," Elana offered. "Anything you need, ask me. In fact, if you start feeling desperate, like you need to cut yourself, call me. I'll come whenever I can, and we'll talk it through."

"Is that how you stopped?" Lacey asked.

Her throat swelled with emotion as she remembered Chloe's loving support. Because as strange as it might sound, using the sharp edge of a razor, and making tiny slices in your skin despite the pain, was as addictive as any narcotic. The cycle had been extremely difficult to break. "Yes. I had help too, from Chloe. She was my foster mother. She took me in after I ran away from several other foster homes."

"I don't think my mother would understand at all, but I'm glad to know you went through this too." Lacey's smile warmed her heart. "It's a deal. I'll call you if I need help kicking the habit."

Elana couldn't help wondering about Lacey's mother. If Lacey had been her daughter, she would have moved heaven and earth to bring her daughter and grandson home. But at least Lacey wasn't alone any more.

She'd be there for Lacey, no matter what happened between her and Brock.

Lacey turned to Brock, who was watching them intently. "I hope you're not too upset with me for leaving."

"No, of course not," he said gruffly. "We were worried something bad had happened to you, that's all."

Lacey slowly nodded. "I know. And for that I'm sorry."

"Are you hungry?" Brock asked, changing the subject. His gaze included Elana. "How about I order out for some pizza?"

This was her cue to leave. "None for me, thanks. I really need to get going."

"Won't you stay?" His gaze clung to hers.

"No, thanks. I have some things I really need to do." She cared about Brock. Cared about Lacey and Tucker too. But she didn't believe in Brock's love. She wasn't even sure he knew how to love.

Lacey was here, and Tucker would be fine.

It was well past time to go home.

Elana tried to ignore the shrill ringing of her phone, the third call within five minutes. Brock's number lit up the face of her phone. Again. Part of her knew she was being childish in refusing to answer, but, truthfully, she wasn't sure what to say.

She'd spent a restless night, tossing and turning, so she wasn't in the best frame of mind. She'd ignored his calls all morning. Was dreading going in to work and seeing him. Working with him as if they were nothing but colleagues.

While her heart ached with wanting the impossible.

When Lacey's number lit up her screen almost an hour later, she didn't consider ignoring the call. Considering how she'd promised to be there for Lacey, she quickly pressed the button to answer. "Hi, Lacey, what's up?"

"Why aren't you answering Brock's phone calls?" she asked in exasperation. "He's driving me crazy, constantly asking me to call you."

Elana sighed. She should have figured Brock would know her well enough to know she wouldn't ignore Lacey's call. "Brock has no right to drag you into our mess."

"I know you didn't ask for my opinion, but I think he's freaking out over your scars," Lacey confided in a low tone. "The look on his face yesterday when you pulled up your sleeves…" Her voice trailed off.

Elana glanced down at her bare arms. It felt weird not to have long sleeves on. She was trying to work up the courage to go to work wearing only her short-sleeved scrubs, but she wasn't sure she could do it. "No, that's not it. Brock has already seen my scars." Her laugh held a trace of bitterness. "Every single one of them."

"All of them?" Lacey echoed. Then her tone changed as she put the obvious two and two together. "Oh, I see. Well, then, what's the problem with you two?"

"It's a long story," Elana said evasively. "And I'd rather not get into it, if you don't mind."

There was a brief pause, and Elana knew she'd hurt Lacey's feelings when she said, "Sure. Whatever."

She closed her eyes, burning with shame. Lacey was trying to be a friend; she deserved better than that. "Lacey, I'm sorry. If you want to know what's going on, here it is. Brock claims he loves me, but I don't believe him."

"Do you think he can't love you because of your scars?" Lacey asked.

How could she explain something she didn't fully understand herself? "No, he says he loves me scars and all."

"But you don't believe him?" Lacey persisted.

"No. I have reason to believe he doesn't really know how to love someone." She didn't want to mention to

Lacey how she'd asked him about adopting Tucker. She didn't think Lacey would take too kindly to Brock's hesitation.

"Hmm. Well, maybe he has some scars too," Lacey said. "Scars you can't see."

What? The truth hit her like a cement block falling on her head. Of course Brock had scars. Deeply hidden scars. Scars that weren't visible to the naked eye.

Lacey was right. She wasn't being fair to him. "Lacey, you're a genius."

"I am?" Disbelief laced her tone.

"Yes. Ah, look, tell Brock I'll talk to him later." If she was going to talk to Brock, she'd rather talk to him in person, not on the phone.

"All right. At least that should make him happy. Take care, Elana." Lacey disconnected from the line.

Elana let the phone slip from her fingers as she stared blindly out the window.

She'd expected Brock to love her in spite of her scars, the undeniable evidence of her troubled past, but she hadn't been willing to do the same for him.

Because she did love him. Had loved him from the moment he'd tried to take responsibility for her scars, rather than seeing them as ugly marks of failure.

But she'd done the exact opposite, by making her love for him conditional on having babies.

Brock tossed aside the cell phone he'd been using to call Elana. It was no use. He'd left half a dozen messages, but she wasn't calling him back.

He was going to have to see her in person. The

moment she'd walked out of his life, he'd realized the depth of his mistake.

He needed to fix things in a hurry.

His front door opened before he'd reached for the handle. "Joel?"

"Hi, Brock. Are Lacey and Tucker here?"

"Yes, I think Lacey's feeding the baby in the spare bedroom." He gave his brother a slap on the back. "Glad you're home, but I have to go and see Elana."

"Elana? Who's Elana?" Joel asked, exasperated. "Don't you want to hear about my job?"

"You got it?" Joel flashed a wide grin. "Hey, good for you. I'm proud of you, Joel. Look, I promise we'll talk more later."

"Wait a minute," Joel said as Brock continued out the door. "Who's Elana?"

"Ask Lacey," he tossed over his shoulder just before he let the door slam shut behind him.

He headed straight for Elana's apartment building, mentally rehearsing what he wanted to say. When he got to the door, Elana came barreling out, practically running into him, much like the day she'd come running out of her mother's nursing home. Only this time she wasn't crying.

He wasn't sure if that was good or bad. Had she really already made up her mind about him? Deciding he wasn't worth her time and effort?

"Brock!" Elana clasped a hand over her heart. "You scared me."

"I'm sorry," Brock apologized quickly. "I'm glad I caught you, though. Do you have a minute to talk?"

She surprised him by nodding. "Sure. As a matter of fact, I was just going to drive over to see you."

She was? Good. That was really good. Wasn't it? Maybe not. "Do you want to go inside or take a walk?"

After a moment's hesitation, she gestured to the apartment building. "We can go inside."

He followed her back up the stairs and into her apartment. Nervously, he sat on her sofa. Her living room was all warm colors and earth tones.

"You're wearing short sleeves," he said, noticing her attire.

She flushed as she glanced down at her bare arms. "Yes, I'm sort of practicing. I'm not sure if I'm brave enough to go to work this way, but I thought I'd give it a try."

Her admission humbled him. "Elana, I think you're the bravest woman I've ever met."

"Me?" Her eyes widened, and she instantly shook her head. "No, I'm not brave. In fact, that's why I told Lacey I'd talk to you. I wanted a chance to explain."

"Lacey?" Brock looked confused. "You spoke to Lacey?"

"Yes. She told me you asked her to call me."

"Yeah, but she refused." Brock let out a low chuckle. "She must have called you anyway. I guess I owe her a debt of gratitude if something she said made you change your mind about talking to me."

Elana sat down beside him, her gaze serious. "She did. I need to tell you that I'm sorry. I shouldn't have gotten so upset when you didn't seem thrilled to adopt Tucker."

"Please, Elana, let me explain." Brock reached over

to take her hand. "You were right that day. I've made dedicating my life to saving patients more important than having a life of my own. To be honest, in some warped way, I didn't think I deserved to raise a child. Didn't have the courage to open myself up to losing someone like that. But being with you, loving you, has made me realize I was wrong."

"How? I'm not courageous," Elana protested.

"You are." Brock tried to make her understand. "After everything you've been through, you opened yourself up to love. With Chloe. With Raine. With Lacey and Tucker." He took a deep breath and let it out slowly. "And I hope with me. Give me a chance, Elana. I love you so much, with my entire heart and soul. Give me a chance to prove how much."

His eyes widened in alarm when her eyes filled with tears. "Brock, I'm the one who should be apologizing to you."

"Why?" He tightened his grip on her hand. Was she trying to tell him she didn't return his feelings?

"You helped me realize that I've been wrong. You asked me to forgive you, and I did. But when you saw my scars, I freaked. Because I hadn't forgiven myself."

"You were young. For heaven's sake, Elana, you had a right to be upset."

"No, you don't understand. I needed to forgive myself for being alive when Felicity wasn't. For loving Chloe while my mother sat day after day in a nursing home. For wishing I could have the family I've always dreamed of."

She paused and then added, "For loving you."

Was she saying what he thought she was saying? "You love me?"

She laughed and threw herself into his arms. He caught her and held her close. "Yes, Brock. I love you. And if you don't want to have a family right away, that's fine with me. Because I love you, and I want you to be happy."

"Elana." He pulled back enough to look into her eyes. "I love you, and I have realized I do want to have a family with you, more than anything else. Will you marry me?"

She smiled, and this time he thought he might be safe in assuming her tears were full of joy. "Yes. I'd be honored to marry you. I love you so much, Brock."

Thank God. He kissed her, knowing that together they could do anything. He held her so tight he didn't ever want to let her go.

"Now my life is complete," he murmured.

EPILOGUE

ELANA stood next to Brock and Joel, the younger brother holding on to a squirmy one-year-old Tucker as Lacey walked across the stage of the technical college auditorium to accept her high school equivalency diploma.

Elana clapped so loudly her hands ached as Brock whistled through his teeth.

"Did you hear Lacey was accepted into college, starting in the fall semester?" Joel said as he helped Tucker wave at his mother as Lacey completed her march across the stage. "She wants to be a teacher."

"I think Lacey will make a great teacher," Elana defended stoutly.

"Me too," Brock added. He glanced down at her, and they exchanged a secret smile. "I heard she got a great scholarship."

"Yeah, she did," Joel said proudly. "All of her tuition is going to be covered, which means we only have to swing the day-care costs. Now that I'm almost finished with my apprenticeship, and will be a full-fledged carpenter, that shouldn't be a problem."

Elana nudged Brock, warning him to keep quiet. She

wanted the scholarship to be a surprise. She didn't want Lacey to know where the money came from, at least not until after she was finished with her degree.

Brock lifted her hand and brushed a kiss across her wedding ring. "Your secret is safe with me," he said in a low tone.

"Oh, really?" Elana said, raising a brow. "And what secret is that?"

Brock simply smiled, putting his arm around her and holding her close. Their wedding had been a small affair, held a few months ago, with only their closest friends and family in attendance. She'd been so thrilled her mother had progressed enough to attend. She'd almost wept when her mother had come to wish them well after the ceremony.

She wasn't sure it was fair for one person to be so happy.

As the graduation ceremony drew to a close, they made their way back out of the auditorium to wait for Lacey.

"You don't know all my secrets," Elana said to Brock when Joel and Tucker rushed over to greet Lacey.

"Sure I do."

She slowly shook her head. "I have one big secret." When he rolled his eyes in disbelief, she added, "I'm pregnant."

For a moment he stared at her in shock. "Pregnant? You're pregnant?"

"Do you mind?" Not that she could do much about it now. They'd slipped a few times with using protection, but Brock hadn't seemed too worried. But maybe he wasn't ready for this.

"No! Of course I don't mind. You're having a baby. Our baby!" He swung her up into a bear hug, sweeping her off her feet.

"Shh, this is Lacey's day." She should have waited until later to tell him the news. But his teasing about secrets had made her blurt out the truth.

Now they didn't have any secrets between them.

"Elana, I can't believe it. We're going to have a baby."

"I'm glad you're happy about it; for a minute you had me worried. I love you, Brock." Elana threw her arms around his neck and kissed him. "I'm the luckiest woman in the world."

"I'm the lucky one," he murmured. "Because you've given me my life. A family." He glanced at Joel and Lacey, who were heading towards them, holding Tucker's hands as he walked clumsily on his own two feet between them. "Let's go home."

EMERGENCY DOCTOR AND CINDERELLA

BY
MELANIE MILBURNE

I dedicate this book to Joe Tucci and Dani Colvin, who first approached me
to be an ambassador for the Australian Childhood Foundation—
a position I accepted with great enthusiasm.

First published in Great Britain 2010
Harlequin Mills & Boon Limited,
Eton House, 18-24 Paradise Road, Richmond, Surrey TW9 1SR

© Melanie Milburne 2010

ISBN: 978 0 263 87877 6

Harlequin Mills & Boon policy is to use papers that are natural,
renewable and recyclable products and made from wood grown in
sustainable forests. The logging and manufacturing process conform
to the legal environmental regulations of the country of origin.

Printed and bound in Spain
by Litografia Rosés, S.A., Barcelona

Melanie Milburne says: 'One of the greatest joys of being a writer is the process of falling in love with the characters and then watching as they fall in love with each other. I am an absolutely hopeless romantic. I fell in love with my husband on our second date, and we even had a secret engagement, so you see it must have been destined for me to be a Harlequin® Mills & Boon author! The other great joy of being a romance writer is hearing from readers. You can hear all about the other things I do when I'm not writing and even drop me a line at: www.melaniemilburne.com.au'

Dear Reader

One of the most rewarding aspects of being a globally published author is the opportunity it gives me to raise awareness of certain issues that are very dear to me. By purchasing this book you are actively helping me help The Australian Childhood Foundation in their quest to stamp out child abuse and neglect in Australia. I will be donating all my proceeds from this book to the Foundation, and hope that in doing so many children's lives will be changed for the better.

It has been said that every childhood lasts a lifetime. The memories some children carry from their childhood are not ones any child should be burdened with. Please join me in helping this great cause as it works to educate and advocate for children who have no one else to fight for them.

With best wishes

Melanie Milburne

CHAPTER ONE

IT WAS the third day in a row that someone had parked in Erin's spot. Not only had they parked there arrogantly, they had done so crookedly, taking up so much space she had to manoeuvre her car into the space near the garbage-disposal unit, which she knew would almost certainly result in a scratch or two on her shiny paintwork.

She rummaged in her handbag for a piece of paper and a pen, and then, glancing around for a flat surface, whooshed out a breath and leaned on the rogue-parker's bonnet to pen her missive: *you are in the wrong spot!*

Erin tucked the note behind one of the windscreen wipers and made her way to the elevator. She tapped her right foot impatiently as she watched the numbers light up as it came down from the fifteenth floor. After a ten-hour shift in the emergency department of Sydney Metropolitan, the only thing she wanted was the quiet, safe sanctuary of her apartment. Her ears were still ringing from the shattered cries of a middle-aged mother who had lost her only son to a fatal stab-wound—yet another drug deal gone wrong.

The doors of the elevator glided open and she came

face to face with a tall man who was wearing blue denim jeans and a white T-shirt that had a dust smear over the right shoulder. He was carrying an empty cardboard box and he smiled at her crookedly as he stepped out. 'Moving in,' he explained with a flash of perfect white teeth.

Erin lifted her chin and gave him a gimlet glare. 'Is that your car in my parking space?'

Something hardened in his green gaze and his smile flatlined. 'I was not aware there were designated parking spaces.'

Her chin went a little higher. 'The numbers are painted on the ground. A blind man could see them.'

One of his dark brows lifted along with his top lip, as if controlled by the same muscle. 'You must be the woman from 1503,' he said, rocking back on his heels slightly. 'I was warned about you.'

Erin felt her hackles rise like the fur of a cornered cat. 'I beg your pardon?'

His eyes moved over her rigid form with indolent ease. 'Erin Taylor, right?'

She tightened her mouth. 'That's correct.'

He smiled a smile that was borderline mocking. 'My landlord told me all about you.'

'Oh, really?' She affected a bored, uninterested tone.

'Yes,' he said, placing the box on the concrete floor. 'You're a doctor at Sydney Metropolitan.'

Erin mentally rolled her eyes. *Here comes another free car-park consultation*, she thought. No doubt he thought he could weasel a flu shot out of her, like one of her neighbours had tried to do as soon as autumn had kicked in last month. 'Yes, that's right,' she said crisply. 'And right now I am off duty, so if you'll excuse me?'

'I'm renting the apartment next to yours,' he said.

'How…er…nice,' Erin said with no attempt to sound sincere.

The man's lazy smile travelled all the way up to his green eyes, making them crinkle up at the corners. 'I guess in the interests of neighbourly peace I should move my car.'

'You should,' she said, stabbing at the call button to reopen the doors. 'But don't use the disabled spot. Mrs Greenaway on level ten uses that.'

'I'll try and remember that.'

Something about his tone made Erin feel as if he was laughing at her behind his urbane smile. She gave the call button an even harder jab, trying not to notice how his T-shirt clung to his lean but muscular frame. She had seen a lot of male bodies over the years so it took a particularly good one to make her do a double-take. This one was seriously fit. No spare flesh, just hard, toned muscle on a six-foot-three, maybe six-foot-four-inch frame. His hair was a rich, dark brown, several shades darker than hers, and his skin was the sort that tanned easily. His twelve-plus-hours-since-he'd-last-shaved stubbled jaw had a hint of stubbornness to it, and his blade of a nose, teamed with those penetrating green eyes, gave him a 'take no prisoners' air that she found strangely compelling.

The elevator doors pinged open, and Erin stepped in and pressed the button for the fifteenth floor. For the sake of common politeness, she forced her lips into a non-committal smile that didn't quite make the distance to her eyes. 'See you around,' she said.

'Yeah, no doubt you will.' He smiled an inscrutable little smile in return.

The elevator doors closed and Erin let out the breath she hadn't even realised she had been holding. She gave herself a mental shake. The tall, dark, handsome neighbour was certainly a welcome change from the previous tenants: a trio of university students who'd partied non-stop and who, to add insult to injury, had put their rubbish in Erin's bin when theirs had been full. It had taken the last two weeks to get the smell of cigarette smoke out of her curtains, since the apartments were linked by a common balcony with only a waist-height glass partition to separate them.

As long as the new tenant stayed out of her way and out of her parking space, Erin was sure they would get along just fine.

'Morning, Erin.' Tammy McNeil, the triage nurse on duty in A&E, greeted Erin the next morning. 'How come you didn't come to the new director's breakfast meeting? He insisted all the A&E doctors on duty today attend. He wants to meet everyone in person, even the cleaning staff.'

Erin placed her bag in the locker under the desk before she straightened to answer. 'I had better things to do—like catch up on some much-needed sleep. I'm sure we'll cross paths sooner or later.'

Tammy perched on the corner of the desk. 'You don't look like you had such a great night's sleep. I know yesterday's death was rough on you. The mum was a bit over-the-top trying to blame you for not saving her son. Are you OK? You look exhausted.'

Erin hated it when people told her she looked tired; it made her feel tired even when she wasn't—although last night had been a rough one, she had to admit, even without the drama of the young man's death. Right until the early hours, she had heard furniture and boxes being dragged across the floors next door, and even though she had put a pillow over her head it hadn't really helped, for when she had finally drifted off to sleep she had woken several times in an agitated state from some vivid nightmares. It always happened after she had to deal with drug-affected patients. The ghosts from the past haunted her when she was most vulnerable. 'I'm fine, Tammy,' she said, reaching for her stethoscope. 'I'm used to patients and their relatives using me as a scapegoat. It's part of the job. It's not as if I have to ever see them again. That's one of the benefits of working as an A&E doctor: I treat them as best I can and then I leave them to someone else to follow up.'

Tammy gave her a wry look as she hopped down off the desk. 'Mmm, well, you might have to have a rethink about that after you hear about Dr Chapman's plan for the department.'

Erin shrugged herself into her white coat, pulling her hair out from beneath the collar and tying it back in a neat bun with an elastic tie she had in her coat pocket. 'I don't care what Dr Chapman has planned for the department. He can't make me work any harder than I do.' She picked up her name-badge and clipped it to her coat. 'If he's anything like our previous director, he'll realise we're all doing the best we can and leave us to get on with it.'

Tammy winced. 'Er…'

Erin frowned at her. 'What's the matter?'

A deep, clipped voice spoke from behind Erin. 'Dr Taylor—a word, please. In my office. Now.'

Erin turned, her eyes widening when she saw the man from the elevator standing there. 'I'm about to start my shift,' she said. 'There are five bays already occupied, waiting for assessment.'

His green eyes were like steel darts pinning hers. 'There are two other doctors and a registrar on duty. I am sure they are well able to cope without you for five or ten minutes.'

Erin pulled her mouth into a resentful line as she followed him out of the department to the office he had been allocated next to X-ray. He held open the door for her and she swept past him, bristling with irritation.

He closed the door and strode over to his desk, which was in a state of moving-in disarray. 'Please take a seat,' he said. 'I won't keep you long.'

Erin hesitated for a brief moment. If she sat down it would give him an advantage she didn't want him to have. He was so tall, standing there looking down at her, making her feel about fifteen years old when she was nearly twice that age. His hard gaze tussled with hers, and she sat like a heavy bag of theatre laundry being dropped. She folded her arms across her chest and swung one leg across the other, in a 'let's get this over with' pose that she knew reeked of insolence, but she was beyond caring.

'Perhaps I should introduce myself properly since I neglected to do so last night,' he said.

'Why didn't you?' she asked with a curl of her top lip. 'You clearly knew who I was given you were "warned" about me.'

Eamon decided against taking the chair behind his desk. Instead he leaned back against the filing cabinet and surveyed Erin Taylor's pursed lips and flashing, chocolate-brown eyes. She was sitting in a combative pose, every feminine inch of her poised to strike. He decided she would be quite astonishingly beautiful if she would smile instead of scowl. She had clear skin with just a dusting of light brown freckles over her uptilted nose. Her chestnut hair was glossy, and even though she had arranged it into a tight chignon at the back of her head a few escaping wisps framed her heart-shaped face. Her mouth was full, although it was currently pulled tight, and her cheekbones were classic, like a model's, sharp and high with a hint of haughtiness about them. Her body was slight but unmistakably feminine; her breasts were pushed up by her tightly crossed arms, giving him a clear view of her cleavage, which he was almost certain was unintentional.

He felt a stirring in his groin which took him completely by surprise. Admittedly it had been a while since he had held a woman in his arms, but somehow he couldn't see Erin Taylor falling into his bed any time soon—although in his head he rubbed at his jaw; there was nothing he liked more than a tough challenge.

'As you already know, I am Dr Eamon Chapman, the new A&E director,' he said. 'You would have received the email about my appointment.'

She didn't answer; she just sat there staring at him with that recalcitrant look on her face.

'You would have also received the invitation to a breakfast meeting this morning which apparently you decided against attending,' he continued.

She sat up even straighter in her chair. 'It wasn't compulsory.'

Eamon pushed his tongue into his right cheek as he fought to keep cool. Something about her reminded him of a defiant schoolgirl with little or no respect for authority. 'No,' he said. 'But it would have been polite to inform me you were unable to attend. As you can imagine, this position is a busy and highly demanding one. I would appreciate every member of the team I am directing to be one-hundred-percent committed from day one of my appointment. That includes you, Dr Taylor.'

Erin raised her chin. 'I worked a ten-hour shift yesterday and a twelve-hour the day before,' she said stiffly. 'I give one hundred and twenty percent to this place.'

'All the more reason for you to be aware of my plans to improve the department,' he said with equal tension.

Erin felt like rolling her eyes. How many times had some bureaucrat come in with a hot-shot plan to revamp the place? It didn't matter what fancy plans Dr Chapman had drawn up; within a few months it would be back to double shifts, patients lying in the corridors and ambulances lined up in the street due to the lack of beds. 'OK, then,' she said, giving him a cynical look. 'Why don't you fill me in now so I'm all up to date?'

He pushed himself away from the filing cabinet and picked up a document from his desk. 'It's all in here,' he said, handing it to her. 'Perhaps you'll do me the honour of reading it at your leisure and getting back to me with any questions or suggestions.'

Erin took the document but in the process of doing so encountered his long, tanned fingers for a fraction of a second. It felt like a lightning bolt had zapped up her arm at the brief contact. She tried her best to cover her reaction by casually flipping through the twenty-page document, but the words, although neatly typed, made no sense at all to her. It was as if her brain had shut down. Her body felt hot and tight, as if her skin had shrunk two sizes on her frame. She could feel her face heating under his silent scrutiny, and she shifted uncomfortably in her chair. The air she breathed in contained a hint of his aftershave; it was lemony and fresh, not cloying or overpowering like some she had smelt.

She heard him shuffle through some papers on his desk and looked up to encounter his emerald gaze trained on her. 'There is another matter I wish to discuss with you,' he said. 'I understand a patient died in A&E yesterday.'

Erin hardly realised she had moved but she suddenly found herself sitting on the edge of her chair. 'Yes, that's correct,' she said. 'He'd virtually bled out by the time he arrived here—he was in grade-four shock and went into asystole. I did his resus by the book.'

'I'm sure you did, Dr Taylor,' he said. 'But a formal complaint has been made by a relative, and as director I am responsible for seeing that it is investigated thoroughly.'

Erin felt her spine give a nervous wobble that travelled all the way down her legs. 'That resus was textbook EMST, Dr Chapman. I've documented the whole episode, and you can watch it on the CCTV as well,' she said, forcing her voice to remain composed and confident.

'The mother of the young man who died...' He glanced at the paper before pinning Erin with his gaze once more. 'The resus might have been technically correct, when it occurred, but what about its timing? Mrs Haddad maintains that you did not respond quickly enough to her son's injuries. She said that they were waiting in A&E for more than an hour before he was properly assessed.'

Erin drew in a scalding breath. 'That is not true! The triage nurse informed me of his injuries and I went straight to him from an asthmatic I was treating. The boy had multiple abdominal stab-wounds and was in hypovolemic shock. I was told that and went straight to the resus bay. I would have seen him within a couple of minutes at most after he arrived. If he was waiting around for treatment, it certainly wasn't here. Maybe they were hanging about in the waiting room, or outside the department. All I know is that as soon as I was told of his arrival I finished injecting prednisolone to a severe asthmatic, made sure she was inhaling the ventolin nebuliser and supervised by a nurse, and went straight to the resus bay. Three minutes at most.'

Eamon Chapman didn't speak but continued to look at her with that piercing green gaze of his.

'You know what some relatives can be like,' Erin argued. 'They don't believe their loved one was involved in something shady. "He's a good boy" and all that. "Someone else did this to him". "The doctors didn't save him". Blame anyone and everyone except the person responsible.'

Eamon put the paper back down on his desk. 'I realise emotions run high in cases like this for everyone involved. Mrs Haddad may well withdraw the complaint after legal counsel. But even so there are still some issues that need to be dealt with in A&E. You will become aware of them once you read my proposal for change.'

Erin rose from the chair, holding the folder against her chest like armour. 'I'll read it and get back to you,' she said.

'You do that,' he said with a half-smile that didn't meet his eyes.

She turned on her heel and was almost out the door when his deep baritone voice stopped her in her tracks. 'By the way, I checked the numbers in the parking area. Unless they are written in Braille, I am very much afraid a blind man could not see them.'

Erin turned back to face him. There was a hint of mockery in his sea-green gaze that made her scalp prickle in annoyance. 'I'll speak to the maintenance guy about having them repainted,' she said with the arch of an eyebrow. 'Or would you like him to paint arrows, or a big, fat, fluorescent "X" so you know exactly where to park?'

A tiny muscle moved next to his mouth. Erin wasn't sure if he was fighting anger or a smile; either way, it made him look even more attractive than he had last night. She felt the tiny flutter of her pulse, and a tingling of her flesh that made her breath catch as his eyes held hers.

'Just my number would be fine, thanks, Dr Taylor,' he said, and reached for his ringing mobile that was clipped on his belt. 'Excuse me. I have to get this.'

Erin spun away and closed the door with a sharp click behind her. She strode back to A&E; for the first time in her career she was immensely glad to see an overflowing waiting room.

It wasn't until Erin was back at her flat with her cat, Molly, on her lap that she picked up the document Eamon Chapman had given her that morning. She absently stroked Molly's thick fur as she read through the proposal, trying to ignore the sound of the sliding doors opening on the balcony next door. She had heard him come home about an hour after her. It gave her a slightly unsettled feeling to think of him on the other side of the wall. To her annoyance she found her thoughts drifting to what his routine might be: would he shower and change before dinner, or would he watch the news on television, perhaps have a beer or a glass of wine if he wasn't on call? Would he cook his own dinner or eat out? Did he have a partner? Was there a Mrs Chapman who would lie next to him in bed at night and be folded into his arms…?

Erin pulled away from her wayward thoughts and focused back on the words printed in front of her. So far there had been some sensible suggestions on streamlining triage and reducing the number of minor cases that should have been handled in general practice. The next section was on follow-through care. Her eyes narrowed as she read the plan for A&E doctors to conduct their own ward-rounds on the patients that had come into the hospital via the emergency department. As she read each word, she could feel a tide of panic rising inside her. She wasn't trained to sit by patients' bedsides and discuss the weather or their personal lives; she was trained to respond to emergencies, to stabilise patients before sending them on to definitive care. She would never be able to cope with all the names and faces, not to mention the added burden of thinking about patients and their lives outside of A&E. She put them out of her mind once they left the department. She had to, otherwise she would end up too involved, unable to remain at a clinical distance.

Erin tossed the document to one side and got to her feet, dislodging Molly, who gave an affronted miaow before turning her back to lick each of her paws with meticulous care.

The doors of the balcony beckoned and Erin slid them open to look out over the view of Sydney Harbour and the city on the opposite shore. Yachts were out, some with their colourful spinnakers up, looking like one-winged butterflies. Smaller craft bobbed about on the light swell and passenger ferries crisscrossed their way through the water, carrying people home from work or into the city for entertainment or dinner.

She gripped the balcony rail with an iron grip and lifted her face to the breeze, breathing in the salty air, wishing she could be on one of those yachts and sail away into the sunset.

'You wouldn't happen to have a cup of sugar, would you?' Eamon Chapman's voice sounded from her right.

Erin swivelled her head to look at him, her heart giving a little free fall. He was bare-chested, his legs encased in dark blue denim slung low on his lean hips. Every muscle on his chest and abdomen looked like it had been carved into place by a master craftsman. She had studied anatomy, yet not one of her textbooks would have done Dr Eamon Chapman justice. 'Um…sugar?'

His mouth tilted wryly. 'Yeah, that sweet stuff you put in coffee. I forgot to get some when I shopped on the way home.'

Erin brushed a strand of hair that the breeze had worked loose from her chignon away from her face. 'The shops are only a short walk away,' she pointed out.

'So you don't have any?' he asked, leaning on the dividing rail with his strong forearms. 'Sugar, I mean?'

Erin tried not to look at the way his biceps bulged as he leaned his weight on the railing. He was more or less at eye level, which was disconcerting to say the least. This close she could see tiny brown flecks in his green eyes that fanned out from his dark-as-ink pupils. 'I…I don't take sugar,' she said.

His mouth tilted even further. 'Sweet enough, huh?'

This time Erin was sure he was mocking her. 'I have five fillings,' she said primly. 'I am not keen on getting any more.'

'Didn't your mother teach you the importance of dental care?' he asked.

She schooled her features into a blank mask, hoping he hadn't noticed the slight flinch at the mention of her mother. 'It wasn't one of her strong points, no.'

Erin felt his silent scrutiny, as if he was reading her

word by word, page by page. She wanted to go back inside but she felt inexplicably drawn to him, like tiny iron filings to a strong magnet.

'It's quite a coincidence, me moving in next door, don't you think?' he asked.

She gave a little shrug. 'There are three nurses and an orderly in this apartment block. Mosman's a convenient suburb. It's close to Sydney Met.'

'Are you renting or do you own your apartment?'

'The bank owns it,' she said. 'I work to keep up the payments.'

Erin had forgotten to close the balcony doors and Molly chose that moment to strut out like a model on a catwalk.

'I didn't realise you were allowed pets here,' he said, looking down as Molly began to weave around Erin's legs.

She grimaced as she scooped up the big fluffy bundle of fur. 'I–I've got special permission from the body corporate,' she lied.

Eamon Chapman cocked his head, as if debating whether to believe her. 'Isn't it cruel to house a cat indoors all the time?'

Erin stroked Molly's silky head. 'She's a Ragdoll. They prefer to be indoors.'

'What's its name?'

'Molly.'

'One of my sisters has a cat,' he said. 'Personally I'm a dog man, but yours looks cute.'

'Thank you.'

He straightened from the railing and stretched. Erin's eyes nearly popped out of her head, like popcorn from a hot pan, as each of his muscles rippled in response.

'Have you had time to look at my proposal?' he asked as his arms came back down to his sides.

Erin had to blink a couple of times to reorient herself. 'Um…yes, I have. I'm not sure it's going to work—that follow-through care thing—it's too complicated. A&E is too busy as it is to expect us to wander off to plump up patients' pillows on the wards.'

'You're missing the point, Dr Taylor,' he said. 'It's not about plumping up pillows; it's about treating the patient from start to finish as a person, not a statistic.'

'I don't treat patients as statistics.'

'Tell me the names of the last five patients you saw today.'

Erin stared at him as her mind went completely blank. She could barely remember faces, let alone names. It had been so frantic, especially when an elderly woman had been brought in with a cardiac arrest at the same time a head injury had arrived. Names hadn't been important; what had been important was saving lives that were hanging by a gossamer thread. 'I didn't have time to memorise their names,' she said, putting Molly down. 'My job is to save their lives.'

'Do you ever wonder what happens to them after they leave you?' he asked.

Erin didn't want to admit how much she wondered about them. She saw it as a weakness in herself, a frailty that should have been knocked out of her way back in medical school. She fought against her human feelings all the time; they kept her awake at night—the sea of faces that floated past like ghosts. 'Not really,' she said, her tone chilly. 'As I said, it's not my job.'

'You might want to have a rethink about that, Dr Taylor,' he said. 'The first trial ward-round begins tomorrow at the end of your shift.'

Erin forced her gaze to remain connected to his. 'Well, I can't see that working. You know as well as anyone that A&E shifts don't end according to the clock—they end when you finish treating your last patient, or at least get them to the point where you can hand them over to the next shift. You can't just breeze out to start chatting with folks on the ward.'

'You're so right. I am quite aware of that,' he said. 'If you read the plan properly, you would see that wind-up on your last patient starts an hour before your shift ends—that gives you at least part of the last hour to do ward follow-through.'

Erin gave him a mutinous look. 'Oh, so we just walk out an hour *before* our shift ends then, and I suppose the next shift starts an hour early to fill in the gap? Or maybe we just abandon A&E altogether for an hour. Look, you can hardly force already overworked staff to take on even more responsibility.'

'If you had read the proposal carefully, Dr Taylor, you would see that new arrangements do not mean more re-sponsibility, just different responsibility. And, as far as implementing this plan, I'm not a great believer in using force to achieve anything,' he said. 'But I am the director, and I would like those working in my team to actually *be* a part of that team. The response from everyone else has been very positive, actually. I think you are going to find yourself out of touch with what everyone else is doing if you simply reject the department's policies.'

She arched her eyebrows. 'So, what do you plan to do, Dr Chapman? Hand-hold every A&E doctor until you're confident they're doing things your way?'

Eamon held her pert look, privately enjoying the way her burnt-toffee-brown eyes challenged his. Her defensive stance made him wonder why she was so against change. None of the other doctors he had briefed that morning had expressed any opposition to his proposal. In fact, three of them had cited cases where if such a plan had already been in place patient outcomes would have been better.

From what he had heard Erin Taylor was not one of the more social members of the department. Apparently she never joined in with regular drinks on Friday evenings at one of the local bars, and as far as he could tell she lived alone, apart from a contraband cat. She was prickly and unfriendly, yet her clinical management of patients was spot-on. She was competent and efficient, although one or two of the nurses had mentioned in passing her bedside manner needed work.

'I have certain goals I would like to achieve during my appointment,' he said. 'One of them is to improve overall outcomes for patients coming through A&E in this hospital. What you might not be aware of is how your expert work in A&E can be undone by isolating later management teams from the acute-care team. When was the last time you did a tertiary survey? It's mentioned in EMST and ATLS, but hardly ever happens. Sometimes injuries and clinical clues get missed in the wards. There is clear evidence that tertiary survey by the doctor who carried out the primary and secondary surveys is more likely to detect missed injuries, and so avoid complications which eat up beds and cost money.'

She continued to eyeball him in that 'I don't give a damn' way of hers. 'So, how long do you intend on propping up the public system before you scoot off for far more lucrative returns in the private sector?'

Eamon cocked an eyebrow at her. 'I could ask you the very same question.'

She held his look for a moment before turning to look at the harbour. The sun was low in the sky, casting a pinkish glow over the sails of the Opera House and the towering skyscrapers of the city on the opposite shore. 'I've thought about it plenty of times,' she said. 'But so far I haven't got round to doing anything about it.'

'You don't like change, do you, Dr Taylor?' Eamon asked.

She turned to look at him, her expression like curtains pulled across a window. 'I can deal with change when I think it's appropriate,' she said, and without another word slipped inside her apartment and shut the sliding doors—locking him out in more ways than one, he suspected.

CHAPTER TWO

ERIN had not long finished stitching a leg wound on a teenager the following morning when Tammy alerted her to a new admission.

'Forty-five-year-old male complaining of severe back pain,' Tammy said, reading from the notes she had taken down. 'His wife found him on the floor of the bathroom. He's nauseous and vomited prior to arriving in A&E.'

Erin twitched aside the curtains in bay four and introduced herself. 'Hello, I'm Dr Taylor. The triage nurse tells me you've got back pain. Can you describe it exactly?'

The man pointed to his left loin. 'Here…' he said somewhat breathlessly. 'Every couple of minutes… I….ahh…!' He writhed and groaned on the bed as his ashen-faced wife clutched one of his hands in hers.

'We'll give you something for the pain and nausea,' Erin said, administering morphine, buscopan and stemetil IV, with Tammy assisting.

'Is he going to be all right?' the man's wife asked.

'How long have you been unwell, Mr…' Erin glanced at the notes '…Aston?'

'I…I haven't been sick for years,' he said, and turned his head to his wife. 'Have I, love?'

Mrs Aston nodded. 'That's right, Doctor. He's never even taken a day off work in thirty-odd years. He's always been—'

'How's the pain now?' Erin asked as she clicked her pen open.

'Eased off a bit,' Mr Aston said, regaining some colour in his face as the pain-relief flooded his system.

'When did you first feel unwell?' Erin asked, pen poised over her patient-history clipboard.

'First thing this morning,' he said. 'I woke up to go to the toilet and then it hit me, didn't it, love?'

'I found him on the floor of the bathroom,' his wife put in. 'I nearly had a heart attack myself.'

Erin acknowledged the wife's statement with a movement of her lips that was neither a smile nor a grimace but something in between. 'I need you to give me a urine sample if you can manage it, Mr Aston,' she said, addressing the patient once more. 'I'd also like you to have an abdominal X-ray. The nurse will organise that while I see to another patient. Once we have the results of the urine sample, we'll know more.'

'Is it cancer?' Mrs Aston asked hollowly. 'Jeff used to smoke, didn't you, dear? He gave it up…what?…ten years ago now, it must be. I remember the day. It was when we went to—'

'We'll know more once we get the results back from the tests I've ordered,' Erin said briskly.

Tammy took over the care of the patient as Erin moved to the next bay. She parted the curtains to see Dr

Chapman standing by the bedside of a young child with his mother. 'Oh, sorry,' Erin said. 'My patient must have been moved into another bay.'

Eamon gave her a formal smile which Erin suspected was for the sake of the patient. 'Mrs Forster has been taken for a CT scan. This is Hamish, and his mother, Karen Young. Hamish here has had a persistent discharge from his right nostril for about a week, but this morning the discharge was blood-stained. We were about to have a look inside, weren't we, Hamish? You don't mind if Dr Taylor watches, do you? I bet she's never seen a braver young man around here.'

The young boy of about three stared wide-eyed but trustingly at Eamon, who picked up a nasal speculum and bright light. Erin was privately a little impressed at how biddable the child became under Eamon's care. She'd had a child with a foreign object up its nose only a month ago, and the floor above had heard its screams when she had tried to retrieve it. In the end she had handed the case over to the ear, nose and throat surgeon who had removed a plastic bead under general anaesthesia.

'There,' Eamon said as he showed the child and his mother the bright blue bead he had found. 'You were a champion, Hamish. I've seen kids twice your age who would have screamed the place down.'

'Weally?' Hamish asked, still a little bug-eyed.

'You betcha,' Eamon said, and then he turned and winked at the young mother. 'You can take him home now, Mrs Young. He's good to go. Just put the ointment Nurse will get for you up his nostril three times a day, and massage it in a bit, until you've finished the whole tube.'

Once the young mother and her son had left, Eamon turned to Erin. 'I'd like a word with you if you are free, Dr Taylor.'

Erin gave him a wary look. 'I have a patient who should be back from X-ray by now.'

'That would be Mr Aston next door?' he asked.

She flattened her mouth at his expression. 'I thought the plan was to have some sort of continuity of care around here,' she said, keeping her voice down in case the patient had returned. 'If I go off for a lengthy discussion with you, who's going to follow up Mr Aston?'

'Meet me in my office once you have finished assessing him,' he said, pushing the curtains aside. 'Unless, of course, anything urgent comes in.'

Erin blew out a breath once he moved past. It would be just her luck that today would be one of those quiet days, leaving her with no excuse to avoid another confrontation with him.

Mr Aston was being wheeled back to the examination bay when Erin returned, after responding to an HMO's phone call about another patient who had been admitted the day before.

Mr Aston's urine sample was positive for blood and his X-ray almost certainly showed a stone at the end of the right ureter. Erin ordered a rapid-sequence urinary-tract CT, which confirmed the finding, and she explained the results to the patient and his wife. 'You have renal colic, Mr Aston, which basically means you have a kidney stone. Very often stones pass spontaneously, but occasionally they don't.'

'What happens then?' Mrs Aston asked.

'If the stone doesn't pass, it may have to be removed under anaesthesia. We'd get a urologist to see you to do a cystoscopy—put a camera up the front passage into the bladder—and use a wire basket to grab the stone and pull it out.'

'Oh dear, it sounds horribly painful,' Mrs Aston said, grasping her husband's hand again.

'He'll be fine, Mrs Aston,' Erin said. 'The ENT specialist is one of the best in the city.'

oh dear! wrong end!

Once she had left the patient's bay, Erin looked at the clock and thought longingly of a cup of tea and a sandwich, even one from the hospital cafeteria. But over an hour had passed since Eamon Chapman had asked her to meet him in his office, so rather than delay the inevitable any further she trudged through the department to where his office was located. She gave the door a quick knock, secretly wishing he had been called away, but she heard his deep voice commanding her to come in.

He was sitting behind his desk but rose to his feet as she came in. 'Have you had lunch?' he asked.

'No,' Erin said, wondering if he could read her mind or hear her stomach in this instance. 'But it can wait.'

'No need to. Why don't we head on down to the cafeteria and grab a sandwich now?' he asked.

She looked at him as if he had gone mad. 'I take it your plans to improve this hospital from top to bottom haven't quite made it to the cafeteria?' she said dryly.

He gave her a rueful smile. 'That bad, huh?'

She felt her lips twitch, but forced them back into

line. 'Keep away from the salami and the chicken. We lost three staff members to a tandoori wrap three weeks ago.'

His dark brows lifted. '"Lost" as in…?'

'Lost as in sick for a week with a reportable disease,' she said. 'A couple of us had to do double shifts to cover them.'

His lips twitched this time, making his eyes crinkle up at the corners. 'There's a café on the other side of the car park,' he said. 'Does that have any black marks against it I should know about?'

'They do a mean salad sandwich with mung beans and alfalfa sprouts,' she said. 'And their coffee's passable.'

He picked up his mobile from the desk and clipped it to his belt. 'Let's give it a try. I'll just let Jan at reception know we'll be within paging distance.'

A few minutes later, sitting opposite Eamon Chapman in the café across from the hospital, Erin wondered how long it had been since she'd shared a meal with a man, even a colleague. She hadn't dated since medical school, and even then it had been an unmitigated disaster. In the end she'd decided she wasn't cut out for the couples' scene. Most of the men she knew were complicated creatures with too much baggage—not that she could talk, given the veritable road-train she had brought with her from Adelaide. But this was hardly a date, she reminded herself. She was pretty certain Eamon Chapman had other things on his mind besides chatting her up. From what she could read from his expression, she was in for a dressing down if anything.

'So,' he said, leaning back in his chair to study

her pensive features. 'How long have you been at Sydney Met?'

Erin was aware of his steady gaze on her as she toyed with the thick froth of her latte with a teaspoon. 'Five years,' she said, meeting his eyes for a brief moment. 'I spent a year in the States before that.'

'Travelling or working?'

'A bit of both,' she said.

'Did you grow up in Sydney?'

Erin's teaspoon gave a tiny clatter as she placed it back on the saucer. 'No. I grew up in South Australia. I moved to Sydney when I was a teenager.'

He took a sip of his cappuccino; her gaze was suddenly mesmerised by the tiny trace of chocolate that clung to his top lip before his tongue swept over his mouth to clear it. She swallowed a little restriction in her throat and quickly dropped her gaze, picking up her teaspoon again and stirring her latte with fierce concentration.

'So, do you have family here or back over there?' he asked.

Erin put her spoon back down and met his gaze. 'Look, I hate to be rude, but what's with the twenty questions?'

His eyes bored into hers for a tense second or two. 'I like to get a feel for the people I will be working with on a daily basis. It's an important part of being a leader, knowing the team's strengths and weaknesses.'

She screwed up her mouth in an embittered manner. 'Do you trust your own judgement on that, or are you usually swayed by others' opinions?'

He accepted her comment with an unreadable look. 'I lean towards the "innocent until proven guilty" philosophy where possible.'

She gave a little snort and reached for her coffee again. 'Yeah, well, I bet it didn't take long for some members of the jury to swing your opinion.'

'What makes you say that?' he asked.

Erin gave her shoulders a gentle shrug. 'Gut feeling; instinct; experience.'

'I wanted to have a word with you about how you handled Mr Aston,' he said after a short silence.

Erin's gaze flicked back to his. 'It was straight-out renal colic. He's got a stone the size of a marble. He's not going to pass it without surgical intervention.'

'I'm not for a moment questioning your diagnosis, Dr Taylor,' Eamon said. 'But I think you could improve on your handling of accompanying relatives. Coming into A&E is stressful for both patients *and* relatives.'

She set her mouth into a defensive line. 'My job is to treat the patient, not pander to their entourage.'

Eamon put his coffee cup back in its saucer, his eyes holding hers. 'Listen, managing the relatives is *part* of treating the patient. Stressed relatives worsen patients' stresses. And accompanying relatives are usually going to be the patient's carers afterwards. One, they need to be well informed. Two, if they are stressed out and decompensate, they won't be good carers. That means more time for patients in hospital, more hospital expense and more loss to the community. I've only been in the department less than twenty-four hours and I have already heard several complaints about your handling of relatives, yesterday's threat of litigation being a case in point.'

Her slim jaw tightened. 'Mrs Haddad's suit will be rejected as soon as the medical council read through my notes and realise the extent of her son's injuries.'

'That is most certainly the case; however, the whole thing may well have been avoided if you had softened your approach.'

'You know nothing of my approach,' she said, shooting him a livid glare. 'You weren't there trying to save the boy's life. When someone is bleeding out before your eyes, it's not exactly the time to ask how his mother or his family are feeling, for God's sake.'

Eamon leaned forward in his chair, his arms resting on the table. Erin moved back, folding her arms across her chest, her chin at a defiant height. 'As you are now aware, I was in the bay next to you when you were assessing Mr Aston,' he said. 'His wife was clearly distressed to see her normally healthy husband in such a state. A reassuring word to her wouldn't have gone astray, not cutting her off in mid-sentence.'

Erin rolled her eyes, and, pushing back her chair, got to her feet in one angry movement. 'I haven't got time for this. I've got patients to see.'

His green eyes hit hers. 'Sit down, Dr Taylor.'

Erin's hands gripped the chair-back with white-knuckled fingers. She was so tempted to shove the chair back underneath the table to drive home her point, but the steely look in his eyes forestalled her.

Several tense seconds passed before she reluctantly gave in. She sat back down, crossing her arms and legs as she sent him a querulous look. 'You said you'd had other complaints about me,' she said. 'Am I allowed to know who they were from?'

He leaned back in his chair, but the hardened look hadn't softened in his eyes. 'That would be unprofessional of me. The complaints were made in confidence; in fact, they weren't even official, just passing comments. No one is out to get you, Dr Taylor, far from it. Generally the staff speak very highly of you, on a professional level.'

'So my bedside manner needs some work,' she said with a petulant huff of her shoulder. 'Pardon me for putting patients' lives in front of politeness.'

'I don't see why you can't manage both,' he said. 'Or do you have a particular reason for being so prickly with everyone?'

Erin felt the probe of his gaze and had to work hard to maintain eye contact. Something about him made her feel exposed. Even though she had only met him the day before, that intelligent, penetrating gaze of his had a habit of catching her off guard. He was seeing things she didn't want him to see, things she had fought hard to keep hidden. She liked her life in its neat little compartments, but she felt as if he was threatening her stronghold, insisting on her being someone she was not, nor ever could be. 'I'm not interested in winning the latest popularity contest,' she said. 'If people don't like me, I don't let it worry me. I have better things to do with my time.'

'Do you live alone, apart from your cat?' he asked.

Erin frowned. 'I thought we were here to discuss issues to do with work, not my private life.'

Eamon draped one arm over the back of the chair that was next to his; his gaze continued to hold hers. 'Sometimes one's private life can have an impact on their professional one.'

She gave him an arch look. 'Sometimes one's boss can put his nose where it is not welcome.'

Eamon felt his lips flicker with a smile. 'I'm not just your boss, Dr Taylor, I am also your neighbour. That blurs the boundaries a bit, don't you think?'

'Not for me,' she said with a flinty glare.

He leaned forward again, his eyes still locked on hers. 'As I said earlier, I don't like the heavy-handed approach, but if it's called for I am not afraid to use it. If you don't lift your game, I will have to take appropriate action.'

She eyeballed him back. 'If you want to fire me, go right ahead, but if you do I'll have the unfair-dismissal commission on your back before you can say Code Blue.'

Eamon felt a rush of blood to his groin at her feisty words. She was like a spitting cat, all claws and hiss, making him want to tame that wild streak by pressing his own mouth to her snarling one. He wondered if anyone had been game enough to come within touching distance of her. She sent out keep-away-from-me vibes like soundwaves. For some reason he found that incredibly attractive. His three younger sisters would think he was crazy taking on someone like Erin Taylor; they were hanging out for a sweet sister-in-law they could take shopping and do girly things with. Somehow he couldn't see the pint-sized Dr Taylor with her touch-me-not glare and barbed tongue going down too well with his touchy-feely family.

'Eamon?' A high female voice sounded from behind their table.

Erin turned her head to see one of the nurses from the surgical ward approaching, bringing with her a wave of heady perfume that irritated Erin's nostrils.

'Hi, Sherrie,' Eamon, said, rising to his feet and sweeping the woman into a brief, hard hug. He held her from him to look down at her flushed features. 'How're you doing? I've been meaning to call you, but things have been pretty crazy since I got back from London.'

'Don't worry about it,' the woman called Sherrie said, with a beaming smile. 'Gosh, you look fabulous. Jet lag and hard work must suit you.'

Eamon gave a self-deprecating smile before turning to introduce Erin. 'Sherrie, do you know Dr Erin Taylor from A&E?'

Sherrie held out her hand. 'No, I don't think we've met properly. I've seen you around, though. Nice to meet you.'

Erin briefly placed her hand in the other woman's before pulling away. 'Thank you,' she said. 'You too.'

'So…' Sherrie turned back to Eamon. 'When are you free for a meal or a drink or something? Where are you staying? Have you bought a house or an apartment?'

Eamon grinned at the barrage of questions, holding up his hands as if to ward them off. 'One at a time, Sherrie. Yes, a meal would be great, and I'm renting my mate Tim Yeoman's apartment in Mosman until the renovations are completed on my house at Balmoral Beach. Tim's still on sabbatical in Edinburgh.'

Sherrie took a pen out of her uniform pocket and scribbled her number and address on a napkin from the table. She handed it to him and smiled. 'Here are my details,' she said. 'I've changed my number since I last saw you. Call me any time. It will be great to hear all about your time in the UK.'

Eamon folded the napkin and put it in the breast pocket of his shirt. 'Thanks, Sherrie; I'll see what I can do for next week. I'm still unpacking, otherwise I'd organise something sooner.'

'No problem,' Sherrie said, and glanced at her watch. 'Oops. Gotta dash. I'm meant to be in Surg A by now. Congratulations on the new job, Eamon. You're exactly what this place needs to whip it into shape.' She turned and smiled at Erin. 'See you around, Erica.'

'Erin,' Erin corrected her.

'Oh, sorry, I'm hopeless with names.' And then, with another beaming smile aimed at Eamon, Sherrie left.

Erin pushed her half-drunk latte away. 'A love interest of yours?' she asked.

He sat back down and drained the contents of his cup before he answered. 'We dated a couple of times a few years ago. Nothing too serious, and fortunately we managed to remain friends after we called it quits.'

'It looks to me like she would like a re-run,' Erin said, not quite able to stop herself from sounding slightly churlish.

One of his dark brows lifted. 'Is that feminine intuition or something else?'

She was the first to shift her gaze. 'What else could it be?' she asked. 'You're not exactly my type.'

'Oh really?' he said. 'What is your type?'

Erin wished she hadn't started the conversation. She

could feel her colour rising as the silence stretched and stretched. How could she answer such a question? She didn't have a type. She didn't even have a social life. She had a cat and a career and a cartload of reasons to keep her life as simple as possible. 'I have to get going,' she said, making a show of looking at her watch. 'I don't want another long day.'

'Big plans for this evening?' he asked as he rose to his feet.

Erin wondered if he was making fun of her. To an attractive man with women falling over themselves to book him for a date, her life must seem pretty dull in comparison. 'Yes, as a matter of fact,' she lied. 'I'm meeting someone after work.'

'About what we discussed over coffee…' Eamon began as he accompanied her back to the hospital.

'Don't worry, Dr Chapman,' she said before he could continue. 'I'll get working on winning friends and influencing people right now.'

Eamon watched as she stalked off down the corridor, her head down, her shoulders hunched and her face like a brewing storm. 'You do that, Dr Taylor,' he murmured, and, blowing out a breath, made his way back to his office.

'Aren't you supposed to be doing the trial ward-round with Dr Chapman?' Lydia Hislop, one of the nurses who regularly worked with Erin, asked. 'The others left over half an hour ago.'

Erin frowned as she checked through the patient's notes she was reading, barely registering what the nurse had said. 'When did Mrs Fuller have a second shot of pethidine?' She glanced at the nurse. 'I don't remember signing for it.'

Lydia peered at the notes, her forehead creasing over a frown. 'That's your signature, isn't it?'

Erin felt a cold hand of unease press against the base of her spine. She closed the patient folder and let out a long, unsteady breath. 'I must be working way too hard,' she muttered. 'I can't even remember what day it is.'

'Tell me about it,' Lydia said with an empathetic eye-roll. 'Have you got time to see Mr Boyle in bay five, or should I get one of the night-duty staff to deal with it?'

Erin glanced at her watch. The ward-round, even if she had wanted to attend, would be winding up by now; it would be over altogether by the time she made it up to the appropriate floor. 'I'll see him,' she said. 'That's the one with the suspected appendix, right?'

'Yes, I've got his history here,' Lydia said, handing her a file. 'He's been in before for a resection of gangrenous bowel about two years ago.'

'That should make for interesting surgery,' Erin said. 'Who's the surgeon on call?'

'Mr Gourlay,' Lydia said. 'Your all-time favourite.'

This time is was Erin who rolled her eyes. 'Maybe I should have gone on that ward-round after all.'

When Erin got home from work, Molly wound her plump body around her legs, mewing in delight. Erin smiled and scooped her up, burying her face in the cat's luxurious fur. The phone rang inside her bag, and she gently put Molly down to answer it. When she saw the number on the screen, she felt a hand of dread clutch at her insides. 'Hello, Mum,' she said in a flat tone.

'Ezzie, I need your help,' Leah Taylor said. 'Things have been tough just lately, you know how it is.'

Erin whooshed out an impatient sigh. 'No, Mum, strange as it may seem, I don't know how it is.'

'There's no need to be nasty,' Leah said. 'All I want is a bit of cash to get me through until my next pension payment.'

Erin began pacing; it was almost unconscious every time she spoke with her mother. Back and forth she went across the carpet, like a caged animal desperate for freedom. She could even see the slightly worn area when she'd last vacuumed. 'Mum, you know what the social worker said about me giving you money all the time,' she said. 'You just shoot it up or drink it.'

'I'm going straight now, Ez,' her mother said. 'I haven't touched a drop for three days.'

Erin rolled her eyes. 'And what about Bob or Bill or Brad, or whatever his name is? Is he going straight too?'

'Just because you can't pull a man doesn't give you the right to slag me off. If you would just tart yourself up a bit you wouldn't be living all alone with just a stupid cat for company.'

Erin felt anger rising in her like the froth of a soda poured too rapidly, threatening to overflow the glass of her control. She had to fight her temper back, knowing from experience it never worked with her mother. There was no hope of a rational conversation with someone in the grip of addiction. She had learned that earlier than any child should have to learn. Some people loved their fix more than their children. Leah Taylor was one of them. The drink and the drugs would always come first, her unsavoury boyfriends a close second. 'Mum, I'm going to hang up now, OK?' she said in a cool, calm voice. 'I'll call you in a couple of days.'

'How can you turn your back on your own mother?' Leah asked in a whining tone.

Erin closed her eyes as she thought of all the times her mother had abandoned her, leaving her to fend for herself until the authorities had finally stepped in. Years of being shunted from one foster home to another, with short periods of being reunited with her mother in some of Leah's all-too-brief periods of sobriety. Yes, Erin could easily turn her back on her mother. It was either that or get hurt all over again. 'I'll call you later, Mum,' she said again.

'Selfish little cow,' Leah snapped. 'You're just like your father.'

'And that would be…?' Erin asked pointedly.

Her mother slammed the phone down.

CHAPTER THREE

ERIN wasn't sure why she went to that particular movie at that particular cinema, but at the time she had figured it was much better than spending the evening alone with her demons. The film was an art-house foreign-language one she had read a review about in one of the weekend papers. She took her seat and sipped at a diet soda; she barely read the subtitles, she just looked at the images flashing across the screen while her thoughts drifted elsewhere.

When she came out of the cinema the streets were crowded with people on their way home from dinner, or on their way to nightclubs for drinking and dancing. The noisy chatter and laughter of everyone having a good time as they enjoyed the balmy autumn evening made Erin wish she hadn't come out after all.

She had never felt more alone in her life.

Eamon picked up his takeaway meal from his favourite restaurant, thrilled that the same people were still running it since he had left to work in the UK a couple of years ago. Right now he could think of nothing better than a cold beer and a madras curry, maybe watching some cricket on television or catching up on some current affairs on the Net.

He suddenly noticed a slight figure in the small crowd that was milling out of the local cinema, her shiny chestnut hair loose about her face instead of tightly pulled back. She was wearing jeans and a loose shirt over a camisole top, with ballet flats on her feet. Her eyes were downcast as she weaved her way through the knots of people, as if she didn't want to be noticed.

Eamon was on his way to her when he saw a boisterous couple coming the other way jostle against her, almost knocking her over.

'Hey, watch where you're going,' the young male half of the couple said belligerently.

Eamon quickly broke through the crowd and put his arm around Erin's waist, pulling her close to his side. 'Sorry I'm late, sweetheart,' he said. Then, turning to look at the obstreperous pair, he gave them the full force of his commanding gaze. 'Is there a problem here?'

The couple exchanged a glance, the young man eventually giving a shrug. 'It's cool, mate. I guess I wasn't watching where I was going.'

'That's what I thought,' Eamon said, and stood with his arm still around Erin's waist until they had moved on.

Erin felt the nerves beneath her skin tingle with feelings she had never felt before. The weight of his arm was unfamiliar, but not in any way unpleasant. With him standing so close to her she could smell his light citrus-based aftershave; she could even see the individual points of stubble on his jaw. The most primal feelings swept over her. No one had ever sprung to protect her before. It awakened such deep yearnings she had trouble disguising how affected she was. To cover her vulnerability, she stepped out of his embrace and dusted herself off, as if his touch had contaminated her in some way. 'Thanks,' she mumbled. 'But the sweetheart thing was a bit over-the-top, don't you think?'

His mouth curved upwards in a smile. 'I don't know,' he said. 'It worked, didn't it?'

Erin found her lips wanting to return his smile, but she controlled them by biting the inside of her mouth.

'So, where's your date?' he asked, looking up and down the street before returning his gaze to hers.

'What date? Oh…' She felt her face colour again. 'Um…they couldn't make it at the last minute.'

'Another doctor, huh?'

'Um…' She looked away. 'No. Just a… Someone who couldn't make it.'

'Story of my life,' he said with a hint of wryness.

Erin looked at him. '*You* got stood up?' Her voice came out slightly incredulous.

'You didn't turn up for the first ward-round,' he said, skewering her with his gaze.

Erin bit her lip and turned away. 'I know. I'm sorry, I had a tough case to deal with. I lost track of time.'

'I realise it won't always be possible to attend each one, but the plan overall is to improve continuity of care,' he said. 'Today's round showed up a few holes in the system, so it will be good to work on those. I can fill you in on what went on so you don't feel out of the loop.'

Erin had always felt out of the loop, but she didn't

tell him so. She hadn't gone to the right school, and she certainly hadn't come from the right family. She didn't mix with the high-flyers; she just got on with her job, hoping to make a difference where she could. 'You seem pretty sure this set-up will work,' she said. 'Is this new system something you experienced overseas?'

'Yes and no,' he said. 'I've worked in several A&E departments now, and I've seen a lot of avoidable problems occur because communication with the medical staff in A&E stopped the moment the patient was rolled out the door of the department—problems that would have been avoided with a structured follow-through plan involving the staff who did the primary assessment.'

Erin suddenly noticed the takeaway bag he was carrying. 'I'm sorry, I didn't realise I was holding you up from your dinner.'

'You're not holding me up,' he said. 'I was just on my way home. Did you drive or walk?'

'I walked,' she said. 'Parking is always a pain down here at this time of night.'

'Like most cities,' he agreed. 'I'll walk back with you. Have you had dinner? I've got enough to share if you'd like to join me.'

Erin felt her cheeks flush. 'Oh no…I wouldn't want to intrude.'

'You're not intruding. Besides, I can tell you how the ward-round went while we eat.'

Erin wanted to refuse but the thought of the rest of the evening alone was suddenly not as welcome as it had been earlier. She told herself she should at least be polite to Eamon after he had come to her rescue so gallantly. Surely she owed him an hour or two of her time? 'Thanks, that would be nice,' she said, glancing at him shyly.

Following the short walk back, Eamon activated the security pass to the apartment block and waited for her to precede him. The elevator ride was swift but to Erin it felt as if it was taking for ever. She didn't know what to say; she didn't even know where to stand. She shifted her weight from foot to foot, half-leaning, half-standing against the bare wall of the elevator. She felt awkward, gauche and out of place, certain he was wondering what was wrong with her. He was probably used to the most sophisticated of women, wining and dining them in world-class restaurants. No doubt he bedded them as well, taking pleasure where he found it, almost certainly giving it back one-hundredfold. She kept her arms folded across her chest but even so she could still feel where his arm had been about her waist.

She began to imagine what it would feel like to have his touch on other parts of her body—her mouth, for instance. His mouth was a sensual one, the lower lip fuller than the top one, making her lips start to tingle in anticipation of feeling its firmness against hers. Would he kiss softly or firmly? Would he cup her face or hold her by the shoulders? Would he…?

The doors of the elevator opening catapulted her out of her wayward thoughts. With her colour still high, she moved past Eamon as he held the doors open with the strong band of his arm, her heart doing little skips in her chest as she breathed in his scent once more. She felt ashamed of her reaction, and hoped to God he wasn't picking up on it. How foolish of her to be so taken in by good looks and easy charm. He was her boss, for goodness' sake! What sort of a fool would she be to compromise her professionalism by becoming involved with a colleague? In any case, given her background, how soon would he stay interested in her? She could hardly take him home to meet her mother and her latest junkie boyfriend. Men like Eamon Chapman dated women from the right side of the tracks, not trailer-park misfits.

'I'm sorry the place is still a bit of a mess,' Eamon said as he opened his apartment door. 'I should be an expert at unpacking by now; I've done it enough times.'

Not as many times as me, Erin thought as she followed him inside. 'Can I do anything to help?' she asked.

'No, just take a seat and I'll get some plates,' he said. 'Would you like a glass of wine? I've got red and white, or beer if you'd prefer.'

'I'm not much of a drinker, so don't open anything specially.'

'One glass of wine won't hurt you,' he said, taking a bottle of chilled white wine from the fridge. 'It'll help you relax.'

Erin pulled at her bottom lip with her teeth. 'Is it that obvious?'

He gave her a reassuring smile. 'Hey, don't be so hard on yourself. That drunken jerk would have frightened most people. He was probably pretty harmless, but these days you never can tell.'

Erin hadn't given the inebriated young man another thought. It was the stone-cold sober, gorgeous one standing in front of her right now that was her real concern. 'I guess I should think about taking some self-defence classes,' she said, taking the glass of wine he handed her.

'Not a bad idea,' he said. 'You're so tiny it wouldn't take much to knock you off your feet.'

Erin felt a shivery feeling move down her spine. How could one casual, throwaway comment make her feel so utterly feminine? She buried her nose in her glass, keeping her gaze averted from his while her heart did funny little somersaults behind her ribcage.

Eamon found plates and cutlery and soon had the food dished up and placed on the kitchen table. 'There you go,' he said, handing her a napkin.

'Thank you,' she said. 'This is very good of you. I was going to have cheese on toast.'

'It's a good standby, I'll grant you,' he said. 'But it'll hardly give you the energy for the sort of hours we work.'

'No, I guess not.'

Eamon watched as she picked delicately at the food. She seemed ill at ease but he couldn't quite decide if it was his company or the experience on the street earlier. He couldn't help comparing her to his three boisterous, extroverted sisters who each sailed through life making numerous friends as they went. Erin Taylor had a guarded air about her, as if she didn't warm to people easily, nor expect them to warm to her. 'So, what did you think of the film?' he asked.

She glanced up from her plate, blinking at him for a moment. 'Film?'

He offered her more curry but she shook her head. He served himself some more as he said, 'The French film you went to see. I saw you amongst the crowd coming out of the cinema. What was it like?'

'Oh…' She put down her fork and dabbed at her mouth with her napkin, not quite meeting his eyes. 'It was…OK.'

'Worth seeing?'

She put her napkin down and briefly met his eyes. 'The cinematography was wonderful.'

'And the storyline?'

She gnawed at her lip in an engaging, little-girl-lost manner. 'Um…it was…it was…'

Eamon laughed. 'It's all right; I get the picture—literally.'

'Oh no,' she said, looking a little shocked. 'I didn't mean to imply it was not worth seeing. It's just that I had other things on my mind…' She gave a little sigh that seemed to come from deep inside her. 'Look, I'm really sorry I didn't make it to the ward-round. I know you probably think I deliberately missed it but something came up and I thought I should attend to it.'

'It's cool, Erin,' he said, watching as she blushed when he spoke her name for the first time.

Her gaze fell away from his. 'I…I guess I should get going,' she said, pushing back her chair. 'Thanks for the meal, it was lovely.'

'You don't have to rush off, surely?' he said, suddenly realising how much he wanted her to stay. 'I'll put the kettle on for coffee.'

She appeared to hesitate, making him wonder if she was as reluctant to leave as he was for her to go. The thought secretly thrilled him. They were two single adults with time on their hands. Sure, they worked together, but that didn't mean they couldn't keep their professional lives separate from their private ones. He'd had relationships with colleagues before; it took a little juggling at times, but he was at a time in his life when he was looking for more. He wasn't entirely sure Erin Taylor was the one to give him the whole package, but she had certainly spiked his interest with her shy, almost gauche manner. She intrigued him, and not a lot of women did that any more. He saw through the flirty come-and-get-me wiles too easily, having witnessed his sisters bring too many men to their knees. No, Erin Taylor was something else—something he was starting to realise was worth investigating a little further.

'One coffee, then,' she said, getting up to help clear the dishes.

Eamon took the plates from her, and their hands met briefly. He saw the way her pupils flared, as if he had sent a current straight from his body to hers. He felt the same current fire through him, lighting a fire in his groin that flickered and then roared. His eyes went to her mouth, the soft cushion of it tempting him to lean forward to taste it. She had not once in the whole time he had known her smiled at him. Suddenly it seemed imperative that she did. 'Has anyone told you what lovely brown eyes you have?' he asked.

She suddenly stepped back. 'I've changed my mind about that coffee,' she said tightly. 'I need to feed Molly.'

Eamon bit back a curse as she stalked to the door. He had never been rejected for a cat before and it stung—badly. 'Erin…' He raked his hand through his hair, feeling as if he had time-travelled back to his hormone-raging teens. 'I didn't mean to offend you. I was just—'

She turned at the door, fixing him with a cold, hard stare. 'You didn't,' she said. 'I just have other priorities right now.' And with that she left.

'Are you sure you want to work a full week of nights?' the nursing supervisor in charge of the rosters asked Erin the next morning. 'I thought you hated night duty.'

'I do, but then who doesn't?' Erin said. 'I just thought I'd get them all over with at once for a change.'

'This doesn't have anything to do with the new director, does it?' Gwen asked, narrowing her gaze playfully. 'I heard he's turning everything upside down in the department.'

Erin felt her cheeks heating. 'I am sure he's well intentioned,' she said, keeping her voice flat with disinterest.

'He's rather gorgeous looking,' Gwen said. 'If I was twenty years younger, I would be making sure I was doing mirror shifts with him.'

Erin took her duty roster from the printer, keeping her expression blank. 'I'd better get going. The waiting room was empty when I left, but who knows how long that will last?'

It lasted all of ten minutes. By the time Erin got back there was a line-up at the door and she didn't surface from assessing, treating and admitting until it was mid-afternoon.

She was on her way to the doctors' room on the third floor when she ran into one of the senior surgeons, Arthur Gourlay. She mentally rolled her eyes and forced her face into a polite mask. 'Good afternoon, Mr Gourlay,' she said.

'What's the meaning of sending me patients without adequate pain-relief?' he blustered without preamble. 'I've had the family on my back for the last hour.'

Erin frowned. 'Which patient are you referring to?'

'That woman you admitted late this morning,' he said. 'The elderly one with bowel obstruction, Mrs Pappas.'

Erin clearly remembered ordering pethidine for the woman in question; she had signed for it, as per hospital regulations, although in this case the nurse on duty had administered it as Erin had been called to another emergency. 'Mr Gourlay, Mrs Pappas had pethidine in A&E and soon after was sent up to Surg B. If she was still in pain, I was unaware of it, as she ceased to be my responsibility once she was admitted to the ward.'

'This is not the first time this has happened,' Arthur Gourlay said. 'I'm going to have a word to the director about it. He's got a point about this follow-through thing. It seems once a patient is out of A&E they cease to exist.'

Erin felt her back stiffen. 'That's not true. It's just that A&E was full all morning. Mrs Pappas was properly assessed and given pain-relief as per my instructions. You can check my notes if you don't believe me.'

'What seems to be the problem?' Eamon Chapman asked from behind her.

Erin felt the hairs on the back of her neck rise as she turned to face him and her heart gave a funny little skip when his eyes met hers.

'Dr Taylor has developed a habit of sending patients

to the ward without adequate pain-relief,' Arthur Gourlay said. 'She seems to think—'

'That is not true,' Erin jumped in defensively.

'Arthur, I will handle this,' Eamon said calmly. 'I need to speak to Dr Taylor about another matter in any case.'

Arthur gave Erin a pompous sneer. 'It's about time someone pulled you into line.' He strode off down the corridor, muttering under his breath as he went.

Eamon swung his gaze to Erin. 'What was all that about?' he asked.

Her cheeks were glowing with anger and her body was stiff, as if she was fighting to keep it contained. 'Arthur Gourlay accused me of not administering pain-relief to a patient this morning,' she said. 'But I clearly remember writing it up.'

'What sort of delay was there before the patient was transferred to the ward?' he asked, stepping aside to allow an orderly go past with an empty gurney.

'I don't know,' she said. 'I was called to another emergency; a cardiac arrest came in and I was with him for the next hour.'

Another orderly was coming down the corridor, this time with a patient in a wheelchair. 'Let's go to the doctors' room and discuss this out of the hearing of the public,' Eamon said.

He shouldered open the door a metre or so down the corridor, waiting until she went in first. The room was thankfully empty except for the fragrant aroma of coffee brewing on a machine next to the sink.

'Coffee?' he asked.

She hesitated, as if she didn't want to prolong the

meeting any longer than she had to, but he saw the way her eyes glanced at the coffee machine and the little up-and-down movement of her slim throat in anticipation of that first reviving swallow.

'I'm going to have one, so I might as well pour you one as well,' he said. 'How do you have it?'

'Black.'

'No sugar?'

She gave him a pointed look. 'Five fillings, remember?'

He smiled lopsidedly. 'Right, how could I forget?' He handed her a mug of the brew and added, 'Is that why you never smile?'

She took the mug with fingers that fumbled in the handover, her eyes averted from his. 'I smile when I think it's appropriate,' she said. 'A&E doesn't seem the place to be grinning like an idiot.'

'So what's the deal with Arthur Gourlay?' Eamon asked after a little pause. 'He's seems to have some pretty heavy angst towards you.'

She gave him a direct look. 'Arthur is like a lot of men with oversized egos. He doesn't like it when he doesn't get his own way.'

Eamon cocked an eyebrow. 'Let me guess, he asked you out and you turned him down?'

Her eyes widened in surprise. 'How did you know? Did he say something to you?'

He shook his head. 'No, but I recognise the signs of a man scorned.'

She looked down at the contents of her mug. 'About last night…'

'Forget about it. I have.'

She looked up at him, her brown eyes wary. 'I wouldn't want you to get the wrong idea.'

'Dr Taylor,' he said. 'We met by chance, we shared a casual meal. That's all it was: a neighbourly get-together.'

She pressed her lips together. 'Right. Of course.' She put her coffee down. 'I'd better get back.'

'Before you go,' Eamon said. 'The pain-management issue Arthur spoke about—he mentioned this has happened before.'

Her eyes took on that guarded look again. 'Are you accusing me of something, Dr Chapman?'

'What would I be accusing you of?' he asked.

She held his look, her mouth pulled tight. 'I have followed the drug protocol scrupulously.'

'No one has suggested you haven't.'

Erin wondered if she should mention the incident the day before where she couldn't recall signing the second shot of pethidine for a patient. But surely that would make her look incompetent if she told him she couldn't remember what she had done and when? 'I suppose you're going to say this proves how important your follow-through plan is,' she said.

'It's pretty obvious there are some gaps in the system,' he said. 'But that's why I'm here to sort them out. I noticed you didn't make it to the second breakfast meeting. We'll be holding them all week and next until I have each A&E staff member up to date.'

'I've read through the document you gave me,' Erin said. 'And, depending on what happens this afternoon, I'll try and make the ward-round.'

'I would appreciate it, Dr Taylor,' he said. 'By the

way, I thought you might like to know, Mrs Haddad—the mother of the young man who died of the stab-wound—has withdrawn her complaint.'

Erin felt her shoulders go down in relief. 'I'm very sorry for her loss, but I tried everything I could to save him. It was just too late.'

'I think she came to realise that,' he said. 'It's sad, isn't it? The waste of a young life—all that potential gone to waste.'

Erin kept her expression blank. 'There's enough drug education around to warn people of the dangers.'

He studied her for a moment with that piercing green gaze. 'You don't have empathy for someone with a drug problem?' he asked.

'Look, Dr Chapman,' she said, expelling a breath of impatience. 'There are lots of really ill patients who need our care. People who self-abuse clog up the system and take valuable resources away from others who are unwell through no fault of their own.'

'It's not our place to make value judgements on patients who come in for treatment,' he said. 'There are a host of reasons why people get hooked on drugs or alcohol. They deserve the same level of care and priority afforded any other patient.'

'I'm not for a moment saying I would treat anyone differently,' she said. 'I just wish more people would take responsibility for their own health.'

'I understand the frustration; I feel it myself at times,' Eamon said. 'But there is only a limited amount of funds to go around. We have to do what we can with what we have.'

There was a beat or two of silence.

Erin heard the ticking of the clock on the wall and the white-noise hum of the refrigerator as it reset its thermostat. She also felt sure she could hear the beating of her heart. It was booming in her chest like a kettle drum with a beat that was as unsteady as it was rapid. She sent the tip of her tongue out to moisten her dry lips, her stomach giving an unexpected little kick of excitement when she saw his gaze slowly descend to her mouth.

Time froze for a moment, and then began to swell with promise…

The door behind Erin suddenly opened and a female voice chimed, 'Oops, sorry, I didn't meant to disturb you both.'

Erin turned and faced the female registrar. 'You weren't disturbing anything,' she mumbled, and quickly made her way out the door, her face feeling as if it was on fire.

CHAPTER FOUR

ERIN was in her kitchen feeding Molly that evening when she heard the sliding doors of next door's balcony open. Her skin automatically tightened, and her heart gave a little thump as she heard the click-clack of footsteps on the tiles.

'Gosh, Eamon,' a feminine voice said. 'It's an absolutely awesome view from here. I wish you'd let me move in with you. Won't you reconsider? *Please?*'

Erin pressed her spine flat against the pantry door as she shamelessly eavesdropped.

'No way, Stephanie,' Eamon said, although his tone was full of warmth. 'We'd be at each other's throats within days.'

'You're so heartless,' the young woman said. 'I don't know why I still love you.'

'It's your job, that's why,' he said.

Erin silently fumed. What an arrogant playboy! No doubt he had woman after woman hanging around for his attention. How annoying, if she was going to have to listen to him every night wooing his latest conquest. She had thought the dope-smoking university students were bad, but living next door to a modern-day Lothario was going to be completely sickening. What if she had to listen to him…? *Oh no, don't even think about it,* she reproached herself sternly. She would get some heavy-duty earplugs and turn up the music or something.

All went quiet for a moment and Erin edged away from the pantry door and sneaked a peek. Her eyes rounded in shock and disgust. The girl called Stephanie was barely out of her teens. What a jerk!

'Have you met any of your neighbours?' Stephanie asked, brushing back her mane of glossy dark hair and looking up at Eamon coquettishly.

Erin stiffened.

'Yes, I have, actually.'

'And?' Stephanie planted one hand on her hip and tilted her head at him.

'And it's none of your business,' he said. 'Anyway, she might be listening.'

Erin sucked in a breath and quickly flattened herself back against the pantry door.

'She?' Stephanie's voice rose. 'There's a woman living next-door? How old? What does she look like? Is she single? Is she nice?'

Eamon laughed. '"She" is one of the doctors at Sydney Met.'

Completely heartless, Erin thought. Had he no consideration for poor Stephanie's feelings? What if the poor girl was in love with him? After all, she had practically begged him to allow her to move in with him.

'Come on, Eamon,' Stephanie pleaded. 'Tell me the rest. You could be dating her for all I would know.'

As if! Erin thought.

'One shared curry hardly constitutes a date,' Eamon said.

'So you've had dinner with her?'

Erin couldn't quite make out the tone of Stephanie's voice. She didn't sound disappointed—incredulous, perhaps, but certainly not heartbroken.

'Just the once but it didn't go so well,' Eamon said. 'Anyway, she's not my type. She's uptight and prickly. And she's stubborn.'

Stephanie laughed. 'Ho, ho, ho, Mr Kettle, have you checked out your shade of black lately?'

'Cute,' Eamon said in a droll tone. 'Real cute.'

'Seriously, though, Eamon,' Stephanie went on. 'Is she pretty?'

Erin held her breath.

'So-so,' Eamon said. 'If you go for that girl-next-door look.'

So-so? Erin fumed. *So-so?*

Stephanie chuckled again. 'So, when do you think I can meet her to check her out for myself?' she asked.

'Well, if you stand over here where I'm standing, you can get quite a clear view of her,' he said.

Erin's eyes widened, and her heart gave a sideways lurch as she turned her head and encountered Eamon's amused emerald gaze.

'Come on out, Dr Taylor,' he said with a knowing smile. 'I'd like you to meet my youngest sister.'

His *sister*? Erin felt her colour rise to the roots of her hair as she peeled herself away from the pantry door. She squared her shoulders with what little pride she had left, and, sliding the doors fully open, walked out onto the balcony.

'Dr Taylor, this is my sister Stephanie,' he said. 'Steph, this is Dr Taylor.'

Erin put out her hand to the young girl. 'Nice to meet you. But please call me Erin.'

Stephanie beamed and shook Erin's hand vigorously. 'Lovely to meet you too, Erin. I've been hearing all about you.'

Erin shot a telling glance in Eamon's direction. 'Yes,' she said. 'So have I.'

Eamon gave her an enigmatic smile. 'Would you like to join us for dinner?' he asked. 'Steph's cooking. I'm pretty sure she won't poison you.'

Stephanie gave him a mock scowl before she turned back to Erin. 'Oh yes, please do join us,' she said. 'I'm doing a hospitality course. I'm trying out my recipes on Eamon. I've brought heaps of ingredients, so there's no shortage of food.'

Erin took a step backwards. 'I don't want to intrude on a family get-together or anything.'

'It's not a family get-together,' Stephanie assured her. 'If it was I would warn you to bring earplugs, right, Eamon?' She shone her winning smile at her big brother.

Eamon grinned back and playfully ruffled Stephanie's hair. 'They don't make earplugs thick enough to block out the Chapman sisters.' He turned his gaze to Erin. 'When the three of them are together, they make a heavy-metal band sound like muzak.'

Erin moved her lips in what was almost a smile. 'It must be lovely to have siblings.'

'Are you an only child?' Stephanie asked.

'Um…yes,' Erin said, conscious of Eamon's steady, watchful gaze.

'I used to long to be an only child,' Stephanie said musingly. 'All that attention, all those presents, not having to share anything and no hand-me-downs.'

'You haven't worn a hand-me-down in your life,' Eamon commented wryly.

Stephanie pouted and gave her brother a playful punch on the arm as she moved past. 'I'm going to check on dinner. Go and open the door for Erin or, better still, lift her over the partition. I'll open some wine for us.'

'How about it, Dr Taylor?' he asked with that same unreadable smile playing about his mouth. 'Do you want to come in the front door or over the balcony?'

Erin ran her tongue over her lips. The thought of those strong brown arms helping her over the partition was a lot more tempting than she wanted to admit. Her mind began to race with images of him lifting her off her feet, holding her against his rock-hard abdomen; the heat of his body seeping through her lightweight clothing. 'Er…I need to freshen up,' she said, brushing an imaginary strand of hair away from her face. 'I'll be five minutes or so.'

His gaze held hers for a nanosecond longer than she could comfortably handle. 'It's a date.'

Erin rummaged through her wardrobe impatiently, tossing clothes on the bed only to toss them to one side in frustration. When was the last time she had bought something new, for pity's sake? She had seen the casual but elegant clothing Eamon's sister was wearing; each piece had probably cost more than her entire wardrobe. She had taught herself to be frugal over the years. She'd had to ignore fashion trends during her teens; it had been enough to get food in her stomach, and even then it had been pretty hit-and-miss. Even now she had money she still wasn't really into the whole shopping thing. She felt too self-conscious; a part of her was frightened she would choose something too young for her, or tarty, like her mother always did.

Erin kept things plain and simple but there were times, especially like these, when she longed to feel more at home with her body, confident enough to wear close-fitting and feminine clothes like other women her age. She was lucky to be naturally slim, and she exercised regularly for the stress relief it gave her. But drawing attention to herself was something she wasn't used to doing; if anything, she did the opposite. Could she break a lifetime habit even if she wanted to?

In the end she settled for basic black: trousers and a shirt, which were both chain-store but comfortable. And, rather than pull her hair back tightly, she scooped it up in a looser style, letting a few strands fall about her face to give her a softer, more feminine look. She managed to eke the last contents of a wand of mascara over her lashes, and, with a smear of lipgloss and a quick spray of her only perfume, she gave Molly a wish-me-luck pat and left.

Eamon opened the door to her soft knock. 'Hi, glad you could make it,' he said, sweeping an assessing gaze over her.

She stepped over the threshold, carrying her keys and a box of chocolates. 'Something smells nice,' she said, handing him the chocolates. 'I'm sorry, I didn't have a bottle of wine in the cupboard.'

'These are great,' he said, taking them from her.

She shifted her weight. 'I didn't buy them,' she confessed. 'A patient gave them to me.'

'Male or female?'

'Male.'

He lifted his brows. 'Your bedside manner can't be all that bad, then.'

She gave him a dry look. 'When you're an eighty-nine-year-old widower who has lived alone for twenty-odd years and dying of prostate cancer, I guess anyone who stands by the bed is going to make an impression.'

Eamon smiled. 'You're being too hard on yourself, Dr Taylor.'

'What's with the formality, Eamon?' Stephanie asked as she poked her head around the door of the kitchen. 'Call her Erin, for goodness' sake. It's such a cool name, unlike Steph-an-ie.' She dragged out the syllables with a roll of her eyes.

'I think it's a lovely name,' Erin said. 'But do you prefer it shortened to Steph?'

'Friends and family call me that, so that would be cool if you do too,' Steph said. 'Hey, bro, can you find me the garlic crusher?'

'Do I have one?' Eamon asked, looking somewhat bewildered.

Erin watched the interplay between Eamon and his youngest sister and felt an ache deep inside for what she had missed out on in not having had a family unit to grow up in. There was an ease about Eamon and his sister, a companionship and camaraderie that was unlike anything she had experienced. Steph obviously adored her big brother and Eamon, although his manner at times was teasing, was clearly protective and very proud of her.

'One garlic crusher.' After rattling through several drawers, Eamon handed it to his sister like a surgical implement.

'Good boy. Now, pour Erin a glass of wine and take her into the lounge,' Steph directed. 'Oh, and don't talk about work!'

Eamon winked at Erin as he scooped up two glasses and a bottle of wine from the bench. 'Come on,' he said. 'We're better out of the way, believe me.'

Erin followed him into the lounge area, which was larger than hers. The decor was minimalist but stylish, reminding her yet again of the different worlds they had come from.

'So,' he said, handing her a wineglass. 'If not work, what shall we talk about?'

Erin took the glass, carefully avoiding his fingers as she did so. 'I don't know…hobbies?'

'Do you have any?'

She cradled her glass in both hands. 'I read.'

'What do you read?'

'Books.'

He gave her a droll look. 'What genre or genres do you like?'

Erin felt her face grow warm. 'I like…er…fantasy.'

'Interesting.'

'What about you?' she asked, trying not to appear flustered by his proximity. 'What do you like to read?'

'Biographies, history, science; that sort of thing,' he answered. 'My sisters are always at me to read other genres but I really like reading for information, not necessarily for entertainment.'

A silence hung in the air for a moment.

'What do you do in your spare time besides reading?' Eamon asked.

'I work out a little. I have a treadmill.'

'Handy.'

'Yes, I don't like running or walking in the dark,' she said. 'I guess that would be one of the benefits of having a dog.'

He smiled lopsidedly. 'I can't quite see Molly defending you from a would-be assailant, but then again I could be wrong.'

She took a sip of her wine. 'I hope you won't let slip that I have her—I mean with the body corporate,' she said. 'I like coming home to her after a tough day. It…it helps.'

Eamon watched as she perched on the edge of the nearest sofa, her wineglass cupped in her hands, her eyes not quite making the distance to his. 'I guess goldfish are not quite the same thing, are they?' he said.

Her brown eyes meshed with his. 'No, they're not.'

Another silence slipped past.

Eamon felt that delicious tug deep in his groin again. He felt it just about every time she looked at him. It was like a direct charge of electricity, zapping him to throbbing awareness. Their rather stilted exchange masked a simmering tension just beneath the surface. He could sense it in the way she held herself, the way her eyes flicked away from his as if she was frightened he would see more than she wanted him to see. He had enjoyed watching her eavesdropping. It had made him realise she did give a damn about what people thought, even though she strenuously denied it. Her face had been so expressive, full of pique, outrage and anger, that it made him all the more determined to get under her guard.

He looked at her mouth, the soft pillow of it looking so very tempting as she sat there sipping occasionally at her wine. He watched the up-and-down movement of her slim throat as she swallowed, and the hesitant sweep of her tongue across her lips. His stomach clenched low and deep with the thought of her doing the same to him. He felt his body swell inside his jeans, the rush of blood that he couldn't control even if he wanted to. God, the thought of slipping into her, having her clutch at him with her tight little body, was making his head spin. He wondered if she would be as hesitant and ill at ease in bed as she appeared in company. Or would she be all hungry tigress, scratching and clawing at him in ravenous need?

She suddenly looked up and locked gazes with him; the air in the room tightened like fencing-wire being strained.

Eamon felt the drum of his blood kicking in his veins, a roaring rush that drove every thought out of his head. He knew if his little sister wasn't banging pots and pans and utensils in the room next door he might very well have closed the distance between Erin and himself and taken his chances on a kiss, as he had been tempted to do the previous evening. As if she knew where his thoughts were leading, Erin sent the tip of her tongue out over her lips, her throat rising and falling again as her eyes slowly slipped out of the reach of his.

'Gosh, it's awfully quiet in here,' Steph said as she breezed in with a plate of nibbles. 'Can't you think of anything to talk about but work?'

'If you put two doctors into a room by themselves, what else do you expect them to do?' Eamon asked, reaching for an olive and popping it into his mouth.

Steph gave him a mock-despairing look before turning her gaze to Erin. 'I hope he hasn't been boring you. He's not the greatest conversationalist in the world.'

'He wasn't boring me at all,' Erin said, wishing she could control her propensity to blush. 'We were talking about…about pets.'

Steph's eyes lit up. 'Eamon told me you had a cat.' She perched on the arm of the sofa next to her brother, crossing one booted ankle over the other. 'So, do you have a boyfriend?'

'Stephanie May Chapman,' Eamon said warningly.

'What?' She looked at him in affront. 'I'm just making conversation.'

'It's all right,' Erin said before he could respond. 'No, I don't have a boyfriend. I don't have much of a social life at present.'

'Maybe we could set you up on a blind date or something,' Steph suggested. 'How about it, Eamon? Do you know of any suitable young men lurking around the hospital?'

He rolled his eyes as he pushed himself out of the sofa. 'Keep me out of it,' he said. 'I don't like people meddling in my affairs, and I'm sure Dr Taylor doesn't either.'

'Spoilsport.' Steph pouted. 'It's so hard for women to meet decent men these days. You could at least offer up a few suggestions.'

'I really don't need—' Erin began uncomfortably.

Steph was undaunted. 'When was the last time you went on a proper date?' she asked.

Erin pressed her lips together, thinking about it. 'Er, it was quite a while ago.'

'How long?' Steph asked.

Erin tried not to look in Eamon's direction. 'It was about seven years ago.'

Steph slapped her hands on her thighs as she looked up at Eamon, who was standing in a brooding manner near the windows. 'See? What's a young single working woman to do?'

'You seem to do all right for yourself,' Eamon pointed out wryly. 'You're only here tonight because your latest squeeze fell through at the last minute. Remember?'

Steph gave her head a little toss as she launched off the sofa arm. 'I'm going to check on dinner and my text messages to see if he-who-shall-remain-nameless has changed his mind.'

The room was as silent as an ancient tomb once the door to the kitchen closed.

'Sorry about—' Eamon said.

'Maybe I should—' Erin spoke at the same time.

'No,' he said. 'Don't let her scare you off. She's cooked for us; we might as well enjoy it. It sure beats cheese on toast.'

Erin picked up her wine again, and the point of her index finger made a pathway through the beads of condensation around the glass. 'She's lovely…' She looked up at him. 'You're lucky to have such a loving family.'

He gave a rueful grimace. 'You do realise we're being set up, don't you?'

Erin felt a frown stitch her forehead. 'Set up for what?'

'My family constantly despairs about me not settling down,' he said. 'When my father was my age—thirty-four—he was already married and had three children. Steph was a surprise package later in life.'

He came over and topped up both their wineglasses before he continued. 'When I hopped on a plane to the UK a couple of years ago, they were convinced I'd break all their hearts by falling in love with an English rose and never come home again.'

'You clearly didn't—not come home, I mean.'

He gave her another long look before he released a slow breath. 'No. I didn't fall in love, either.'

Erin couldn't quite work out why she felt such a flooding sense of relief at his words. 'Is it what you want to do?' she asked. 'I mean, settle down and have a family?'

He twirled the contents of his glass, took a sip and then answered. 'Yeah, I would like that. I've enjoyed my freedom as much as the next guy, but I must admit I'm a bit tired of coming home to an empty apartment after a gruelling day in A&E.'

'Maybe you should get a cat,' she suggested.

He smiled an enigmatic smile as he raised his glass back to his mouth. 'Maybe I will.'

Steph came bursting back into the room. 'Sorry, guys, but I have to dash. Last-minute change of plans. I've left everything ready for you. All you have to do is serve it once it's cooked. It should only take another twenty minutes.'

'Todd—or is it Tom?—changed his mind, huh?' Eamon asked.

Steph gave him a glowering look, but it wasn't long before a sheepish smile broke through. 'It's Todd and, yes, he did. I'm going to meet him for a drink.' She turned to Erin. 'I'm sorry about this. I hope you don't mind.'

'Of course not,' Erin said, starting to rise to her feet. 'It was nice of you to cook for your—I mean, us.'

'Don't get up,' Steph said, waving her back down. 'I know my way out. Stay here and chat to Eamon. Have a nice night.' She blew her brother a kiss and slipped out.

Erin met Eamon's amused green gaze once the front door clicked shut. 'She's so full of life,' she said. 'I feel incredibly staid and boring in comparison.'

He sat on the arm of the sofa his sister had vacated earlier. 'You're not boring,' he said. 'I find you rather intriguing as a matter of fact.'

Her brows lifted. 'You *have* been leading a quiet life. I can assure you there is nothing interesting or intriguing about me.'

He studied her for a lengthy moment. 'Why haven't you been on a date in seven years?'

Erin glanced at the wine in her glass. 'Too busy, too tired, too hard to please.' She lifted her gaze back to his. 'I'm not into the casual-fling scene. I'm not into settling down, either.'

'You sound quite adamant about that.'

'I am.'

'Who hurt you?'

Erin felt her defences go up like a swish of rapidly unsheathed swords. She had to work hard to hold his steady gaze. Her heart gave a stomping kick against her breastbone, and her stomach clenched as if a hand had snatched at her insides. 'Why do you ask that?' she asked in her best cool and controlled tone.

He lifted one shoulder in a shrug-like movement. 'Instinct. Intuition. Gut feeling.'

'I didn't know there was such a thing as male intuition,' she said, trying to keep her expression bland and her tone even. 'I thought that was the special domain of women.'

'Let's put that to the test.' He got up from the arm of the sofa and came and sat beside her. 'What's your intuition telling you now?' he asked, pinning her with his gaze.

Erin sat very still, but the surface of the wine in her glass rippled with her underlying apprehension. Her mouth was dry and she had to moisten her lips with her tongue in order to speak, an action that his all-seeing gaze closely followed. 'Um…I get the feeling you're going to make a move on me,' she said. 'But I would strongly advise against it.'

He raised one of his brows. 'Are you warning me you'll slap my face if I do?'

'I don't believe in using violence to get a message across.'

His eyes went to her mouth for a beat or two before slowly coming back to hers. 'So, no slapping if I kiss you.' He rubbed at his jaw, the scrape of his palm across his light stubble clearly audible in the pulsing silence. 'Now, that's tempting.'

Erin swallowed. 'D-don't even think about it,' she

said; her voice didn't sound strong and assured, however, but soft, hesitant and slightly breathless.

'I've been thinking about it since I ran into you when I came out of the lift.' His voice was a deep burr of sound that made the hairs on her scalp prickle with sensation.

'S-surely not.' She moistened her lips again. 'I was positively rude to you.'

His mouth tilted in a little half-smile. 'Are you apologising for that or just stating a fact?'

Erin was feeling more and more out of her depth. He was within touching distance. She could smell his clean, male scent. She could feel his body warmth. She could reach out and touch his chiselled jaw. She could reach out and run a fingertip over his lips. She could lean forward and meet his mouth halfway...

Or she could be sensible and get off the sofa.

'Don't even think about it,' he said softly, taking one of her hands before she could use it to lever herself upwards.

Erin drew in a breath, feeling it rattle all the way down into her lungs like loose change in someone's pocket. She looked down at her hand encased in his. She wondered how many lives those long, clever fingers had saved. Or how many women he had tempted into his arms and into his bed. 'This is not a good idea, Dr Chapman,' she said, still looking at the stark contrast of her lighter toned skin with his.

'What's not a good idea?' he asked in that sexy, deep baritone.

She met his gaze and then wished she hadn't. Intimate possibilities swirled around them like a heavy fog. She could so easily lose her way.

So very easily.

'You. Me. Us,' she said. 'It would never work.'

'What makes you so certain about that?' he asked. 'You've only known me a couple of days.'

'The work thing…' Her teeth savaged her lip. 'It…it always complicates things.'

His thumb began a mind-numbing stroke across the back of her hand, each lazy slide of his warm flesh against hers heating her to the core. She felt the slow melt of her resistance, and vainly tried to stop it. It would be so easy to give in to the eroticism of the moment, so easy to lap at the pool of longing, to dive beneath its rippling depths, to feel the pulse of his pounding blood within her silken cave.

'Maybe you're thinking way too much, Dr Taylor,' he said, bringing her hand up to his mouth.

Erin held her breath as she felt his lips brush against her fingertips. She felt the slight graze from his evening stubble, the brazenly intimate contact sending a shock wave of reaction through her belly and beyond. His eyes locked on hers as his mouth moved against each of her fingers in turn. She felt mesmerised by his touch. It brought such heat to her body, making it tinglingly alive. She gave a little gasp when his lips opened over her index finger, drawing its knuckle into the warm, dark, danger-ously tempting cavern of his mouth. She felt the sexy rasp of his tongue as it curled around her sensitive fingertip, her senses almost exploding in response. She could hear ringing in her ears, a buzzing sound that made her wonder if she was losing control of her mind, drawn into such a whirlpool of longing that nothing else made sense.

'Damn it,' Eamon said as he released her hand and got to his feet.

Erin blinked herself back to reality. Of course he would stop this nonsense; someone had to be sensible about this. It wouldn't do to let this go any further. It was crazy to think otherwise. It was crazy to think…

'Great timing, don't you think?' he asked as he moved towards the kitchen.

Erin frowned as she realised the buzzing wasn't coming from inside her head at all. It was the oven timer telling them dinner was ready. 'Er, yes,' she said. 'I guess it is.'

'Do you know how to switch it off?' he called out from the kitchen. 'I haven't used it before. I don't want to call Steph; I'll never hear the end of it.'

She got off the sofa on legs that felt like not-quite-set jelly and made her way to the kitchen. Eamon was leaning over the oven, peering at the dials, giving her a wonderful view of his jean-clad, taut behind. She came as close as she dared, reaching past him to press the button which should have had a tiny bell symbol on it but in this case was worn away from use. 'That's the one,' she said. 'It's exactly the same model as mine next door.'

He straightened and looked down at her. 'Amazing.'

Erin shrugged. 'You would have worked it out eventually.'

'I wasn't talking about the timer.'

She drew in a shaky little breath as he came closer. She didn't step away; in a galley kitchen there wasn't anywhere to go, or so she told herself later. 'Oh?' Her voice came out like a mouse squeak.

His arms settled either side of her, his hands resting on the bench, creating a cage for her body. His eyes meshed with hers, holding her entranced as each sensually charged second pulsed by.

'So, Dr Taylor,' he said in a low, deep rumble. 'Where should we go from here?'

Erin carefully inflated her lungs but even so she felt as if a handful of thorns had gone down with the air she breathed in. 'Um, you step back. I step back. Easy. Sensible. No harm done.'

His lips curved upwards. 'You think?'

Erin didn't know what to think. Her mind seemed to have switched off several minutes ago. Her senses were on high alert, each one screaming for more of his touch. Her tongue darted out to moisten her tombstone-dry lips; her heart lurched when she saw his eyes drop to her mouth.

Time slowed, frame by frame, as his head came down, lower, lower, the warm caress of his breath skating over the surface of her lips, heating her blood to a slow boil. Her breath mingled with his, an erotic union that sent her senses reeling even further. She closed her eyes as his mouth brushed hers, like a sable brush against a precious canvas, soft, light, careful. He did it once more, just as lightly, the barely there touch making her lips tingle for more pressure.

He lifted his head a mere fraction, his eyes heavy-lidded as they tethered hers. 'How's that intuition of yours?' he asked. 'Do you reckon it's time to stop or should we risk one more kiss?'

The winds had never had so much caution thrown at them as Erin stepped up on tiptoe, her hips brushing against the rock-hard wall of his. 'Maybe just one more…' she whispered.

'Better make it a good one, then,' he said, and covered her mouth with the explosive heat and fire of his.

CHAPTER FIVE

IT WASN'T as if Erin had anything in recent memory to compare it to, but she was sure she had never been kissed quite like that before. His mouth was commanding but not too controlling, warm and moist, but not slippery and sleazy. It was experienced, exciting and erotic. It was daring and even dangerous at times when he used his tongue to call hers into a duel-like dance that had blatantly sexual overtones. She was swept away with it, the pull of attraction like an undertow around her lower body. She felt the pounding of his blood against her pelvis as his erection hardened to steel, a thrilling reminder of his potency and power, and her vulnerability to it. Her body melted into his heat, the barrier of their clothes doing nothing to detract from the sensations she was feeling.

His mouth continued its sensual assault, not once lifting, just changing position until she was breathless and dizzy with whirling sensations.

His hands left the bench, cupping her face instead, adding a touch of tenderness that was unexpected and, because of it, all the more enthralling. His tongue circled hers, gently, cajolingly, until she found a rhythm that matched his: slow and sensual, then fast and furious, backing off to pace the passion and then grinding down again with ravenous need.

Erin's lips felt swollen but she kept on kissing him, her heart thumping like a madly swinging anvil when his hands moved from her face to settle just below her ribcage. His splayed fingers were so close to her breasts, making them pulse with an ache she had never felt before. Her nipples were tight and sensitive; just the pressure of his chest against hers was enough to make every nerve ending twitch in fevered response.

His mouth softened on hers, slowing down the hectic pace as his hands gently cupped her breasts. She dared not breathe in case he stopped; the slow roll of his thumbs over her distended nipples made her head reel.

She whimpered into his mouth as he moved aside her clothing, that first touch of skin on skin making her insides quiver. His hand was warm and dry and very, very determined. She loved the feel of him exploring her softness, the way she was a perfect fit for his palm. She loved the way his fingers were slightly calloused, as if he was no stranger to physical labour. It reminded her of his arrant masculinity, of the way he was so overwhelmingly male and not for a moment ashamed of it.

His mouth hardened as he deepened his kiss; the grind of his hips against hers and the low, deep groan he gave made her skin tighten with pleasure. It was reckless and foolish to respond so wantonly but she couldn't help it. It was like trying to stop a runaway train; the momentum was gathering inexorably as each second passed.

His hands moved from her breasts and settled against her hips, pulling her against his burgeoning heat with unmistakable purpose. She felt the frantic flutter of her pulse as his body signalled its need of hers, the increasing pressure of his mouth and the sexy stab and thrust of his tongue against hers sending her into a wheel-spin. Her body was slick with moisture; she could feel it pooling like warmed honey between her thighs. She had never felt such an overwhelming response; the sheer force of it took her completely by surprise. Was it her hormones raging out of control? Was it because she had not experienced red-hot passion like this before? Did she want him just because she *wanted* him? Was there no other reason than just the most basic pull of primal need to mate with someone potent, to be tamed by the leader of the pack, to be brought to sobbing submission in mind-blowing pleasure?

It was all of that and more, but it didn't mean Erin was going to give in to it. She had good reason not to. All her adult life she had fought against the instincts of the flesh, knowing how damaging they could be to one's freedom in the long run. She had seen it first-hand: the devastation of not being able to withstand temptation, the way a life could suddenly spiral out of control, never to be the same again.

She pushed her hands against Eamon's chest, fighting with herself all the way as she felt the play of hard muscle under her palms. She tightened her resolve, pulling her mouth out from under his. 'Sorry,' she said, her voice, not surprisingly, sounding husky.

'Time to stop?' he asked, still holding her by the hips.

Erin could feel the throb of his hardened flesh, so close to the achingly empty heart of her. 'Um…possibly shouldn't have started,' she said, running her tongue over her swollen lips, tasting him, tasting temptation, and only just resisting it.

He gave a chuckle of laughter that rumbled against her chest. 'Don't you like to live a little dangerously sometimes, Dr Taylor?'

She slipped out of his hold, folding her arms across her chest as she faced him. How like him to laugh at her. To make fun of her, to make light of what to her was so significant she didn't dare take it further. 'No, I don't,' she stated flatly.

'Erin…' He raked a hand through his hair in an endearing, almost boyish manner. 'Maybe I overdid it a bit. I'm sorry, but you have a very kissable mouth.'

Erin tightened her arms like whalebone stays across her body. 'There are plenty of kissable mouths you can choose from, but this one is now off-limits.'

He shook his head at her as if admonishing a small, recalcitrant child. 'You were the one who gave me the go ahead, remember?'

She summoned up a glare but it wasn't her best effort. 'One kiss, not a marathon. My lips feel bruised.'

He closed the distance between them, lifting his hand to trace the outline of her lips in a touch so gentle she could only just feel it. 'Maybe you're a little out of practice,' he said. 'When was the last time you were kissed?'

Erin felt her colour rise. Had he thought her responses clumsy and inexperienced? How embarrassing! No doubt he was used to very experienced, streetwise lovers, women who knew how to take and give pleasure. 'I don't have to answer that,' she said, stepping away from him again.

'You don't have to be ashamed of not putting it out there, Erin,' he said. 'I'm forever telling my two still-single sisters they should hold back. Men respect it, believe me. We might try it on, but deep down we don't want the woman we have a one-night stand with to end up being the mother of our children.'

Erin felt a funny sensation in the pit of her stomach as she looked at him. He would make some lucky girl a wonderful husband and father of her children. He had all the qualities that counted, and besides that he came from a rock-steady background. She knew how important good role-modelling was. She had seen the results of generational violence or addictive behaviour or both. Eamon was so lucky to have a solid foundation to build on. It made her feel the loneliness and isolation of her situation all the more acutely. 'Thanks for the morality lecture, but you've been preaching to the choir,' she said. 'I don't do one-night stands and I have no intention of having children.'

He gave her one of his thoughtful looks. 'Funny, but I didn't have you pegged as a career girl.'

'What makes you say that?' she asked, frowning at him. 'My career is very important to me. It always has been and always will be.'

He continued to hold her gaze as if he was peeling back the layers to the truth. 'If your career was so important to you, it would make sense that you would do everything in your power to enhance your chance of promotion. But word has it you've had issues with every director you've worked under. Not very wise if you want to advance your career.'

Erin pulled her lips into a tight line. 'If for once a director was hired who had less of an ego and more of a desire to bring about genuinely good outcomes for patients, I would not hesitate to follow orders.'

'I am all about good outcomes for patients,' he said. 'As to the ego, well, don't all good leaders need one in order to lead solidly and dependably?'

'Time will see,' she said with an arch look. 'So far all I've seen is great inconvenience to staff.'

His brows drew down over his eyes. 'That's rather rich coming from you, isn't it? You haven't yet attended one ward-round or information breakfast.'

She pressed her lips together before responding. 'I am under no obligation to do so when I'm on night duty.'

His frown became darker, more threatening. 'You've switched to nights?'

She raised her chin. 'I read in the document you passed around that the follow-through-care proposal didn't apply to doctors on night duty. The handover will remain as it stands, given the activity at that time of morning on the wards with the changeover of staff and breakfast and so on.'

His expression tightened, making a white-tipped nerve flicker like beating wings beneath the skin at the edge of his mouth. 'You really are determined to do things your way, aren't you?' he asked.

'My way works for me.'

'But what if it doesn't work for the patients?' he

asked. 'You lose all contact with them the moment you hand them over. You've been lucky so far, Erin, but what if the next patient suffers as a result of something you missed in the primary or secondary survey?'

Erin held his challenging look although she dearly would have liked to shift her gaze from the steely probe of his. 'I am always very thorough in my assessment and management of patients.'

His eyes became more intent on hers, more focused. 'What about the pain incident Arthur Gourlay referred to? Mrs Pappas, wasn't it?'

She opened her mouth, and then closed it, thinking carefully before she spoke. 'I know for a fact I signed for her pain-relief. I remember doing it.'

'Are you saying there are times when you *don't* remember?'

Erin heard the suspicion cleverly stitched in between each word of his question. Had Lydia Hislop spoken to him about their conversation in A&E about Mrs Fuller's follow-up pethidine shot? She liked Lydia—she was one of the few nurses she could see herself having a friendship with outside of work—but it didn't mean the nurse might not have used a private conversation to score some brownie points with the new boss. 'A&E, as you know, is a busy, often frantic place at times,' she said, choosing her words with care. 'And at those times it is a little difficult to remember every single detail—that's why the drug documentation protocol is in place.'

'That's if everyone is using it as it should be used,' he said.

She frowned. 'What are you implying? That I'm somehow not following hospital procedure?'

His penetrating eyes surveyed her for a pulsing moment. Erin felt as if she was under a powerful microscope. Every flaw, every chink in her armour, was being pulled apart and examined under intense scrutiny.

It worried her that she had become less meticulous due to the long hours she had worked recently. She had always set such high standards for herself. She hated thinking she might not have performed her job at maximum capacity. It had been a trying time with the death of the young man the other day; her concentration might have slipped. It was understandable; there had been such a lot going on, especially with the news of a new director arriving. And now she had made herself seem even more unprofessional by responding to Eamon Chapman's kiss with such wantonness.

Sydney was a big city but the medical world was small. It would only take one person to see them together and it would be all over the hospital. She already hated the gossip the hospital fraternity generated; she hated the stupid innuendoes that people went on about once they suspected two people were involved. Besides that, she hated mixing her private life with her professional one. She liked her life in neat, ordered compartments. She didn't like blurred boundaries. It made her feel insecure. And kissing Eamon Chapman made her feel very, very insecure. He was clearly toying with her. How convenient was it for him to have her living right next door to call over to play doctors with him whenever he felt like it? And what if he was only flirting with her to get her to see things his way? Did he see her as a challenge to conquer? A trophy he had to collect to show how proficient he was at his job? If so, he was in for a bigger challenge than he realised.

'That is not what I'm implying at all,' Eamon said into the tight silence. 'I am merely saying the system is not completely foolproof.'

'I know exactly what you're implying and why.' She scooped up her purse and keys. 'I've changed my mind about dinner.'

Eamon frowned. 'Hey, wait a minute. You can't walk out just like that. Steph's gone to a lot of trouble. What am I supposed to say to her?'

She gave him a hard little glare as she opened the front door. 'Tell her she's right—you were starting to bore the hell out of me.' And before he could say another word she shut the door in his face.

CHAPTER SIX

WHEN Erin arrived for night duty A&E was already full and had been for several hours. Michelle Oliver was the senior nurse on duty, a woman she had worked with many times before. Michelle was competent and steady under pressure but the downside was that she was one of the main arteries of the hospital gossip-network.

'Well, well, well, aren't you a lucky girl?' Michelle said as soon as Erin placed her bag in the lockable drawer at the doctors' station.

Erin kept her features as blank as possible as she straightened from the drawer. 'Why is that?'

Michelle folded her arms across her chest and gave her a conspiratorial smile. 'A little bird told me you had dinner with the new director last night.'

Erin felt a muscle ticking in her cheek but fought it back under control. *What little bird?* she wondered. Or had it been the man himself? 'Dr Chapman rents the apartment next to mine,' she said. 'His sister was visiting and invited me over. But your source is wrong because I didn't stay for dinner.'

Michelle's light blue eyes twinkled. 'Word has it he's

determined to win you over to his plans for the department, it seems, by fair means or foul.'

Erin looped her stethoscope around her neck, trying to keep her expression coolly detached. 'Excuse me,' she said. 'I have patients to see.'

'There's a bet running on how long it will take him to do it,' Michelle called out after her.

Erin stopped and turned around to face the grinning nurse. 'A…a *bet*?' she asked with cold incredulity.

Michelle nodded. 'The residents and registrars set it up. You're the only one who's against the changes. There's a carton of beer riding on how long it will take Dr Chapman to get you on side.'

Erin aligned her shoulders in a rigid stance. 'Does Dr Chapman know about this bet?'

Michelle met her gaze with equanimity. 'Who do you think is providing the beer?'

Erin threw herself into seeing the line-up of patients, determined not to think about what Michelle had said, but even so whenever she had a spare moment her anger would kick in like a hot blast of fuel near dry tinder. To think Eamon Chapman was secretly reeling her in for the sake of a game, a puerile locker-room joke that would no doubt be laughed about for months on end. Each time she encountered a resident or registrar in the department, she felt as if they were sniggering behind their professional façades. How many people knew about this stupid bet? Was everyone laughing at her, like they had done in medical school after her one disastrous date?

She ricocheted with fury, determined to take Eamon Chapman on head-to-head. He was not going to make a fool of her—not professionally, and certainly not personally. Not if she could help it.

Just when Erin thought she had things more or less under control in A&E, news came in of a high-speed-motorcycle-accident victim due to arrive via ambulance within minutes. She felt the rush of adrenalin flood her system as she mentally began to prepare herself. Motorcycle accidents were often serious, especially high-speed ones. It would take all of her concentration and professional training to set aside her private issues while she dealt with a life-and-death situation. This was not the time to be ruminating over Eamon Chapman's despicable ploy to get her on side. A patient's life was about to be placed in her hands; the responsibility had never felt more daunting. Only her experience at dealing with similar situations bolstered her confidence. The staff working with her were competent, especially Michelle, and the registrar, Tom Brightman, was one who had shown great promise right from his intern days.

The doors to A&E swung open as the ambulance personnel wheeled in the male victim, the more senior officer calling out the patient's details.

'Approximately twenty-five-or-six-year-old male involved in a motorcycle accident. He was found twenty metres from the bike, which appeared to have struck a guardrail after clipping a car. He was unconscious with a GCS of seven; the helmet was badly damaged. His right thigh was angled at thirty degrees with a compound fracture—we've splinted it and bandaged it to control blood loss. His left ankle was at forty degrees and also compound, and the foot pulse is weak. His pulse was a hundred and forty and BP eighty systolic. We've put in a fourteen-gauge canula and run in two litres of saline. He's been bagged and masked with high-flow oxygen. It took fifteen minutes to stabilise him and the trip took another ten.'

'Thanks,' Erin said, donning gloves, a mask and a face shield.

The patient was on a spine board and had a Donway splint on his right leg and a blow-up splint on his left ankle. He had been fitted with a hard collar to stabilise his neck. With the staff's help they shifted the victim to a resus bed as Erin prepared to intubate him, suctioning the mouth to clear his airway.

Tom Brightman came in after being called up to the ward by the nursing staff. 'What's going on?'

Erin filled him in as she began to intubate the victim, which was proving more difficult than she had first realised, as his face was so badly injured. She felt the tension build in her body; beads of perspiration trickled down between her shoulder blades as each precious second passed. 'He's not intubatable. I'm going to do a cricothyroidotomy,' she said. 'Michelle, get me a scalpel and size-six tracheostomy tube, stat. Tom, undo that collar, but keep his neck stabilised. What's his BP?'

'Seventy systolic,' the other nurse said. 'His shock is getting worse.'

Erin stabilised the trachea with her left hand and made a transverse stab incision into the cricothyroid membrane. She lengthened the incision, then spread it open using artery forceps and inserted a size-six tracheostomy tube and connected it to the oxygen. Relief flooded her as the patient's chest inflated with each squeeze of the bag. 'We've got an airway, thank God,' she said.

'Good work.' Eamon's voice sounded from just behind her. 'I'll bag him.'

'OK.' Erin forced herself to remain focused on the patient, even though her own airway felt as if it was obstructed. Why was he here? He wasn't on night duty according to the roster pinned to the cork-board in the office.

The second nurse had already adjusted the leg splint and re-bandaged the fracture site. 'The bleeding seems under better control,' she said. 'His BP has come up to ninety systolic.'

'You'd better check his chest, Dr Taylor,' Eamon said. 'He feels hard to ventilate.'

Erin listened to the patient's chest. There was good air-entry on the left but none on the right, which was hyper-resonant to percussion. There was bony crepitus all over the right chest. 'I'll check his trachea before you put the collar back on, Tom,' she said to the registrar. 'His neck veins are elevated. He's got a right tension pneumothorax. Michelle, get me a couple of fourteen-gauge cannulas.'

'If you want to switch places I can do that right tension,' Eamon said.

For a split second Erin wondered if he wasn't confident she was up to the task. Had he somehow guessed how stressed she felt? She thought she had masked her feelings well. Her emotions were on lock-down; she couldn't afford to think about this young man's parents or family waiting outside. She couldn't bear to think about facing them if he didn't make it. She had done it many times; she had walked the seemingly endless corridor time and time again, facing human devastation at its worst. Raw emotion; people gutted by the dreadful pain of loss. She had never got used to it; she wondered if she ever would.

'Dr Taylor?'

Erin met his gaze with gritty determination. 'It's fine,' she said in a clipped tone. 'I've done heaps of these.'

She proceeded to do a right-needle thoracocentesis in the second intercostal space. There was a distinctive hissing sound as the trapped air was released.

'That's it,' Eamon said. 'His ventilation's improved markedly. What's his pulse and BP?'

'Pulse one hundred, BP one hundred. I've got pulse oximetry on. Sats are ninety percent,' the nurse said.

'OK, we've got airway and breathing sorted for the moment. I'll take blood for path and cross-match, and we'll start a couple of units of O-negative. Dr Chapman, can you do GCS? Michelle, get these clothes off for full exposure, then set up for catheterisation and an NG tube,' Erin instructed, remaining in control of the resus.

After completing the secondary survey, Erin spoke to the general, orthopaedic and neurosurgical registrars, organised a head-to-toe CT scan once she was sure the hypovolaemia was managed and stable, and then formally handed the patient over to the general surgical team for definitive management.

Erin stripped off her gloves and bloody gown and

placed them in the bin. She felt a wave of exhaustion swamp her as she washed her hands at the sink. Every bone ached with tiredness and strain. She was running on empty, and she still had six hours left on her shift. It was a depressing thought that this was night one of five. What had she been thinking?

'Dr Taylor.' Eamon put down the patient's notes he was flipping through at the doctors' station when Erin came back from the bathroom. 'Can I have a quick word?'

Her brown eyes flickered with something. 'I still have patients waiting,' she said, shifting her gaze slightly.

'I just checked, and you're due for a half-hour break,' he said. 'Besides, Tom's a good registrar. He's quite capable of holding the fort for a few minutes. There's nothing urgent in there. I've already checked with the triage nurse.'

A second or two passed in silence.

'All right,' she said, still with that off-centre, guarded look.

He led the way to his office, aware of her stiff carriage—such a change from last night when she had been like a warm kitten in his arms, until she had slammed the door in his face after he'd pressed too many of her buttons. He hadn't been able to sleep for thinking about her, for wanting her. His body had throbbed for hours with the memory of holding her against him. He couldn't remember a time when he had been more turned on. Although it had been a while since he'd been intimate with anyone, he was a normal, red-blooded male in the prime of his life. He enjoyed the physicality of sex; he had never sought more than that with previous partners, but something about Erin Taylor made him want more. He hadn't worked out if it was because she was more of a challenge than most, or whether it was something more elemental. All he knew was he wanted to taste that soft mouth again, to feel her in his arms responding the way she had the night before.

He closed the door once they were both inside his office. Erin was standing with her arms folded across her body as if it was cold. 'I should apologise for last night,' he said. 'Things didn't exactly go according to plan.'

Her eyes hardened like brittle toffee. 'No, obviously not.'

Eamon closed the distance until he was standing just in front of her, not touching, but close enough to smell her light, feminine fragrance. 'What's going on?'

Her chin came up. 'Why don't you tell me?'

A frown pulled at his brow. 'You seem a little uptight. I've apologised for last night, but for most of the evening I thought we were getting on just fine. I even considered that we might start seeing each other a little more regularly, or at least that was the impression I got from you until you stormed out.'

Her mouth tightened. 'Sorry. I don't think that's a good idea.'

'What changed your mind?'

Her eyes glittered with sparks of anger. 'A case of beer has changed my mind.'

His frown deepened. 'What?'

She rolled her eyes in disdain. 'Oh, come on, Dr

Chapman, surely you don't need me to spell it out for you? I know about the bet.'

Eamon felt like scratching his head. Had he missed something somewhere? 'A bet? What bet? What are you talking about?'

She put her hands on her slim hips, in a pose that reminded him of his mother telling him in no uncertain terms what would happen if he didn't do his homework when he was about ten. 'The residents and registrars,' she said tightly. 'Apparently you are supplying the prize.'

Eamon raked his hand through his hair. 'Who told you that?' he asked.

Her eyes glittered with lightning flashes of anger. 'It doesn't matter who told me. Is it true?'

'Of course it's not true,' he said. 'I don't know anything about a bet. What's it about?'

She was still glaring at him. 'The bet on how long it would take you to get me to agree to your plans for the department. That's what last night was all about, wasn't it? The softening-up approach: a little flirtatious dinner by candlelight, a kiss or two to make me let my guard down. And then, hey presto, the one-and-only offsider finally capitulates and you punch your fist in the air in victory.' She stabbed a fingertip on his sternum. 'What a pity it didn't work, Dr Chapman.'

Eamon snagged her hand before she could pull away. 'Hey, wait a minute,' he said. 'I don't know anything about this.'

Her expression was livid as she tugged against his hold. 'Michelle Oliver told me all about it. And, let me tell you, if she knows then everyone knows. She also knew I was at your flat last night. How on earth would she know that unless you told her or someone else on staff?'

Eamon let out a long, low sigh as he let her hand go. 'I think I know how she might have found out about that.'

She cocked her brows expectantly, her hands on her hips in a combative pose. 'Well?'

He shoved his hand through his hair once more. 'I ran into Sherrie Mason earlier today—you know, the nurse I introduced to you when we were having coffee the other day?'

'Your ex-but-still-best-friends girlfriend?' she said with a sarcastic edge to her voice.

Eamon flattened his mouth. 'Sherrie goes to the same gym as Steph. Steph obviously said something, as Sherrie asked me this morning how my dinner-date with you went.'

She glowered at him. 'What did you say? That you got to work on me with a few kisses before I saw through your seduction plan and left?'

'Look, I realise this is exactly what you wanted to avoid—and me too, if it comes to that,' he said. 'I don't like people speculating on my private life, but sometimes it's unavoidable.'

She flashed him another fiery glare. 'If you don't call off that stupid bet, I will resign without notice.'

Eamon took a moment to compose himself. The department was short-staffed as it was. Erin was one of the best A&E doctors he had seen. Her competence dealing with the motorcycle-accident victim showed just how valuable a part of the team she was. She was clear and concise in her directions, and she had handled the drama with enviable calm. The last thing he wanted was for her to storm out during his first week on the job, and not just for professional reasons.

'I'll have a word with the residents and registrars,' he said. 'I'm sure it's just one of those things that got blown out to be more than it was. It was probably an offhand comment that got misconstrued.'

Her expression remained sceptical. 'Then it had better be sorted out, and quickly. I don't appreciate being the butt of puerile jokes amongst the junior staff.'

'Perhaps if you hadn't been so against working within the new guidelines none of this would have happened,' he said.

Her eyes widened in affront. 'So it's my fault, is it?'

'Don't put words in my mouth, Erin.'

She dropped her hands from her hips. 'I need to get back to the department. It's been a long shift.'

'Tell me about it,' Eamon said on a weary sigh. 'I've been here since seven-thirty this morning.'

Her expression softened a fraction. 'Why have you stayed back so long?'

He pointed to the pile of paperwork on his desk. 'I'm going through some patient records,' he said. 'It's tedious, but it needs to be done. I need to cross-check some information from the wards.'

Her eyes flicked to the papers on his desk before they came back to his. 'Is there something wrong with the records?' she asked.

'Not as far as I can tell, but then I'm nowhere near

finished,' Eamon said. 'It'll take me another couple of days to get through that lot.'

She opened her mouth but then pressed her lips together, as if she'd been about to say something but had changed her mind.

'Erin, about last night…' he began.

'I'd rather not talk about it.'

'We need to talk about it.'

She averted her gaze. 'There's nothing to talk about. We had dinner. We kissed. End of—'

'Don't say it.'

Her eyes flicked back to his. 'Don't say what?'

'End of story,' he said. 'That's what you were going to say, wasn't it? You like those short, sharp, to-the-point statements, but that's not really who you are, is it, Erin? Underneath that frosty façade you put up is a very warm and very sensual young woman.'

She pursed her lips like an old-time schoolmistress, shifting them from side to side for a beat or two, but even so he could see the way her cheeks bloomed with colour. 'I should get back to finish my shift,' she mumbled.

She made a move towards the door but Eamon stalled her with a hand on her arm. 'Wait, Erin,' he said. 'There's something I want to do.'

He brought her hand up to his mouth and pressed his lips against her stiff fingers, all the time holding her eyes with his. He felt the tension slowly ease out of her hand, her fingers finally relaxing against the curl of his.

Her eyes dipped to his mouth, hovering there for an infinitesimal moment, before coming back to his. He watched as the tip of her tongue came out in a sweeping motion, leaving a fine sheen of glistening moisture over her lips. He felt a punch-like jolt of desire deep in his groin, his blood leaping in his veins as he imagined her soft mouth pleasuring him, her tongue tasting him, stroking his length, curling around him tantalisingly before she gave him the ultimate sensual delight.

He suppressed a shiver as he brought his head down, and her soft gasp filled his mouth as it covered hers. Her lips were soft and malleable, eager to give and to receive. Her tongue met his as soon as he went in search of it, dancing around him shyly at first, and then with greater boldness. His blood hummed through his body, thickening him as he pressed against her. She melted against him, her arms snaking around his neck, her fingers tangling in the back of his hair, making him groan as he deepened the kiss.

He had never felt so totally bewitched by a woman. She was such an enigma—uptight and prickly one minute, soft and yielding to him the next. He felt as if he could never have enough of her. She tasted so sweet and yet so sexy, a heady combination that made his head spin with erotic possibilities. He wanted her so badly his body ached with it. The surging heat of his blood was like rocket fuel in his veins.

He turned her in one movement, pushing her back against his desk, his mouth going to the scented, smooth, velvet skin of her neck, his tongue tasting her before he nipped at her with his teeth in a playful little tug that evoked a whimper of pleasure from her. His hands went to her hips, holding her to his heat, relishing the feel of her so close. He brought his mouth back to hers, savouring its feminine allure, relishing in the way she responded to him so feverishly.

Her teeth nipped at his bottom lip, tugging on it before sweeping over it with the soft, moist salving glide of her tongue. He wanted to feel her skin, the silky smoothness of her breasts, the tightly budded nipples he could already feel digging into his chest. His hands went to shape her, the soft whimper of pleasure she gave thrilling him as he searched for the buttons on her shirt.

There was a knock on the door, jolting both of them upright. Eamon met Erin's wide-eyed gaze before he called out in a voice that was distinctly gravelly, 'Just a minute.'

Erin fumbled with her clothing, her breathing so ragged she felt as if she had just run a marathon with lead weights strapped on her legs. Her heart was beating madly, her mind was scrambled and her insides were quivering with unmet needs.

'Sit down and look relaxed,' Eamon instructed as he went to the door.

Erin mentally rolled her eyes. Relaxed? Who was he kidding? She had never felt more on edge in her life. Her nerves were jumping like live wires and her flesh was tingling from where he had touched her.

She sat on the chair opposite his desk and picked up a patient's file, pretending to read it while Eamon spoke with the staff member at the door over a matter to do with a patient in Intensive Care. She listened with one ear, but then her eye was drawn to the patient's name on the document in her hands: Mrs Melina Pappas. Her heart gave a little stumbling movement in her chest as her gaze went further down the page to a section where someone had circled her signature in yellow highlighter and placed a question mark right next to it…

CHAPTER SEVEN

'SORRY about that,' Eamon said, coming back to the desk. His eyes went to the document in Erin's hands, the tension in the room suddenly palpable.

'Why is my signature circled?' Erin asked, rising to her feet. 'What's going on?'

He met her flinty look without wavering. 'Nothing's going on. I am merely checking the records, as I said.'

Erin felt her heart pick up its pace. 'That's Mrs Pappas's file.'

'Yes, I know. I wanted to make sure Arthur Gourlay's accusation was dealt with quickly,' he said. 'I can find nothing in the notes to suggest anything untoward. That is your signature, I've already checked it.'

Erin compressed her lips, the lingering doubts circling in her head like a flock of pigeons looking for somewhere to perch. It made her feel uneasy to have uncertainty of any sort hanging over her. The thought of Eamon checking through the notes, studying her signature and every other detail to do with the patients she had treated, made her feel very ill at ease. What if there was a mistake? What if she had missed something? It was certainly possible. No one was perfect. No one could be one-hundred-percent focused all the time, especially in a place like A&E, where there were so many distractions as critically ill patients were ferried in and out. And then of course there was the trainee staff she had to keep an eye on, residents and interns, and even registrars at times didn't always follow directions. They were not the ones who had to take responsibility for any mistakes, however; it was the doctor who was ultimately in charge who had to step up to the plate.

'Maybe the patient just needed more than the standard dose of pain-relief,' Eamon said. 'She had a gangrenous bowel obstruction, after all, a painful condition.'

'Yes…' Her eyes fell away from his.

He took the file and placed it with the rest of folders on his desk. 'I've taken up enough of your break. You haven't even had a cup of tea.'

Erin met his eyes briefly. 'I don't want you to think that I'm the sort of person who does this…' she grimaced as she hunted for the right word '…you know, fraternises with colleagues during work time.'

He smiled as he sat on the edge of his desk, his arms loosely folded over his broad chest. 'I won't tell anyone if you don't.'

She chewed at her lip, her hand fidgeting with her ID badge. 'I feel embarrassed about what just happened.'

'The kiss thing?' he asked.

She nodded, her throat feeling tight as she swallowed. 'That and the bet thing. I'm sorry for shooting first before asking questions.'

He unfolded his arms and pushed himself off the

desk, coming to stand in front of her again. He brushed her cheek with the back of his knuckles in a feather-light caress. 'Forget about it, Erin,' he said. 'I would have jumped to the same conclusion, especially given what you'd been told. But I can assure you I had absolutely nothing to do with it. I admit I want you to commit to my plans for the department, but no doubt you have your reasons for not wanting the change. My job is to find out what they are and help you overcome your doubts.'

Erin lowered her gaze from his. 'It's not that I don't care about the patients. I do. They are someone's son or daughter, mother or father, uncle or aunt, cousin or niece, nephew—whatever. I never forget that while I'm treating them. I'm always thinking of the people waiting on the other side of A&E's doors: what they're feeling, the hope, the dread and the disbelief that something terrible has happened to the person they love, that they might never be the same again, or even worse not survive.'

'I know,' he said, resting his hands on her shoulders. 'I feel that too. But that's why I'm so committed to improving the system.'

She looked up into his clear, green eyes. 'I don't want you to think I'm deliberately being obstructive. It's just that I…I don't think I have anything further to offer than initial assessment and treatment.'

'I think you're once again underestimating yourself, Erin,' he said. 'I realise you're not as comfortable as some of the others at relating to the patients and their relatives, but that is a skill that can be worked at over time.'

'I've never been a people person,' she said. 'I like my own company.'

'You seemed to enjoy mine a few minutes ago,' he said with a wry smile.

Erin gave him a look of mild reproach. 'Yes, well, you do have a rather persuasive manner about you at times.'

He grinned at her again. 'Just you wait until I really lay on the charm. You won't know what hit you.'

Erin tried to suppress a little bubble of excitement that rose in her, but even so it was impossible to ignore the flutter of her pulse at his words. She was already floundering in an unfamiliar sea of sensual temptation. She had lost her bearings the first time he'd kissed her, and each of his subsequent kisses had made her cling to him like a raft. She had never experienced anything like it before. Her response to him was so out of character. She had certainly been attracted to the occasional man in the past, but only in a passing manner. She had never been in love. She wasn't sure if she had the capacity to allow someone to get that close to her. If they did, and then abandoned her, she knew she would be devastated, just as devastated as she had been each time her mother had let her down in the past. She had learned to rely on no one but herself. She felt safe that way.

Eamon Chapman, however, was threatening to disrupt that sense of safety. From the moment she had met him, he had challenged her. It was like fire meeting ice. She could feel herself melting a little further every time he was near her. Like right now, standing with his warm hands resting on her shoulders, his intense green eyes meshing with hers, the promise of passion in the sensual curve of his mouth. His body was half a step away from touching her from chest to thigh. If she let her breath out fully, her breasts would be almost brushing his chest.

'I'm not sure this is what I need right now,' she said, unable to hold his gaze in case her eyes belied her words. 'Maybe it's not what either of us need at this point. You have an important job to do. I don't want to distract you from it. I don't want to be distracted from my work, either.'

He seemed to wait a beat or two before he spoke, his eyes steadily holding hers. 'Erin, how would you feel about looking at my suggestions for the department on neutral ground?'

She looked at him warily. 'What do you mean?'

'There's a meeting being held this Saturday in the Southern Highlands,' he said. 'It's a one-day conference I've organised for A&E specialists in the area on follow-through care. You might have seen it advertised in the doctors' room. I want you to think about coming. You might find it more useful than the breakfast meetings here. I've invited a couple of specialists from interstate to speak on how their departments have coped with the changes so far.'

She drew her bottom lip into her mouth, holding it there for a moment before she released it. 'I don't know.'

He took her hand again and gave it a gentle squeeze. 'Think about it, Erin. We could drive down together early on Saturday. I could take you to meet my parents after the conference. They're only a few kilometres away from the hotel where the meeting is being held. I have my own cottage on their property, which has two bedrooms, so you don't have to feel too crowded. It would only be for one night in any case.'

Her brown eyes eyed him narrowly. 'Why would you want me to meet your parents?'

He smiled at her. 'Isn't that what a guy does when he's seriously attracted to a girl?'

She bit her lip again. 'I don't know. I'd have to find someone to feed Molly for me.'

'If you can't find someone, you could always bring her along. My parents wouldn't mind. They love animals.'

She let out a sigh. 'Are you always so intent on getting your own way?'

He raised her chin with his fingers. 'You know something, Erin? You have a habit of pushing me away with one hand while tugging me towards you with the other.'

'I'm not even touching you,' Erin argued. 'You're the one holding me.'

He dropped his hands. 'I'm not touching you now.'

'It feels like you are,' she said without thinking.

He smiled a disarming smile. 'Now, that's really interesting, because I can still feel your lips on mine.'

Erin looked at his mouth, and her insides turned to mush all over again. He was so heart-stoppingly gorgeous. His smile could melt steel; just one look from those forest-green eyes could send her pulse soaring out of control. His body was so vitally alive, so intensely male. She could still feel his hard male contours against her softer ones. Her body was still reverberating with the pounding of his blood where he had pressed his need to hers. It made her wonder what would happen if they actually did make love. She was a trained doctor;

she knew the female form, she understood sexual response. But somehow she knew making love with Eamon Chapman would be far more enthralling than anything she had felt or imagined.

But why was he pursuing her when he could have anyone he wanted? She'd seen the way the women on the staff looked at him. She had even heard some of the racy comments in the staff toilets about his physical assets. She was the last person he should be interested in, which made her wonder if he had an entirely different motive. Could she risk a relationship with him no matter what the cost?

She brought her gaze back to his. 'I guess I must be quite a novelty to someone like you.'

'Why do you say that?' he asked.

She gave a little shrug. 'I'm not able to offer you anything other than, well, you know…? An affair.'

His eyes darkened as they held hers. 'So you're considering having an affair—as you call it—with me?'

Erin disguised a little swallow. 'That's what you want, isn't it?'

He continued to hold her gaze with the mesmerising force of his. 'I would be lying if I said I wasn't interested in taking our relationship to the next level,' he said. 'You've seen and felt the evidence for yourself.'

She gave him a wry look. 'Indeed.'

He smiled as he brushed a strand of her hair back from her forehead. 'We don't have to rush into anything you're not ready for. I get the sense you're not very experienced. You can't be, if you haven't dated for seven years. But I respect that. In fact, I find it rather sweet.'

'The novelty factor.' She let out her breath on an exaggerated sigh as she lowered her eyes. 'I knew it.'

He raised her chin, locking his gaze with hers, his expression serious. 'No. Don't keep underselling yourself like that. You are a very beautiful and desirable young woman. Why do you have such low self-esteem? Has someone hurt you in the past?'

Erin moved out of his hold, hugging her arms across her middle. 'I can't help being the way I am. I've just never seen myself locked into a long-term relationship. I don't think I could handle the whole suburban thing: prams and pets, picnics on the weekend. I like my own space.'

'I'm not offering you "for ever", Erin,' he said. 'It's way too early to be thinking along those lines. I'm just talking about "for now".'

She drew in her lips as she surveyed his features. 'I can't help feeling this is more about your goals for the department than anything else. Michelle Oliver intimated as such. "By fair means or foul", she said.'

Eamon shook his head. 'No, that's not what this is about. I admit, I do want you to adopt my strategies for change, but do you see me kissing anyone else around here?'

Erin wanted to believe this was for real, that his attraction to her was just as genuine as hers for him. 'I'm just trying to be sensible about this,' she said. 'We want different things. How could a relationship between us work?'

'It will work because of what happens when we do this,' he said, placing his mouth over hers in a lingering kiss.

Erin felt her lips swell with immediate longing, and as he slowly pulled away her lips clung to his as if they never wanted to let go. She looked up at him, her heart feeling a squeezing tightness as she thought of the day when he would walk away from her and take up with someone else—someone more attractive, someone who wanted to settle down and play happy families, someone who would fit in with his well-to-do family. How would she feel if she was to run into him from time to time, like Sherrie Mason did? Could *she* see him as a friend, someone she had once dated but had moved on from without ill feelings or regret? Erin couldn't see how she would be able to do it without feeling robbed of something, without feeling insanely jealous that someone else was enjoying his kisses and his touch, experiencing his lovemaking. What was wrong with her? It wasn't as if she was prepared to offer him anything permanent. If the grapes she eventually reaped were too sour for her taste, wasn't that her problem, rather than his?

Erin's beeper sounded, fracturing the silence with its shrill pulse of urgency. She glanced down at the small screen and grimaced. 'I need to get back. There's another MVA on its way.'

When Erin got home she felt too wired for bed. She had never been particularly good at sleeping during the day. The street she lived on was relatively quiet, but in the distance she could still hear the rumble of traffic, the occasional tooting horn, or, because the hospital was only a couple of suburbs away, a police or ambulance siren. Each time a siren sounded, she would jerk upright, her heart jump-starting with adrenalin.

After she fed Molly she got on her treadmill and ran

for forty minutes, enjoying the mindlessness of running nowhere. But, once she was finished and had showered and put on her pyjama bottoms and a cotton T-shirt, she still didn't feel anywhere near ready to switch off.

She drummed her fingers on the balcony rail as she watched the harbour with all its bustling activity, a restlessness consuming her that was unlike anything she had felt before. Her eyes kept wandering of their own volition to next door. She knew there was no possibility of Eamon being home at this hour. She hadn't seen his car in the car park downstairs, which meant he had left before she got home. He wouldn't have had much sleep, she thought in empathy. He had left A&E soon after the MVA victim had stabilised enough to be transferred to Intensive Care, which would have given him two hours, three at the most, to rest before he was back at the department.

She wandered back into the apartment, but just as she was about to lie down her phone began to ring from the charger on the kitchen bench. She picked it up, her spirits plummeting even further when she saw her mother's name on the caller ID. 'Mum, how are you?' she said in a toneless voice.

'Ez, I've got a big surprise for you,' Leah Taylor said.

Erin felt her spine stiffen in apprehension. 'Oh? What is it?'

'I'm here in Sydney,' Leah said in excitement. 'I got one of those cheap flights. It cost less than the taxi from the airport. I flew in first thing.'

Erin's palm moistened against the phone she was holding. 'So…where are you staying?'

'*Ez-zie!*' Her mother's voice had a whining edge of reproach to it. 'Where do you think I'm staying? With you, of course. I'm downstairs right now. I wanted to surprise you. Are you surprised?'

'Totally blown away,' Erin said flatly.

'So are you going to let me in or not?'

'Are you alone?' Erin asked.

'Yeah, I got rid of that creep Brad. He was pinching my… Er, I mean, he was cheating on me.'

Erin closed her eyes as she leant back against the pantry door. 'So how long are you going to be in Sydney?' she asked, silently dreading the answer.

'I haven't made any firm plans,' Leah said. 'Hey, are you going to open the door or what?'

Erin pushed herself away from the pantry door and reached for the security pad with dread weighing heavily in her chest. 'I'm on the fifteenth floor, apartment 1503. And don't smoke in the lift.'

When she opened the apartment door to her mother's knock, Erin tried not to show any emotion, but inside her heart felt as if it had been seized by an artery clamp. Her mother was stick-thin; her once-chestnut hair was now bottle blonde with grey roots showing through, like the silver trail of a snail. Her skin was wrinkled beyond her years, weathered by too much sun, too many cigarettes and too many illicit substances. She was wearing black jeans that were so tight they looked like they had been sprayed on, her leopard-print top showing what would have been a cleavage if her weight was in the normal range.

Leah stepped past her into the apartment and, turning, put her bag down and placed her hand on one hip, jutting it forward like a catwalk model. 'Aren't you going to give me a hug?' she asked.

Erin closed the door. 'Sure,' she said, stepping forward and hugging her mother in an embrace that felt awkward and unnatural and heartbreakingly unfamiliar. How many times had she longed for affection as a young child and been pushed away? How many times had she cried herself to sleep at night in yet another stranger's house, not knowing where her mother was or even if she would ever come back to claim her?

'Well, then,' Leah said. 'Let me look at you.' She placed her index finger against her mouth, the rest of her fingers propped beneath her chin. 'You certainly don't do much to enhance your features, do you, Ez? What *is* that you're wearing?'

'They're called pyjamas, Mum,' Erin said, folding her arms across her chest. 'I was about to go to bed.'

Her mother's eyebrows, plucked to a single line of hair, rose. 'At this time of day? What have you been doing all night? Partying?'

Erin rolled her eyes. 'No, strange as it may seem, I've been working. I'm on night shift for the rest of the week.'

Leah plonked herself down on the sofa, swinging one broomstick-thin leg over the other. 'That's a pain, because I wanted to spend some time with you.'

'How nice of you to think of me, Mum, but you're about three decades too late.'

Leah pursed her lips. 'You don't ever give me a break, do you, Erin? You always want to blame me for everything that's not right in your life.'

Erin unfolded her arms, trying her hardest to rein in her temper, to hold back the avalanche of hurt feelings that was threatening to consume her. 'Everything is just fine in my life,' she said. 'I have a roof over my head, something other than junk food on the table, a full-time job and—'

'And a cat,' Leah cut in disparagingly.

'*And* I have a man I'm seeing.' The words spilled out before Erin could stop them. Once they were spoken she felt as if she had committed herself. It felt strange, and yet right somehow.

Leah's hair-thin brows rose again. 'Who is it? Another doctor?'

'Yes, as a matter of fact. He works at Sydney Met. He's my boss.'

'Careful, Ez,' her mother said, hunting in her handbag for cigarettes. 'You don't want to complicate your life with men who can hold something over you, like your job. Before you know it, he'll have you fired for some paltry reason when his interest in you runs out.'

Erin snatched the cigarettes out of her mother's hand. 'No smoking in my apartment,' she said. 'If you have to poison your lungs, do it outside on the balcony, but close the sliding doors.'

Leah rolled her eyes as she got off the sofa. She snatched the cigarettes back and went towards the balcony. 'God, you're such a party pooper,' she said. 'How could I have had a daughter so straight-laced?'

How could I have had a mother so unlike the mother I most needed? Erin thought with an ache deep inside her chest. 'I'm a doctor, Mum,' she said, pointedly closing the balcony doors as she joined her mother outside. 'I have to deal with the results of years of smoking. It's not a pretty sight, let me tell you.'

Leah blew a plume of smoke past Erin's right shoulder. 'You only live once, love,' she said. 'Might as well make the most of it.'

'Well, you've certainly done that,' Erin said, waving a hand in front of her face.

Leah's weathered face became pinched. 'You're so quick to judge. You don't know what it was like for me.'

Erin folded her arms again. 'Don't start, Mum, I haven't got the violin tuned.'

Leah tossed her cigarette butt down onto the balcony tiles and ground it out with the heel of her snakeskin boots, her mouth pulled so tight it looked like a drawstring purse. 'One day you'll be sorry you've treated me the way you do. One day when you're old and all alone with no one who cares about you. That's what you're going to end up like, Erin. Do you realise that? You might have a man interested in you now, but how long will that last? You don't know how to keep a man in your life. You push them away just like you push everyone away. You're incapable of loving anyone. You don't even like yourself.'

Erin stalked back inside the apartment. 'I'm going to bed. Make yourself at home.'

'I want us to become close, Erin,' her mother called after her. 'It's what I've always wanted.'

Erin sent a glance heavenwards and turned back around. She opened her mouth to fling back a stinging retort, but something in the expression on her mother's gaunt face stopped her. She blew out her breath on a sigh. 'I want that too, Mum,' she said, so softly she wasn't sure her mother even heard it. 'I want that too.'

CHAPTER EIGHT

ERIN didn't see Eamon in person for the rest of the week. He was attending a course in Melbourne on hospital management, which meant she hadn't had to worry about introducing him to her mother. He had texted her several times, reminding her about the conference on the weekend in his last one, to see if she had made up her mind about attending.

She hesitated before she texted him back with her answer. She wanted to go to show she was keen to develop her skills professionally, but the prospect of being with him for most of the weekend was a huge step for her to take. He had assured her his cottage had separate rooms, but how many kisses would it take before she was in his arms and in his bed? It wasn't that she didn't trust him—it was herself she didn't trust.

It didn't help that her mother's words had echoed in her head over the last few days. Would she end up alone and lonely unless she lived a little now? What was the harm in seeing where things with Eamon went? She was young and healthy and, after working so hard, surely deserved some fun in her life?

Erin had deliberately not mentioned to Leah that the man she was dating was living next door. That would have been asking for the sort of complications she could well do without. She could just imagine her mother sashaying over there with a wine cask and cigarettes in hand, looking for a chance to party.

Her relationship with her mother was still on shaky ground. Erin worked hard at toning down her bitterness, and she could see Leah was making an effort not to get in the way. In any case, Leah slept late most days, and pottered about the apartment for the afternoon before going out at night. Erin didn't ask where she went or what she did. She didn't really want to know. She had laid down some ground rules: no men, no drugs. She'd had to compromise on the smoking and drinking. She knew it would be impossible to police it with her being on night duty.

Just before Erin began her last night on night duty, the receptionist in A&E informed her that a patient's relative was waiting to see her.

'I've sent her to wait for you in the counselling room,' the receptionist said. 'I thought it would be more private than the waiting room, with the patients listening in.'

Erin made her way to the small lounge-like room set up for relatives of seriously ill patients. Going in there nearly always made her feel a sense of dread. She had witnessed so much pain in there, the walls almost seemed to sag with it. When she got there the door was ajar, and when she pushed it open she found a young woman in her mid-twenties sitting there, very obviously pregnant.

'Dr Taylor?'

Erin nodded and offered her hand. 'Please don't get up,' she said. 'What can I do for you?'

'You treated my boyfriend the other day,' the young woman said. 'Josh had a motorcycle accident. Do you remember him?'

'Of course,' Erin said, sitting on the edge of the nearest sofa. A wave of guilt washed over her as she thought about the young man. Why hadn't she gone upstairs to see how he was getting on? Wasn't that what Eamon Chapman was fighting for—the ongoing care of critically ill patients as people, not bodies on gurneys? They were people with lives, with hopes and dreams, and with people who loved them. 'I'm sorry,' she said. 'I should have gone up to the ward to see him. I've been so busy I—'

'Please don't apologise,' the young woman said. 'I'm just so grateful for what you did. Josh wouldn't be alive if it wasn't for you.'

Erin felt uncomfortable with the praise, and shifted in her seat. 'I work as part of a team,' she said. 'I can't claim any special attention for helping Josh pull through. I had some great people working with me that day.'

'Yes, I know, but Dr Chapman told me you were one of the best A&E doctors he'd ever worked with,' the woman said. 'I'm Alice, by the way.'

'I'm Erin,' Erin said. 'It was nice of Dr Chapman to say that but, really, he was just as skilled, if not more so.'

'He's been lovely to me through this ordeal,' Alice said, her hand going to her protruding belly. 'I was so scared Josh wouldn't live to see our baby being born.'

Erin swallowed, dragging her eyes away from the swollen belly. She had seen a tiny foot—or was it a hand?—move under the close-fitting garment Alice was wearing. A lump formed in her throat, dry and boulder-sized, and for some strange reason she felt like crying.

She hadn't cried in decades.

'How is he?' she asked in a hoarse-sounding voice.

'Josh is still in a coma,' Alice said. 'But the neuro-surgeon, Mr Blackwood, is confident he'll wake up in a day or so.'

Erin wondered if Ben Blackwood was being overly positive, given Alice's pregnant state. Ben was a top-notch neurosurgeon, in fact he and his lovely wife, Georgie, were two of the most highly qualified and experienced neurosurgeons in town. But they were com-passionate too, and would not want to burden a distressed relative with more information than was necessary. It was important to offer whatever hope one could. 'Josh is in very good hands,' she said, feeling hopelessly inadequate.

'I have something for you.' Alice opened her large handbag and took out a neatly wrapped rectangular parcel. 'I made it myself while I was sitting by Josh's bedside over the last couple of days and nights.'

Erin took the parcel with fingers that felt almost numb. She untied the pretty pink ribbon, her thoughts going to all the birthdays when there had been no present for her, not even a card. It wasn't her thirtieth birthday for another couple of months, but she felt a thrill rush through her as if it was the first present she had ever received. She peeled away the sticky tape and unfolded the paper to find a beautifully framed piece of cross-stitch of a terrace house similar to the sort that parts of Sydney were well known for. 'I don't know what to say…' Erin traced her hands over the frame. 'It's absolutely beautiful. No one's ever made me something like this.'

Alice beamed. 'I'm so glad. I was going to bring you chocolates or wine, but that's not something that will last. I wanted you to remember me and Josh. I know you see a lot of patients, you probably forget all the faces and names over the years, but I wanted you to know you will never be forgotten. If we have a girl we're going to call her Erin, and if we have a boy he's going to be Eamon. We haven't been told the sex. We wanted it to be a surprise.'

Erin bit the inside of her mouth. She could feel her bottom lip quivering even though she bit down until she tasted blood. The pretty terrace house blurred in front of her and she hardly realised she was crying until a tear fell like a raindrop on the little row of flowers Alice had painstakingly stitched.

Alice leaned forward placed a hand on her arm, her expression clouding with worry. 'I didn't mean to upset you.'

Erin looked at her through watery eyes. 'You haven't. It's just that I feel very honoured and very touched you've gone to so much trouble, especially when you're going through such a harrowing time.'

Alice smiled. 'You're a very special person, Dr Taylor. When Josh wakes up, would you be able to come up to Intensive Care so he can thank you in person?'

'I'll come up when I've finished my shift,' Erin promised.

When she went up to Intensive Care the following morning, Alice was sitting beside Joshua Reynolds's bed, looking at him lovingly. The ventilator hooked up to him to keep him alive until he could breathe on his own was hissing and groaning, and the various tubes and lines coming out of his body reminded Erin of how lucky he was to be still alive so far. She hadn't seen the CT of his brain, which made her feel another wave of guilt. The least she could have done was call Ben Blackwood to see how Josh was doing.

'Dr Taylor!' Alice greeted her warmly.

'Hi, Alice,' Erin said with a little smile. 'How's he doing this morning?'

'Well, he's not awake yet, but the day has only just started,' Alice said cheerfully.

Erin admired her positive attitude. It was so refreshing, and it made her feel a little more hopeful herself. She had become so jaded over the years, not allowing her hopes any ground in case she had to relinquish it later. Maybe it was her personality and not so much her background, she thought. Maybe her mother was right—maybe she didn't really like herself.

Erin looked at the chair Alice had been sitting in. 'Shouldn't you be sitting in something a little more comfortable than that?'

'It's all right; I don't want to be a nuisance.'

'You're not being a nuisance,' Erin insisted. 'I'll have a word with one of the orderlies to see if they can bring in one of the armchairs from the doctors' room.'

Within a few minutes an orderly had brought in a comfortable armchair and, after another chat, Erin left Alice to have a quick word with the senior nurse on duty about making sure Alice was provided with proper nutrition and drinks. She explained to the nurse that Alice was so devoted to Josh that she barely left his bedside.

'I'll see what we can do,' the nurse said. 'I'll have a word with the kitchen.'

'Thanks, I'd appreciate it,' Erin said. 'She's at least five or six months pregnant and has been through a very worrying time. And it's not over yet.'

'I know,' the nurse said on a sigh. 'I just hope he makes it.'

Erin glanced back at Josh's cubicle. 'He'll make it,' she said, borrowing a little of Alice's confidence.

Erin was putting Alice's gift on the front seat of her car in the hospital car park when she saw Eamon getting out of his car a couple of spaces away.

He smiled at her as he came over. 'How are you, Erin?'

'Fine.' She self-consciously tucked a strand of her hair back, knowing how wrecked she looked from a night on duty. She already knew from her last visit to the bathroom her eyes had suitcases under them, and her skin was pale, making her freckles stand out like brown felt-marker points. 'How are you? How did the seminar in Melbourne go?'

'It was OK,' he said. 'I just flew in. I haven't even been back to the apartment.'

Great, Erin thought. He hadn't run into her mother. Yet.

'Have you had breakfast?' he asked. 'Do you fancy a quick tea and toast across the road before you go home to bed?'

Erin was far more in need of his company than the tea and toast. Just seeing him face to face made her realise how much she had missed him. He looked so gorgeous in his white shirt, red-striped tie and dark trousers with their razor-sharp creases. His eyes looked fresh and clear, his skin smooth from a recent shave and his dark hair neatly groomed. 'That would be nice,' she said, giving him a small smile.

'Of course, we'll have to risk the gossip,' he said as he led her by the elbow across the busy street. 'By the way, I had a word to the persons involved in that bet you were telling me about.'

'Yes, I know,' she said. 'A couple of them apologised when I crossed paths on duty.'

'Good.' He shouldered open the café door, his eyes sweeping over her face. 'Hey, you look tired.'

'I hate it when people tell me that,' she said. 'It always makes me feel far more tired than I actually am.'

'I know, but five nights on duty is a tough call.' He held out a chair for her. 'Do you find it hard to sleep during the day?'

'A bit,' she said as she sat down. 'The first day is the worst. After that I kind of get into a routine.'

The waitress came over and took their orders. Erin sat back and watched as Eamon's easy charm brought a tide of colour to the young girl's face. She knew the feeling, that heady rush of sensation at having his undivided attention. Those intense eyes with their ink-spot pupils were enough to make any woman go weak at the knees, whatever her age or marital status.

The waitress moved away and Eamon met Erin's gaze. 'So, tell me what you've been doing while I've been out of town.'

'Um…working and sleeping.'

'How's Molly?'

'She's good.'

A little silence passed.

'Steph says hello.'

'Please say hello back.'

'You haven't changed your mind about tomorrow, have you?' he asked.

Erin gave him a sheepish look. 'Only about a hundred times.'

He smiled at her. 'I knew you'd be madly thinking up excuses why you couldn't come. You'll enjoy the break from the city. And I know you'll love my parents' place.'

'Where do they live?'

'They live about five kilometres out of Bowral,' he said. 'My mother is a very keen gardener. The place is amazing at this time of year, with the autumn leaves.'

'So you didn't grow up in the city?'

'Yes and no,' he answered. 'Cloverfields was our country residence. We spent our holidays there but we had a house in the city, in Turramurra. My parents sold it when they retired and now live exclusively at Cloverfields.'

'It sounds lovely,' Erin said, thinking again of how different their backgrounds were; they couldn't have been more disparate. His family's wealth and status in the community, both city and country, was something he probably took for granted. Most of the wealthy people she knew did, they didn't have a clue how the other half lived.

'You've got a wistful look on your face,' he said.

'Have I?'

He smiled and reached for her hand. 'Did you miss me?'

Erin felt a warm sensation pool in her belly as his fingers wrapped around hers. 'A little, I guess.'

His eyes darkened as they held hers, his voice gravel-rough as he said, 'I missed you too. I wish I could have squirreled you away from work to come with me.'

Erin thought of how nice it would have been, secreted in a luxury hotel room with him: no prying eyes, no ribald jokes, no gossip and innuendo, just the two of them getting to know each other. She felt a little shiver tiptoe down her spine. What would it be like to be a normal young woman for once, to have a love affair and not agonise over when it might end?

'How about we head out of town after I've finished work this evening?' he said. 'That way we can have two nights away, not just Saturday.'

Erin hesitated as she thought about it. She couldn't remember the last time she'd had a weekend out of town. Somehow the thought of spending the weekend at her apartment with her mother was not all that exciting, and certainly not as exciting as being with Eamon. 'Er…are you sure?'

'Of course.' He released her hand, picked up his coffee and took a quick sip. 'Did you find someone to feed Molly?'

Erin cupped her tea cup in her hands. 'Actually, I do have someone who could feed her for me…'

'So it's all settled, then,' he said. 'You can go home and sleep, and once I finish work I'll quickly pack and we can get going. We might even miss most of the traffic if we're lucky.'

They walked back to the car park together, his longer stride shortening to match hers. Erin felt his broad shoulder brush against her once or twice, and as they crossed the road he cupped her elbow again in a protective manner. Her skin leapt at his touch even through the lightweight fabric of her cardigan. He stood waiting for her to drive off; the last sight of him from her rear-view mirror was him lifting his hand in a wave, a smile creasing up the corners of his eyes.

'Mum?' Erin closed the door of the apartment. She wrinkled up her nose at the smell of cigarette smoke. Even though she had insisted her mother go out on the balcony to smoke, Leah didn't always remember to close the doors. The stale, acrid smell was starting to permeate the curtains and soft furnishings. 'Mum, are you home?' She raised her voice a little as she slid the balcony doors open to let in some fresh air.

She tossed her keys on the counter and wandered through the rest of the apartment, opening windows as she went. A feather of unease brushed the base of her spine as she checked each of the rooms. How many times during her childhood had she come home to this air of the unknown? It was like an odour in the air, a pungent premonition of something not quite right.

Erin found the note on her bedside table. It was scrawled in her mother's distinctive hand, as if a hen with a pen in its beak had pecked at the piece of paper haphazardly. She joined the dots as best she could, finally making out that her mother was going to stay with a friend for a few days. There was no address, no contact details, and no 'I love you' either.

Erin sat on her bed with a sigh, her foot banging against something that jutted out from beneath the valance. A frisson of alarm rushed like a startled gecko up her back. She stood up and dropped to her knees, her heart racing as she pulled her doctors' bag the rest of the way out from under her bed, where she kept it unless she was driving further than to and from the hospital. The bag was partially unzipped, as if someone in a hurry had not quite completed the task. Erin glanced over the airway equipment, the neatly wrapped bandages, the little packets of sutures, the stethoscope coiled like a two-headed snake, and the place where the syringes should have been but weren't.

Her eyes flashed to the drug compartment, her heart giving a knockout punch to her chest wall when she saw it was empty: no morphine, no diazepam, no adrenalin and no hydrocortisone.

She sat back on her heels and put her head in her hands. 'Oh, Mum!' she cried. 'How could you do this to me?'

'How's he doing, Alice?' Eamon asked as he visited Intensive Care towards the end of his shift.

'He squeezed my fingers!' Alice said with a rapturous smile. 'It was only slight, but it was the first time he responded to my voice. Mr Blackwood says we might be able to turn off the ventilator as soon as he shows more signs of waking up.'

'Alice, that's fabulous news,' Eamon said. 'He'll have

a long road ahead in rehab, but it looks like he's going to make it. You've done a brilliant job supporting him. He's a very lucky man.'

Alice smiled. 'Dr Taylor came to see him. She got this special chair brought in for me. Wasn't that lovely of her?'

Eamon glanced at the leather chair with its comfortable padded arms and lumbar support. He felt a little hook-like sensation tug at something deep inside his chest. Erin Taylor might like doing things her way and in her time but there was no doubt she cared about the patients and, yes, even their relatives and loved ones. She just didn't like showing it. 'That was very kind of her,' he said. 'I'm sorry I didn't think of it myself.'

'That's OK.' Alice smiled. 'Are you off home now?'

'Just about.' Eamon clipped Josh's file back on the end of his bed. 'Can I get you a coffee or tea or something before I head off?'

'No, thanks, I'm fine. The nurses have been looking after me. I think Dr Taylor might have said something to them, because they've been bringing me extra snacks when the meal trolley comes round.'

'You need to keep your strength up,' Eamon said, feeling that hitch again. 'I'll be in on Monday to see how things are going.'

Eamon gave Erin's door a knock and waited, his packed weekend bag at his feet. He felt a delicious thrill of anticipation about this weekend. He loved visiting his family, but having the shy and unworldly Erin Taylor with him was doubling his delight. He felt like a teenager going on his first date: nervous, excited and convinced he was falling in love. He laughed at himself; no, it was too soon to be talking like that. Besides, she insisted she was a career girl, and he wasn't going to marry someone who didn't want to have his kids. He wanted what his parents had: long-term love and commitment to family.

Of course, if he could get Erin to change her mind…

The door opened a sliver and half of her face peeped out. 'Hi… Look, I'm really sorry, Eamon, but I can't make it after all.'

Eamon frowned. 'Are you OK?'

'I'm fine. Well, maybe not fine. I think I'm just over-tired from night duty.'

'Open the door, Erin.'

It was a full five seconds before the door opened. He counted them. He was shocked at her appearance. Her face was pale and her eyes were red-rimmed as if she had been crying. 'Hey, sweetheart,' he said, closing the door as he stepped inside. 'What's on earth's the matter?'

She bit down on her trembling bottom lip and he reached for her, holding her against him, his chin resting on the top of her silky head. 'You've been crying, haven't you?' he asked.

She nodded against his chest. 'Sorry, I'm not normally this emotional.'

'You're tired and all out of whack,' he said. 'What you need is a dose of my mother's cooking and nurturing.'

She pulled back from his hold and looked up at him. 'I haven't got anyone to look after Molly.' Her gaze fell away from his. 'The person I had in mind had…other plans.'

'No trouble,' he said. 'Have you got a cat-carrier thing?'

She nodded.

'Then we'll take her with us.'

A little frown creased her brow. 'I wouldn't want to put anyone out. Not everyone is a cat person and Molly sheds a lot of hair.'

'My parents love animals and they're no strangers to pet hair. Now, go and pack a bag.' He turned her in the direction of her bedroom and gave her a little pat on the behind. 'Go on. I'm not leaving without you. Oh, and have you got your doctor's bag?'

She gave him a funny look over her shoulder. 'Yes…'

'Can you bring it? I haven't had time to get one together since I got back. I don't like to drive any distance without a trauma kit.'

Erin sat back in Eamon's car a few minutes later, Molly safely and rather indignantly ensconced in her pet carrier. The traffic was heavy until they made it to the freeway, and after that it was more or less free-flowing. The further along the freeway they went, the more she felt as if by leaving the city and its fumes behind she was leaving her cares and concerns behind as well. Well, perhaps not all of them, she conceded as she thought of her mother and her new stash of narcotics. It had been an awkward moment when Eamon had asked her to bring her doctor's bag. She just hoped they wouldn't encounter anything that would need the administering of drugs. How could she explain their absence from the kit?

'What sort of music would you like to listen to?' Eamon asked.

'Um…I don't mind. What do you like to listen to?'

'Depends,' he said. 'On drives like this I like classical, but in the city I usually listen to the radio.'

'My previous neighbours—you know the ones who were in your apartment before you came?—they loved heavy metal. It was awful. I'm glad they weren't there this week while I was trying to sleep.'

Eamon sent her a smile. 'I promise you I won't play any heavy metal while I'm living next door. Anyway, my place is going to be ready in a couple of weeks, or so the contractors said. It could be longer; you know what tradesmen are like.'

Erin felt a sinking feeling in the pit of her stomach. She would only see him at work once he moved out. There would be no glimpses from the balcony, no spontaneously shared meals. He would no doubt be looking for someone to settle down with by then, someone to fill his nicely renovated house with a sweet-smelling baby or two. Erin thought of Alice waiting back at the hospital beside Josh's bedside, their tiny child growing inside her womb. She felt a fleeting sense of panic at the thought of never feeling the movement of a tiny foot or elbow inside her. No little rosebud mouth would hungrily seek her breast and no little arms would ever reach up for her.

'Is something wrong?' Eamon glanced at her again.

Erin forced her lips into a smile. 'No, of course not. I was just thinking how nice it is to get away from work.'

'Just wait until you see Cloverfields,' he said. 'You'll never want to come home, I guarantee it.'

CHAPTER NINE

EVEN though the sun had well and truly set by the time Eamon drove into his parents' gateway, Erin could see what a spectacular property it was as the fingernail clipping of the moon cast a magical, silvery glow over the sweeping paddocks. The tall poplar-lined driveway led the way to the large colonial house, surrounded by European trees and lush gardens.

The house was lit up with a warm, welcoming glow of lights, and as soon as Eamon tooted the horn the front door opened to reveal a couple in their early sixties, their hands linked as they waited for their son and his guest to walk up the steps. A silky-coated elderly Irish setter appeared by their side and, pricking up its ears, gave a happy bark and gingerly made its way towards Eamon.

'Hey there, Bridget,' he said, gently ruffling the dog's floppy ears.

The dog came over to Erin and licked her hand, wagging her tail in greeting. 'She likes you,' Eamon said, smiling at her.

'Darling, how wonderful to see you!' Eamon's petite mother stepped forward to hug her son tightly.

Erin watched as Eamon lifted his mother off the ground as he returned the hug. 'Hi, Mum,' he said, grinning at his father.

'G'day, son,' his father said, taking his turn to hug his son.

'Mum, Dad, I'd like you to meet a colleague of mine, Erin Taylor,' Eamon said, placing a gentle hand on the small of Erin's back. 'Erin, my parents: Henry and Grace.'

Erin shook both of his parents' hands in turn. She was struck by the warmth of their grasp and their genuinely friendly smiles as she returned their greeting shyly.

'So lovely you could make a weekend of it,' Grace said. 'Now, where is this gorgeous cat of yours? We'd better get her inside and fed. Don't worry about Bridget, she's used to cats. We have a couple who live in the barn. I found a tray and bought some kitty litter for Molly to save you the trouble.'

'That was very thoughtful of you,' Erin said.

'I'll bring her in and take our bags to the cottage,' Eamon said. 'You go in with Mum, Erin. Dad, want to give me a hand?'

'Sure,' Henry Chapman said and followed Eamon back to the car.

Erin stepped inside the country mansion with Grace. The smell of autumn roses and furniture polish was paramount; the cosy warmth of a crackling fire in the grate in the formal sitting room off the long, wide hall reminded her of many of the stately homes she had visited when she had toured England on her way home from the States a few years ago.

'I'll show you through to Eamon's cottage first, shall

I?' Grace suggested. 'Then once you've settled Molly in we can have a drink before dinner.'

'That sounds lovely,' Erin said, following her through to the back of the house to where a wisteria-covered walkway led to a separate building. 'You have a beautiful home, Mrs Chapman.'

'Grace, please,' Grace said, sending her a friendly smile. 'Eamon tells me you live next door to him. I hope he's a good neighbour?'

'He's very quiet compared to my last ones,' Erin said.

Grace smiled as she opened the front door of the cottage. 'I've made up both beds in each of the bedrooms, but don't feel you have to sleep separately.'

Erin felt her cheeks grow warm. 'Er…we…there's nothing…'

'I was young once,' Grace said with a twinkle in her hazel eyes. 'I remember all too well what it was like in the early days of Henry courting me.'

She moved over to an antique wardrobe. 'Now, here are some hangers to hang up your things. There is a bathroom the other side of Eamon's room. I put the litter tray in there. I'm sorry there isn't an *en suite*. These old homesteads weren't designed for modern-day luxuries and, this being the original servants' cottage, we didn't want to spoil its authenticity with too many renovations.'

'Of course,' Erin said. 'Anyway, it's just perfect the way it is.' She swept her gaze over the white-and-grey wallpaper and sweet-smelling vase of roses on the dressing table. The bed was a double, covered in a handmade quilt following the same white-and-grey theme.

There was a little writing desk under the window over-looking the paddocks at the back of the house, and a wing-chair in a matching striped fabric was set in a corner, providing a cosy nook for reading.

'Ah, here's Eamon now,' Grace said. 'I'll leave you two to get Molly acquainted with her surroundings. She's very welcome to have the run of the main house if you think she'd cope.'

'I'll see how she goes,' Erin said. 'She's never met a dog before.'

'Bridget is too old to be much of a threat,' Grace said. 'See you both in a few minutes.'

Eamon put the carrier on the floor and Erin opened it, coaxing an affronted Molly out. She eventually stalked out, giving Erin a 'how could you subject me to that?' look, before she sat and licked each of her white-socked paws in turn.

'Better show her where the conveniences are,' Eamon suggested. 'She might want to powder her nose.'

Erin couldn't help smiling. 'I'm sure she does.'

His eyes returned her smile. 'I'm going to throw my stuff in my room. I'll meet you back here in five to take you to the sitting room for drinks.'

'OK.'

Once Erin was sure Molly knew her way around, she came back to the bedroom assigned to her. She went over to the window and looked out over the moonlit paddocks; the tall trees were like sentries guarding the boundaries. The whole property reeked of family and traditions that went back over two hundred years. She could almost imagine the pioneer settlers taming the land, the sun beating down on their backs in the summer, the cold, snow-driven winds of winter no doubt reminding them of the home country.

She heard the soft knock on the open door and turned to see Eamon waiting to take her back inside the main house where her parents were waiting to have drinks before dinner. 'This is such an amazing place,' she said as he accompanied her along the wisteria walkway.

'It's great, isn't it?' he agreed. 'It's been in the family for seven generations.'

'So what happens after your parents can no longer run the place?' Erin asked. 'As the eldest and only son are you going to take over?'

He gave a loose shrug of one shoulder. 'Who knows? Maybe I'll appoint a manager like my folks did until they moved down, or maybe I'll relocate here and become a country A&E director. It all depends.'

Erin wanted to ask 'on what?' but they had reached the sitting room where his parents had laid out drinks and pre-dinner nibbles.

Within moments a glass of champagne was placed in Erin's hand. She took the sofa on the right-hand side of the fireplace. Eamon sat beside her, his parents seated opposite, and the russet-coloured dog lay in front of the fire. Erin watched as Henry slipped an arm around his wife's shoulders in a loving embrace. It was such a simple gesture, but it spoke of an enduring love that she found deeply moving.

'So when are the girls and co arriving?' Eamon asked, offering Erin the plate of nibbles his mother had passed across.

'Steph, as you know, isn't coming until Sunday. Sophie can't make it, but sends her apologies. I think there must be a new man in her life. And Kate and Simon said they should be here for afternoon tea, just after you wind up your conference. Kate will want to feed Emily first before they drive down, I expect.' Grace smiled at Erin. 'Emily is only two months old,' she explained. 'She's our first grandchild.'

'How lovely for you both,' Erin said. 'Do you get to see her often?'

'Not often enough, is it, darling?' Grace said to Henry.

'No, indeed,' Henry said. 'But then we don't want to interfere. Young parents need to find their own way of doing things, just like we did, right, Gracie?'

'Of course,' Grace said. 'But I do think young mums need a lot of practical support in those early few months. It's such a huge change, having sole respon- sibility for a baby, even though Simon is a wonderful father and support.'

Erin listened with one ear as the conversation moved on to other subjects, but her thoughts kept drifting back onto the subject of young mothers. She couldn't help thinking of her own mother, pregnant at the age of sixteen. Leah had told her snatches of things, like how her parents had thrown her out when she'd announced she was preg- nant. But then she'd also told Erin she had slept with her first boyfriend at the age of fourteen and had smoked her first cigarette the year prior. Erin couldn't help thinking there were some things that were better left unknown.

'What about you, Erin?' Grace's voice broke through Erin's ruminations.

'I'm sorry?' Erin blinked. 'I didn't quite catch that.'

'Poor darling, you're probably exhausted,' Grace said. 'Eamon told me you've been on night shift for days on end.'

'Yes.'

'Mum was asking if you had any family living in Sydney,' Eamon said.

'No,' Erin said, mentally crossing her fingers at her little white lie. 'There's just me. My mother lives in Adelaide.' *Or, at least, that is where she is supposed to be living.*

'Oh well, perhaps she'll move across when it comes time for you to settle down and have little ones,' Grace said.

'Mum.' Eamon's voice had a hint of warning to it.

Grace gave him a guileless look before getting to her feet. 'I'll just go and check on dinner.'

Henry cleared his throat, winking at Eamon as he rose from the sofa. 'I'll give you a hand,' he said, and followed her out of the room.

Bridget the dog pricked up her ears, but gave a sigh and lay back down and closed her eyes. It was apparently too much effort to move from the comfort of the spot in front of the fire.

Eamon turned on the sofa so he was facing Erin, his expression wry. 'My mother will have you married with three kids before you can say "engagement ring".'

Erin lowered her gaze to look at the trail of bubbles rising in her glass. 'I'm sure she means well. After all, it's worked for her: a happy marriage, four happy, grown-up children and a grandchild, with no doubt more to follow.'

She felt the weight of his gaze and slowly turned to look at him. 'I'm not the only woman in the world who doesn't see that for herself,' she said.

'No, but somehow I don't think you really want to live the rest of your life alone,' he said, his gaze steady and thoughtful on hers. 'I think you want much more out of life but, because you're frightened you might not get it, you tell people the opposite so they won't feel sorry for you.'

Erin disguised the direct hit of his assessment by arching her brows and affecting a sarcastic tone. 'I didn't know you had specialised in psychoanalysis as well as emergency medicine.'

His eyes remained locked on hers. 'Why do you push everyone away, Erin?'

Her mouth tightened. 'Why do you insist on coming too close?'

'I intend to come a whole lot closer,' he said in a husky tone. 'There's something happening between us, Erin—you know there is.'

She gave a little up shrug of her shoulders. 'It'll pass one way or the other.'

He brushed his fingertips down the curve of her cheek, stopping just shy of her mouth. 'You think so?'

Erin felt the nerves in her lips jump to attention, so she sent her tongue out in an effort to settle them down.

The air seemed to tighten. The distance between their bodies was now almost no distance at all. His knee was touching the lower end of her thigh, and her mind began to run with images of their limbs entangled in the throes of passion. Her heart banged against her ribcage, huge expectant beats that made a roaring sound in her ears. Was he going to kiss her? she wondered. Here, when any second his parents could wander back in and discover them? The possibility was both thrilling and nerve-racking. She wanted him to kiss her. She wanted much more than his kisses. She wanted to feel the full-throttle force of his desire; she wanted to feel the explosion of the senses that signified the ultimate in human pleasure. She wanted to be lost to common sense, swept up in an intimate world of longing and fulfilment.

His eyes darkened immeasurably as his fingers danced over her cheek again, but this time his index finger stopped to linger over the outline of her lips, in a fainéant movement that sent a waterfall of sensation down the length of her spine. 'Do you have any idea of how much I want you?' he asked.

Her throat tightened over a dry swallow. 'This is…this is crazy,' she whispered.

His mouth tilted in a wry smile. 'Maybe, but it's a nice crazy, don't you think?'

'Actually, I stopped thinking about five minutes ago.'

'That long, huh?' The corners of his eyes crinkled in amusement. 'I should've made a move when I had the chance.'

'You can hardly make passionate love to me in your parents' sitting room,' Erin said.

His fingertip moved over her lips again. 'My parents already think we're sleeping together.'

Erin felt her face heating as she remembered his mother showing her to the cottage earlier. 'Yes, I know.'

'Don't be embarrassed.' His fingertip brushed back

and forth over her bottom lip. 'They might be in their sixties, but they're quite progressive in their outlook. They met and fell in love within days. They married within six months.'

'Wow, that is fast.'

'When you know, you just know, or so they say.'

'Who are "they"?'

'Those who know.'

Erin let out a shaky little breath as his fingertip did its rounds again. 'That tickles.'

'You're very sensitive,' he said, returning his gaze to hers, holding it, searing it. 'I reckon we'll be dynamite together.'

Erin felt a power surge between her legs at his words. Her mind went on another imaginary sprint, conjuring up images of how it would be in his arms, feeling every stroke and glide of his mouth and hands, and very male body in full arousal. 'You seem pretty certain about that,' she said, working hard to keep her voice from wobbling.

His eyes smouldered. 'I am.'

'Dinner is ready!' Grace called diplomatically from the doorway.

Erin jumped up from the sofa, her face aflame.

Eamon rose with the sort of languid grace she found attractive in a man so tall. He placed his palm in the small of her back, sending another bolt of reaction through her body as he led her through to the formal room across the hall.

The dining room was a beautiful room complete with chandeliers over a long, rectangular cedar table which could seat at least twenty people. Grace had set one end of the table up with highly polished silver and what looked to Erin to be Wedgwood china and Waterford crystal. A cluster of fragrant roses was set amongst the pendulous fronds of some maidenhair fern as a centrepiece, giving the table an old-world elegance that made Erin feel she had stepped back in time.

Once Eamon had seated her, he went round to the opposite place-setting, his long legs almost touching hers beneath the table once he took his seat.

Henry was in charge of pouring the wine as Grace fussed over serving a beautifully prepared meal of locally grown beef in red wine, served with fluffy mashed potatoes, and green beans she proudly declared were home-grown.

Erin sipped at her wine as the meal progressed, marvelling at the close, easygoing relationship Eamon enjoyed with both of his parents. For some reason it made her determination not to fall in love with him all the harder to maintain. She began to think how wonderful it would be to have a man in her life who knew how to love and respect women, a man who also respected and adored his father, the sort of role model that would give children the best possible start in life. She thought of some of the foster homes she had been in. Certainly some of the couples had been stable enough, but she had never seen this sort of love between parents and children.

Every time Eamon looked Erin's way her heart leapt, and her belly nose-dived when his feet bumped hers under the table. Those amazing eyes of his were a shade darker than his father's, relaying a secret message that made her pulse soar.

After a mouth-watering dessert of home-made lemon delicious and thick, country cream, Grace suggested they move back to the sitting room for coffee and liqueurs.

Erin was feeling the effects of the wine she had consumed at dinner, so politely declined a liqueur. She rarely drank, not just because of her mother, but because she liked to feel in control of all of her faculties. But, exchanging glances with Eamon, she realised that with or without alcohol she was not exactly in charge of anything, least of all her self-control.

The fire crackled and spat as Henry placed another log on it, the sparks shooting up the chimney like the sparks Erin felt shooting up her spine when Eamon came and sat beside her on the sofa. His arm rested on the cushions near the back of shoulders, not touching, but close enough for her to feel the magnetic force of his body. She could so easily lean her head back and rest against his arm. She could so easily turn her head and encounter his gaze, smile at him, communicate everything she was feeling bubbling up inside her. But instead she kept her eyes trained on the flames licking at the logs of wood, thinking of how the desire inside her was exactly like those long tongues of flame.

'Well,' Henry said, getting to his feet and reaching for his wife's hand. 'I think it's time we oldies left you young ones to chat while we get our beauty sleep.'

'Yes, indeed,' Grace said, slipping her arm through

her husband's. 'Will you let Bridget out for a last walk, Eamon, before you go out to the cottage?'

'Sure,' he said. 'Night, Mum, Dad. Thanks for dinner. It was great.'

'Yes, thank you so much,' Erin said. 'Thank you for making me so welcome.'

'Not at all,' Grace said with a smile. 'It's lovely to have you. Don't let Eamon keep you out of bed too long.'

'I won't,' Eamon said with a teasing glint in his eyes.

Erin sat on the far end of the sofa once Eamon's parents had left.

'Come back over here,' he commanded softly.

'I'm fine where I am.'

'Frightened you mightn't be able to say no?' he asked.

Erin wondered if he knew how close to the mark he was. 'Maybe I should go to bed. It's been a long day…a long week, actually.'

He rose from the sofa and, offering her a hand, pulled her upright. 'Come with me while I let Bridget out for a walk. We can have a look at the night sky.'

Erin followed him out of the house. The sound of crickets and frogs and the distant hoot of a barn owl sounded like music to her ears. Bridget wandered off to what appeared to be her favourite patch of lawn in the middle of the circular driveway, and obediently squatted.

'It's so peaceful here,' Erin said, looking up at the black-velvet blanket of the sky with its pinholes of stars.

'Mmm, it's quite a change from the city,' Eamon agreed. 'Hey, did you see that?'

Erin leaned closer to follow the line of his pointing finger. 'What? Where? What did you see?'

'A meteor—just a small one,' he said, his shoulder brushing against hers. 'Wait a few minutes, there's bound to be another one. You'd better get a wish ready.'

She glanced up at him sceptically. 'You believe it works?'

He grinned at her. 'Why not? It's worth a try, surely?'

She looked back at the sky, her shoulders lowering on a sigh. 'I used to think some dreams and wishes would come true if I wished and dreamed hard enough, but they never did.'

'What did you wish for?' he asked after a short pause.

Erin crossed her arms over her chest, not so much because of the chill of the autumn air, but more to control the pain she felt deep inside her chest. 'I don't know. Just things.'

Bridget came back over to where they were standing, her plumy tail wagging softly. Eamon bent down and ruffled her ears. 'Maybe it's all about timing,' he said, straightening. 'When the planets are aligned, maybe your dreams will come true.'

Erin looked at him again. 'So you're a romantic, Dr Chapman, are you?'

His gaze went to her mouth. 'You'd better believe it, Dr Taylor,' he said, and covered her mouth with his.

CHAPTER TEN

ERIN had never been kissed in the moonlight before. It had a lot to recommend it, she thought as her senses went into overload. The magic of his mouth as it slowly but surely explored hers made her head feel light, and her body lost its guarded stiffness as he drew her against his hardened form. She felt the ridge of his arousal, the heat of his body shielding her from the cool night air. One of his hands cupped the nape of her neck, the other rested gently but purposefully against the base of her spine. Shivers of delight cascaded down her back, weakening her resolve even further.

After a few breathless minutes Eamon lifted his mouth off hers. 'We should go in. You're starting to shiver.'

Erin was shivering in anticipation and need, not the cold, but she felt too shy to tell him. She envied her peers, the ones who could casually do the next steps in this dating dance. They wouldn't baulk at following him to his room, slipping off their clothes and joining him in his bed. They wouldn't think twice about taking and giving pleasure. Why did she have to be so damned inhibited when all she wanted was to experience the thrill of his touch?

He lifted her chin, angling her head so the light falling from the front windows spotlighted her features. 'We don't have to take this any further right now,' he said. 'I'm OK with that. I want you, but I can wait.'

She pressed her still-tingling lips together. 'This is new territory for me.'

He brushed the pad of his thumb over her chin. 'I know it is,' he said softly. 'Take your time, sweetheart.'

Erin felt her heart swell in her chest. Most men would have been pressuring her by now, insisting on her following through on the promises communicated in the way she had returned his kisses, but because he didn't it made her want him all the more. She suddenly wasn't fighting off his desire, but the tumultuous drive of her own. It was a much harder thing to control. It was foreign to her, an unknown entity that threatened everything she had put in place to protect herself from hurt. She felt the pulse of it in her fingertips; it was like a back beat in her body, quietly keeping time until he claimed her as his.

He took her by the hand and led her back into the house. 'If you need anything during the night, just give me a shout,' he said. 'Come on, Bridget,' he called to the dog, who was sniffing around the base of a standard rose. 'Time for bed.'

Eamon saw Erin to her room in his cottage and after planting a soft-as-a-brush kiss to her mouth left to lock up the main house. She traced her lips with the point of her tongue once he had gone, tasting him, tasting the temptation she had so very nearly caved in to. She released a little sigh and, gathering up her toiletries bag, made her way to the bathroom the other side of Eamon's bedroom.

When she came out the cottage was quiet apart from the ticking of an old carriage clock on the hall table. She went into her bedroom, where Molly was curled up on the end of the bed. Molly opened one blue eye before closing it again. The soft sound of her purring made Erin smile; at least her cat felt right at home.

The bed was soft and comfortable but it took ages for Erin to relax enough to sleep. Her body rhythms were out of sorts after her stint of night duty. She felt on edge, wired for action instead of drowsy and relaxed. She tossed and turned for a while then, reaching for the bedside lamp, rummaged in her overnight bag and retrieved a book she had brought to read. She propped herself up on pillows and began reading, but she wasn't really following the storyline.

After about an hour she tossed it aside and, throwing back the covers, she slipped on a wrap and tiptoed out to use the bathroom.

On her way back down the hall a tall, shadowy figure appeared in front of her. She put a hand up to her throat, momentarily taken by surprise, but as the moonlight poured in from the windows she could see it was Eamon.

'Can't sleep?' he asked.

She shook her head. 'I hope I didn't wake you. I've been reading for the last hour. Night duty always does this to me. It takes me another week to get back into rhythm.'

'Would you like some hot milk or something?' he asked. 'I was on my way into the house to get one in any case.'

'Couldn't you sleep either?'

He gave her a rueful look. 'How did you expect me

to sleep after stirring me up in the moonlight the way you did?'

Erin felt her cheeks warming with colour. 'I'm sorry, I didn't mean to give you the wrong impression. I'm not the sort to lead someone on and then leave them…you know…?'

He flicked her cheek with the lightest touch of his finger. 'You worry too much. Come on, let's raid the kitchen.'

Erin followed him back into the main house, suddenly feeling like a child at boarding school colluding with an inmate to have a midnight feast, although it was closer to two in the morning. The kitchen was just as cosy as the other rooms of Cloverfields. It had a large wood-fired cooker that was still burning on low. She went and stood in front of it, warming her hands as Eamon found two mugs and a pan to heat the milk.

Bridget looked up from her basket near the range but, after giving a long-drawn-out doggy sigh, put her head back down on her paws, her eyes drifting shut once more.

'She's getting old,' Eamon said, nodding towards the dog. 'She's nearly fourteen. It'll be a sad day when she passes on.'

'I can't imagine losing Molly,' she said. 'I know she's only a cat, but she's the first pet I've ever had. I didn't realise how much I would come to love her. Maybe I wouldn't have bought her if I'd known how I would feel.'

He looked at her thoughtfully. 'You can't protect yourself from deep feelings. They sort of sneak up on you when you're least expecting it.'

She looked down at her hands splayed in front of the

cooker. 'I don't want to get hurt. I hate feeling vulnerable. I like to know what's going to happen and when. I need to know so I can prepare for it.'

'Life isn't like that, Erin,' he said. 'You can't always prepare for stuff. Life has a habit of throwing things out of left field. Look at Joshua Reynolds, for example. One minute his life was going along perfectly, the next it's hanging by a thread in Intensive Care.'

Erin turned from the range to look at him. 'I went to see him and his girlfriend.'

His eyes softened. 'I know. Alice told me.'

She looked away. 'It doesn't mean I agree with your plans. It's just Alice made me a gift and I felt obliged to look in on Josh's progress.'

'You really helped her, Erin,' he said. 'Not only did you save Josh's life, you really made Alice feel supported. That's what I want both patients and relatives to feel. You're more than halfway there.'

Erin sipped at her drink, conscious of him on the other side of the table watching her with that all-seeing green gaze. She had told him far more than she had told anyone about her insecurities. She couldn't imagine why she had done so. Was she falling in love with him? He had certainly turned her small, tightly contained world upside down. Here she was spending a weekend away with him in the country. Who would have thought she would have agreed to such a thing even a week ago?

She met his gaze and felt a ripple of something indefinable go through her. Her heart squeezed, her breathing intervals shortened and her throat felt dry as she saw his gaze slowly dip to her mouth.

She put her mug back down on the table and rose to her feet. 'I should try and get some sleep.'

'I'll tidy up here while you go back out to the cottage,' he said, gathering up the mugs. 'I don't want to tempt myself beyond endurance. Just knowing you're a room away is enough to have to handle.'

Erin bit her lip. 'Eamon…'

He came up to her and placed a fingertip over her lips, his eyes meshing with hers. 'Don't make this harder than it already is,' he said huskily.

She moved closer, her hips brushing against his, her arms going around his waist, holding him to her. 'I think I've changed my mind,' she said in a soft whisper. 'I want you to make love to me.' As soon as she said the words out loud, she realised how much they were true. She ached to have him hold her, to show her the passion she could feel simmering between them.

His pupils flared and his hands tightened on her hips. 'Erin, you're tired. You might regret it in the morning.'

She pushed herself closer. 'So what if I do? What harm is done? We're both adults. We can be sensible about this. It's just sex, right?'

He twisted his mouth. 'But what if it's not? What if it's something else entirely?'

She frowned. 'You mean something more serious?'

He nodded. 'I want the whole works, Erin. Not just a quick, furtive scramble under the sheets. I've done plenty of that in the past. I'm sick of it. I want to build a future, a family just like the one my parents built.'

Erin felt her shoulders stiffen as she pulled away. 'I

can't promise you any of that. I told you—I don't want that sort of commitment. It's just not me.'

'What *is* you, Erin?' he asked. 'The uptight A&E doctor who ticks off everyone she meets? Or is she a lonely little girl who is frightened about getting hurt by what life might throw her way?'

Erin threw him a withering look. 'You don't know anything about me, Eamon Chapman. You think you do, but you don't.'

'I know enough to know you are hiding from life,' he said. 'You've locked yourself up in an ivory tower where no one can reach you. Do you dislike yourself so much that you don't think you deserve a bit of happiness and stability in your life?'

His words were so close to those her mother had spoken a couple of days ago, they made her feel all the more defensive. 'I don't have to listen to this,' she said, swinging away.

'You can't run away for ever, Erin,' he called out after her. 'Eventually someone is going to get through your armour and make you see what you're throwing away.'

She threw another caustic look over her shoulder before she stalked out.

Eamon let out a rough sigh as her heard her footsteps on the path outside. 'Well,' he said, addressing the sleeping dog on the floor. 'I handled that brilliantly, didn't I?'

When Erin came through to the house the next morning breakfast was in full swing. The delicious smell of bacon drew her like a magnet, so too did the aroma of freshly baked bread and brewed coffee.

Eamon was sitting at the table next to his father, both of them with newspapers propped up in front of them. He looked up as Erin entered the room, but his expression gave nothing away. 'How did you sleep?' he asked.

'Fine…eventually,' she answered.

Grace came over with a plate of toast. 'You poor love,' she said as she set a rack of toast on the table. 'You doctors work too hard. It's no wonder you're tired all the time.'

'What time does the conference kick off?' Henry asked his son.

'It starts at nine and finishes at four,' Eamon said. 'I thought on the way back I might take Erin out to The Gib.' He turned and addressed Erin. 'That's Mount Gibraltar. Once we get to the top there are great views over Bowral and Mittagong and the rest of the Southern Highlands.'

'It sounds like fun,' Erin said. 'I enjoy walking.'

'It's a lovely time of year to see Bowral,' Grace said, stirring her tea. 'In the late 1880s a tree-planting programme was started. There are avenues of beautiful deciduous trees and private gardens. In September there's a tulip festival in Corbett Gardens. You'll have to make sure you come down for that. Kate and Simon got married there two years ago. It was the most beautiful wedding, so romantic. I'll dig out the photos to show you later.'

Erin gave Grace a small smile. 'That would be lovely.'

Once breakfast was over Eamon led the way out to his car. The drive to the hotel where the one-day conference was being held was conducted in snatches of banal conversation. Erin got the feeling he was avoiding any mention of the night before. She was rather relieved, and quietly took in the passing scenery, content to enjoy the autumn colour and the crisp, bright morning once they ran out of things to say.

Eamon's colleagues greeted him warmly once they arrived at the conference venue, and once name tags were on and introductions carried out the day's program began. Erin watched from the back of the small conference-room as Eamon presented a PowerPoint presentation of some of the innovations that had been trialled in other hospitals he had visited whilst he was in the UK. She kept a low profile throughout the day, quietly taking in the information, listening with interest to the question and answer session at the end of the morning's session.

Lunch was a casual eat-while-you-mingle-and-chat affair. Erin was balancing a glass of orange juice and a sandwich when one of the female delegates came over and introduced herself.

'Hi, I'm Tracey Bolton,' she said. 'I trained with Eamon at Sydney University. I live in the district as a rural A& E specialist.'

'Hi, I'm Erin,' Erin said, juggling her food and drink to offer her hand.

'I think it's great you've come along to the meeting with Eamon,' Tracey said. 'I hear you're staying with him at his parents' place.'

'I'm just…we're not…I mean…'

Eamon came over at that point and stole a triangle of sandwich off Erin's plate, sending Tracey a quick, boyish grin. 'Hi, Trace, enjoying the meeting?'

'Of course,' she said, smiling back. 'It's great to see you so happy, Eamon.' She turned her smile on Erin. 'He's a great guy. I would have snatched him up myself, except his best mate got in first.'

'I've forgiven him for that,' Eamon said, still grinning. 'How is Rob?'

'He's great,' Tracey said. 'He's at home with the twins.' She smiled at Erin again. 'We have twin boys, eight months old.'

'Come on.' Eamon beckoned with his hand. 'Show us the photos. I know you're dying to.'

Tracey gave him a sheepish look, and, handing Eamon her plate—which he proceeded to steal food from—rummaged in her purse. She handed Erin a photo of beautiful blond, blue-eyed twin boys, chubby cheeked, glowing with good health, their little limbs bare and brown from the previous summer's sun. Erin felt an acute sense of loss hit her as she handed the photo back. 'They're gorgeous,' she said. 'What are their names?'

'Bryon and Bailey,' Tracey said, sighing as she looked at the photo before putting it back in her purse. 'I haven't had a decent night's sleep since they were born, but I've never been happier. And I was such a career girl, wasn't I, Eamon?'

'Yep, you sure were,' he said. 'Just shows what a good man can do to your ideals, doesn't it?'

Tracey gave him a playful poke in the ribs. 'Watch him, Erin,' she said. 'He'll have you barefoot and pregnant before you know it. The man's ruthless when it comes to getting what he wants.'

Erin felt her face light up like a furnace and buried her nose in her glass of orange juice. The conversation drifted to other topics, and within a few minutes the last session was announced and everyone began filing back into the meeting room.

Eamon held open the car door for Erin once the conference had ended. 'Do you still feel up to a walk up The Gib?' he asked.

'Sure,' Erin said. 'I need to stretch my legs. I'm not used to sitting all day.'

'Did you get much out of the sessions?' he asked once he was behind the wheel of the car.

'It was very interesting,' she said. 'I can see how follow-through has its advantages.'

'But?'

She met his quick glance. 'I have my reservations.'

'Because?'

Erin gave a shrug and looked down at her hands. 'I'm still thinking things through. I need time to adjust. I don't usually rush into things. When I do, I end up regretting it later.'

Erin felt his glance but didn't look his way. He remained silent and she was glad for it. Maybe he understood how embarrassed she was about last night and was being gracious enough to let things slide.

For now.

The climb to the top of the mountain was well worth the view. Some other walkers had already made it to the top and were busily taking photographs. Erin used the camera in her phone to take a few shots, surreptitiously capturing an image of Eamon looking out over the Southern Highlands with a look of deep concentration on his face.

'Time to go?' he asked as he came back to where she was standing.

'Thank you for bringing me here,' she said on the way down. 'I can't remember the last time I breathed in such gorgeous fresh air.'

'It's a world away from the city, isn't it?' he said, taking her hand over a rough patch of ground.

The solid grasp of his fingers sent a shiver of reaction through her flesh. How different this afternoon might have been if he had taken her up on her offer to sleep with him last night, she thought. She found it hard to look him in the eye, wondering if he thought she had come across as too easy or so pathetically desperate for physical intimacy she would sleep with the first man who showed an interest in her. The fact was she *did* want to sleep with him—not because he was interested in her, not because he was attractive and available, but because she had never felt this way before about anyone. She was so frightened of admitting to her feelings, even to herself. Love was not something she had ever trusted. Everything she had loved had been taken away from her. Why would this be any different?

Eamon was still holding her hand when they got back to the car. He began stroking the back of her fingers with his thumb as his eyes met hers. 'About last night…' he began.

Erin grimaced. 'No, please don't remind me of how

appallingly I behaved. I must have been much more tired than I realised. I hope you weren't embarrassed. I'm deeply ashamed about practically throwing myself at you like that. I can't think what came over me.'

He lifted his hand to her face, brushing the back of his knuckles down the curve of her cheek in a light-as-air touch. 'You don't have to apologise. I wanted it too. I still want it. I want you, Erin. If you don't want to take things further, then fine. Maybe we should just go with this for now. No strings, no commitment, just the way you want it.'

Erin swallowed. Is that what she wanted? She was so confused. All she knew was she wanted him. She wanted to feel his arms around her, to feel his mouth on hers, to feel the pulse of his blood inside her body, to feel him move with passion to the explosive point of release and beyond. She was about to tell him so when a shrieking cry pierced the brisk morning air.

'Help! Oh God, my ankle! Oh God....'

A woman in her sixties was lying groaning on the ground near where the cars were parked, and appeared to have fallen heavily on her ankle. Her husband was trying to get her back on her feet, but she was wailing in pain. 'No! I can't get up. Stop it. Leave me. *Oh God!*'

Eamon snapped to attention. 'Quick, Erin,' he said, handing her the car keys. 'Run and get the trauma bag from the car. I'll assess the situation and call an ambulance.'

Erin came back with the emergency kit to where Eamon was doing his best to calm the woman who was now close to hysterics. The pain she was in was obvious. She was sheet-white, and when Eamon tried to examine her ankle she screamed in agony and then began to hyperventilate.

'It's all right,' Eamon said soothingly. 'We're both doctors. Just try and stay calm. It looks like you've broken your ankle. We'll do what we can to ease the pain until the ambulance arrives.'

'How far away is the ambulance?' the worried husband asked.

'About half an hour,' Eamon said. 'Apparently there was an accident on the freeway earlier. But we've got medical supplies to keep your wife in relative comfort until they get here.'

Erin felt her throat tighten in panic when Eamon turned his gaze on her.

'We'd better administer some morphine while we wait,' he said.

'Um…I don't think there's any in the kit.'

The space between his brows narrowed. 'What about some diazepam? That might take the edge off it.'

She bit her lip. 'Sorry, the drugs were past their use-by date. I…I forgot to replace them.'

He gave her another frown before turning back to the patient. Erin listened as he eventually calmed the woman down, getting her into a more comfortable position while he removed her shoe and sock in preparation for the ambulance arrival. The woman whimpered in pain while her husband hovered about helplessly.

A small crowd had gathered, which made Erin feel all the more inadequate and uncomfortable. Guilt struck at her with powerful blows. She should have known something like this would happen. She should never have left her bag in reach of her mother; it was like leaving candy out near a child. Leah Taylor just couldn't help herself. And now a poor, innocent woman was suffering unnecessarily because Erin had not had the foresight to take adequate precautions.

The wail of an ambulance had never been more welcome to Erin's ears. It seemed to be hours since Eamon had made the call, but as it happened it was only about twenty minutes. The paramedics quickly and competently took over, thanking Eamon for his help before they drove off with the patient loaded in the back and her husband following in his car.

Eamon picked up the trauma kit where Erin had placed it earlier. 'We'd better get back for dinner,' he said, leading the way to the car. 'Kate and Simon should have arrived by now.'

Erin waited until they were on their way before she spoke. 'I'm really sorry about that. I should have re-stocked the kit.'

'It can happen to anyone,' he said graciously, although Erin noticed there was a small frown pulling at his forehead all the way back to Cloverfields.

As soon as Eamon pulled up in front of the house a slim woman who looked like Steph but a few years older came rushing over. She barely waited until he was out of the car before she hugged him tightly. 'It's *sooo* good to see you,' she said. 'Wait until you see how much Emily has grown.'

Eamon hugged her back, before releasing her to open

Erin's door. 'Katie, this is Erin. Erin, Kate, the eldest of my three sisters.'

'Hi, Erin,' Kate said with a friendly smile. 'Lovely to meet you. Steph told me how gorgeous you are.' She grinned up at her big brother. 'Well done, bro, a great improvement on the last one. I thoroughly approve.'

Erin watched as he tugged at his sister's hair as if she was five years old instead of a married woman with a two-month-old baby. Another little pang of envy assailed her at seeing how much love there was between the siblings. But when Kate's husband, Simon, came over and handed baby Emily to Eamon, Erin felt an even deeper pain-like sensation. Eamon cradled the tiny baby in his strong arms, holding her gently but competently, as if he did it every day of his life.

'Hello, gorgeous girl,' he said. 'My, you have grown. Are you keeping your mummy and daddy on their toes?'

'And then some,' Simon said with a wry smile.

Kate slipped her arm through one of Erin's. 'Come and tell me all about how you met my brother,' she said, leading the way to the house.

That evening was one of the most pleasant Erin had ever experienced. She was enveloped with the Chapman family's friendliness and warmth, her shyness gradually easing as she felt more and more at home.

One of the most poignant moments was when Kate handed Emily to her to hold while she helped Grace with something in the kitchen just before everyone was about to head off to bed. Erin sat in the sitting room with the fire crackling in the hearth, the baby cooing up at her, waving her little starfish hands about, a bubble of saliva dribbling out of her tiny rosebud mouth. Erin felt a flood of emotions wash over her as she cradled the child. This was just part of what she would be missing, she thought. Not just the experience of giving birth, but nurturing that child, watching it grow and mature, bonding with it along with its father, as Kate and Simon had so securely bonded.

Erin captured one of the little flailing hands and pressed a soft kiss to each of the tiny fingertips. The baby smiled a gummy smile, and Erin felt her chest constrict again. Had her mother ever felt like this with her? she wondered. How could she have? Within days of her birth Leah had been back on the streets looking for the drugs she craved.

'She's beautiful, isn't she?'

Erin looked up to see Eamon had come in. She had been so lost in the moment she hadn't heard him approach. 'She certainly is,' she said, looking back down at the baby, whose little eyelids were fluttering as she fought against sleep.

Eamon sat next to her on the sofa and, reaching out, brushed one of his fingertips down the baby's cheek, close to where she was cradled against Erin's breast. 'It's a pity they have to grow up so fast,' he said.

'Some have to grow up faster than others.' Erin hardly realised she had said the words out loud until she saw the way Eamon was looking at her. He had that thoughtful look on his face, as if he was trying to put the pieces of a complicated puzzle together.

'Things were pretty tough on you growing up, weren't they?' he said after a long moment.

She looked back down at the baby lying in her arms. 'It wasn't anything like your childhood, that's for sure.'

'I recognise how lucky the girls and I have been,' he said. 'It's not something I've ever taken for granted.'

Erin wanted to tell him everything; the words were hovering on her tongue, but something held her back. Pride, shame, perhaps a combination of both. Her background was so disparate from his. The experiences she'd had were unthinkable in his family context. Would his family be so welcoming to her if they knew the truth about her upbringing?

'You absolute darling!' Kate whispered as she tiptoed into the room. 'You've got her to sleep. You must have a magic touch because she doesn't usually settle for anyone but me.'

Erin carefully handed over the sleeping baby. 'She was a little angel,' she said. 'I could have sat here all night with her.'

Kate gave her a grin. 'I'll remember that at three in the morning when she wakes up and won't go back down. I'll come in search of you and hand her over.'

Kate left with the baby and Eamon turned to Erin. 'Do you fancy a nightcap?' he asked.

Erin didn't really want a drink, but she did want to prolong the evening with him. Because there had been people around all day, they hadn't had a moment by themselves. It had been so hard, seeing him but not touching him, watching his sensual mouth curved upwards in a smile but not being able to kiss it. The thought of a few stolen minutes with him now was too tempting to resist. 'That would be nice,' she said, adding after a little pause, 'I had a lovely day today. Not just at the conference but here with your parents, sister and brother-in-law, and of course little Emily. I've never met a nicer family. Everyone has been so welcoming to me, so friendly and open.'

Eamon smiled as he handed her a cognac. 'They're pretty special, aren't they? I'm glad you like them. They've certainly taken a shine to you.'

Erin dropped her gaze to the cognac glass cradled in her hands. 'Eamon, I've been doing some thinking about…' she snatched in an uneven breath '…about us.'

He took the seat next to her on the sofa, one of his arms going along the back, his fingers idly playing with her hair. 'Go on,' he prompted.

She looked at him, feeling her heart tighten as his eyes darkened with desire. 'I've never met anyone quite like you before. It's been amazing to spend time with someone who is so…' she paused to search for an adequate word '…so well-balanced.'

His fingers caressed the back of her neck in a bone-melting touch. 'I'm not perfect, Erin. I have lots of faults just like anyone else.'

She grimaced ruefully. 'Not as many as me. You're the first man who's taken the time to get to know me. I can't tell you how much that means to me.'

He sent the point of his index finger on a sensual discovery of her lips. 'I'd like to get to know you even more,' he said. 'I've been kicking myself over how I handled last night.'

'Oh?'

He brushed his thumb over her bottom lip. 'Yeah,'

he said. 'I should have carried you off to bed while I had the chance. You wanted me. I wanted you. I blew it.'

'I still want you,' she said unashamedly. 'I can't believe how much I want you.' She gave him a self-deprecating look. 'I can't believe I'm even admitting it.'

He took the cognac glass out of her hand and placed it alongside his on the coffee table, his eyes smouldering as they came back to mesh with hers. 'Not here. I want us to be alone, totally alone. So, how about it? Tomorrow night. My apartment. My bed. A date?'

Erin felt her belly flip over as his head came down. 'It's a date,' she whispered as his mouth covered hers.

CHAPTER ELEVEN

THE drive back to Sydney the following afternoon was full of simmering tension. Erin could feel the anticipation building in her body. It had been building all day. Each time Eamon caught her glance, she felt a hot spurt of longing fill her; every time he brushed against her or linked his fingers with hers she would feel as if her bones had liquefied. She wondered if that was why he hadn't taken her to his room the night before, to ramp up her desire for him so she would have no second thoughts later tonight once they were alone in his apartment. He had kissed her for endless minutes on the sofa, he had kissed her outside her bedroom door, but then he had stopped.

And it had worked.

For now all she could think of was finally being alone with him, to feel his skin under her fingers, to explore every plane and contour of his body with her hands and her mouth.

By the time he drove into the apartment car park Erin's heart was beating like a drum. The journey up in the lift made her pulse soar, the extra time it took to deposit Molly next door stretching out the tension to snapping point. The air vibrated with it when Eamon opened his apartment door for her to pass through, his eyes dark with promise.

Erin barely waited for him to close the door. She fisted a hand in the front of his shirt at the same time his head came down, his mouth crushing hers beneath the passionate pressure of his.

This was no tender, tentatively exploring kiss. This was a kiss that stated implacably what was going to happen next. Flames of need flashed through Erin's veins as he backed her further into the room, almost toppling a lamp on the way.

'God, I nearly went crazy back there,' Eamon said, breathing heavily.

'Back where?' Erin asked, planting a hot, moist kiss to his neck.

He nibbled at her earlobe, his low, deep voice sending shivers through her. 'At Cloverfields. In the car. In the lift. All of it. I couldn't wait to get back here and do this…'

Erin gasped as he worked at her clothes, removing them with heart-stopping deftness until she was in nothing but her bra and knickers. She fumbled with his shirt buttons, but in the end he shrugged it off without undoing the last ones.

He lifted her in one effortless movement and carried her into his bedroom, sliding her down his body, making her feel his arousal all the way. 'Tell me to slow down,' he said in a ragged tone.

'I don't want you to slow down,' she said as she went for his belt.

She heard him suck in a breath as she slid the belt out of his trousers, her fingers lightly skating over him before she lowered his zip. She was going on instinct, taking her cue from his reaction; the thrill of feeling the satin-covered steel of him in her hand was breathtaking.

He pulled her hand away when he could take her caresses no more, pushing her back on the bed until they were a tangle of limbs and hungry, searching mouths.

Erin arched her back as he found her breasts, his mouth a hot, sweet torture as he suckled and stroked and laved in turn. He went lower to the cave of her belly button, his tongue dipping into the tiny whorl of sensitive flesh until her senses were skyrocketing. He continued on, lower and lower, his warm breath dancing over her feminine folds. What he did next lifted every hair on her scalp; the feel of his lips and tongue in such an intimate caress was almost too much for her. She whimpered and grasped at his head, not sure she could cope with the whirlpool of sensations threatening to consume her.

'It's all right,' he coaxed gently. 'Just relax and let go.'

She felt her flesh flutter with the first wave of pleasure, and then an avalanche followed. She felt the aftershocks ricochet through her, spasms of delicious feelings that made her mind empty of everything but ecstasy.

He moved back over her, his hair-roughened legs entrapping her beneath him. He reached past her right shoulder to the bedside table drawer, taking out a condom. She held her breath as he put it on, the anticipation of him finally possessing her making her heart pump with excitement.

She placed her hands on the front of his shoulders, meeting his eyes with colour flooding her face. 'Eamon,

I know this is really bad timing, but…' She bit her lip before continuing, 'The thing is, I've never really done this before. Not the whole way.'

His eyes softened. 'Are you telling me you're a virgin?'

She winced in embarrassment. 'I feel like a pariah.' She put one of her hands over her eyes. 'God, how pathetic it sounds. Nearly thirty years old and never had sex.'

Eamon tugged her hand away from her face, his expression meltingly soft. 'Hey,' he said in a husky tone. 'It's nothing to be ashamed of.'

She screwed up her face. 'You don't think it's pathetic?'

He smiled and pressed a kiss to the middle of her forehead. 'I think it's the most beautiful thing that you want me to be your first. Are you sure you want to go through with it? Do you need more time to think about it?'

Erin linked her arms around his neck. 'Maybe I think too much. I worry too much about what could go wrong instead of concentrating on what is going right. This feels right.'

He kissed her again, softly, tenderly. 'It feels right for me too,' he said. 'It felt right from the moment I met you.'

Erin brought his head down and sighed with pleasure as he kissed her deeply. She knew he was working hard to pace himself; she could feel the tension in his body and the increasing urgency of his mouth as it captured hers again. His erection was against the feminine seam of her body and she opened to him instinctively, that first smooth, cautious glide of his body making her spine unhinge vertebra by vertebra. Her body tightened around him, gripping him, delighting in the feel of him moving slowly but surely within her. He was so patient with her, pausing until he was sure she was able to take him inch by inch, her body adjusting to his thickness, her senses crying out with delight at feeling his total possession. He slowly began to build his pace, his inexorable climb to the summit of release carrying her along with him. She felt her body swell and pulse with need, the inner muscles of her core hot and moist as he drove through, time and time again. Her fingers dug into his taut buttocks, the sensations building until she was writhing beneath him, swept up into another vortex of earth-shattering rapture as she felt him finally let go. She held him tightly as he shuddered, emptying himself with a low, deep groan of primal male pleasure.

'Am I too heavy for you?' he asked after his breathing had steadied a little.

'No.' Erin settled against him, her fingers playing with his hair as she looked into his eyes. 'I like the feel of you right where you are.'

'I like the feel of it too,' he said. 'You were amazing, sweetheart. You nearly blew the top of my head off.'

She smiled softly and traced his mouth with her fingertip. 'I never knew it could be like that…you know… so fulfilling. At least not the first time.'

He grabbed her finger and sucked on the end of it, holding her gaze with the burning heat of his. 'It will only get better,' he said. 'Practice makes perfect, right?'

Erin felt a playful smile tug at her mouth. 'So does that mean we get to do it again?'

His eyes darkened. 'Damn right it does,' he said and, swooping down, covered her mouth with his.

* * *

Erin felt as if she was floating when she arrived at work the following day. Her body felt so different, so alive and tingling all over after spending the night curled up in Eamon's arms. He had left early for work, and she had spent an extra half-hour lying in his bed, surrounded by the smell of him on the sheets and on her skin.

Although they had made love several times she had made no promises to him; she had said nothing to him of her feelings. She had felt too shy to confess how much and how deeply she loved him. She didn't want him to think his passionate awakening of her senses had made her fall in love with him out of a pathetic sort of gratefulness. It had started a long time before that, she just hadn't realised it at the time. The moment she had met him had been life changing. How could she have known that the tall man getting out of the lift that day would cause her to question her adamantine stance on remaining single and childless? Ever since she had seen him holding his tiny niece she had felt the stirring of deep, maternal urges within her. They had lain dormant for all this time, but it had taken that tender moment to make her realise she *did* want it all. The only question was: could she have it?

The first couple of hours of her shift in A&E were so hectic, Erin didn't have time to think about her relationship with Eamon. A cardiac arrest came in at the same time as a multi-trauma. She worked tirelessly with the staff as she carefully assessed and prioritised patients, not stopping until the last patient was taken up to Theatre.

Erin was writing up the last of the notes when Tom

Brightman, the registrar, came over carrying one of the department phones. He placed his hand over the mouthpiece, his expression grim. 'Dr Taylor, it's Mr Gourlay. He says it's urgent.'

Erin inwardly groaned as she took the phone. 'Erin Taylor.'

'What the hell do you think you're doing down there in A&E?' Arthur blasted her without preamble. 'That last patient you sent up went into respiratory failure. We only just managed to salvage him.'

Erin straightened in her chair, her hand tightening around the phone. 'Mr Yates?'

'Yes, the man with the flail segment,' Arthur blustered. 'He was screaming in pain by the time he got up here.'

Erin frowned. 'Mr Yates was given pethidine on arrival. The x-rays showed five ribs broken in two places so we gave him another shot before he was taken up to Theatre. If you don't believe me, check the notes. It's written up.'

'Who gave him the injection?' Arthur asked.

Erin thought back to the pandemonium in A&E when Mr Yates had come in with his wife and daughter, all seriously injured from a motor-vehicle accident, at the same time an elderly man had come in with chest pain and had subsequently arrested. Lydia and Tom as well as two residents and an intern had worked alongside her, following her directions, bringing her equipment and performing procedures under her guidance. 'Lydia Hislop gave him the second shot,' she said. 'I gave him the first.'

'I'm having another word with the director about

this incompetence,' Arthur said. 'Just about every time you're on duty patients are compromised by inadequate pain-management.'

Erin opened her mouth to defend herself but the line went dead as the surgeon hung up.

Tom gave her a look of empathy as she handed him back the phone. 'I tried to tell him we did it by the book, but he wouldn't listen,' he said.

Erin sighed as she pushed back her chair to stand. 'I'd better have a word with Dr Chapman.'

'Do you want me to have a word with Lydia?' Tom asked. 'Maybe she made a mistake or something.'

Erin shook her head. 'No way,' she said. 'Lydia is one of the most competent and switched-on nurses in this department. In any case, I saw her inject the patient.'

Tom shrugged. 'Maybe it's a problem with the batch.'

Erin looked at him for a long moment.

'What did I say?' Tom said.

'Never mind,' Erin said, moving past him. 'Keep an eye on things until I get back.'

Eamon drummed his fingers on his desk, his brow creased into a network of lines. Arthur Gourlay's accusations were still ringing in his ears. A little niggling worry kept eating at him. He didn't like where his thoughts were leading him, but as director he had a responsibility to put personal issues aside in order to make objective judgements about the level of care patients were receiving. Was it just a coincidence that Erin's trauma kit had had no drugs in it at the weekend? He physically winced as he thought about the possibility of her siphoning off narcotics for personal use. It was unthinkable…or was it? Was he allowing his feelings and attraction for her to cloud his judgement? More to the point, had *she* used his attraction to her to muddy his thinking?

The documents from the previous incident were in front of him; her signature had been verified. There was no doubt she had signed for the drugs, but the question was *had* she administered them to the patient?

He had read of this type of scenario before. There were several cases where a doctor or staff member had stolen drugs from the department for personal use. Although strict guidelines were in place, A&E at peak times was harder than other departments to monitor. There was a lot of activity when multiple cases came in; junior staff often had to perform procedures such as injections while the more senior staff managed resus or bleeding control. Eamon had experienced the bedlam first-hand but had always been stringent in checking and double-checking the paperwork.

If only Erin wasn't so prickly and defensive. He couldn't help feeling she was hiding something, which made it even harder for him to know how to approach this sensitive situation.

There was a knock at the door, and when he issued the command to come in he felt a jolt of reaction zap him when Erin entered his office.

'Erin.' He rose to his feet. 'I was just about to call you.'

'I had to see you,' she said. 'Has Arthur Gourlay called you?'

'Yes. It seems there's been another incident of inadequate pain-relief, this time almost resulting in a death,' Eamon said gravely.

She worried at her bottom lip. 'Look, I know I should have told you earlier, but I had another incident a few days ago. I should have mentioned it when we talked about the Pappas incident, but I thought you would think… Well, I should have mentioned it regardless.'

Eamon kept his gaze steady on hers. 'Go on.'

She moistened her lips. 'I had a patient with a bowel obstruction come in—a Mrs Fuller. A&E was busy and I had a lot to keep track of. I…I looked through the notes once things had quietened down and I saw where I'd signed for a second shot of pethidine.'

'And?'

Her brow furrowed further. 'The thing is…' her throat rose and fell '…I don't remember signing for it, although it is definitely my signature.'

Eamon chose his words carefully. 'So what you are saying is you are not sure if you signed for it or not?'

She bit her lip again. 'I don't know what I'm saying. I just can't explain how patients have ended up without the pain-relief I thought we'd administered. It doesn't make sense.'

Eamon let a small silence pass. He wanted to believe her. Was he so in love with her that he couldn't be objective any more? 'Do you have any explanation for what's happened with these patients on transferral to Mr Gourlay's care?' he asked.

'Tom Brightman suggested something just before I came to see you,' she said. 'He said maybe something was wrong with the batch of pethidine.'

'If so then why are only select patients you have treated experiencing inadequate pain-relief?' Eamon asked. 'There have been no other cases outside these.'

She chewed at her lip again. 'I don't know.'

'Is there anyone who you suspect who could be using you as a shield?' he asked after another pause.

She frowned at him. 'What…you mean like forging my signature or something?'

'It could be done, Erin. You don't have a particularly complicated signature. I could do it myself at a pinch.'

Her eyes moved away from his. 'I'm not sure. Why would someone do that?'

He let another silence pass, watching as she shifted her weight from foot to foot as her hands fidgeted in front of her body.

'Erin.' He drew her gaze and then locked down on it with his. 'Why didn't you have any narcotics in your trauma kit?'

Her eyes widened and her face blanched. 'Wh-what are you suggesting?'

Eamon tightened his resolve. *Keep it professional. Forget the personal. This is about patient care.* 'It is your responsibility to make sure your kit is fully stocked. You know the protocol—you sign for the drugs at the pharmacy, documentation is kept on all that are issued and all that are handed in past their due-by date.' He waited a beat before adding, 'It can all be checked by a simple phone call.'

Her body stiffened. 'You think *I* am taking drugs from the department? You think I am using drugs from my *own* bag?'

He folded his arms across his chest. 'You tell me.'

She blew out a forceful whoosh of air. 'I can't believe you would think that. What sort of person do you think I am?'

'Dr Taylor, these are very serious accusations that I—'

'So it's back to Dr Taylor, now, is it?' she asked with a flash of her toffee-brown eyes. 'That's quite a change from last night, isn't it?'

Eamon drew in a calming breath. 'I have to investigate this situation without allowing my personal feelings to get involved. I'm sorry, but that's just the way it is.'

She set her mouth. 'I quite understand, Dr Chapman. But let me assure you I am not stealing drugs from the department. The drugs from my trauma bag were stolen.'

Eamon kept his eyes trained on hers. 'Did you report it?'

She dropped her gaze, and he felt an arrow pierce his heart. 'No.'

He tightened his folded arms but the pain in his chest didn't lessen. 'Why not?' he asked. 'It's a reportable offence, Dr Taylor. Those are restricted drugs. If they are in the hands of someone who doesn't have the authority to use them, who knows what could happen. If someone dies you could be held responsible.'

She brought her gaze back to his, flashing with defiance. 'I didn't report it because…because I knew who took them.'

'Are you going to tell me who that was?'

Her mouth tightened like a knot in a piece of string. 'No, I am not.'

Anger filled Eamon's body at her intractable expression. 'Then I am afraid I am going to have to suspend your contract until this is cleared up,' he said.

Her eyes flared in outrage. 'You're firing me?'

He kept his gaze hard on hers. 'You heard me, Dr Taylor. I cannot have someone working in my department with the suspicion of drug use hanging over them. Your contract is suspended until such time as you feel able to explain to me where the missing drugs are.'

She pulled her slim shoulders back, her eyes shooting daggers of hatred at him. 'You don't have to suspend my contract, Dr Chapman.' She all but spat the words at him. 'I am resigning as of this very minute.'

Eamon watched as she spun on her heel and stalked out of his office, the door slamming in her wake, making the qualification certificates he'd only just hung on the wall rattle in their frames.

He raked a hand through his hair, a deep, ragged sigh deflating his chest. In spite of her reaction he made a vow to himself he would do everything in his power to clear her name. She couldn't possibly be responsible. He knew it in his gut. She was a perfect foil for such a scam—already known for being difficult and touchy, she would be an easy target to lay the blame on. No one would question it. Her career would be ruined while the real culprit escaped the hand of the law.

At least he would be able to see her away from the hospital—perhaps then she would open up to him, trust him enough to tell him who she was protecting. Who could it be? She lived alone, she didn't socialise and she'd never had a serious boyfriend.

His stomach clenched as he thought of the intimacy

they had shared the night before. He let out another rough-around-the-edges sigh. He only hoped she would come to see he had no choice but to suspend her over the allegations. Otherwise the first relationship he had considered to be one he wanted to last for ever was going to be over before it had a chance to begin.

As much as it pained her to do it, Erin booked Molly into a pet boarding centre so she could escape for a few days. The thought of running into Eamon in the lift or in the street was unbearable. She couldn't believe he hadn't trusted her. Sure, perhaps she should have told him about her mother, but she had felt it was too soon in their relationship to reveal the still-living skeleton in her family cupboard.

She had not long returned from dropping Molly off at the boarding centre when the phone rang. She looked at the receiver as if it was a bomb about to go off, but when she picked it up it turned out to be the lesser of two evils, for once. 'Mum,' she said, laying on the sarcasm without restraint. 'How nice of you to call. Is this call to apologise for raiding my doctor's bag, or is this a request for more?'

'Get over yourself, Ez,' Leah slurred. 'You weren't using them, why shouldn't I?'

'Because it's against the law,' Erin bit back. 'I could get you arrested. Do you realise that?'

'You wouldn't do that to your own mother.'

'Oh yeah? Well, what sort of mother are you?' Erin asked, as tears burned at her eyes. 'You're as high as a kite and you're drunk. And I lost my job because of you.'

'Told you not to sleep with the boss,' Leah said.

Erin gritted her teeth. 'What do you want?'

'I want to stay at your place for a few nights.'

'No. Absolutely not.'

'You don't mean that,' Leah said.

'Yes, I do.'

'But where will I go?'

'How about rehab?' Erin suggested coolly.

'Rehab sucks.'

'So does being stoned and drunk when you're forty-seven years old.'

'I'm your mother, Erin. You should respect me. I gave birth to you, didn't I?'

Erin felt like screaming. It was as if every childhood hurt and disappointment had gathered in her chest. It felt like a pressure cooker about to explode. She loved and hated her mother at the same time. She wanted her mother to die. She wanted her mother to live. She wanted to save her mother, and yet she wanted to be relieved of the responsibility she had been carrying for so long alone. 'Mum…' Her voice came out hoarse. 'Please don't do this to me. Not now. You can't stay here. I'm going away. I'm leaving town for a few days, maybe a few weeks.'

'Then let me house-sit for you,' Leah said. 'But before you go can you stock up on some of that brandy you had in the pantry the last time I was there? It was real special. Much nicer than the stuff I usually get.'

Erin bit the inside of her mouth to control her spiralling emotions. This was too much. Why was her life so complicated? Why couldn't she have had a milk-and-cookies mum? If destiny insisted her life had to be tough, why not just an alcoholic or just a drug user for a mother, why did she have to have both? 'Mum, I don't think you heard what I said,' she said as if speaking to a particularly inattentive child. 'I am going away and I might not be coming back.'

There was a long silence broken only by the sound of Leah sipping something from a bottle.

Erin closed her eyes against the stinging tears. 'Mum?'

'Can you lend me the money for my fare back to Adelaide, then?' Leah asked. 'I'll pay you back as soon as I get back on my feet.'

Erin let out a sigh that shredded her chest. 'I'll transfer the funds right now.'

'Thanks, Ez. I knew I could rely on you. You're the best daughter a mother could have.'

Long after her mother had hung up, Erin held the receiver against her cheek. The cold, hard phone was no substitute for the loving touch of a mother but for now, as always, it would have to do.

CHAPTER TWELVE

ERIN spent two weeks at a cottage on the Central Coast. She missed Molly dreadfully and she missed Eamon even more. She walked for miles each day, no matter what the weather dished up, trying to restore some peace to her troubled mind. She turned her phone off and resisted every temptation to switch it on to see if Eamon had tried to call her. Every way she looked at the situation, she began to see the difficult situation he'd been in as unit director. If she had told him of her worries over the second pethidine shot in the beginning, perhaps he might not have been so hasty in suspecting her. And of course if she had trusted him enough to tell him about her mother he would have seen what an impossible situation she was in. Her pride had ruined everything, just as it always had.

Maybe her mother was right: she needed to get over herself. Running away wasn't going to achieve anything. She had been running away all her life, and look where it had ended up. It was time to face things like the professional adult she had worked so hard to become. Someone was trying to sully her name and reputation and she was hiding away up here, letting them get away with it. No wonder Eamon thought she was guilty. She was acting it, and had done so from the outset.

Erin quickly packed her bags, paid her bill, left the cottage and was home with Molly within the space of a couple of hours. She went out on the balcony but her heart sank like an anchor when she saw Eamon's flat was empty. The furniture was gone, everything no doubt shifted to his newly renovated house at Balmoral Beach. She bit down on her lip until she tasted blood, the thought of having to meet him at the hospital with all those accusatory stares and whispers taking all the courage she could muster.

Somehow she managed it. She held her head high and walked through the hospital entrance and down the corridor past a couple of nurses who turned their heads as she went past to Eamon's office. It was only as she raised her hand to knock that she realised she should have phoned first.

The door suddenly opened and Eamon almost knocked her over. 'Erin!' He grasped her by the upper arms to steady her. 'Where have you been? I've been calling you for the last two weeks. Why haven't you had your phone on? I've been out of my mind with worry about you.'

Erin blinked back tears. 'I had to see you.'

He pushed open his office door and led her inside, closing it firmly behind him. 'Sweetheart, can you forgive me for how I handled things? Pulling rank on you like that.' He scraped a hand through his hair. 'God, what a jerk I've been. I should have been concentrating on getting to the bottom of this, not pointing the finger at you.'

Erin blinked at him in surprise. 'You don't suspect me any more?'

'I didn't suspect you at all, not really. I just wanted you to tell me your side, but you refused to do so. I felt I had to take a stand before things got out of hand. You know what hospitals are like. Your career would be over if word got out about this.'

She frowned at him. 'You mean it hasn't already been ruined? It's been two weeks. Surely everyone's been talking about me by now, especially with me leaving like I did?'

'Erin, I did what I could in terms of damage control,' he said. 'I had a word with the CEO and somehow managed to get Arthur Gourlay off his high horse. I pointed out to him how he could find himself with a slander case on his hands if some other explanation came to hand. The staff have been told you took some much-needed leave. You had a month owing to you in any case.'

Erin was overcome with emotion. 'I should have told you right from the start. I feel so stupid now. I should have trusted you.'

'Trusted me with what?' he asked.

She looked down at her hands clutching the strap of her handbag. 'My mother is a drug addict,' she said. She lifted her gaze back to his and continued, 'All my life I've been covering for her drug and alcohol problems. I've spent more time in foster care than with her, but she's my mum and I love her. She's not ever going to be shortlisted for Mother of the Year or anything, but she's had a tough life and I can't give up on her.'

'Oh, baby.' That was all he said. Two little words,

softly delivered, but they contained a wealth of support and understanding.

Erin dropped her bag and stepped into his out-stretched arms, the feel of those strong, protective limbs coming around her making her feel as if she had finally come home. 'I should have told you. I was just so em-barrassed. I can't remember a time when I haven't been embarrassed by her. I feel guilty about it. Perhaps if I was a better daughter…'

Eamon cupped her face in his hands. 'Don't blame yourself, sweetheart,' he said. 'You're a wonderful daughter. It's about her issues, not yours. Has she ever told you why it all started? Why she began drinking and doing drugs?'

Erin looked into his sea-green eyes. It felt so good to have someone to lean on for once, someone to listen to the pain of her childhood without judging. 'I think I might have told you earlier, she got pregnant with me while she was still at school. I realise it must have been tough for her. She came from a strict, conservative family. My grandparents kicked her out of their home, but I'm not sure if it was because she was sleeping around or pregnant or because of the drugs. I suspect all three.'

'Was she using before she got pregnant?'

'She was using before and during pregnancy. I was born addicted to heroin. I was in Intensive Care for three weeks. Apparently I almost didn't make it.'

His thumbs stroked her tear-stained cheeks. 'Darling girl, you really didn't get the best start in life, did you?'

She gave him a wry look. 'It gets worse.' She took a little breath and told him of the repeated stints in and out of foster care, the unsavoury boyfriends her mother had surrounded herself with, the dealers, the addicts, the drunks and the violence. Even as she told him she wondered yet again how she had survived it.

'You're an amazing person, Erin,' he said, his voice warm and full of admiration. 'You've had so much thrown at you and yet you've risen above it. You're a brilliant doctor; you've devoted your whole life to helping people. So many others would have gone the other way, following the bad example set by their parents, but you broke the cycle.'

Erin felt comforted by his words. It helped her to finally accept what she could change and what she couldn't. 'I haven't quite given up all hope for my mother,' she said. 'I would like to think that one day she'll be able to get her life in some sort of order. It's just so hard doing it all alone. She's like a child. I feel like I've been the parent all along.'

'In many ways you have,' he said, taking her hands in his. 'Is that why you are so against having children?'

She looked into his eyes for a long moment. 'Yes and no.' She sighed again and looked back down at their joined hands, her fingers so small encased in his. 'I guess I was scared about her influence on any children I might have. What if her addiction is genetic? It's also one of the reasons I haven't dated. How do you explain to the person you've just met that your mother's a drug addict?'

He gave her hands a squeeze. 'No one should judge you for what your mother does. I certainly don't.'

'Thank you for saying that,' Erin said. 'I can't tell you how much it means to me.'

'Erin, darling.' His forehead creased in a frown. 'Does anyone at the hospital know about your mother's issues?'

She shook her head. 'No, I've never told anyone. You're the first person I've ever trusted enough to tell.'

He placed his hands on the tops of her shoulders. 'I'm going to get to the bottom of this drug thing, Erin. You have my word on that. I've been thinking it over, going through every possible scenario. But first I want your permission to have your signature analysed.'

Erin frowned. 'You mean by a forgery expert or something?'

He nodded. 'I have a mate in the police force. He specialises in this sort of thing. It's a pretty exact science. He'll be able to tell if it was you that signed for that second shot of pethidine or someone else.'

Erin was still having trouble realising he believed her to be innocent, but the more she thought about it the more it looked like she had been deliberately targeted. But who hated her that much? She knew she wasn't best friends with everyone on staff, but surely no one would set out to deliberately sabotage her career? She said as much to Eamon, but he reassured her again that he wasn't going to rest until he had cleared her name. He had already tried so hard to keep her name from being dragged down. Why had she run off without speaking to him first? She should have known he would handle the situation with the professionalism she had come to admire in him.

'Go home and rest,' he said. 'I'll drop by later tonight and take you out to dinner. I want to show you my new place. I moved in a couple of days ago.'

'I felt so disappointed when I came home to find your place empty,' she said. 'It's not going to be the same without you there.'

He kissed her in the middle of her forehead. 'There's one way to fix that, you know.'

She looked at him quizzically. 'How?'

He kissed her on the mouth this time. 'I'll tell you later.'

A couple of hours after Erin had left, Eamon looked back through the stack of patients' notes yet again. He had already faxed through the information for his friend in the police force and now wanted to check and double-check in case he had overlooked anything. It was nearly seven o'clock, and Erin would be expecting him to pick her up, but he just couldn't rest until he was absolutely certain he hadn't missed anything.

And then he found it.

It was so obvious a ten-year-old child could have solved it. He could have kicked himself for missing it. Two whole weeks had passed, and he should have picked up on it on day one when he'd first gone through the files.

How could Erin have signed for pethidine on a day she hadn't even been on duty?

His mobile buzzed on his desk and he picked it up to answer it. 'Eamon Chapman.'

'Eamon, it's Matt. I've done that analysis for you. Your girl is all in the clear. Someone's been forging her signature.'

'Yeah, I know,' Eamon said, clicking his pen on and off. 'Now all I have to do is find the real culprit.'

'Our people will have a look through the CCTV

tapes,' Matt said. 'It might take a few days but something should come up.'

It had better, Eamon thought as he ended the call. Otherwise he hadn't got a hope of keeping this thing quiet for too much longer. If word started to spread, it would be like wildfire and Erin, although innocent, could get seriously burnt. Her career could be totally ruined by this type of allegation. If someone wanted to destroy her, they couldn't have thought of a better way to do it. The only question that begged to be asked was who hated her *that* much?

There was a knock on the door and he sighed as he closed the documents in front of him. It was probably Rob Craig, the CEO. No doubt he had heard something in the loop and was coming to warn him the news was about to break in spite of his best efforts to keep things quiet.

But to Eamon's surprise it wasn't the CEO who came in and nervously took the seat opposite his desk.

'Dr Chapman? I'm sorry to disturb you, but there's something you should know about the question over pain management…'

Erin was trying to cajole Molly into forgiving her for sending her to cat crèche, but to no avail. Molly pointedly ignored the treat Erin hovered under her uptilted nose, her whiskers twitching in affront.

The doorbell rang and she left the treat on the carpet next to Molly and went to answer the door.

Eamon was standing there with a huge bunch of red roses. 'Hey, gorgeous,' he said, swooping down to plant a lingering kiss on her mouth. 'How's my girl?'

Erin could feel herself glowing at being 'his girl'. It made her feel secure in a way she had never felt before. 'I'm fine,' she said, feeling a shy blush steal over her cheeks.

He brushed one of her cheeks with his fingertips. 'God, I love it when you do that,' he said. 'It's so adorably sweet.'

Erin placed her hand over his and held it against her face. 'It's so good to see you.'

He turned over her hand and pressed a gentle kiss to the middle of her palm. 'It's good to see you too, sweetheart.' He put the roses down and pulled her into his arms, kissing her until she was breathless.

'Wow,' she said as she leaned back in his arms. 'That was certainly worth waiting for.'

'Erin.' His hands slid down her arms and encircled her wrists as if he was physically warning her that what he was about to say would be painful to hear. 'I got word back from my mate in the police force.'

She felt her breath screech to a halt. 'And?'

He gave a heavy sigh. 'Someone has been forging your signature. Just a couple of times, but it's a serious offence, given the circumstances.'

Her stomach felt queasy as she saw the gravity of his expression. 'You know who it is, don't you?'

He gave a single nod. 'I went through every roster, hoping I would find something to narrow it down, and then I saw it. I don't know why I didn't pick up on it the first time I looked. You know when you abruptly changed to night duty?'

She nodded.

'Well, that first day—in the morning, actually—your signature was on a patient's file for pethidine. But you weren't at work that day. I went through the duty roster and finally it came to me. I was about to confront the person when they came to me and confessed. That's why I was late. She came to my office just as I was leaving.'

Erin's heart gave a little lurch. 'She?'

'Lydia Hislop,' he said.

She swallowed tightly. 'Lydia?' She swallowed again. '*Lydia?*'

'I'm sorry, Erin, I know you are fond of her. And she's a damn fine nurse. But it seems she didn't do it to bring any disrepute on you. Your signature was the only person's she felt she could successfully imitate.'

'But why?' Erin asked in a cracked voice. 'Is she using? She doesn't seem the type. She's so competent. I've never seen her miss a step. Not once.'

'They weren't for her,' Eamon said soberly. 'Her mother has MS. She's in the advanced stages of the disease. Her mother made Lydia promise to assist her suicide. Lydia has been stockpiling vials of pethidine. She's been very careful, and may well have got away with it if Arthur Gourlay hadn't made such a fuss over the patients who came in under him.'

'But I saw her give Mr Yates an injection.' Erin was still trying to get her head around it all. 'I was there. I saw her administer it.'

'She swapped the vial with saline,' Eamon said. 'She felt terrible about Mr Yates almost dying. She never intended something like that to happen. She tried to select patients who would not be adversely affected, but in this case she got it horribly wrong.'

Erin felt ill. *Lydia*. Of all people! It was so hard to believe, and yet was it? Lydia was a compassionate nurse. Perhaps watching her mother's agonising decline had tipped her over. The emotional ties had blurred her judgement. How tragic that she had felt that was her only option to ease her mother's suffering. 'What will happen to her?' she asked.

'It will now become a police matter,' Eamon said. 'Lydia at least had the courage to come forward. She said she heard a couple of nurses talking about you in the restrooms this afternoon. They apparently saw you heading towards my office and thought you must have been called in over it. Some rumours must have already been circulating. She didn't want you to get the blame. It's sad, but that's the law. She will be prosecuted, but who knows? The courts may take into account her mother's plight. The irony is in some countries assisted suicide is legal.'

'Poor Lydia,' Erin said. 'I feel so sorry for her. I wish I'd known about her mother. I wish I'd been more supportive.'

'Erin, you're not responsible for everyone you work with,' he said. 'But then maybe that's what I love about you—the way you try to hide how much you care. You pretend to hold people at arm's length when deep down you're just as compassionate, if not more so, than anyone else.'

Erin blinked at him and then blinked again. Had she heard him correctly? No, of course not. She was imagining it. She had to be. She had heard what she wanted to hear. She longed to hear he felt something for her, but how could he? They had only known each other such a short time.

'Aren't you going to say anything?' he asked.

She snagged her bottom lip with her teeth. 'Um…I'm not sure what I'm meant to say.'

'Did you even hear what I said?'

'What did you say?'

'I love you.'

Erin stared at him, her mouth falling open. 'I thought I'd imagined it.'

He stroked her cheek with his thumb, his eyes meltingly soft as they held hers. 'You didn't.'

Erin was still lost for words. She just stood there, looking into his eyes, wondering if she was dreaming. He loved her. For all her faults, all her insecurities, in spite of her difficult background, he loved her.

She didn't hesitate to reciprocate. 'I love you, too.'

His eyes twinkled. 'Well, that's a very fine start. When did you decide that?'

She smiled back at him. 'I think it happened the very first moment I met you. I didn't believe in love at first sight. I didn't even really believe in love, period. But now I believe it all. I *want* it all.'

Eamon's thumb stopped moving mid-stroke. 'You mean if I were to ask you to marry me and have my babies, even though we've only known each other a ridiculously short time, there's a remote possibility you might say yes?'

Erin felt her smile widen. 'I guess you'll have to ask me to find out.'

He got down on one bended knee and took both of her hands in his. 'Erin Taylor, will you marry me?'

Erin felt her heart swell to three times its size. 'Yes. Yes *Yes!*'

He rose and pulled her to her feet, wrapping his arms around her, holding her against him as if she was the most precious thing on earth. 'What changed your mind?' he asked.

She looked up into his eyes again. 'You. Your parents. Your sisters. Your little niece. You most of all. Just you.'

He kissed her tenderly, lingering over her mouth as if he never wanted to let her go. 'My beautiful, brave little Erin,' he said. 'I can't wait until you're wearing my ring and carrying my child.'

'Me too.' Erin wrapped her arms around his waist, her face pressed against the fortress-like wall of his chest. She felt safe for the first time in her life, safe and loved and protected.

And happy.

Blissfully, deliriously happy.

Her life might not have been easy, and the struggles with her mother were certainly not over yet, but somehow Erin knew that with Eamon's strong support and unwavering love they would make it.

And they did.

 MEDICAL™ 2-in-1

Coming next month

THE SURGEON'S MIRACLE

by Caroline Anderson

Nurse Libby Tate had very good reasons for thinking that a high-society ball and an unexpected night of passion with paediatric surgeon the Hon. Andrew Langham-Jones couldn't possibly end with a pregnancy! But now that it has, Libby has a secret that could put their miracle baby and new-found happiness at risk...

DR DI ANGELO'S BABY BOMBSHELL

by Janice Lynn

Dr Darby Phillips needed a temporary date fast, and delicious doctor Blake Di Angelo seemed the perfect choice. But their little charade turned into romance for real – and now Darby must tell Blake he'll soon be hearing the pitter-patter of tiny feet!

NEWBORN NEEDS A DAD

by Dianne Drake

Brooding doctor Neil Ranard steers clear of relationships, but new (and pregnant) colleague Gabrielle Evans has somehow thawed Neil's guarded heart. And when he delivers her little son, Neil wants more than anything for them all to be a family!

HIS MOTHERLESS LITTLE TWINS

by Dianne Drake

Nurse Dinah Corday has received a warm welcome from everyone at White Elk – except from pediatrician Eric Ramsey! Yet this brooding doctor and his twin girls soon get under Dinah's skin...

On sale 7th May 2010

MEDICAL™

Single titles coming next month

WEDDING BELLS FOR THE VILLAGE NURSE
by Abigail Gordon

When Jenna Balfour returns home to Bluebell Cove, she's welcomed back into the local community with open arms. The only person who keeps his distance is enigmatic Dr Lucas Devereux. But warm-hearted Jenna longs to soothe the pain she glimpses beneath his abrupt exterior…

HER LONG-LOST HUSBAND
by Josie Metcalfe

A&E doctor Olivia never expected to see her husband again, until she hears his voice on her wedding day and turns round to see Gregor, the love of her life… alive! Working as an army medic has left Gregor unable to walk, but he's as handsome as ever. Does he still love Olivia – or has Gregor only returned to say goodbye…?

On sale 7ᵗʰ May 2010

0410/03b

millsandboon.co.uk Community

Join Us!

The Community is the perfect place to meet and chat to kindred spirits who love books and reading as much as you do, but it's also the place to:

- Get the inside scoop from authors about their latest books
- Learn how to write a romance book with advice from our editors
- Help us to continue publishing the best in women's fiction
- Share your thoughts on the books we publish
- Befriend other users

Forums: Interact with each other as well as authors, editors and a whole host of other users worldwide.

Blogs: Every registered community member has their own blog to tell the world what they're up to and what's on their mind.

Book Challenge: We're aiming to read 5,000 books and have joined forces with The Reading Agency in our inaugural Book Challenge.

Profile Page: Showcase yourself and keep a record of your recent community activity.

Social Networking: We've added buttons at the end of every post to share via digg, Facebook, Google, Yahoo, technorati and de.licio.us.

www.millsandboon.co.uk

mc

2 FREE BOOKS
AND A SURPRISE GIFT

We would like to take this opportunity to thank you for reading this Mills & Boon® book by offering you the chance to take TWO more specially selected books from the Medical™ series absolutely FREE! We're also making this offer to introduce you to the benefits of the Mills & Boon® Book Club™—

- **FREE home delivery**
- **FREE gifts and competitions**
- **FREE monthly Newsletter**
- **Exclusive Mills & Boon Book Club offers**
- **Books available before they're in the shops**

Accepting these FREE books and gift places you under no obligation to buy, you may cancel at any time, even after receiving your free books. Simply complete your details below and return the entire page to the address below. You don't even need a stamp!

YES Please send me 2 free Medical books and a surprise gift. I understand that unless you hear from me, I will receive 5 superb new stories every month including two 2-in-1 books priced at £4.99 each and a single book priced at £3.19, postage and packing free. I am under no obligation to purchase any books and may cancel my subscription at any time. The free books and gift will be mine to keep in any case.

Ms/Mrs/Miss/Mr _____ Initials _____

Surname _____

Address _____

_____ Postcode _____

E-mail _____

Send this whole page to: Mills & Boon Book Club, Free Book Offer, FREEPOST NAT 10298, Richmond, TW9 1BR